PAISLEY HANOVER ACTS OUT

CAMERON TUTTLE

illustrations by Alli Arnold

DIAL BOOKS

DIAL BOOKS
A member of Penguin Group (USA) Inc.
Published by The Penguin Group
Penguin Group (USA) Inc., 375 Hudson Street, New York, NY 10014, U.S.A.
Penguin Group (Canada), 90 Eglinton Avenue East, Suite 700, Toronto, Ontario, Canada M4P 2Y3
(a division of Pearson Penguin Canada Inc.)
Penguin Books Ltd, 80 Strand, London WC2R 0RL, England
Penguin Ireland, 25 St. Stephen's Green, Dublin 2, Ireland
(a division of Penguin Books Ltd)
Penguin Group (Australia), 250 Camberwell Road, Camberwell, Victoria 3124,
Australia (a division of Pearson Australia Group Pty Ltd)
Penguin Books India Pvt Ltd, 11 Community Centre, Panchsheel Park,
New Delhi - 110 017, India
Penguin Group (NZ), 67 Apollo Drive, Rosedale, North Shore 0632, New Zealand
(a division of Pearson New Zealand Ltd)
Penguin Books (South Africa) (Pty) Ltd, 24 Sturdee Avenue, Rosebank,
Johannesburg 2196, South Africa
Penguin Books Ltd, Registered Offices: 80 Strand, London WC2R 0RL, England

Library of Congress Cataloging-in-Publication Data
available upon request

For Barbara, one of the cool moms—Un of a Kind,
UnFinished, UnForgettable

CHAPTER ONE

I took a deep breath outside the door to Yearbook class and then sauntered—yes, I actually sauntered—into the room, doing my best imitation of calm, confident me. I was totally nervous. I had butterflies in my brain. But it was good nervous, excited nervous. I was one of the chosen people.

Have you ever had the feeling that you were destined for greatness? Not that you would ever admit that to anybody. But have you ever heard the all-in-your-head voice telling you that you're special, that the whole reason you're even on the planet is not just to annoy and bankrupt your parents, that it's also to do something unique and totally amazing?

I had that feeling as I sauntered into Yearbook on the first day of sophomore year. The soundtrack in my head was indie groovy and super danceable—and that was even before I saw Eric Sobel.

There he was, fiddling with the settings on his camera.

No way. Eric Sobel in Yearbook? Using my awesome power of deductive reasoning, I figured he was a staff photographer this year. Eric Sobel, the star of varsity soccer—*varsity*—sitting here in Yearbook. I was at the championship soccer game last year, when he was just a freshman, and he scored not one but two goals in overtime. We won the game, and when they gave him the MVP trophy, his eyes got all watery, and he almost cried. I could tell. I had binoculars.

There's something irresistible about a guy who cares enough about something—even if it's soccer—to almost cry.

And just seeing him sitting there in Yearbook cranked the volume on my internal sound system way up. I pictured us studying together after school at Freddie's Pizza, leaning close over our homework, whispering dreamy words like *sine* and *cosine* and *tangent*. He'd laugh, and I'd lovingly push his dirty-blond bangs out of his eyes. Then he'd smile at me all sweet, and tenderly wipe a small piece of tomato-y pepperoni off my cheek.

I knew immediately that this year was going to be the best year of my life.

Then I walked into the side of a desk.

Ugh, embarrassing. OMG. I was such a high school cliché, and it was only third period.

"Take a seat, people," said the Yearbook advisor, Ms. Madrigal. She was perched on a stool behind the podium, starting to take attendance. I turned around in a full circle looking around for an empty seat. But every desk was taken. So I made my way over to the far side of the room and hopped up on the windowsill. Public school budgets—there are never enough desks for everyone.

I hadn't thought of Eric Sobel as a Yearbook type. But I

figured there were a lot of things I didn't know about him—yet. The classroom was filled with student leaders and arty-smarty types, cool brains, people who obviously had intelligent, informed opinions about things like hybrid cars and the best cafeteria food at Ivy League schools, people who went to foreign films on a Friday night and drank too much coffee on purpose. I was in heaven. I was going to learn so much from these people—but more importantly, my seven-point plan was falling perfectly into place.

See, I have this killer seven-point, college-application action plan. It's not like I'm totally neurotic or uptight or anything. I'm just very practical. I've got to have it all worked out if I'm going to be Yearbook editor senior year. I've mapped out the things I need to accomplish over the next three years so I can have a sick college application and lots of options for schools. Life is all about options, right? At least that's what my mom keeps telling me. I want options.

My seven-point action plan is not just about getting straight A's or being the best at soccer or joining Yearbook or running for sophomore class vice president. That would be insanely stupid and boring. My plan is to distinguish myself as a highly motivated, unique individual with quirky, creative habits, diverse goals, and quality personal values.

How did that sound? Did you buy it? Did it sound real? I don't want to lay it on too thick—just thick enough to stick in the acceptance pile at the admissions offices.

I checked out the other sophomores in class, assessing my

competition for Yearbook editor senior year. Yearbook is mostly seniors and juniors with only a handful of sophomores. You have to submit a writing sample and an application to even be considered for the class. Right now, my sophomore competition was Dwight Cashel, a brainiac, but so squeaky clean that he's kind of uptight and annoying. No one would want him to be editor. Then there was Bentley Jones—not only super smart but also a superior human being with so many different talents it pretty much made you sick. I couldn't imagine her wanting to be Yearbook editor when she could be playing the sax in the jazz honor band *and* running the anchor lap for the mile relay team at State *and* choreographing and starring in the spring modern dance show. Eric Sobel? No, he was way too shy to want to be editor. It had to be me. I could so feel it.

Ms. Madrigal had stopped talking. She poked at the air with her index finger, counting each student. "That's strange," she said. "Whose name *didn't* I call?"

I looked around the room a little confused, and cautiously raised my hand. And then you'll never guess who else did—Candy Esposito. What was Candy Esposito doing in Yearbook?! She already controlled all the popular categories at school. Wasn't that enough?

"And you are?" asked Ms. Madrigal, looking at me.

"Paisley Hanover."

"Oh, right. Hanover? Hmmm . . . " She scanned her attendance list, shaking her head. "Candy, I don't see you on my list either. Well." She looked around the room with an embarrassed grin. "This is a little awkward, ladies. It seems that this class is over-enrolled by one student. Normally that wouldn't be a problem, but this is an application and invitation only class. If I let both of you in, that wouldn't be fair to the many other students who applied."

A fizzy wad of nervousness ricocheted around my stomach. Was my seven-point master plan already about to collapse into a wimpy, wobbly six-point plan? Eric Sobel looked over at me and kind of smiled. Or did he wince? Oh God, I think he winced.

Ms. Madrigal called the main office on the phone by the door and tried to sort things out. While she talked, Candy Esposito shot me an excited can-you-believe-this? expression, like we were suddenly bonded by this disaster and the best of friends. I gave her an I'm-so-excited-and-confused! look right back. I mean, she's Candy Esposito. What else could I do? I struggled to hear what Ms. Madrigal was saying, but everyone was being extremely selfish by yakking away.

"Okay people," Ms. Madrigal said as she hung up the phone. "Listen up! Paisley and Candy," she said, giving each of us this intense look, "you both submitted excellent writing samples. But apparently there was some clerical error." She swept her gaze around the room. "Now, I could make an arbitrary decision here, but I have a much better idea." As she spoke, she weaved her way between the desks trying to make a personal, Oprah-ish connection with everyone. "Being a member of *The Highlander* staff requires collaboration. It requires teamwork, probably more than any other class at this school. It also demands the ability to work under pressure, often on a deadline with not nearly enough time to do your best work but having to deliver your best work anyway."

A few seniors laughed. "Don't remind me," said this year's editor, Max Chapin. He was probably going to Stanford.

"There is a space for either Candy or Paisley—but not for both, I am sorry to say." Ms. Madrigal actually looked sorry, which made me feel kind of hopeful. Candy already had enough wins. "But I don't think this should be my decision," she said with a glint in her eye. "I think it should be *your* decision." She paused, looking around the room.

Oh no. Oh please no.

"Are you in? Are you with me, people?"

The room erupted in hoots and cheers. Oh no, no, no. This was not good. My fizzy wad of nervousness morphed into a bubbling blob of nausea.

"Candy, Paisley, come on up to the front. You've got a quick assignment. I want each of you to come up with a headline that best describes you and your personality."

What?! Clearly, Ms. Madrigal had been watching way too many episodes of *Survivor*. Everyone groaned, except for all of the people who laughed nervously, including me.

"Think pithy, think clever," she continued. "Don't be shy, be precise. Have fun with it. And then, in a well-crafted sentence or two, summarize the unique talents and skills that you, and only you, would bring to the Yearbook staff. Then we'll take an anonymous vote. The person with more votes gets the last spot in this class. The other person gets to take Drama instead."

Drama?! No way! I am not getting stuck in Drama with the socially disabled and hair-impaired. I felt my nose break into a sweat.

Candy Esposito is not only a junior and a varsity volleyball and track star, she's super cute and super popular, and the worst part—she's super nice! Everyone likes her, everyone! She's impossibly pretty with these pouty lips and a cute, perfect nose that look like they were sculpted by like Michelangelo. And she has this little scar under her right eye that's beautiful like body art and somehow makes her even more unique. And she has sparkly brown eyes, and dimples, and long shiny hair the color of sun-kissed honey. (I know that because certain girls are always trying to get their hair to be the color of hers, and the closest color in a box is called sun-kissed honey.) And if that wasn't horrible enough for me, her father used to be a professional baseball player and now owns a bunch of Burger Kings, so Candy's always treating her friends to free Whoppers and inviting them to games where they get to sit in her family's box seats.

I looked around the room searching for allies I could count on. Bentley Jones stared at me, shaking her head. She looked really sorry for me. And she *likes* me.

I'm doomed. I'm so totally doomed. How did my seven-point plan turn into a razor-sharp seven-point weapon that's about to obliterate me in front of my peers?! I blinked my eyes trying to focus. Get it together, Paisley. You can do it. You can do it!

I realized that if I had any hope of beating Candy Esposito, I would have to swing big and knock one out of the park. My headline would have to dazzle and delight with unexpected wit and genuine confidence. My well-crafted argument would need to seal the deal, letting everyone know how dedicated I was, how much fun I could be, how much I loved hard work and words of all sizes.

I can do this. I can do this, right? Yes! I *can* do this! What does my terminally positive Dad always say? "Visualize success!"

Candy came over to me and shook my hand. "Good luck, Paisley. I know you'll do great." She had this big smile on her face. God, why did she have to be so *nice*? After that, I didn't have any trouble visualizing success. Unfortunately it was Candy's.

"Okay ladies. Remember, have fun with this. You've got three minutes—"

Three minutes?! Now I know why Ms. Madrigal has a reputation for sadistic, subversive forms of student torture.

"—starting right now."

My butt puckered. I flipped past the doodles of Eric Sobel to a blank page in my notebook. I stared at it. Headline, headline, clever headline describing me. Headline, headline, three-minute deadline? Lifeline! Help! Okay, okay, stay calm. Breathe. Breathe. I looked up in a bug-eyed panic just as Eric Sobel snapped a few pictures.

Oh great.

I started scribbling frantically.

Paisley Hanover—
Something clever
Something clever
Something <u>cleverer</u>
Anything!
Welcome to Never Clever Land
Clever is Crazy Being Polite
Paisley Hanover—Crazy in Polite Ways
Ugh.
Brainy Babe
Quirky Turkey
Strange but True
Hope on a Rope
Dork on a Fork
Fun for All, All for Fun!
A Punny, Funny Friend
Funny Weird
Funny Ha Ha
Funny Weird <u>and</u> Funny Ha Ha
More Laughs than a . . .
More Fun than a Barrel of Sophomores
Sophomore of the Good Stuff
Sophomore of a Good Thing
Paisley—Not Just Those Sperm-Shaped Thingies

Help. Help! Brain freeze. Can't think. Can't think! Dear Universe, please help me think! I should get up and walk out of here right now.

I looked over at Candy. She was slowly tapping her pen against her naturally soft, pink lips. I could tell she was thinking of something really amusing just from the look on her face. OMG! She's cracking herself up. Crap! Focus. Focus. You can do it! Candy doesn't love words as much as you love words. She loves everyone and everyone loves her, but that is not the same as being a good writer. Right? Focus!

Focused on Fun
Focused, Fun, Fabulous!
Little Miss Funshine
Freckles and Funshine
Freckles Are Fun
One of a Kind
Fun of a Kind
Fun of a Kind Girl
Fun for Your Life
Tickled Think
The Sizzle and the Steak
Functional and Fashionable
Smart, Stylish, and . . . totally stupid!
Shigoogley!
What?
Irony. Irony. Try irony.
Paisley Hanover—I Should Have Overslept!

That's good. That's kind of funny.
No, not so funny.
Paisley Hanover—Write On!
Will Write for Clothes
I'm Dying Here!
Not as Popular as Candy
Will Write for Candy
I'd Vote for Candy

"Okay, time's up!" called Ms. Madrigal as if that was good thing. I looked up in a panic.

If only I'd known then what I know now, I definitely would have thought of Sidebra* and Panties, and I would have owned the whole situation with total supreme confidence. But then this would be a very different story.

"Who wants to go first?" Ms. Madrigal asked, looking from me to Candy.

"Paisley does," said Candy all cheery and nice. Thanks a not, Candy.

I wish I couldn't remember exactly what happened

*SIDEBRA

Okay, I should probably just explain this right now. No, that's not a typo—that's a sidebra. I admit it was a typo the first time. I'm kind of a bad typer. But I've learned that sometimes it pays not to use spell-check or look in the mirror before leaving the house. I mean, some of your best stuff can come from your quote-unquote mistakes. Trust me. I know. It's called a happy accident.

So, what *is* a sidebra? No, it's not for women with three boobs. And it's not like an under-arm-holster-purse-thingie. Although that would be kind of cool. I should doodle that one. Anyway, no, a sidebra is actually one of my best happy accidents. It's one of the weird things I'm known for at school. But that's all I'm going to say for now.

next. I mean, isn't your brain supposed to be your friend and protect you from the pain of horrible trauma by forgetting it? My brain is definitely not my friend.

I don't know why I chose the headline I did. It just jumped out at me from the list. And then it popped out of my mouth. I do know that I believed in it at the time. It was sort of clever (I thought) and informative (I guess), and it seemed like me (whoever that is).

There I was, standing in front of the class, clutching my notebook, looking around the room at all of these dying-to-judge-me faces. I tried to visualize success. But all I could visualize was pain. I could feel it in the air. I could feel my pain, I could feel everyone else's pain, and I could feel everyone else feeling my pain. Stop. You can do this. *You can do this!* cheered my all-in-your-head, personal rah-rah. Believe it. Just believe it. Sell it to the back of the room! Then I set my notebook down on the podium and went for it.

I jumped out toward the class like some demented clown. "Paisley Hanover—*Fun* of a Kind Girl!" And then I punctuated my headline with some bizarre manic gesture that could only be described as spastic jazz hands.

A camera snapped like crazy. People laughed. A lot of people laughed, actually, including Ms. Madrigal and Candy. For a second, I thought it would work. I really thought I could win. Some people even took notes when I read my well-crafted supporting sentences.

But I was no match for the tantalizing possibilities of

"Sweet, Nutty, Mouth-Watering Candy" delivered with Candy Esposito's irresistible blend of cute and confidence. And when she mentioned free Whoppers, onion rings, and golden-brown french fries on every work weekend? It was all over.

How embarrassing. How—ugh! What an idiot. I never had a chance against someone as popular as Candy Esposito. What was I thinking? Everything was over—the assignment, our little competition, the vote, my love connection with Eric Sobel, my shot at being Yearbook editor, my seven-point master plan, my hopes of getting into the college of my dreams, and the best year of my life.

And it was *still* only third period.

CHAPTER TWO

I must have been having an out-of-body experience as I trudged down the hall to Drama. I was repeatedly and mercilessly scuffing the heels of my new suede boots along the concrete. I would *never* do that to new boots if I were actually inside my own body.

Why? Why? WHY did I have to act like such a weirdo at that exact moment? If only I had gone with my second choice, "Paisley Hanover—I'd vote for Candy!"

How could I possibly end up in Drama and not Yearbook? I'd been planning and prepping and—and I didn't even have anything in *common* with Drama geeks! There was no way I could spend an entire year in third period with a bunch of weird-ass freakazoids.

I texted Jen.

OMG Humili8d! ES saw it! Must di.

Suddenly, Drama class actually seemed like the ideal place for me to go and quietly die. I mean, no one would know me there. I grabbed the cool metal handle, pulled open the door, and made my not-so-grand entrance into Drama.

Mr. Eggertson was standing in front of the stage, talking in this booming theatrical voice. Everyone turned and stared at me. Everyone. I stopped.

"New student?" asked Mr. Eggertson.

I nodded, holding up the yellow registration slip that I had just picked up in the office.

"Grab a seat."

Wow. The room was completely filled with Pleasant Hill High extras. Who were these people? Did they even go to my school? Wow. What weirdness—weird bodies, weird hair, weird clothes, weird hats. It was like I just walked into Weirdos "R" Us. Perfect. I should fit right in.

I slumped down in the nearest chair and tugged at a loose brown thread in my skirt, pretending I wasn't eyeing every other person in the room. Mr. Eggertson was going on about the origins of theater in ancient Greece and somewhere else really old. He had short dark hair and looked more like a dancer than a teacher, really muscular and lean.

I tried not to move my head while I checked out the other kids. This one girl—at least I think it was a girl—was wearing an orange and yellow knit elf hat with big earflaps, and it was like eighty degrees out. Next to her was Mime Guy. He had this blond Afro and was wearing a long black cape and a battered top hat. He might as well have worn a sign that said "Please Beat the Crap Out of Me."

I casually looked to the left. Teddy Baedeker, aka Special Ted, was sitting straight up in his chair staring at me. Teddy is a learning-disabled kid who's been in the class ahead of mine since forever. He's always been sweet and really harmless, but now he's sweet and really horny and gets boners in class all the time. Like right now, he sat up even straighter in his chair and nervously scratched his you-know-what.

I quickly looked away.

I prayed to Our Lady of Perpetual Boners for protection. She's this secret patron saint that Jen and I made up last year. Jen is Catholic, so she knows all about praying to saints and stuff. I closed my eyes. *Please, please, please, don't let me be sitting anywhere near Teddy Baedeker when he pitches his next pants tent. Thank you. Amen.*

When I opened my eyes, I saw a few kids I actually recognized. That weird retro lesbian Cate Maduro held her phone in her lap speed-texting someone. She looked over at me, then back to her phone. What's up with her freaky fifties hairdo? That bright red lipstick? Those pointy-toed Keds? Was she living in a time warp?

SIDEBRA

Why do guys scratch their little friend all the time—in public?! Do they think they're invisible? Do they think no one notices? Do they not even care? They should care. It's disgusting. And frankly, I'd rather not be reminded that some guys even have one. But if they can't help doing it, there should at least be some universal sign to warn innocent bystanders. You know, like those baseball hand signals—ear tug, right elbow pat, double nose wipe, left elbow pat, everyone look away now!

Cate and I kind of used to be friends when we sat next to each other in seventh-grade Spanish. We got A's all year and got in trouble all the time, always moving crazy Señora Pillsbury's glasses or hiding all of her chalk or setting her clock radio to go off really loud in the middle of class. But we had totally different friends and never really talked outside of class. And now, I don't know. Last year she got all retro and weird and next thing you know she was making out with some girl at an after-game dance and telling everyone she was a lesbian.

I looked around again, still trying not to move my head. Way off to the side, Mandy Mindel, this shy girl who plucks out all of her eyelashes, was slumped in a chair looking even more lost than usual. Whenever I see her, I always wonder about her parents. I wonder if they named her Mandy thinking it would become this cute, popular girl name. But instead Mandy Mindel ended up being shorthand for a painfully shy and lonely nervous wreck. I always thought her parents must be bummed.

Then I spotted Jean Merrill sitting with one long, gangly leg crossed over the other. She was looking all granny-chic wearing this little cardigan over a vintage polka-dot blouse with these wrinkly linen wide-leg floods and what looked like orthopedic dancing shoes. I couldn't decide if the shoes were thrift-shop cool or just tragic. Wow. She's got to be over six feet tall now. No wonder she can't find pants that fit.

I still felt bad about accidentally on purpose calling her String Bean Merrill over the loudspeaker at the eighth-grade dance because she had grown like a foot and a half that year. My mom, who unfortunately now is best buds with her mom, told me that Jean had to see a shrink because of it. I guess "Bean" kind of stuck. So now when I see her, I always go out of my way to be extra nice to her.

I gave her a short wave, trying to play it cool. She rolled her eyes and turned away, then leaned over and whispered something to a couple of Library Girls sitting next to her. They all kept turning and looking at me, laughing their glasses off.

So much for Drama being a place to go and quietly die. I had to get out of this class. This couldn't be good for my sanity or my popularity.

Mr. Eggertson was drawing something on this big white board, so I tried to appear interested and engaged.

But just then, the door behind me squeaked open. I turned.

Clint Bedard.

He quickly slid into the chair right next to mine and sniffled hard. Mr. Eggertson didn't even look. What was Clint Bedard doing in Drama? I would've expected him to take an elective like Bomb-Making or Car-Jacking—something, you know, career-related.

I looked down at his hands. I think you can tell a lot about a guy from his hands. They were almost elegant, like artist hands, with long slender fingers and dirty fingernails. Maybe he worked as a mechanic after school? He had this woven black rope bracelet around one wrist and two chunky silver rings on his index fingers.

I should probably tell you that I don't know Clint Bedard, even though he's in my grade, but I know his reputation. He's the kind of guy who freaks out most dads and turns on certain moms. Can I say that? Oh well, I did. Anyway, last year, he set the school roof on fire shooting bottle rockets, and all classes were canceled for three days. He has this hair, this sexy dark thick hair that's always messy and sticking up, like some hot senior babe has been running her hands through it in the backseat of a car. I always thought he was bad news and kind of felt sorry for him. But that was before he was sitting right next to me, close enough that I could smell his hair product. Hair product? That's weird. I expected him to smell like cigarettes or Taco Bell.

He kicked both feet out and leaned back in his chair, folding his arms behind his head. Nice biker boots. I inched my chair away from him a little so I could get a better look without being totally obvious. He had this amazingly detailed tattoo on his upper arm. What was that? It looked like some crazy maniac sticking out his tongue. He caught me staring at him and flashed this naughty, flirty grin—and *what* was *that*?

I tried not to laugh as I scribbled in my notebook.

Dude, you've got glittery lip gloss on.

I held my notebook out in front of him and tapped my finger on the page. He took my pen and started writing.

Watermelon. Wanna taste?

Before I could even think, he grabbed the notebook again and wrote:

Who's that?

He drew an arrow pointing to—OMG! A doodle of Eric Sobel kicking a heart-shaped soccer ball.

I calmly pulled my notebook back, closed it, and looked back at Mr. Eggertson. I pretended to concentrate, but I was pretty much dying inside.

Mr. Eggertson pointed up above the front of the stage. "The proscenium arch serves as a window through which the audience views the actors on the stage." He paused and looked around the room. "Am I losing you?"

Silence.

"Okay, everybody up! On your feet. Shake out your arms. Shake out your legs. Good. So, what is acting?"

"Faking it," Cate Maduro yelled out. A few people laughed.

"That's part of it. What else?"

"Performing on stage!"

"Playing a role and memorizing lines!"

"Good, what else?"

"Pretending to be someone you're not!"

"That's high school!" shouted Jean Merrill, cracking herself up and everyone else too, including me.

"Okay, okay," said Mr. Eggertson. "Acting is all of those things. But more than anything else, acting is *reacting*. Being present in the moment and really paying attention to what the other person is saying and doing. Let's try an exercise. Partner up with someone you would never normally speak to."

I glanced around the room. Well, that would be about everybody. I took a few steps toward Jean Merrill. "Partners?"

She looked at me skeptically, twirling a long piece of blond hair over and around her index finger. "Yeah, fine. Whatever."

Mr. Eggertson went on. "I want you to be as honest as you

can be in a short, spontaneous conversation. Talk about anything, but keep it real. Pay attention to the words, intonation, *and* body language. Don't act—*react*. And begin!"

She just stood there staring at me, looking slightly disgusted.

"So, um," I started. "How was your summer, Jean?"

"Look. Just call me Bean, okay? Everyone else does now. Thanks to you."

"Oh. Okay." I nodded. Was she still mad at me? Yup, pretty sure she was. I tried to win her over. "Cute shoes."

"Thanks." She pushed her glasses up with the back of her hand. "But don't call me String Bean, Bean Stalk, Bean Stalker, or Beano. Got it?"

"Got it."

"And whatever you do, don't call me anything over a loudspeaker or I will stab you in the eye with a dull number two pencil." She laughed. "God, I crack myself up."

"And switch!" Mr. Eggertson had a deep voice like some TV announcer. "New partners. No friends!"

Believe it or not, I felt really relieved when skinny Charlie Dodd ran up to me and wiped his forehead with the bottom of his maroon XXL polo shirt. Charlie and I aren't really friends, but I know him from carpool. He's kinda nerdy and used to wear only polo shirts tucked in. He had them in like a million different colors. Then last year, he switched to XXL polo shirts, untucked. So, I guess now he's like Gangsta Nerdy or something. I never thought I'd be so happy to see him.

"And begin!"

"Thanks, Charlie."

"Charles, please," he said in this British actorly way. "It's my stage name."

"I didn't know you were into Drama."

"Yeah, I want to expand my nerd rep in new, exciting ways. You can only go so far with Chess Club and the French horn."

I laughed. "How come you're not this funny in carpool?" I asked.

"I am. You ignore me." He said it like it was no big deal.

I almost blurted out, "No, I don't!" That would be reacting, right? But I decided to take an insane risk and actually be honest. "I do? Sorry." I really meant it.

"And stop! Find a new partner, please!"

"No worries," said Charlie before walking off.

Whenever anyone says "No worries," I get the distinct feeling I should be worrying. I stood there trying to think. Do I ignore him? I don't think so. I just never notice him much because I'm always half-asleep or listening to my iPod or doodling in my notebook—I have a little doodling obsession—or cramming for a test or texting someone. Is that the same thing as ignoring him? I decided to have a real conversation with Charlie in carpool at least once a week. Then I turned around, hoping to find Clint Bedard, and smacked right into—

"And begin!"

Oh crap. Cate Maduro was standing right in front of me with her hands on her hips.

"Paisley Hanover," she said, oozing attitude. "What are you doing in Drama? Shouldn't you be in the gym at some Pep Squad meeting?"

Oooh, she was nasty. And Pep Squad? What a cliché. I looked at her like I was beyond bored. Her skin was even paler than usual against her bright red lipstick, and her dark hair curled around one side of her face like a question mark. She was wearing these tight, way-out-of-style pants with a high cinched waist.

I tried to stare her down. But she had these crazy blue eyes that shot through you like demonic lasers. Must be colored contacts. So I went with Plan B—sneak attack.

"So, are you like really a lesbian now?"

She didn't look the least bit flustered as she leaned into my face and whispered, "Who wants to know?" Her breath smelled like spearmint Tic Tacs. I didn't even flinch. I was a little sorry I had gone there, but I was not about to be intimidated by some sketchy social misfit. I stared right back.

"Everyone. People can't stop talking about you."

"Really? What people?"

"What do you think we talk about at Pep Squad meetings?" For an instant, Cate Maduro looked terrified, then she laughed at me in that nice-try way.

"And stop! Okay, grab a seat! What did you notice?" Mr. Eggertson asked. Everyone just sat there. "Come on, people. What was consistently happening in all three conversations?"

I raised my hand. "Most people say the opposite of what they really mean?"

"Exactly!" Mr. Eggertson smiled and even looked a little impressed. "Which is why body language and intonation are so very important. The key to acting is not simply understanding the words—it's understanding the emotions *behind* the words." He paused. "I want you all to keep this in mind, because in a week or so, I'll be assigning you a partner and a scene. The two of you will be rehearsing every day for two weeks, after which you will perform your scenes for our fall drama night production, *Acting Out*."

Muffled groans and twitters from around the room. I felt my lungs drop into my stomach.

"*Acting Out* is open to the public to make sure that we have a good-sized audience." Mr. E. paused. "And always great fun."

Yikes! I hoped none of my friends found out. Just then my phone vibrated. I pulled it out fast. A text from Jen. Finally.

r bench @ mrng brk. BIG NWS!

I texted her right back.

Me 2! c u

Cool. Our munch bunch was on.

I turned around to find everyone suddenly lying on the floor. What had I missed? I got down and stretched out awkwardly.

"Now breathe," Mr. Eggertson was saying. Everyone started making these strange humming and vibrating sounds. "This is how we warm up and tune up our instruments," he said. Apparently, that's what you call your body when you're an actor—your quote-unquote instrument.

"Continue exhaling, people!"

I exhaled, but my instrument sounded permanently out of tune.

What could Jen's big news be? Maybe she got the inside scoop on Cindy Kutcher's new boobs? Maybe Bodie dumped her? A girl can dream, can't she?

"Keep it steady," Mr. Eggertson called out. "Now slowly raise the pitch until you can feel the vibration in your nose and the front of your face like a mask of sound."

Someone made a big fart noise. Everyone laughed, even me. Then the whole room began to swell with the hum of vibrating noses and faces. It sounded like a giant mosquito.

"Perfection, people! You are all going to be famous!" Mr. Eggertson shouted. "I can hear it in your noses."

When we finally stood up, Mr. Eggertson divided the class into two groups, and we did this lame trust exercise, where one by one, everybody had to stand on the edge of the stage and fall backward into the arms of the other students. You had to trust that the group below would work together to catch you and not let you hit the floor and crack your head open. If you asked me, it was a lot to ask on the first day of school.

But weirdly, it wasn't. There was this chill acid jazz playing from Mr. E.'s iPod. The windows were open, and you could get a whiff of that sweet green smell coming from the cut grass in front of the school. The room felt warm in the morning sun and kind of cozy. I was starting to think I could get used to Drama.

Fortunately, I was in the catching group first. Some people had to be coaxed. But most people just leaned back and went for it. The more people trusted you, the more you really didn't want to let anyone down, the more you wanted to catch everyone safely and lower them gently to the floor, even the fat kids. Especially the fat kids. And everyone really did work together. It was kind of amazing.

I was having this warm and fuzzy, people-are-beautiful moment, and then Clint Bedard took a diving leap into the crowd like it was a mosh pit. He would've broken his neck if he hadn't landed right on top of me. A bunch of us ended up in a pile on the floor groaning and laughing.

And then, without even getting off of me, Clint said in the most innocent voice, "Air male delivery for Paisley Hanover." He laughed. I laughed. What else could I do? I had to do something. Then we all laughed so hard that someone farted for real. And no. It wasn't me.

Mr. Eggertson was royally pissed. "That's one, Mr. Bedard. Two gets you a fast pass to the vice principal's office. Three and you're out of here." Clint flashed his flirty little grin at me. He seemed quite pleased with himself.

We all regrouped in front of the stage in our human catcher's mitt formation to finish up the trust exercise. Bean Merrill went next. All six feet of her—light as a tall, skinny feather. Then Teddy Baedeker went. I was shocked. The way people gently caught him and slowly lowered him to the floor, you would have thought he was the secret lovechild of our star quarterback and homecoming queen—not Special Ted, the weirdest kid in school. It was really cool. Really.

Then it was my turn. So I'm up there, standing on the stage with my back to the crowd, wondering if everyone can see up my skirt, but I'm also feeling full of trust and like cotton-candy luv fuzz. Then people started saying super encouraging stuff like "Come on Paisley, we've got you." "Relax!" "Just let go, lean back, and trust." So I did.

But just as I was beginning to fall backward, someone shouted, "Nice butt, you rah-rah!" And then people started to catch me, and for a second I thought everything was going to be fine. But then someone pinched me in the butt. Hard. And I yelped because it really hurt and I squirmed to get away. And then people started laughing. And then they basically dropped me. On my hip.

"Whoops!"

"Are you okay?"

"Sorry, Paisley."

"Bummer."

I lay there staring at the floor, waiting for the pain in my hip to subside, trying to ignore the shidiots still laughing at me.

"Hey, people, that is no way to build trust!" Mr. Eggertson shouted.

You can see little faces in the pattern on the linoleum floor tiles. There's a blockhead boxer with a flattened nose, a sleeping lady with long swirling hair, and a smirking, baby cupid angel. You can see little faces in the linoleum until your eyes start to water and fill up with tears.

No. I will NOT cry.

"Paisley?" asked Mr. Eggertson, kneeling down next to me. "Are you all right? Do you need to go to the nurse's office?"

"Fine. I'm fine!" I jumped up really fast and walked it off, rubbing my hip with the heel of my palm. I kept staring out the windows. I didn't want to see anyone, and I didn't want anyone to see me.

Bean Merrill touched my shoulder like she was tagging me it. "You okay?"

"Yeah. Fine. Whatever." I picked up my backpack and limped out of class. I so wasn't fine. But it wasn't my hip that was really hurting.

CHAPTER THREE

When I limped out of Drama, I was so in my own tortured head that I actually walked right past Yearbook just as class was letting out. It was the last place on the planet I wanted to be, and that was before Bentley Jones, Dwight Cashel, and Eric Sobel, the three lucky smarty sophomores who had gotten into Yearbook instead of me, bounded into the hall, bursting with superior college-application energy.

I wanted to strangle them. Instead, I ducked into the sticky bun line.

Every day at morning break, Jen, Amy, Carreyn, and I always shared a sticky bun. It was a tradition. Today it was my job to wade through the lines and pick out the biggest one with the most sugary goo on top. I struggled upstream from the cafeteria toward sophomore hall, my hip still throbbing, protecting the sticky bun with my life—if anything could cheer me up, it was sugar with friends.

We had all agreed to meet at my locker to download about morning classes. I couldn't wait to vent about my tragic life to Jen. I spotted Amy and Carreyn straddling the bench in front of my locker, reserving our prime location. I ducked under the hall railing and cut across the lawn where sophomores were grouped together in little conversational pods.

I should probably tell you a little about my school so you can picture it. Where I live, it never gets super cold. Like maybe it's snowed once and that was totally freaky. We basically have an outdoor campus. It's not like one big tall building. It's a bunch of one-story buildings in rows with covered hallways in between. There's a huge parking lot in front of the school and then once you get past the main offices and the main quad and the cafeteria, there's senior hall, junior hall, sophomore hall, and then freshman hall stuck out in the boonies near the band room. Does that make sense? Maybe I'll just draw a picture.

"Hey Paisley," said Charlie Dodd, waving at me sort of sympathetically. I waved back. I hoped I didn't see anyone else from Drama out here. A few other kids said hi too. I smiled and waved, but I kept walking—limping—maneuvering my way through the pods.

SIDEBRA

Yes, I know it's about time I addressed my weird name. Paisley. Paisley Hanover. And don't even bother. I've heard them all—Pains Me, Parsley, Spazley, Lazy Paisley, Crazy Paisley, Crazily Paisiley, Paislini, Paislini Bikini, Paisley Poo, Pays Late, Never Pays, Paised & Confused, blah, blah, blah. But it's been my name for my whole life, so it seems totally normal to me. And no, I wasn't named after that fabric with the sperm-shaped thingies on it. I was named after Paisley, Scotland, this town where my mom's family used to live like a million and two years ago. I've never been there, but I've checked it out online. I was kind of bummed to read that Paisley the town actually *was* named after the fabric with the sperm-shaped thingies on it. But I wasn't. Remember that. You'll be quizzed later.

"Hi Pais!" Amy and Carreyn called out at the exact same time.

Amy is tall and pretty with straight brown hair and big eyes and a really big personality. And she also has what Mom calls big bones. So she's literally been on a diet since the sixth grade. All that dieting and she still has big bones. She's usually super funny, but she can also be a little crabby, probably because she's constantly hungry. I don't know why she's so hard on herself. Well, actually I do. Her mom is sort of an uptight starvoholic perfectionist freak. She even makes *me* feel nervous. Anyway, we're always telling Amy that her body is great, that there's nothing wrong with it, but it's hard to convince her.

Carreyn eats enough for both of them but somehow stays way skinny. I guess she has a super fast metabolism, which is a blessing considering the incredibly bad perm she just got. Carreyn isn't the cutest face-wise, but she has a good bod. And she's always working it. "Go with your strengths," she says. "Go with your strengths." Her hair is the color of sun-kissed honey (told you) and she has big white teeth and a huge goofy smile that makes you want to smile with her. Sometimes Carreyn can be a little insecure about her looks. Actually, a lot insecure. But I admire her creativity and fierce determination to look better. Really, I do. She's always trying different things and she's truly fearless in the beauty and self-improvement department.

"Hi, guys," I called back.

"Oh my gag," Carreyn whispered. "Have you seen Cindy Kutcher's new boobs?"

"No thank you," I said. "But I heard all about them. Nice birthday present from your parents."

"Can you say impending back surgery?" Amy asked.

"That's so awful." Just the thought of it made me cringe. "Hey, have you seen Jen?"

"Nope," said Amy. "I'll bet she's with Bodie."

I looked around. "What? She just texted me and said she'd meet us here."

"Paisley, take a relaxative! If she said she's coming, she's coming. Cute outfit," said Carreyn, nodding with approval.

"Thanks." I dropped my backpack and casually posed. Then winced. Who wanted a hip fracture the first day of school? But my outfit was pretty cute. I was wearing this short lime green and brown mod patterned skirt and this super cute clingy brown top with a scoop neck that was tight but not slutty tight. And, of course, my new chocolate brown suede boots.

"I didn't know we were wearing boots today," Carreyn whined, looking confused and a little deflated. She had on satin ballet flats and quickly pulled her feet under the bench and out of view.

"We're not wearing boots. I am."

Amy looked down at her size eleven feet jammed into her size ten ballet flats and shook her head. "I can't believe I fell for this. I don't even like ballet flats. On me, they look like ballet *fats*!"

"Amy, stop. You're not fat," I said, poking her in the rib cage.

"But if you're *feeling* fat, can I have your quarter of the sticky bun?" Carreyn asked.

Amy ignored her. "Even my feet are fat. Look, look!" She pointed at her toes. "I have fat pockets between my toes."

"Amy!" I said, exasperated. "You're starting to sound like you have fat pockets in your brain."

Amy got all serious. "Is that possible?"

"Oh my God!" I had to change the subject. "You'll never guess what happened to me this morning."

"Is it a guy? Did someone ask you out?" asked Carreyn, flapping her hands in front of her.

"Was it Teddy Baedeker?" said Amy, trying to look sincere.

Carreyn laughed and a chunk of half-chewed sticky bun flew out of her mouth.

"Uh, no," I said. Poor Teddy Baedeker.

"Well, Eric Sobel sort of looked at me in Yearbook," I said slowly, not wanting to disappoint, and not really wanting to confess the horrid details.

Their eyes got kind of big and they both sighed, "Wow."

"Yeah. Wow." I plopped down between them on the bench. But you know, why ruin three people's mornings with my sad story? So I leaned in. "Amazingly, he's even hotter than last year," I whispered, as if delivering insider info. "His hair is a little longer, a little shaggier, and sexy. And . . ." I paused for dramatic effect. "He's taller."

They both stared at me like they were having a personal moment with the new and improved Eric Sobel.

Finally Carreyn whimpered, "It's not fair. He's already too gorgeous."

Amy nodded, nibbling on a grape. "More please."

"He just looked at me and kinda smiled! There isn't any more." I looked at Carreyn and then Amy. "Yet!" I giggled, hoping it didn't sound forced, knowing I was completely deluded.

My chances with Eric Sobel were, like, nonexistent. The most we had in common was being on the same page of the school newspaper at the end of freshman year for that stupid Spring Superlatives thing. Eric Sobel was "Best Dressed." And I was "Best Laugh." Unfortunately it's because I've kind of developed a reputation for laughing so hard I sometimes pee a little in my pants. Some people, especially really hilarious people, won't let me ride in their car anymore. Okay, not really. But that was the joke for a while last year.

Now I checked down the hall in both directions. "Where is Jen?"

"I guess she *is* with Bodie." Amy shrugged and took a sip of Diet Coke.

"She's got Bodie on the brain twenty-four/seven." I pulled off a little piece of sticky bun. "It's so strange for her."

Jen first started hanging out with Bodie at Bigwood, this swanky athletic club that looks like a big ski lodge, where they both worked over the summer. After Bodie broke up with Candy Esposito, he started flirting with Jen like every day while she was folding towels. She loved it. And I was excited for her. At first.

"Well, if you ask me," Carreyn said, "she's been acting beaucoup bizarro ever since Hutch's pool party."

"It started way before that, like when they moved into that little house," I said.

Carreyn and Amy nodded. I knew they were picturing Jen's new house because they had these pained, slightly grossed-out looks on their faces.

Jen's parents were getting divorced, so they had to sell their house at the beginning of the summer. It was depressing enough that her parents were splitting up, but you should have seen where Jen and her mom and her little brother were living now. It was this tiny little house down behind the Save Mart—and they were *renting*. Her dad moved into some apartment in the next town over to be closer to the girlfriend he supposedly didn't have. What a creep. Jen had seen them together at least twice, and the girlfriend was way younger. Gross.

"Hey, Pains Me!"

Hilarious. I've never heard that one before.

Peter Hutchison strutted over. Oh great. Hutch is this big obnoxious loudmouth jock. The sad thing—he's supposedly one of the smart ones. Unfortunately, he's friends with everyone I'm friends with, so I have to tolerate him. Hutch was wearing his black and gold letterman's jacket, as always. His freshman year he lettered in football and basketball, even though he sat on the bench the entire basketball season. He never went anywhere without that jacket.

I rolled my eyes. "Hi, Hutch. New jacket?"

Amy and Carreyn laughed.

"You miss me?" He tried to put his arm around my shoulder, but I stood up and spun out of reach.

"Yes, I missed you," I said sweetly. "What's your name again?"

Hutch laughed way too hard. "You also missed a sick party at my house, know what I'm saying?"

"Really? You had a party? When?" Of course I was invited, so I knew about the stupid party, but I was at a spa retreat with my grandmother over Labor Day weekend—I totally love my Grambo, but there are some things about a grandmother it's just better not to see.

"Like you didn't hear about it. Right," he said.

Charlie Dodd walked toward us down the hall sipping a smoothie and listening to his iPod, probably some Gangsta Nerdy tune. In one smooth athletic move, Hutch stripped the ear buds from Charlie's ears, swiped the cup from his hand, ripped the straw and lid off the cup, and swung the smoothie up to his mouth.

Charlie just stood there.

Hutch slammed it down in about three chugs, then wiped his hand across his mouth. "Thanks, little dude." Hutch handed the empty cup back to Charlie.

Charlie had experienced this type of respect for most of his life and took it like a man—a smart and scrawny man. "My pleasure." He smiled. "Can I get you anything else? Breakfast is the most important meal of the day."

"Thanks, I'm good."

"I really hope the Fem Boost doesn't make your man-boobs bigger." Charlie clutched his backpack like a football and bolted down the hall.

"You little rectal wart!" Hutch took off after him, blasting his way through the mid-morning crowd.

"What a moron," I said, watching Hutch chase Charlie down the hall.

"Really? I think Charlie's looking kinda cute this year," said Carreyn, sounding a little crushed out.

"Gross!" said Amy.

"I meant that Hutch is the moron," I said.

Carreyn was suddenly all freaked out. "Amy, I was totally kidding!" She laughed in her semi-manic way. "God, I can't believe you thought I was serious. Charlie Dodd's gross!"

"*Hutch* is gross," I said. "What a skeezer buttcap." I sat down on the bench in front of my locker and checked my phone for messages from Jen. Nothing. I texted her.

Wat up? Whr r u?

"So what happened at that party?" I asked Amy and Carreyn. "Jen's definitely withholding details, but I can't figure out why."

"I don't know." Carreyn popped the last piece of sticky bun into her mouth. "But it was a lot of fun in the hot tub."

"Fun?" asked Amy. "It looked like a varsity grope-fest to me."

"Don't be such a B with an itch! They're great guys." Carreyn wiped sugar slime off her upper lip. "If you'd fit into your new bathing suit, I'm sure you would've been sitting there right next to Jen."

"Actually, no. I wouldn't," Amy snapped. "I don't just let any guy grab my butt the way you do."

Carreyn's mouth dropped open and her hands fell to her hips. "What are you saying? Are you calling me a slut?"

Fortunately, just then the warning bell for fourth period rang. Amy gave Carreyn a you-would-know look and walked off to her next class before I had to break up a brat fight.

Jen texted me back.

w/ BoD

sorry. c u @ lunch

Unbelievable. I would never blow off my best friend for some guy on the first day of school. Would I? No. I would not.

Well, okay, Bodie isn't just some guy. He's a junior. He's Bodie Jones, star running back. Bodie Jones, power forward and awesome three-point shooter. Bodie Jones, all-state sprinter. Bodie Jones, brother of Bentley, herself a superior human being. And, on top of all that, he's a really great guy—funny, cute, nice, and extremely well groomed. He volunteers at the local nursing home, he's willing to be hypnotized and make a fool of himself at school assemblies. He's Bodie Jones, total A-lister. I slowly turned the combination lock and opened my locker. I hate Bodie Jones.

I don't know if your school is like this, but at our school, popularity works a lot like celebrities in Hollywood. There's the A-list, the B-list, the C-list, the D-list, and the indie darlings. And then there's everyone else. The extras.

Basically, I've always been a B-lister. There was the year I had to wear headgear, which dropped me to the C-list, but that was a long time ago. Then last year, something truly amazing happened. I became a B+-lister. I had never been so popular, and it felt awesome. It was this weird lucky bunch of things that all came together.

First, I have red hair, which not everyone goes for. But I grew it longer over the summer before ninth grade, and that definitely helped. And my brother Parker was a senior and really cool in an indie darling way, which gave me an all-access pass to some parties and stuff that most freshmen would never even know about. And then the other lucky thing that happened—Jen got boobs. Huge, round, full, bounce-when-you-run boobs. And every guy in school started noticing her and wanting to find out who she was. And since I'm her best friend, a lot of those guys started talking to me. So I suddenly had tons of face time with older cute

SIDEBAR

A-list: Varsity Jocks (guys), Varsity Poms (cheerleaders), BPs (beautiful people), Yearbook editor, and student body officers. (Only juniors and seniors allowed!)
B-list: Freshman and sophomore Jocks, Poms, BPs. Cool kids who just moved here. Stars of boys' teams. Sporty, cute stars of girls' teams. JV Poms. Anyone dating an A-lister.
C-list: Uncool kids with really nice cars, brains who unexpectedly got really cute or surprisingly good bods, baton twirlers, and leads in school plays.
D-list: Mathletes, AV Guys, Library Girls. Clueless kids who try way too hard to be popular and always end up making total fools of themselves (i.e., people only know their names because they're idiots).
Indie Darlings: Kids with special skills or weird talents. Like Tracy Monroe, our very own Olympic swimmer, or Clint Bedard, our very own arsonist. (Everyone likes an indie darling at least for a week. They have crossover appeal because they do whatever they want and they're good at it.)
Extras: Everyone else.

guys and I didn't even have to flirt or fake-laugh at any dumb jokes.

But then something happened. Her parents' divorce, this party at Hutch's . . . I don't know. It's like, where did Jen go? Literally.

Ugh. Could this day get any worse?

I jerked open my locker and grabbed my American History textbook. As I pulled it out, a folded-up piece of paper flew out of my locker and landed on the ground between my boots. I picked it up.

FRECKLES ARE SEXY

OMG! What?! I casually looked around to see if anyone was watching me. It had to be a joke. No one thinks freckles are sexy. Do they . . . ?

Who?

CHAPTER FOUR

I cut fourth period. I wasn't planning to. It just
kind of happened.

As I walked down the hall, I studied the note for clues—all
capital letters written in black ink on plain notebook paper. Not
much to go on. But that's weird—all the E's looked like backward 3's.

The hall was starting to get crowded. I looked up, and there
they were again! What was it with these three? Were they all best
buds now?! Bentley Jones, Dwight Cashel, and Eric Sobel had
turned the corner and were headed in my direction, talking and
laughing like the world were made of lollipops and midgets. I
waited for them to hook arms and skip down the hallway singing *Follow the Yellow Brick Road! Follow the Yellow Brick Road! Follow,
follow, follow, follow, follow the Yellow Brick Road!*

I wanted to sic my flying monkeys on them. Crap. No time.
I walked backward and turned into the library.

They were supposed to pass by, and then I was going to
go straight to American History. But they didn't. They stopped
right in front of the library, and then all three turned to see

"Sweet, Nutty, Mouth-Watering" Candy Esposito come bopping down the hall. And then they followed me right into the library! I mean, what?!

I lunged behind the magazine rack to scope out an escape route. While I was hiding, I noticed a flyer on the bulletin board announcing that sign-up sheets for class officers would be posted in the main hall. I made a mental note. Thank God Candy Esposito was a junior and couldn't run against me for vice president.

When the coast was clear, I made a beeline for the back wall, bent double as if I were looking for something—only really, *really* fast. I wasn't in the mood to hear Candy Esposito go on and on with fake modesty about how she really didn't deserve to win the Yearbook spot, but when you're so well liked and have so many friends, people always just vote for you.

I hid behind the thick reference volumes and spied on them through the shelves. They were standing across the room, talking to who I guessed was the new librarian, but it was hard to see. They were probably introducing themselves as the next generation of Yearbook Royalty. Ergh. I was about to make a break for the door, when the final bell rang.

Oh no! I collapsed against the back wall. When I'd asked if this day could get worse, I wasn't looking for a sarcastic answer.

Parker had warned me about Mr. Yamaguchi, my American History teacher. It was better to break your own leg than show up late to his class. I looked around for the thickest reference book I could find, inched it off the shelf, and let it drop directly onto my foot. Silent library scream!!!! It hurt like crazy, but sadly, nothing broke. That's the downside of nice boots. So . . . I just kind of . . . didn't go to fourth period.

I made myself comfortable, hiding in the reference section, and started reading about beetles. Did you know that there are more species of beetles than plants? There are over like 350,000 species of beetles, not counting the unnamed ones. And they're surprisingly well accessorized.

That's when I heard Candy Esposito's voice coming from the other side of the reference shelf.

"Hi, so are you almost done with the computer?" she asked.

I peeked through the encyclopedias. Candy was talking to this junior girl, kind of a C-lister, not totally unpopular but definitely *not* a pop.

"No."

"Are you sure?" Candy asked, smiling. "Because I *really* need to use it, you know, like right now."

"Why don't you ask one of them?" The girl pointed down the row. Dwight Cashel and Bentley Jones were sitting at the other computers, probably researching papers that wouldn't even be assigned until next year.

"Well, I could, but I know them and I know they're working on really important stuff."

Holy shiitake mushrooms! Did Candy actually just *say* that—and with a huge smile on her face?!

The girl didn't say anything back. I mean, what could she say? She just looked up at Candy and then down at the keyboard. I couldn't see her face, but I watched her shoulders sink down. She saved and closed her file, then got up and walked away.

"Thanks!" Candy waved, all super sweet.

That was . . . gross. And I thought Candy was supposed to be one of the *nice* ones.

I turned back to my book on beetles and wondered if the cute popular beetles took advantage of C-list beetles, but I couldn't find anything. I was totally absorbed in the feeding habits of tiger beetles when she found me.

"Are you researching a particular species of beetle? Can I help?" an unfamiliar voice asked.

I looked up, I'm sure with a painfully guilty face. "Uh, no. Thanks. I'm okay."

"Hi. I'm Ms. Whitaker, the new librarian."

Librarian? I'd heard of Ms. Whit, but she did *not* look like a librarian. She looked like some brainy babe hipster. She wore these cool chunky glasses and a bunch of bright-colored bangle bracelets and this beaded necklace and . . . Whoa. She had a tattoo. A librarian with a tattoo? Is that even allowed?

"Hi." I went back to my beetles and concentrated very hard, hoping she would respect my appreciation for arthropod knowledge and move on.

"I love beetles too. See?" She held up a clear hunk hanging from her necklace. There was a big green shimmering beetle frozen in resin. "*Cotinis mutabilis*, a fig-eater beetle."

I wrinkled my nose and leaned in to examine it. "Wow. That's really . . . dead."

"Yup." She smiled. "So, who are you?" she asked innocently, looking down at some list.

Uh-oh. "Paisley? Paisley Hanover?"

She ran a finger over her eyebrow a few times. She had these wild blue-green eyes. "I don't see you on my list for study hall."

Busted! I didn't have the energy to make up some elaborate story, so I went with the truth.

And guess what? Ms. Whit was pretty cool. She even laughed when I mentioned Mr. Yamaguchi.

"Yeah. I've met him. You don't want to start the year on his bad side."

She let me hang out in the library for the rest of fourth period, just this once, as long as I agreed to come to her "Real Research in the Digital Age" lunch seminar next week and bring friends.

"Yeah, sure," I said. That was easy. Ms. Whit was definitely my kind of librarian.

There were rumors about the faculty at Pleasant Hill as well as the students. Mr. Eggertson had been a truly talented actor with a real agent and everything, and then his wife had gotten pregnant with twins, and he'd been teaching full-time ever since. Our vice principal, Mr. Canfield, was secretly gay, but don't tell his 300-pound wife or their two kids. Mr. Yamaguchi was a big-shot corporate lawyer who burned out and started teaching because he thought it would be relaxed and far more rewarding. Now he was more unrelaxed and burned out than ever. Our head custodian had actually gone to Pleasant Hill High. And foxy Señor Abbott's wife was a Bolivian heiress.

But one of the best rumors revolved around Ms. Whitaker, the new librarian. Someone had heard that she was a radical socialist, and while certain people at our school liked to throw that term around, no one (other than Toby and Kobe Bach-Avery, whose parents really were socialists) really had any idea what being a socialist actually meant—i.e., no iPhone, no Xbox, no cable TV.

My mom told me that Ms. Whit wasn't a radical socialist—she was a radical social*ite*. Her family owned the county's big newspaper and, apparently, she walked away from millions simply to piss off her snooty parents. When I first heard this, true or not, I immediately liked Ms. Whit. I had never thought of anyone over thirty as even having parents, at least not having parents enough that you would want to piss them off. And then to find out she had a tattoo? Like I said, my kind of librarian.

I stealthily maneuvered my way around the library, acting all I-Spy, trying to avoid the Yearbook Royalty. As I inched along the side windows, I glanced outside—and there was my locker.

Hmmm. What a perfect place to set up a stakeout. Maybe I could catch a glimpse of my locker stalker in action.

Then I made a break for the magazine lounge and hid behind a *National Geographic*, which is not that easy to do, considering its size. I looked up just as Eric Sobel sat down next to me on the couch, picked up a *Sports Illustrated*, and conspicuously held it up in front of his face just like me.

"Hey," he whispered from behind the magazine. "Hey you, behind the herd of endangered elephants."

I peeked at him from behind my magazine, trying to hide my face from Candy, who had just reached right past me for this week's *The Economist* and then returned to her computer.

Was Eric Sobel talking to me?

"Check this out." Eric surreptitiously slid a neon yellow flyer in my direction. "It might work for you. Instead of Yearbook."

Yes, Eric Sobel was talking to me!

I tried to concentrate on the headline. *The Fly is Open!* Wait. Was he serious? I looked back at him. He had the most intense green eyes and dark, dark, long lashes.

"I shot some photos for them last year," he whispered. "Not Yearbook-related, but still. It's a wacked out but fun crew."

I took the flyer from him and skimmed it. I could hardly believe he was talking to me, let alone making suggestions for electives.

The Fly is Open!
for business this year

Despite senseless draconian budget cuts,
The Fly is still in business.
Come to a lunch meeting to learn how
you can join our new all-volunteer staff
and discover the many joys of journalism—
long hours, no pay, great parties.
We need writers, editors, field reporters, columnists,
photographers & coffee sherpas.

No experience or scruples required.
WHERE: Room 107
WHEN: Friday @ noon
**You can kill the budget
but you can't silence the pen...
or the computer...
or the website...or whatever.**

I looked at him kind of amazed. He was trying to help me. He was seriously trying to help me. "Thanks," I whispered.

"Sure." He slowly lifted his magazine to cover his face.

I shoved the flyer into my bag. He's got to like me, right? I mean, not necessarily *like me* like me, but at least like me as a friend. I mean, maybe not as a weekend friend, but as a school friend, right? God, I sounded like a needy gooberish girl. I was not going to think about him or wonder about him or obsess about him or fantasize about him until he gave me a sign. I looked over at him.

Nothing.

Ergh.

Some of you may think that a school library is the center of the boring universe. And the only reason to go there is to avoid people or read magazines for free or take a nap where it's air-conditioned.

All I'll say is this: What ended up going down in our library was definitely *not* boring. But that's all you get. For now.

CHAPTER FIVE

Finally the bell for lunch rang. I leaned against the window, waiting for the library to clear out, and spied on my locker. Nothing unusual. And then the crush of loud, rowdy, hungry kids surged into the hallway, blocking my view.

And there was Clint Bedard, walking across the grass. I started to go, but something made me turn back and watch him for a second. He was long and lean and moved with this easy, relaxed rhythm. Clearly, he had his own internal sound system too. And it was good. As he walked down the steps and away from all the yelling, chasing, obnoxious sophomorons, I wondered where he was going and what was playing on the soundtrack in his head. I barely remembered him from last year. Maybe now I'd be seeing him everywhere, like a new vocabulary word.

I could see Amy and Carreyn already parked on our bench. And there was Jen standing with them. Yay! I looked inside the little pocket in my bag to make sure I still had my freckles love letter. There it was. I threw my bag over my shoulder and headed out.

But by the time I got to our bench, Jen was gone. I checked down the hall in both directions. "Where did she go?"

"Oh, it's very sad." Amy shook her head and took a sip of Diet Coke.

Carreyn nodded. "We weren't sure how to tell you. We've lost her again."

"What? No."

"Yup." Amy looked disappointed, for real. "She left us. She's in the main quad eating lunch with Bodie. Sorry."

"But we agreed to meet right here!" I pulled out my phone as if waving around proof would change anything. "What did she say? Is she mad at me or something?"

"I don't think so," said Amy.

"She seemed fine to me," Carreyn added.

"I'm going down there."

"Where?" asked Carreyn. "To the quad?" Her eyes bulged. I nodded.

"No way," said Amy. "Are you sure you want to do that?"

The main quad at lunch is kind of scary. There are benches on all four sides, and there's a huge bronze statue of our mascot, The Pleasant Hill Hornet, right in the middle surrounded by this low round brick wall that everyone sits on. At lunch and break, the main quad is packed with Jocks and Poms and BPs. You pretty much have to be a junior or a senior, or dating a junior or a senior, or insanely confident, to hang out there.

At the beginning of every year, there's always some poor clueless freshman who's stupid enough to walk across the quad, gets chased down and duct-taped to the bronze hornet, and then crowned with a brown paper lunch bag. My brother Parker told me about this girl a few years ago who was running across the quad at lunch carrying her flute case, when she wiped out in her clogs and went flying. She landed splat on the bricks surrounded by her books and her lunch and her open flute case. Everyone just laughed at her. He said she never got over it and ended up transferring to another school. Isn't that awful?

And I could relate. I used to play flute. I chose it because it was the smallest instrument and the case would be really easy to carry to school. But I had to give it up because I kept hyperventilating and passing out whenever I practiced. Anyway, when Parker told me that story, it really freaked me out, and I had this dream that it was me wiping out in the quad, only it wasn't a flute, it was a tuba, and I was totally naked—except for the tuba. Aren't crazy anxiety dreams the best? By the way, I look really good in a tuba.

I couldn't believe Jen was eating lunch in the main quad on the first day of school. I mean, we were

SIDEBRA

I admit that a big bronze hornet with its four front legs up, like a boxer in fighting position, is totally ridiculous. The bronze hornet was donated to Pleasant Hill High a few years ago by alumnus Monty Montego. According to anyone who remembers him, in high school Monty was a total dweeb with bad teeth and greasy, already-thinning hair. Now he's a local celebrity—the anchor guy on Evening News 7—and has big, blinding white teeth and a thick, expensive head of hair. He not only donated the statue, he did a three-part on-air story about the design, forging, and installation of the big bronze hornet so we'd all know exactly how much he'd spent.

Weight of the hornet:
approximately 3,500 lbs.
Height of the hornet: 93"
(that's almost eight feet!)
Cost of the hornet: $50,000
Supplying the quad with a monstrous, self-congratulatory bug: Priceless.

definitely popular, but only B+-list popular. Either Jen had a death wish, or she and Bodie were even tighter than I thought.

Jen's been my best friend since she moved here from Michigan in fifth grade. And we've eaten lunch together every single day, except for that month in sixth grade when we were in lunch suspension for faking a screaming, hair-pulling girl-fight during recess in front of a substitute yard monitor. We got in big trouble, but it was worth it.

Different friends have cycled in and out of our lunch bunch every year. But Jen and I have always stuck together—until today. I was starting to get a really bad feeling about this thing with Bodie. The old flat-chested Jen would never do anything like this. I pulled my phone out of my bag to see if she had called or texted. Nope.

I stuffed most of my sandwich back into the Ziploc bag. I wasn't feeling very hungry anymore. Actually, I was feeling pretty sucky. Maybe she had a good reason for blowing me off. Maybe something had happened. But I definitely wasn't going to risk going into the quad. I just wanted to scope it out from a safe distance.

If you stand in the main hall, you can look out the windows past some bushes and get a perfect view into the quad. I tried to act casual, like I was just early for sixth period and not like I was spying on my best friend.

Wow. There she was, right near the hornet, standing in a small group with Bodie and Candy Esposito and a few other juniors, looking all fabulous and popular. Jen was laughing and obviously in on whatever joke Bodie was telling.

I leaned against a pole, pulled out my phone, and hit Jen's speed dial. I was going to tell her that she was looking totally popular and BP. I looked back out the window. I wanted to see the expression on her face when I said it. It took a few seconds for her phone to ring. I couldn't help smiling as I watched her dig into her tote bag. She pulled it out, checked the caller ID, and then dropped the phone back into her bag.

I'm sorry, what?

I quickly hung up and watched her say something and laugh and fake hit Bodie on the arm in this girlie flirtatious way. Candy Esposito suddenly got all animated and talky and then—no she *didn't*—started waving her hands around in a crazy, manic gesture.

Spastic jazz hands.

What? No. No! A few people laughed. Then Bodie spastic jazzed her back, adding some fancy footwork and turning it into a bad *High School Musical* dance move. Everyone burst into hysterics. My so-called best friend Jen was actually bent over, gasping with laughter. I just stood there, mortified. I was already feeling totally loserish. But being ignored, gossiped about, and laughed at all at once was threatening to put me over the edge. And wasn't Bodie supposed to be one of the nice ones? Wait. Why did I suddenly feel like I was having déjà vu?

How could this day have gone so wrong?! I turned away and sunk down onto the shiny linoleum floor. It felt cool and smooth against my palms, and oddly comforting. I greeted the faces in the linoleum. Hello blockhead boxer with a flattened nose. Hello sleeping lady with long, swirling hair. This was the only thing that felt right so far about my first day of school.

"Repugnant."

I looked up. Charlie Dodd was standing in front of me, shaking his head.

"Repugnant?" I repeated.

"I didn't want to say anything at morning break with all your friends around. But yeah. What happened to you in Drama class. Repugnant."

Huh? I must have been staring at him with a this-does-not-compute expression.

"PSAT vocab word. Offensive. Repulsive. Disgusting. You studied for the PSATs over the summer, right?"

"No."

"Really? Wow, Paisley. You're way behind." He turned and walked up the hall, the tail of his XXL polo shirt flapping like a dress.

Normally, I wouldn't even care what Charlie Dodd thought. But Charlie is a total brain and he knows what he's talking about when it comes to grades and tests and all things nerd. Plus, after our "conversation" in Drama, I was trying to take Charlie Dodd more seriously.

Repugnant. Repugnant. I sighed. It was the first day of school and I was already way behind, on top of being a total weird-ass freakazoid loser. I was pretty sure I wouldn't have any trouble remembering the word repugnant, though, since it perfectly described my first day of sophomore year.

CHAPTER SIX

And things only got worse. For the rest of the afternoon, I prayed that this was just some twisted first-day-of-school anxiety dream and that soon I'd wake up and laugh about it as I went off to live my fabulous sophomore life. Of course, the only dream part was that I *had* a fabulous sophomore life.

As the last bell rang, my phone started buzzing. Another text from Jen.

Grls lkr rm. 3:15 Rly!

I texted back.

ok c u

In the locker room, I pulled my hair back into a ponytail and sat down on a bench to lace up my cleats. Still no sign of Jen. Carreyn had transformed her wild permed hair into two poofy pigtails. I watched her tie a black ribbon around one and a yellow ribbon around the other. Whatever Carreyn lacked in skills on the field, she more than made up for in school spirit.

"We're so gonna be late," said Amy to her own reflection as she quickly applied lip gloss and passed it to Carreyn. Amy believed that if you look your best on the field, then you'll definitely play your best. Carreyn had a whole different take. Who cares if you aren't that good if you look good doing it, which explained her short shorts and tight tank top. Carreyn is the only one of the four of us who wasn't a starter, but she still made practice every single day. She hated to be out of the loop.

It was already 3:25. If we weren't dressed and on the field by 3:30, we'd have to run a lap for every minute we were late. Coach Sykes loved to torture us. She pretended to hate us and told us we were all spoiled rich kids, which we weren't. Most of us were actually middle-class kids, and only some of us were *really* spoiled. But when we scrimmaged, she thought it was hilarious to divide our team into two groups, the Haves and the Have A Lots. We pretended to hate her back. But I knew her hard-ass routine was all an act. She loved us—at least she did right after we won the district championship last year.

"I'm gonna go," said Carreyn apologetically. "I don't want to get in trouble."

"Me too," added Amy. "I'm feeling too bloated to run extra laps. And I cannot deal with Coach Psycho today."

They both looked at me, waiting to see if I was coming.

"I'll wait for Jen," I said, slamming my locker shut and hooking the lock through the latch. "I want to hear her big news. We'll run late laps together."

"You're such a good friend, Paisley," said Carreyn. "See you out there!" Her pigtails bounced like little pom-poms as she trotted out the door after Amy.

I really wanted to tell Jen about the horrors of Yearbook and Drama, and I especially wanted to show her my

FRECKLES ARE SEXY note and see who she thought could've written it. I loved Amy and Carreyn, but I knew if I showed the note to them, everyone would find out about it and I'd probably never get another secret note—or I'd start getting stupid copycat notes like PICKLES ARE SEXY. No thanks.

I tightened and retied my laces and looked at the clock. I washed my hands, splashed water on my face, and looked at the clock. I did a few quad stretches and looked at the clock. It was already 3:34. By the time I got out to the field, I was already looking at five late laps. Where was she? It was bad enough that Jen was late herself on the first day of practice. But making me late too? Coach Psycho was going to kill us—we were supposed to be team leaders.

I'd wait three more minutes.

I waited five and then stopped for a drink on my way out the door. I was slurping the cord of water arcing over the drinking fountain when I heard footsteps running outside and a familiar laugh.

"Hey Pais!" Jen shouted like she had just won the lottery. She ran through the open locker room doors and gave me a quick hug. "Sorreee! Sorry I'm so late."

"No big. Cute tote."

"Marc Jacobs. Roger bought it for me. Can you believe it?" Roger is her scummy, cheatin' dad.

"That's awesome," I said, thinking it was a total waste of money and a pathetic attempt to buy Jen's approval. Too bad Roger didn't want to buy *my* approval. She didn't seem mad at me, though. Everything seemed normal. Except her cheeks were really flushed, and she had tiny beads of sweat across her nose and a few hairs stuck in her lip gloss.

She ran her pinky along one cheek to free the hairs and tucked a few white-blond strands behind one ear. "I had to move Bodie's car for him." She shook her head, giggling. "I could not get it into gear."

I frowned at her. "What are you now, like his personal assistant?"

"No." She stepped back. "I'm his *girlfriend*, Paisley," she said in this really condescending voice. "That's what girlfriends do."

I rolled my eyes. "Thanks. I'm not some noob. Hurry up and change. I waited for you, and now we're both late."

"What is your problem?"

"*My* problem? You blew me off at morning break. You blew me off at lunch! Then you told me to meet you here before practice for some big news. Now you're so late, we'll both be running laps until dark!"

"Enough with the bitch-me-out, okay?"

I just glared at her. You've got to be kidding me.

"All right, sorry about break and lunch." She so didn't mean it. "I said I'd be there, then I changed my mind. I wanted to hang with Bodie."

"Obviously," I said coldly. "So is that your *big* news? That you just want to hang with Bodie? Come on, hurry up and change."

"Well . . . " Jen had this strange look on her face. She turned her back to me and started digging through her fab designer tote. "Don't be mad, okay?" She hesitated. "But I'm not going to practice."

"What?"

She looked up and shot me a quick glance in the mirror, then looked away. "Sorry. But I've decided I'm not gonna play soccer this year."

I stood there for a second. I should probably explain that Jen is one of our best forwards. She can shoot with her left and her right foot better than I can. She has awesome ball skills and she's really fast. And the best part, we know each other so well, it's like we can read each other's mind on the field. I never would have scored all those goals last season without her.

She *had* to be kidding.

"Right." I nodded with a fake smile. But then—wait. Where was her soccer bag? I suddenly had a nasty feeling in my stomach.

"Paisley, I'm serious!" She turned around. "I've been thinking about it for a couple weeks . . . But I decided for sure today. I'm gonna try out for cheerleading instead."

I laughed, like really laughed.

"What is so funny? God!" She threw down her fists and stomped her stacked-heel boot. "No one takes me seriously anymore!"

I stopped laughing. OMG. She *was* serious.

"Jen, why would you want to jump up and down on the sidelines cheering for the stars of some other team when you can *be* the star of our team?"

"I don't expect you to understand."

"Why not?"

"Well, you can't see! I'm just not that into soccer anymore. Sorry, but you'll just have to accept that we're growing in really different directions."

I laughed again. Was she for real?

"You know, you shouldn't laugh. When I make cheerleader, I'll be mucho popularo. And guess what? You probably will be too."

"And that's all you think I want?"

She dropped her head and gave me her duh look.

"What if you don't make cheerleader?" I asked.

"I'll make cheerleader. Bodie's on it. He's tight with the Varsity Poms and asked a couple of them to teach me the routine before tryouts next Tuesday." She smiled like this was the greatest thing.

"Jen, I don't get you. Are you like Bodie's little doll now?"

"Paisley, he loves me, really loves me, and I love him, and I want to spend as much time with him as possible. What are you, like jealous?"

"Jealous?! Ever since you started hanging out with him, you've been all . . . " I shook my head, trying to figure out what to say that wouldn't insult her.

"Bored with you?"

I wanted to explode. I couldn't believe this! I blinked my eyes and took a deep breath. "Jen, sometimes I— Right now I just— Ugh! I just really can't stand you right now." So much for not insulting her.

"Oh Paisley, you are *so* back-in-the-day. Grow up."

CHAPTER SEVEN

"Wait. She actually used those words? Mucho popularo?" asked Amy with disgust.

"Yep."

Amy and Carreyn and I were doing this passing drill where you start in a triangle and have to chase your own pass. We kept passing and running and passing and running farther and farther from the other groups so no one could hear our conversation.

"I don't know," said Carreyn, passing the ball to me. "I think we could use a Pom in our group. It might be fun."

"Don't you get it?" I blasted the ball back to Carreyn. "If Jen makes cheerleader and becomes a Pom, she won't *be* in our group anymore."

"Oh, right."

"Think she'd really do that?" asked Amy. "Just drop us?"

"She's not thinking about us. She's thinking about Bodie. This whole cheerleader thing is all about Bodie. She would never quit soccer for *cheerleading* if it weren't for him. And if she makes it, even if she wanted to stay friends with us, think her new Pom BFFs would let her hang with us? Think not."

Amy trapped the ball with her foot. "Pais? How come you

didn't know about this?" she asked sincerely, which was weird for Amy. "I mean, you're her best friend." She kicked the ball to me just as Coach Sykes blew her whistle. I stood there wondering the same thing and watched the ball roll past me.

"I've seen one-legged sixth graders with better ball skills!" Coach Sykes barked. "I am not here to babysit a bunch of gossip girls every afternoon. If you're not here to work your little stingers off, then go to the mall tomorrow and don't bother coming to practice." She threw her hands on her hips, looking around to see if she had scared us even a little. "Okay, let's hear it, ladies!"

We all ran together into a big swarm of black and yellow pinnies and cheered like Kool-Aid-drinking freaks. "Buzz! Sting! Win! Go, Lady Hornets!"

Coach Sykes clapped and hooted. "Yeah! That's what I like to hear!" Then she turned to me. Her eyes were filled with faux hatred. I tried not to laugh. "Parsley, where's your evil twin Jen Sweetland?"

I knew where the evil Jen was. I had just talked to her. What I didn't know was where the good Jen had gone—the one who used to make me laugh, the one with the smart mouth and kooky antics. I couldn't tell Coach Sykes the truth about Jen. She would totally freak. And besides, I was still hoping to talk Jen out of cheerleading. "Cramps," I told her. "Really bad cramps."

"That's no excuse!" she barked. "Women have been menstruating since the beginning of time. Life must go on, ladies. It's still survival of the fittest, which reminds me." She pointed her finger in my face and yelled, "Give me fourteen laps now. Fourteen!" She glared at me. "Remember, I'll be watching you even when I'm home with my feet up on the couch drinking a cold beverage and watching *Extra*."

I started running my late laps as everyone else cleared off the field.

Three down, eleven to go. The girls' field was now empty except for me.

Pais? How come you didn't know about this? How come? How come? How come?

Why *didn't* I know Jen was going to do this? It's true. I *should* have known. I was her best friend. At least I used to be.

I kept running, and more and more questions I couldn't answer filled my brain. Why did I care if someone thought I was a rah-rah and dropped me on my butt? Why did I care what Jen did? Jen *wanted* to be a Hornette. Why did I care what anyone thought at all? And why did I keep thinking about Clint Bedard? Maybe I *was* jealous of Bodie? Maybe I *was* jealous of Jen? And why did I always do what I was supposed to do? Coach Sykes

SIDEBAR

Our cheerleaders were officially called the Hornettes—the delicate, feminine version of the Hornets, named decades ago in a far more innocent time when no one would make the obvious association and start calling them the Hos, which of course everyone did now. As a popularity power cluster, our cheerleaders were the Poms, but behind their backs, everyone but their closest friends called them the Ho'nettes—the Hos for short. And not just because they were totally obnoxious about flaunting their popularity and lording it over everyone else, but also because they had really hot uniforms and a reputation for being as easy as pie.

But Jen wasn't easy. I knew her. So why would she want to be now?

wasn't watching me. No one was watching me. I was running double-digit late laps on the honor system like an idiot.

But the really impossible question was why Jen would even *want* to be a rah-rah Hornette. Was it really worth it, just to be more popular?

I stopped running at nine laps, walked a little, and then collapsed on the ground. Who cared if I got in trouble? The grass felt cool against my sweaty cheek. I lay there trying to catch my breath. My lungs burned along with everything else in my body. It was September but it still smelled like summer and still felt warm even though the sun was about to drop behind the roof of the library. I kind of wanted to cry, but I was too tired and too mad.

All the other girls were long gone, but the boys' team was scrimmaging on the next field over. I closed my eyes and got lost in the sounds of their scrimmage.

"Time! Got time!"

Thump.

"On your back!"

Thump! Thud.

"Hey!"

Whistle.

"Down the line!"

Thump. Thump.

"Gotcha back!"

Then a long triple whistle and a few celebratory whoops, followed by the sounds of guys talking and then clearing the field.

After a while, I lifted my head and turned to cool my other cheek on the grass. I watched a few guys practicing corner kicks.

I closed my eyes again and imagined that I was invisible. I had a feeling that this could be my new favorite hobby, and I was determined to get really good at it. Finally, it was quiet, so quiet I could hear my heart pounding through the ground.

And then I heard the hard thump of a soccer cleat against a ball and the satisfying slap of a ball hitting the back of the net. I opened one eye. Some guy was standing alone on the next field. His hair was damp with sweat and his shirt was drenched. It was Eric Sobel.

With one eye I watched him line up a bunch of soccer balls at different points across the top of the penalty box. He stepped back and attacked each ball. Left foot, right foot, left foot, right. He blasted each ball into the back of the net, leaning over the ball and following through every time, just like I know I'm supposed to do. He was incredibly focused and serious until he nailed the last ball into the left corner of the net.

"Gooooooooooooooooal!" he yelled like that lunatic South American soccer announcer, running around in a circle. And then he pulled off his shirt and threw it into the air and did this goofy little dance.

Wow. I had seen pictures of him on Facebook, but he never looked like this.

He jogged toward the goal to retrieve the balls. Just as he got there, he jumped up, grabbed the cross bar with both hands, and did fifteen pull-ups. I know, I counted, which was why I couldn't be bothered to breathe.

Eric Sobel is much more than gorgeous. He's gorgelicous. I knew he had good legs. All soccer players do. But his torso was . . . amazing. It was like he had grown so much over the summer that his smooth tan skin barely fit his body anymore, like his skin had been shrink-wrapped over this perfect male anatomy. He could have been on the cover of one of those catalogs that are supposedly selling casual clothes but are really selling shirtless boys at the mall. I wanted to lick Eric Sobel's chest. OMG, did I just say that? OMG, I so did.

I closed my eyes and smiled. This serendipitous sight had quite possibly saved my entire day. Maybe everything was going to be okay. Or maybe not. But even if I got dropped on my head tomorrow in Drama and died a humiliating, horrible high school death without a single real friend, I'd die happy with that image of a shirtless Eric Sobel in my brain.

Eric collected the balls in a yellow mesh bag, reached down to grab his sweaty shirt off the grass, and started walking in my direction. OMG, *he was walking in my direction!* What should I do? What should I *do*?! I couldn't get up now because I'd look totally stalkerish. Maybe if I just didn't move and prayed that the sun was in his eyes and that he was having some deep soccer thought, he wouldn't even notice me. I put my head down, closed my eyes, and held my breath. I could hear his footsteps getting closer and closer.

"Hey," he said. I opened one eye and he did the cool-guy head nod.

"Hey," I squeaked, not moving an inch.

"You okay?" he asked without stopping.

"Uh, yeah. I'm just . . . listening, to the earth. I want to be a good friend to the earth and good friends are good listeners, right? And this spot right here"—I pointed at the ground—"this is a really good spot. To listen." I took a deep breath. Oh my God. I was ridiculous!

Eric stopped and nodded slowly, like he was actually trying to understand me. "Okay, cool. I'll try that spot sometime." He smiled and pushed his sweaty bangs off his forehead.

As I watched him walk away, I did the silent all-in-your-head shriek. *Aaaaaaaaaaaaah!* I wanted my whole body to melt like hot wax through the grass, into the ground, and drip down into the core of the earth because . . . the earth is my friend.

Aaaaaaaaaaaah!

CHAPTER EIGHT

Before you meet my parents, I want to tell you a little about my town, which is technically a city but feels more like a town, a small town. It seems like everyone either knows everybody else or knows about everybody else. My mom says that in our town, gossip is currency. So even if you don't have the biggest house or the nicest car, or even a car at all, you can still feel rich if you have good dirt on someone.

I guess our town is a lot like other suburban towns outside a big city. Except it has a pretty embarrassing name, so I'm not even going to tell you what it is. Yep. It's that embarrassing. Let's just say that if you passed the sign for our town on the freeway, you'd either think that it was the most beautiful place on earth or the name of a cult. Sometimes it feels like both.

Anyway, we've pretty much got all the things we need. And anything we don't have, like a real mall or a multiplex theater, is in the next town over. But not a lot happens in our town at night. You can pretty much lie down in the middle of our main drag after 10:00 on a school night and not be in any danger of getting flattened. I know. I've done it. One night, Jen and I stretched out in the street for over an hour and counted eleven shooting stars.

If you turn off the main drag at the bank and go about three miles up this long winding road, you'll eventually pass our old elementary school, Charlie Dodd's house, and Jen's old house on the way to my house, which is where I was headed now.

I dropped my soccer bag and my book bag and my muddy cleats on the kitchen floor and opened the refrigerator.

"Hey Pais! How'd it go today?" My dad was standing in front of the kitchen table wearing his dorky neon yellow running vest and doing his usual stretches while he skimmed the *Wall Street Journal*. He's way into multitasking.

"It sucked." I looked around for something to drink.

"Are we being ironic?" He switched feet and started another quad stretch. "Is sucked a good thing this year?"

I pulled my head out of the fridge just long enough to roll my eyes at him and then went back to my search. "We're out of sparkling water," I grumbled.

"It couldn't have been that bad." He switched legs. "Could it?"

I filled him in on a few highlights of my day, which were actually all low points. (No, I didn't mention Eric Sobel's shrink-wrapped, lickable torso. He's my dad!)

"What you need, Paisley, is a shot from Doctor Positivo!" He pretended to give me an injection in my shoulder. I ignored him. It's one of his usual routines. "A little positivo potion will kill off those negative thought germs."

"I don't have negative thoughts, Dad. I had a sucky day. Okay?"

My Dad is all about having a super positive attitude. He actually believes that that's the solution to everything. Obviously, he's way too old to remember what it's really like to be a teenager. But it's impossible for me to argue with him about it. He works really hard and he's always doing these big real estate deals, he's always running marathons, so he's in really good shape, and he's always annoyingly happy.

And then there's my mom.

"Hello, my lovelies!" My mother entered the kitchen as if she were walking onstage for her cabaret act. Only she was wearing very big sunglasses and a very small white tennis dress. Thank God she's been using that self-tanning lotion on her thighs. "Was everyone's day as delicious as mine?" She didn't wait for a response. "We won!"

I closed the refrigerator door, hopped up onto the counter, and started pulling at a piece of string cheese.

Mom did this little dance move around the kitchen island, giving me a quick hug as she passed by, then she danced her way over to Dad and kissed him hard on the lips. Do I really need to see this? No.

"Mmm. An oaky Chardonnay," said my dad, licking his lips.

"We stopped for a celebratory glass of wine after our match. Did I say glass? I meant bottle. We clobbered them!" She looked over at me. "Shoulders back, Sweet P! You're slouching."

I sat up straight and stuck out my poor excuse for boobs.

"That's it," she cheered. "Back rest, no chest. Spine straight, chest great!" She gave my ponytail a love squeeze and started rubbing the back of my neck. It felt really good. I didn't move, hoping she wouldn't notice she was doing it and would keep going while she talked. "And they must have been at least ten years younger than we are. *And*—get this—they had all of this fabulous matching crapola. You'd think they were sponsored by Nike. But we were awesome!" she said, swatting the air with an imaginary two-handed backhand. "We really were. We played like Venus and Serena on Advil."

My dad laughed. "Congrats, babe. Let's go out to dinner and keep celebrating. What do you say, Pais?"

"Okay," I mumbled.

"I'm only doing six, so I'll be back in"—he checked his running watch—"forty-four minutes."

Only six miles? See what I mean about his annoyingly positive attitude? He ran through the kitchen and right out the back door.

I waved at no one. "Bye, Dad."

"Hon, how was your first day?" Mom asked.

"Good." I didn't even hesitate. "It was really good." I just smiled and slid down off the counter.

"Oh, I'm so proud of you. I want to hear all about it at dinner." She grabbed me and gave me a hug and a kiss on the cheek. I leaned back, trying to pull away. "Mo-om!"

She started tickling me. "Admit it! Admit it, you love me!" My mom laughed.

"Mo-om!" Okay, I was laughing a little. "Get away. You are so weird." Finally, I broke free and picked my stuff up, lugged it upstairs, and took a long, environmentally unfriendly shower.

That's pretty much what it's like at my house. We're all busy, doing our own thing. And as long as we all act like everything is going great, then everything goes great. Does that make sense?

After dinner, I went upstairs to do my homework and some cyber-stalking. I had to push my cat Dyson off of my laptop again. He's gotten in the habit of curling up and sleeping on it all the time, I guess because it's warm.

Dyson jumped up on my lap and settled in, power-purring while I stayed up late on Facebook. I studied Jen's profile, reading through her list of friends and—OMG! I wasn't a Favorite Friend anymore! What?! When did that happen?

I followed her trail of faves to Bodie's page, Candy Esposito's, Amy's, Carreyn's, Hutch's. There was a zoomed-in photo of Jen and Bodie making out on Hutch's page. It had to be from that party last weekend. They really *did* hook up. Wow. And how. It was like graphic. Actually, there were a lot of kissing photos on Hutch's page. Weird. Also, a bunch of shots of Jen with Bratty Sasshole #1 and Bratty Sasshole #2, laughing with their

SIDEBRA

No, I didn't name him Dyson. When I adopted him at the SPCA, Dyson was the name on his cage, and I was dumb enough to think that really was his name. But then my brother Parker told me that the SPCA people just make up the strangest names they can think of and he was probably named after a vacuum cleaner. I didn't believe him. But I went back a few days later, and saw three cats named Eureka, Hoover, and Electrolux. Oh well. It was too late. He was already Dyson to me.

mouths wide-open and looking pretty drunk. Classy. When did Jen get so tight with the Sassholes? They were total A-list McMeanies.

I should explain that Bratty Sasshole #1 and Bratty Sasshole #2 is my personal shorthand for these two nasty Varsity Hornettes. Here's all you need to know: They're juniors in Bodie's group, so they're total pops, and they're super tight with Candy Esposito, and they're basically joined at the hip. They talk alike, dress alike, and act alike, and if BS1 didn't have dark hair, and BS2 didn't have blond hair, I probably couldn't tell them apart. I don't know if anyone really likes them or if everyone's just afraid of them and *pretends* to like them. But you definitely don't want to get on their bad side. They will crush you. And they will do it with a smile.

My attention snapped back to Jen's profile. Wow, somebody definitely had it out for her. There were some truly nasty anonymous things posted in her Honesty Box. *Careful girlie, you're drinking your own cool-aid!* What does that even mean? *You think you're so hot—but you're snot.* I said nasty, I didn't say original. *Better watch your cute little backside, Sweetland.* Okay, that sounded ominous. I had no idea who wrote these things. And no—it wasn't me. Like I would ever.

That night I slept outside by the pool. I wanted to feel like it was still summer when everything really *was* good, when Jen and I hung out almost every day, and sophomore year was nothing but a happy fantasy, something to shop for and plan for and dream about. I scrunched down in my sleeping bag and stretched back on the chaise longue so I could look up at the stars, the same stars that Jen and I had stared at all summer.

It was a really clear night. The jumbo crickets were chirping like crazy. Schirp-schirp, schirp-schirp, schirp-schirp. That sound filled the whole sky. It hung from every tree branch, every telephone wire, the edge of every roof. Schirp-schirp, schirp-schirp, schirp-schirp. I don't know why, but it gave me a really good feeling.

I watched for shooting stars and tried to imagine what Jen's life was like since her parents split. Maybe that would explain why she was acting so un-Jen-like.

Her dad is a certifiable creep who cheated on her mom and now doesn't seem to care about anyone but himself. Her mom is going back to work selling real estate, so she's studying for some big test all the time. And—this is weird—she got her eyes done over the summer. It was spooky seeing her with two black eyes, like someone had beaten her up. Jen was totally freaked out and she practically lived at our house for a few weeks. Her mom said it's an investment in their future and that she needed the surgery so she could keep her eyes on the prize.

I don't know. If my family were having a major meltdown, maybe I'd be getting super drunk at parties and clinging to my new boyfriend like my life depended on him too. I should ask Jen's mom what she thinks is going on. I love Jen's mom. She is definitely one of the cool moms and always says brutally honest, funny things like, "It takes a very small man to drive a truck that big" or "Gossip is the opium for the asses" or "If you ever find yourself, Roger, I hope it's nowhere near me."

I think she'd be honest with me if I asked her about Jen. But my mom says not to bug her. She thinks Jen's mom is having a midlife crisis because her husband has replaced her with a younger, thinner version of herself. My mom has a theory for everything—

Shooting star!

—but what is a midlife crisis, anyway? Maybe *I'm* having a midlife crisis. Maybe my neurotic self is really, really mature for its age. Or maybe I'm actually halfway through my life and I'll be dead when I'm 30. That would mean I only have . . . I closed my eyes . . . 5,475 days left, that's . . . 131,400 hours, of which . . . 43,800 I'll probably be asleep. So I might only have . . . 87,600 hours left to get stuff done. Yeah, I did that all in my head.

But wow. 87,600 hours. I'd better get going. I have a lot to do.

CHAPTER NINE

I woke up early, so early that the sky was still violet-blue. That's one of the things I love about sleeping outside—I never need an alarm. I just lay there, all cozy in my sleeping bag, and listened. A few birds were chit-chatting away, a car started, and sprinklers danced back and forth across somebody's lawn. The air tasted cool and crisp and sweet. Considering yesterday's hellishness, I felt great.

And I decided that I was going to feel great all day—no matter what happened. I swiped a handful of morning air and closed my fist tight, holding my secret stash of positivity particles. Okay, a little lame maybe. But I'm my father's daughter.

After rolling up my sleeping bag, I went inside and up to my room, turned on some music, and assessed the outfit situation. I wanted to feel confident but casual and definitely not be trying too hard. Jeans, sandals, and this cute little top with hand-stitched detailing on the neck and sleeves. Perfect.

In carpool, I made a point of sitting next to Charlie Dodd so we could have a real, meaningful conversation. I looked around the minivan. Most kids were listening to music, trying to sleep, or staring out the window in a catatonic stupor.

"So Charlie, I was wondering. What's your opinion of *The Fly*?" I asked, doodling a cartoon fly in my notebook.

He looked at me kind of weird. "Button fly or zipper fly?"

"No! Our school newspaper, *The Fly*?" I pulled the flyer Eric Sobel had given me out of my bag and showed it to him. "I might go to this meeting."

Charlie read through it and shrugged. "The editors seem genuinely iconoclastic, but their product is fairly bourgeois. Are you thinking of joining the staff?"

"Maybe."

He nodded. "School newspaper always looks good on college apps. And if it's not a real class, then maybe you can sign up but not have to do anything."

"I'd kinda like to do something, actually. I thought I was going to be in Yearbook, but . . . " I didn't want to finish my sentence.

"Yeah, I heard about that headline slam in Yearbook yesterday. Bummer."

"*You* heard? How did *you* find out?"

"Dwight Cashel wrote about it in his blog. He's in love with Candy Esposito."

I sighed and looked out the window.

Mr. Eggerston didn't waste any time in Drama. Thank God. People had been lobbing weird, sympathetic looks at me since the moment I walked in—except for Clint Bedard. He stared at me with this knowing smile. I just had no idea what it was he knew.

"Okay, people! This is what's called an open-scene exercise,"

Mr. Eggertson called out. He stood on the stage waving a stack of index cards. "These words don't actually mean anything. Each of you has to *give* them meaning through your delivery, through your intonation, through your instrument. It's not merely about *saying* the words, it's about communicating the subtext." He slapped his palm with the stack of cards. "And if you don't know what that means, look it up or ask someone who does know. Okay, people, partner up!"

Everyone scrambled, searching for a partner that they liked or could at least stand to look at.

I dropped my notebook on my chair and turned to Bean Merrill, who had been right next to me. "Bean? Wanna . . . "

"Um, nothing personal, but . . . " She pointed with her head toward this genius AV geek, one of the few tall guys in the room, and then smiled conspiratorially and loped off in his direction. I had to smile too.

I quickly looked around for Charlie Dodd. But he was already talking to Clint Bedard. Who happened to be looking really good today. Stop it!

I looked to the left and then to the right in what I hoped was not an obvious panic. Oh no. The only two people left were Teddy Baedeker and Cate Maduro. Crap.

Cate glanced at Teddy, then back at me. She shook her head, not even trying to hide her disgust at being stuck with me, and walked slowly in my direction. She was wearing this little pearl choker and tight sweater set—oh, and a beauty mark. Whatever. Teddy ran a hand through his short, overly gelled hair, scrunched up his nose, and nodded. He was used to this.

Cate was a few feet away from me when she abruptly turned a hard right and threw out her arms. "Teddy!" she exclaimed, like she was greeting a dear old friend. "Howdy, partner."

What a freakin' psycho.

"Okay Paisley," said Mr. Eggertson. "You're with me. Up here. We'll demonstrate."

I glared at Cate as I walked by. What was her problem?

I hopped up onto the stage, and Mr. E. handed me an index card. It said: *Shake before opening. Naturally and artificially flavored. Triggers sudden slim-down of as much as seven pounds.* Oh crap. This was going to be hard.

Mr. E. leaned over and whispered in my ear, "I just called off our engagement. Got it?"

I nodded.

I took a few seconds and thought hard about the time my old cat Scamper got hit by a car and I buried him in the backyard in a cardboard TiVo box. Then I looked up at Mr. E. with real tears in my eyes.

"Shake before opening." I trembled, obviously in pain. And then I pleaded, "Naturally?"

He looked at me and shrugged. "Was the staff."

"And artificially flavored." My lower lip quivered. I was amazed. "Triggers? Sudden slim-down?" I started to cry for real. I had no idea where this was coming from.

He looked really, really sad and took my hand. "Respectful, supportive, and . . ."

I pulled my hand away and touched my heart. "Of as much as seven pounds," I whispered, and turned away.

"And scene!" yelled Mr. E. The class clapped, like *really* clapped.

Cate Maduro just stared at me coldly with her arms crossed. But Bean flashed me a big goofy smile with an I'm-impressed! nod.

"Okay, people! What was going on in the scene?"

"Breaking up!"

"He dumped her!"

"He broke her heart!"

"Yes, exactly, all those things. Any questions? Okay!" Then Mr. E. turned to me. "Nice work, Paisley." He seemed genuinely impressed. I kinda was too.

At lunch, I was headed to my locker when I passed Bodie and some Varsity Jocks in the hallway. It made me think of those photos I'd seen on Facebook the other night. Something strange definitely happened at that party. But what? And why wasn't anyone spilling? I was lost in my own head space until I heard Amy's booming laugh.

Jen and Amy were standing in front of my locker giggling about something. I was partly relieved but mostly annoyed to see Jen hanging out with us at lunch again. I was still spinning on what she'd said yesterday. It's not like I was just going to *forget* about it, you know? But she couldn't have meant all that . . . Could she?

I slipped into perky girl character and put a smile on my

face. I'd just use my new drama skills and play along. "Hey, you guys!"

"Hey Paisley!" they said together. Then they both waved at me doing the exact same manic hand gesture that I had done in Yearbook. I stopped cold and watched them burst into hysterics.

"Thanks a *not*, you guys!" I was really pissed.

"What?" asked Amy. "We're just rippin' on you."

But Jen was still rippin' *into* me. "It's way adorable, really," she added acidly, then smiled and did the spastic jazz hands wave to Carreyn, who was bouncing down the hallway toward us. Of course, she spastic jazzed right back with her big goofy grin.

"It's not adorable!" I fumed. "It's embarrassing! Does everyone on the planet know what happened to me in Yearbook? Ugh, stupid spastic jazz hands!" I was so flustered, it took me like three tries to get my locker combination right.

"Spastic jazz hands?" Jen asked snarkily, one eyebrow cocked.

"Yes! The whole thing was totally humiliating," I said, ignoring her taunting.

"That's not what Candy said." Jen acted all in-the-know. "She told me you were awfully cute and funny and then, when you did your *spastic jazz hands*, it was hilarious. I think it's Candy's new favorite dance move."

The three of them all started bouncing their hips and doing the move with cheerleader enthusiasm, chanting, "Spastic jazz hands! Spastic jazz hands! Spastic jazz hands!"

I slammed my locker door shut.

Then all of a sudden, Jen went into full-blown-freaky-cheerleading mode. "Come on, Paisley! Don't be mad! It's really funny! Don't feel sad!" she yelled, then high-kicked and dropped into the splits.

I stared at her. Had she completely lost her mind? She raised her arms above her head. Oh no. *Again?* I turned and stomped off down the hall before I could find out.

She cheered after me. "Roll on, Paisley! You're our girl! Just relax or you might hurl!"

"*Hurl?*" I heard Amy ask.

"Whatever," Jen replied. "I was improvising. *You* find something that rhymes with girl."

I tried to stay positive, I really did. But Candy Esposito not only took my spot in Yearbook, she also took my positivity stash. That girl was so greedy! I just wanted to get as far away from my hilarious friends as possible. If I did a big loop around the whole campus, by the time I got to the tennis courts near the band room, maybe lunch would be over and I'd be calm enough not to want to kill my friends.

Spastic jazz hands . . . Spastic jazz hands?! Where did that even come from? It's not like that move is part of my usual repertoire. If only I had calmly and casually said, "Paisley Hanover—I'd vote for Candy," like I didn't even really care about Yearbook, like I understood the popularity equation and had a firm grasp on irony instead of just my desperation. Why? Why? WHY?

"Paisley?"

I stopped my all-in-your-head self-torture and looked around. Mandy Mindel was actually talking—talking to *me*. She leaned against the wall near the double doors that opened onto the front lawn, looking like she might collapse if the wall weren't there.

"Hi, um. I was . . . um. I was wondering if you were, if you were going out, out to the front lawn?" she asked, obviously in psychic pain.

The front lawn is where the Drama geeks and other freaks gather at lunch, where no one can see them doing whatever they do.

"I wasn't planning to."

She nodded. "Oh, okay, never mind. Sorry."

"Why? Are you going out there?"

"Well." She scratched her nose really hard, pushing it around with the back of her finger. It looked like it was made of rubber and might pop off her face.

Mandy wears glasses all the time, which is lucky because it helps hide the fact that she had no eyelashes. I tried really hard to look at her eyeballs and not her eyelids.

"Do you want to go out there?" I asked.

"Well." She blinked nervously. "Only if you do. I mean, if you did, I would. I would walk with you if you . . . if you wanted."

Wow. For a second I had a sense of someone else's constant high school hell. Suddenly spastic jazz hands didn't seem like such a global crisis.

"Yeah, you know. I do want to eat lunch on the front lawn. Come on." I pushed open one of the doors. "Thanks for walking with me."

She didn't say a word as she followed me out into the bright noon sunlight.

It took a few seconds for my eyes to adjust. Wow. There were lunch pods for the Pleasant Hill extras too. Who knew? There was a cluster of junior and senior Drama Queens, some AV Guys and YouTubers passed around a video camera, a few NILs stretched out in couples feeding each other. Gross. NILs are what we call nerds in love, two fugly social misfits who somehow found each other and fell in love, or at least in lust. The Goths were gathered in the shade under the tree. A bunch of Emos were lying on the grass too depressed to eat.

I turned to Mandy. "Come on." We slowly weaved our way through the various groups. Mime Guy in the cape was playing Scrabble with some other Drama dweebs and the uncool foreign exchange students. Teddy Baedeker was juggling two oranges and an iPhone. Hold the phone—he wasn't bad.

Mandy dropped to her knees and inched over into their group. I kept walking, taking it all in, and then I spotted Bean Merrill and Charlie Dodd sitting with Cate Maduro and a few Library Girls near the school sign.

"Yo, Paisley!" said Charlie, waving me over.

Cate Maduro looked up at me and then fell back on her hands. "Oh my God, it's everyone's favorite rah-rah." She was dressed in her usual fifties-style drag. I couldn't figure out who she was trying to be.

"Hey Paisley," said Bean, looking sort of curiously at me. "Sit down."

I plopped down next to Bean and crossed my legs on the fringes of their pod and dug into my lunch.

"Are you lost, Paisley?" asked Cate Maduro.

"Just ignore me, okay?"

"That's easy."

I ignored her.

Bean pointed toward my feet. "Sweet sandals."

"Thanks." I slowly unwrapped my sandwich—smoked turkey with sun-dried tomatoes and arugula on a baguette. I made it myself. "So, are you guys nervous about doing our first scene?" I took a bite and looked around the circle.

"I'm not," said Bean. "As long as I don't get Mandy Mindel or Special Ted as my scene partner."

"Oh, I hope he's *my* partner," said Cate Maduro all seductive. "I'll bet he's an amazing kisser."

Everyone laughed.

"That's disgusting," said LG Wong. She's the queen of the Library Girls and a total goody-goody. Most people think LG stands for Library Girl, and now it kind of does. But it really stands for Lydia Georgette. No wonder she goes by LG. Anyway, she plays classical piano and at least three other instruments, gets straight A's, and reads so much she has to carry all of her books around in one of those rolling suit-cases. The weird thing, she has this cool chopped-out anime-girl haircut.

"I hope I get Clint Bedard," said Bean with a smirk. "Have you seen him lately? He's lookin' hot in a lost boy kinda way."

"I know," I agreed. "Where was he last year?"

"Probably in jail!" said Charlie.

"What, are you jealous?" I asked.

He scoffed. "Highly unlikely. Why would I be jealous of some brainless, subordinate lowlife?"

Cate dropped her head and peered at Charlie over her cat-eye sunglasses. "Because he's hot."

"So's a pile of dog crap. And I'm not jealous of that."

"Charlie!" Cate pretended to be shocked. "You are so cute when you're mad. Did he beat you up? Or just steal your lunch?"

"I'm not mad," he said, sucking hard on the straw sticking out of his juice box. "I'm more . . . " He turned and looked right at Bean. "Disappointed."

"What?" she asked, all exasperated. "Don't be such a nerda-thon."

LG Wong jumped in to change the subject.

"So, Paisley, what's it like being one of the chosen people at PH?" She looked at me as she cleaned her glasses. Then she put them back on. "I've always wanted to know."

"Leave her alone," said Bean.

"No, I want to hear this," said Cate Maduro. "Does it hurt

your head being so popular? Does the pressure just make you want to kill yourself?"

Charlie Dodd chimed in. "She's not *that* popular."

"She's A-list, total insider," said LG to Charlie. "I'm serious. I really want to know what it's like."

"Hello? I'm sitting right here. I can't believe you guys. You're totally clueless if you think I'm A-list popular," I said. I was trying to stay positive and bond. "No one is *that* popular. At least I'm not. I really relate to you guys," I said earnestly. "I don't always say the right thing or wear the right thing."

Silence.

Okay, that didn't come out right. "What I mean is, everyone at this school struggles to fit in. Even me. Especially me."

They all laughed, except for Charlie, who just stared at me like I was insane.

"Yeah right," said Cate Maduro. "Oh no, who do I sit with today? The Poms or the BPs?" They laughed again.

"Or the Sporties or the Perfect Girls?" said LG, throwing her hand over her forehead like some cartoon damsel in distress. "Gosh, it's so darn confusing being popular."

"Do I go out with the varsity football star on Friday night," said Charlie, acting all girlie, "or the varsity soccer star?"

"Or maybe I'll be really generous and go out with both!" added Cate Maduro, all cheerleader perky. Everybody thought that one was hilarious. The Library Girls couldn't stop laughing. All their glasses almost fell off.

I just sat there feeling depressed. For some reason, I didn't expect the unpopulars to be so nasty too. At least the populars *pretended* to be nice to each other—sometimes. I looked away. Mandy Mindel and Teddy Baedeker were laughing at Mime Guy pulling himself across the grass with an invisible rope. Why did I even come out here?

I started to pack up my lunch. "Well, you'll be happy to know you're just as nasty as the most popular people at this school."

"Come on, Paisley," Charlie groaned. "We're just raggin' on you."

"Whatever."

"Well," said Cate, sitting up and tucking her legs under her, "you'll be happy to know you're just as vain as the least popular people at this school."

I couldn't believe Cate actually said that right to my face. I glanced around the circle with this is-she-for-real? look. Charlie and Bean seemed a little uncomfortable.

"So, um, Cate, why do you hate me so much? I mean, what did I ever do to you?"

She shrugged, suddenly acting all blasé. "I don't hate you, Paisley. You're just . . . *so* Pleasant Hill."

I glared at her. "What is *that* supposed to mean?"

"Oh my God!" Bean reached over and grabbed something out of my bag. "*The Fly* meeting. I totally forgot!" She jumped up, waving the neon yellow flyer, and grabbed my hand. "Come on, Paisley, we're gonna be late."

She pulled me up and we ran across the lawn toward the

door. We didn't stop running until we were inside the main hallway.

"That was totally weird," she said to herself, shaking her head. She opened the flyer she was clutching in her hand and started reading.

"Thanks, Bean." That *was* weird. I tried to think of what I could've done or said to Cate Maduro. Nothing. I haven't even talked to her since seventh grade.

Bean looked up from the flyer, all innocent. "For what? I really wanted to go to the meeting. Room 107. Come on." She took off up the hall.

I stood there for a second, trying to understand what had just happened. And then I chased after her. I figured if Yearbook wasn't in the cards for me this year, then I might as well check out our school's tacky, unprestigious alternative, *Fly Paper*, aka *The Fly*: "All the news that sticks to print."

CHAPTER TEN

The meeting was already going on when Bean and I walked into room 107. Everyone turned and stared. Why is everyone always staring at me these days? Someone handed each of us an issue from last year, and we slipped into seats in the back row.

Miriam Goldfarb was sitting on a desk in the front row talking. She had smarty arty glasses, dark curly hair, and a nasally voice.

"And you won't be the only ones volunteering to produce our un"—she dropped her head and gazed over her glasses at the room filled with people as if she were seeing us for the first time—"our un-award-winning news rag, *Fly Paper*, affectionately known as *The Fly*."

She spoke in this strange singsongy rhythm, pausing like she didn't know what she was going to say next, although she obviously did. Miriam Goldfarb was the editor of *The Fly* and a total brain.

"Our new librarian, Ms. Whitaker, has kindly offered to volunteer"—pause—"her time as our faculty advisor."

"Hello," said Ms. Whitaker, waving. A few people clapped.

"Thanks to the prevalent football fascist mentality here at Pleasant Hill High— Gooooo Hornets!" Miriam yelled. "*The Fly* is no longer an accredited class. It's a *club!*"

A wave of boos followed. The room was a bizarre mix of kids from all four grades. I couldn't get a read on how to describe them or how they all happened to end up in this room for this meeting. But they all had a lot to say.

"Journalism—not jingoism!" someone shouted.

"Hey, when's the first party?"

"It'll be a cold day in Pleasant Hell before the pen is silenced!" yelled Logan Adler.

Then some guy playing the bongos started drumming and chanting, "*The Fly* will never die. Nev-er die, nev-er die, nev-er die," and everyone joined in.

I scrunched down low in my chair and hugged my backpack. What was I doing here?

"Okay! Okay!" Miriam raised her arms and her nasal voice. The crowd immediately quieted down. "Just because we don't have a budget doesn't mean we won't have fun!" Miriam continued. "We'll be doing a lot of"—pause—"fundraising throughout the year, like bake sales and car washes, and of course begging our parents." She cackled. "As you know, *The Fly* parties are legendary." Everyone cheered like maniacs. "So we'll start charging non-staff to get in." Miriam looked around the room, smiling like a proud parent. "*The Fly* may be the ugly, obnoxious, unloved, uncoordinated, unpopular stepchild here at Pleasant Hill High, but we are the *only* newspaper this school has—and our voice will be heard!"

More cheers and bongo drumming. The "nev-er die" chant started up again.

"Miriam, may I add something?" called Ms. Whitaker over the noise.

"Of course. Please do." The room quieted down.

"We have a huge challenge this year, no doubt, but it's worth it to keep the paper alive. Yes, *The Fly* is our only school newspaper, which means it's the only school publication to reach people on a regular basis. That means *your* words can reach people—and that's power!" You could tell she was getting really into it. "Each one of you has the opportunity not only to report the news here at school, but also to inform people about global issues, inspire readers, and get them thinking about new ideas. If you decide to get involved and write for *The Fly*, which I hope you will, that power is yours."

"Hear, hear, Ms. Whitaker! Hear, hear!"

Miriam Goldfarb was a weirdo. No wonder they killed the budget, with her as the editor. But still, there was something about her . . . It was like she didn't go to our school every day. She just went to her life.

While Miriam talked on, I flipped through the issue from last year. There was a cute photo of Charlie Dodd blowing a gigantic bubble out of his French horn at some carwash for new band uniforms. And something about Bodie Jones catching air and dunking the ball at the buzzer to win the game. I kept flipping. *The Fly* was filled with sports scores and photos with bad punny captions, hard-hitting stories about trash in the quad, fluffy profiles on standout faculty members and students, and controversial op-ed pieces intended to pad college admissions packages more than change minds. One op-ed headline read: "Can't We All Just Not Get Along?" Hilarious. By Miriam Goldfarb. That figures.

This year, with no budget, *The Fly* would probably be even worse.

"As you know, I am the editor, and that"—Miriam gestured grandly toward the back of the room—"adorable dumb blond is my assistant"—she paused again—"editor Logan Adler."

Logan walked up to the podium, smiling like a giddy beauty pageant finalist, and waved to the group as if he'd just been crowned rather than insulted. "Thanks, Mim"—he air-kissed her sweetly—"for that flattering introduction. You are far too kind." He wore a black T-shirt that said DUMBE BLONDE across the front.

Bean reached for my notebook, flipped to a blank page, and scribbled something. Then passed it back to me under my desk.

They're a couple! ♡♡

I looked at her, hoping for visual confirmation. She gave me a knowing nod. All I could think was, thank

SIDEBRA

Even though she was a senior and he was a junior, and she was nasal-neurotic brainy, and he was adorable-funny brainy, somehow Miriam and Logan *were* a couple. They went to journalism camp over the summer and fell madly in love in the fact-checking seminar. He wrote a really funny piece about it on his blog.

Oh, and he's not really blond. He bleached his hair the week before school to protest the big cut in our school district's arts budget. And now he was starting a protest group called the Dumbe Blondes. Their mission: to attend all varsity games and school events and cheer like ditzy idiots, showing district administrators the future of Pleasant Hill High if all the cool arts classes were cut. Signs with grammatical errors and misspelled words were emphatically encouraged.

God they found each other. I held my notebook on my lap under the desk and wrote, How do you know?

Bean grabbed it and scribbled another note, then passed it back to me.

Read his blog. It's hilarious!

Logan Adler flipped open his notebook and looked down at the podium. "Okay, let's get down to business." Then he looked up with a big love-crazy grin. "By the way, ignore her. She's off her meds and she's about to be accepted early-admission to Yale, so she's obnoxious as hell."

As I doodled his T-shirt design in my notebook, Logan read off a bunch of jobs that needed to be filled—writers, editors, photographers, production supervisors, columnists, reporters in the field, party planners—with a brief description of each job.

"Sign-up sheets are here." He pointed to the front row. "And hey, regardless of whether or not you join *The Fly*, I hope you'll *all* join the Dumbe Blondes!"

There were a few beauty-pageant-quality shrieks of joy. I guess some people were already in the club.

SIDEBRA continued

FYI: You don't need blond hair to be a Dumbe Blonde. You just have to be an authority-questioning, arts-loving activist.

PS FYI: Dumbe is misspelled on purpose. You know, it's like satire? Because so many people mix up blonde and blond or never even bother to learn the difference? So anyone who spells dumb with an "e" is even *dumber* than a dumb blonde. Get it?

PPS FYI: *Blond* is an adjective, as in "She has unnaturally curly blond hair."
Blonde is a noun, as in "He had a morbid fear of beautiful, tall blondes."

And I'm pretty sure blonde is only used to describe a female with blond hair. Are you confused yet? Just remember: Blonde with an "e" is always for she.

And Blondie is not a person—it's a band.

"You'll not only get one of these snazzy T-shirts for a mere ten dollars"—Miriam slowly waved her hand up and down his side like a game show prize girl—"you'll also get the satisfaction of driving the administration bonkers!"

More cheers and squeals of blondish joy.

"And if we make enough noise this year, we can save electives like Art, Band, and Drama from extinction."

Wait. Drama? They were maybe going to cut Drama?

"Remember kids, protesting is good, clean fun!"

The room rumbled to life as everyone started talking and moving toward the sign-up sheets.

"What do you think? Wanna sign up for something?" Bean asked me.

"Um, I don't know." I didn't want to hurt her feelings if she was totally into it. "It could be fun. But I'm pretty busy with soccer and stuff." I hesitated. "Did you know Drama was in trouble?" I asked her.

"No, but it figures. They want to fry anything remotely creative."

I chewed a cuticle but didn't say anything.

Bean didn't seem to care if I wanted to sign up for *The Fly*. She did. So she signed up to be a field reporter for Drama. Then she joined the Dumbe Blondes. And you know what? So did I. It was only ten bucks. And I got a snazzy T-shirt. Bean looked at me sort of surprised. I didn't blame her. I was surprising *myself* today. And guess who bought a shirt right after me? Ms. Whit!

On our way back to our lockers, Bean and I were holding

up our T-shirts, acting all goofy and ditzy like the dumbest of the Dumbe Blondes, cracking each other up. Bean started doing these funny, idiotic cheerleading moves. I joined in, doing the moves I'd seen Jen practicing earlier.

Then I looked down the hall and froze. Jen and Carreyn were standing there, staring at me coldly.

"Oh, *that's* really nice, Paisley." Jen said my name like it tasted bad.

"What?"

"What are you trying to say, that we're dumb?"

OMG! This was getting insane. "Jen," I said slowly, "it's *not. About. You.* It's the name of a protest group we just joined. God, not everything is about you."

Jen stared at me all bug-eyed. Carreyn lifted her chin and crossed her arms, adjusting her nearly identical, cheapo version of Jen's designer tote bag.

Bean looked from them to me, me to them. "Excuse me?" Bean waved. "Excuse me? Not sure if you noticed, but I'm blond too?"

Carreyn and Amy glanced at her like they couldn't care less, then turned back to me.

"Oh, so then I guess you're saying *all* blondes are dumb." With that awesome comeback, Jen turned and stalked off in the opposite direction.

"Yeah," Carreyn said, stink-eyeing us, then following Jen down the hall.

I sighed. Unbelievable.

"I really like your friends." Bean smiled sweetly.

CHAPTER ELEVEN

I called a powwow. I had to. Before things spiraled totally out of control with Jen, and took Amy and Carreyn with it, we needed to talk—all four of us, face-to-face, and definitely not at school. Maybe if we had a pool powwow, everyone would remember how much fun we had over the summer. Maybe we could get it back.

So the four of us agreed to meet at Amy's house on Saturday afternoon for a pig-out party and a heart-to-heart. Or so I thought.

I was a little late because I had to ride my bike and it was super hot that day. When I got there, Amy was stretched out on her huge pink bed, flipping through a magazine, drinking a Diet Coke, and eating cookies and edamame, this strange Japanese diet food she was all into. Carreyn was on the carpet in the splits position, bouncing away her muscles or tendons or whatever, along with her self-respect.

See, Carreyn had gotten the brilliant idea of trying out for cheerleading too. I admired her enthusiasm, but sometimes she could be such a clone. I mean, what would Carreyn even do if she didn't have someone else to imitate? As I walked in, she was trying to enlist Amy—again.

"Come on, Amers," Carreyn begged. "We'll have so much fun. If we make it, we can all cheer together at the opening game next Friday and then go to the dance with all the Poms!"

"No way." Amy held up a hand without taking her eyes off her magazine. "I'd rather be on YouTube dancing topless than be a cheerleader. Oh, my bad! That is being a cheerleader." She looked up and guffawed.

"That only happened once!" Carreyn sounded all insulted. "Pleeeease? We really need girls like you for the base of the pyramid."

Amy gave her the smack-down look, and Carreyn shut up.

"Jen's not here yet?" I asked, wiping my face with the sleeve of my T-shirt.

Amy and Carreyn looked at each other.

"Nope. Not yet," Carreyn said. "I think she had to go by her house or something." Carreyn reached for a brush on the bedside table and began frantically brushing her hair. She had been trying to brush out that crazy perm all week. Now her hair just looked frizzy and damaged like she stuck her finger in a light socket every night before bed.

Amy shrugged. "Or she's probably late 'cause she's talking with Bodie."

Carreyn paused her hairbrush attack. "Like if she's with Bodie, they'll really be talking? Think not."

"Ugh, Bodie! I am so sick of Bodie!" I kicked off my shoes and pulled off my sweaty Peds and flung them on the carpet. "I'm boiling. Let's go swimming."

Carreyn looked at Amy before saying, "No, let's wait here for her. I'm sure she'll be here soon."

I flopped down across the foot of Amy's bed on her pink angora throw blanket, reached for a pink frosted animal cookie with sprinkles, and took a bite. Being in Amy's room was like being inside a big poof of cotton candy. Everything was pink and soft and fluffy. She even had a pink aromatherapy candle that *smelled* like cotton candy. Not what you'd expect from a big girl with a big voice and a monster goal kick.

"How come you're so sick of Bodie?" Carreyn asked. Amy didn't even look up from painting her toenails—guess what color?

"I don't know." I took another bite of the cookie and thought about it. "It's not him, really, it's just . . . He's changed everything."

"Yeah," Carreyn agreed. "Think he's changed Jen?"

"Duh. Big-time."

"Yeah. I think she's changed too," Amy agreed.

"Do you think she's conceited now?" Carreyn asked. Amy looked up from her toes to see what I would say.

"No." I shook my head. "It's not that."

"You have to admit, though, she's gotten a little conceited," said Carreyn. Amy looked back at her toes.

"It's something else," I said. "I don't know. I just wish she'd talk about it. She's like totally ignoring me."

"Selfish?" asked Carreyn. "You must think she's being selfish, right?" She nodded.

"I don't know. Not really."

"Not at all?" Carreyn asked.

"Well, I guess a little." I sighed. "But I think it's more like she's confused. Like she's trying to be someone else but has no idea who. I think her parents' divorce has really messed her up. And Bodie, he's someone she can cling to."

"So you're saying she's clingy?" asked Carreyn.

"Static clingy." I shook my head. "This isn't the Jen I know."

"Maybe Body Snatchers got her and turned her into a zombie?" Carreyn asked with big eyes.

"Invasion of the *Bodie* snatchers!" Amy added. We all laughed—Amy laughed so hard Diet Coke came out her nose. She pinched the tip—"Burning, burning"—and then wiped it over and over with the back of her hand.

"Well maybe, in a way, that *is* kinda what happened," I said, reaching for another cookie. "I think she hooked up with Bodie at that pool party and now it's like she can't think for herself."

"No way? They *hooked up* hooked up?" asked Carreyn. "They weren't even together then. You think she's become a slut?" She shoved a fistful of popcorn into her mouth.

"I hope not," I said. "But she's definitely been really different since that party. I don't know . . . I'm not sure I really trust Bodie. I know he's supposed to be a great guy and all. But what if he's just using Jen? He's definitely the kind of guy who can get away with that."

"*What?!*" a voice screamed from under Amy's bed.

Oh my God. What was that? I sat straight up. I looked from

Amy to Carreyn and then down at the floor. What the . . . ?
Jen was scrambling out from underneath the bed like an angry
crab.

"You think I'm messed up and clingy?!" she yelled at me,
red-faced and spitting mad.

"What?" I looked at her and then quickly at Amy and Carreyn again. I sat up on my knees. "No!" I said, breaking into a
fresh sweat. "I didn't say that! I just—"

"And that Bodie's just *using* me?!"

"No! Jen, what are— Why are you—"

And then I stopped.

I was having this long, slow, horrible realization. My pulse
pounded in my ears. I looked from Jen to Amy to Carreyn. And
then I lost it.

"Oh my God. I can't believe you guys!" I felt a huge lump in
my throat. "I can't believe you!" I jumped off the bed. "What
is your problem?! God, you're supposed to be my *friends*!" I
stood there in the middle of Amy's bedroom. And no one said
a word.

Then Carreyn started to laugh. "Come on, Pais. We're just
kidding. Whatever."

"Whatever?!" I screamed and threw a cookie at the wall as
hard as I could.

Jen just glared at me, blinking away tears. Amy wouldn't even
look at me.

I so didn't want to—I willed myself not to—but I totally
started to cry. My best friends had set me up. There was nothing

left to say. I threw open Amy's bedroom door so hard it smashed against her dresser. I ran down the hall and out the front door. Then I jumped on my bike and pedaled as hard as I could.

I was crushed. And then I was mad. And then I was totally crushed. And then I was unbelievably, raging mad. Was that all Jen's idea? Or did Carreyn plan it to get on Jen's good side so she'd be totally in with her and I'd be totally out? And why did Amy go along with it? I replayed the conversation in my head, and then burst into tears all over again.

I was pedaling so furiously with my head down and crying like the Bionic pissed-off Woman that I didn't even see the storm drain. Before I knew what was happening, my bike suddenly stopped cold. I went flying over the handlebars, doing this perfect slow-mo backflip for, like, ever.

Thud.

I landed really hard on the pavement and skidded to a stop on my shoulder just off the road. I blinked my eyes a few times. I couldn't move. I couldn't breathe. Was I dead? No, unfortunately. I lay there on the hot dirt sputtering, gasping for air, waiting for my lungs to come unpuckered. And I had this rich flash fantasy of Jen and Amy and Carreyn sobbing at my standing-room-only funeral and feeling beyond horribly guilty for the rest of their miserable lives.

No such luck. My lungs came unglued. I sucked in air. And I finally caught my breath. It smelled nasty over here, like some animal had been hit by a car and was decomposing in the dry grass a few feet away.

I stood up slowly. Ow. And brushed some of the dust and gravel off. Ow. My back hurt, my shoulder hurt. And my bare feet were burning up! Ow! Ow! Ow! I hopped from foot to foot trying to pull my bike out of the storm drain. I finally wrestled it free. But the front wheel was totally mangled and bent. And the tire was flat. I had to make a run for some shaded dirt under a big bush. I hopped from foot to foot in the tiny patch of shade. Why why WHY did I leave my shoes and phone at Amy's house? I ran back to my bike, picked it up, and started the wobbly push toward the shade of a pathetic little tree. Ow. Ow! OW! I spotted a mailbox down on the other side of the road and ran for it.

By the time I hopped and hobbled to the top of the drive-way, I felt like I'd been dancing on red-hot coals. The driveway opened up into this big flat area in front of a huge modern house. I dropped my bike and sprinted for a tree by the lush green lawn, howling all the way.

I was bent over panting and sweating like a pig when I heard the front door open. I looked up. Oh God. Oh God, no.

Cate Maduro was standing in the doorway.

CHAPTER TWELVE

There she was, wearing flip-flops, sweatpants, and a tank top. And looking surprisingly normal.

"What are you doing here?" I blurted out, as if she were barefoot and sweating in *my* driveway.

She casually put one hand on her hip. "I live here. What are you doing here?"

I wiped the sweat out of my eyes and checked the soles of my feet for blisters. "Can I use your phone?" I asked.

Cate looked at me like I was insane.

"Please?"

She followed the you're-insane look with one of her you-pathetic-loser head shakes.

"Never mind." I turned around and tiptoed to the edge of the lawn psyching myself up for my red-hot coal dance, take two.

"Wait."

I turned around. She pointed to my shoulder. "You're all bloody," she said.

I looked over my right shoulder. Blood had seeped through my white T-shirt. It looked kind of like the shape of a pork chop. "Yeah, I wiped out in a storm drain and flipped over the handlebars."

"Really? I always wanted to see someone do that." She stepped back inside and waved me toward the door. "Come on."

I left my crippled bike on the lawn and followed her into the house. "Wow." I stared up, gaping at this giant wall of glass. The living room dropped down a few steps and there was a round fireplace suspended from the ceiling in the middle of the room. "This house is intense. It's like something you'd see in a magazine."

"What, did you think I lived in a double-wide?"

"No. I . . . I just, I don't know." I followed her into the kitchen. It was huge and spotless. I decided to keep my mouth shut.

She handed me the phone and watched me call my mom's cell. I left a message with the address. "She's probably still at Yogilates. It's her new thing."

Cate leaned back against their big stainless steel Sub-Zero fridge and crossed her arms. We stared at each other. This was bad. I looked away.

"It won't be long," I sputtered like an idiot. "I hope."

It was really bad, beyond awkward bad. And then the strangest thing happened.

We both started laughing.

A little at first, and then more, and soon we were both bent over with these big sloppy rolling laughs, the kind that make your cheeks hurt and your eyes water. I thought I was going to pee.

Finally, I stopped and sighed. "Do you have a bike I could borrow?"

She burst into hysterics again. "No."

I tried not to laugh. "Are your parents here? Maybe one of them could drive me home?"

"They're at work." She laughed even more. "They just love to work." She slowly stopped laughing.

"Oh." I stood there. It was awkward again. "Should I wait outside?"

She didn't answer. But she did fill a glass with cold water from the fridge door and pushed the glass down the counter in my direction. Then she handed me a wet paper towel folded neatly into quarters.

I reached over my shoulder and carefully blotted my pork chop stain. "Ow."

"Let me see," she said. I tried not to watch as she lifted the bloody T-shirt flap away from my oozing, shredded skin and peeked at it. "Ew," she said, pulling her head back and making this grossed-out face.

"What?"

"It's got gravel in it."

Cate has her very own bathroom and it's extremely cush. She filled the bathtub with a few inches of cold water so I could soak my scorched feet, and then we sat on the side of the tub while she plucked out pieces of gravel with tweezers. I felt a little weird taking my shirt off in front of her, so I held a bath towel to my chest. She acted like it was no big deal. She just sterilized Mr. Tweezerman and went to work like she performed roadkill surgery every day. And it was the weirdest thing . . . I actually told her everything that had happened at Amy's house.

"I never liked those girls," she said like she wasn't the least bit surprised. Plink! She dropped another tiny rock into this mod glass soap dish.

"They're not usually like that. Really. Ow!" I flinched and pulled away.

"Sorry." She gently blotted. "Maybe not to you."

I didn't say anything and tried to remember a time when Jen or Amy or Carreyn had even talked to Cate Maduro. I couldn't think of anything, but maybe I hadn't been with them. Were my friends all turning into a bunch of mean girls? Or had they always been like that and I never noticed? Was *I* like that?

I wanted to ask Cate, but I didn't have the guts. And besides, she had pointy tweezers in her hand, and I was half-naked.

"Popularity is poison," she said. Plink!

"Come on, you wouldn't say that if you were popular." Whoops. That just slipped out. But Cate surprised me.

"I wouldn't *want* to be popular at Pleasant Hell," she said.

I was quiet. Was she just saying that because she was bitter? Or was she for real? I stared at my puffy pink feet in the water. Wait. Was *I* for real? I had been doing so many bizarre things over the last couple days because of Jen. Trying to avoid her, trying to act like everything was fine, trying to act like I didn't care or miss her when I did and I do. And Jen was doing bizarre things so Bodie would like her more. And Carreyn was trying to be just like Jen so any guy would like her at all. And Amy was just going along with it all. Were *any* of us for real?

Cate spread a glob of antibiotic ointment over my scrape. "Muy gooey, chica!" We both laughed. It was one of the dumb things she used to say in Spanish class, and it turned into one of those all-purpose sayings that could mean anything we wanted it to, depending on how you said it. I had forgotten about that.

Then she taped a big square gauze thingie over it. "Here. You can have these." She handed me the box of gauze squares. "I haven't used them since I got my scorpion tattoo last year." Scorpion tattoo? Oh, right. I'd almost forgotten that she was the McNasty who loved to sting me. It's amazing how different people can be away from school. "Did you know that some scorpion species reproduce without mating?"

"Nope." I shook my head. "How . . . convenient."

"Wanna stay for dinner? LG is coming over. I rented *Heathers*."

Whoa. I couldn't believe she'd just asked me to stay for dinner. "You're good friends with LG Wong?"

I heard my mom's car honk outside.

"Yeah. She's nothing like she seems at school. LG's got the best goody-goody schoolgirl act of anyone I know."

Schoolgirl act? "I can't tonight. We're . . . " What? What were we doing? "We're having a family dinner. My brother's home from college." Why did I just lie?

My mom honked again. I turned and hobbled toward the front door.

"Here." She kicked off her flip-flops. "Wear these."

"Really? Thanks." I slipped them on. "And thanks for the clean shirt and, you know, everything."

She nodded. "See ya." She almost looked sad.

I think we were both wondering the exact same thing as I got into the car. What would it be like on Monday when we saw each other? Would we be any different? Or would we act the same as always, like we had absolutely nothing in common? One girl pretending she hated everyone, and the other girl pretending she liked everyone. Just because that's what everyone expected.

CHAPTER THIRTEEN

When I got home, I went up to my room and closed the door even though I knew my mom was dying to interrogate me and squeeze out every juicy detail of my tragic day. Dyson was curled up on my laptop as usual. I picked him up, carried him over to the bed and snuggled with him, feeling like he was the only friend in the world that I could trust.

Why is it that someone like Cate would be so much nicer to me than my own quote-unquote friends?

I listened to Dyson's power-purr and tried to make sense of what had happened at Amy's. What could Jen have said to them to make them do that to me? I was convinced now that it *had* to have come down from Jen. But why?

I must have fallen into a deep emotional coma, because I woke up in my clothes on Sunday morning. My shoulder ached like crazy. And then a wave of dread swept over me as it all came flooding back. I wasn't getting up today. No way. Finally around 1:00, my mom knocked gently on my door.

"Hey, can I come in?" she asked. "I brought you waffles since you were sound asleep by dinnertime last night."

Okay, that was so not fair. I love waffles.

"Thanks." I sat up in bed, and Mom propped me up with a few pillows. Then I started inhaling my waffles.

Mom hovered at the foot of my bed and watched me eat. "Pais, what's wrong?"

"Nothing."

She just looked at me. Why can they just stare at you and make you break? What is that?

"Jen hates me," I blurted. My mouth was full, but the floodgates had opened. I gave my mom the short but full-strength-agonizing version of the story.

"Oh, honey, she doesn't hate you. She's going through a difficult, painful time now. Scoot over." She sat down next to me on the bed and gave me a big hug, and I actually let her.

"It was awful, Mom," I said into her shoulder.

"Honey, there are so many things in life that you can't control, like what other people do, or say, or feel," she said, stroking my hair. "All you can do is try to control how *you* feel about it."

"Well, I'm mad!"

"I know you are. I don't blame you. And I'm not saying that you shouldn't feel your feelings. But Jen may not be able to handle all of your anger and disappointment right now. I'll bet she really needs you to be a friend."

"I've tried to be her friend!"

"Hey, why don't you write her a letter, a letter that you're never going to send, where you get to express all of your feelings—your anger, hurt, frustration, jealousy, disappointment, whatever. I guarantee that you'll feel much better. It always works for me."

"Mom, I'm not jealous."

"Okay. I was just making suggestions."

I figured it couldn't hurt.

> Dear Jen,
>
> Let me introduce myself since you may not remember me. My name is Paisley Hanover. I'm your friggin' best friend for the past five years!!! Remember? What is going on with you?! God, you just seem like a totally different person these days. And can I just say, the new you is NOT an improvement. You're selfish, you're insecure, you're nasty, you're fake, and you're obviously pretending to be someone you're not just because of Bodie and your new wanna-be "fab" friends. Gag! Barf! Puke in a purse! What happened at that pool party?! And who am *I* supposed to talk to now? We used to

I wasn't even finished venting and I was already feeling so much better. When I came back from the bathroom, Dyson was settling down on my laptop again. "You crazy kitty," I said in my cat voice as I lifted him off the keypad.

I sat down, ready to finish my vicious letter, and stared at an empty screen. OMG. It was gone! I clicked around trying to find it. Oh no oh no oh no. I clicked desperately, hoping it was saved as a draft or something. Finally, I clicked SENT MAIL.

Oh no.

Oh crap.

Oh puke in a purse.

CHAPTER FOURTEEN

When I saw her at school the next morning, Jen refused to talk to me, except to say, "I'm not talking to you." She gave me the wave-off and looked the other way. Like I even *wanted* to talk to her. I mean, really—*she* was mad at *me?* Ergh!

"I'm not talking to you either," Carreyn snarled.

I waved, like, see ya, and watched her follow Jen down the hall.

Amy just looked at me like I was an idiot. "Let me get this straight." She hoisted her hands onto her hips. "You wrote a vicious hateful vent letter in an *e-mail* with Jen's address in the To line, and your *cat* accidentally sent it?"

I nodded. Even I had a hard time believing it when she said it like that. But whatever! Amy had gone right along with Jen's nasty plan. I was about to call her out, when—

"How come your cat never e-mails *me?*" she asked.

I wasn't sure if I was allowed to laugh, but I did anyway. So did she. Then she straightened her face. "Obviously, I'm not talking to you *or* your cat." And she stormed off like a soap opera actress, making a goofy face at me over her shoulder. At least Amy wasn't completely bonkers.

I walked into Drama not knowing what to expect from Cate Maduro. I tried to make eye contact with her, but she ignored me. Figures. Just as the bell for third period rang, Bean came rushing over to me with a big smile on her face. She was wearing her Dumbe Blonde T-shirt.

"I got you something at the thrift store."

"You did?"

She handed me a crumpled brown paper bag. I looked inside and pulled out a western-style shirt with this wild faded paisley pattern and square pearl snaps.

"Paisley. Get it?" Bean laughed like a total goofhead.

"Thanks, Bean. I love it." And I meant it.

She smiled even bigger. "It's kinda worn and a little frayed on the edges, but that's what makes it cool."

"Yeah. Thanks." I put it on right over my top. "It fits perfectly."

We sat down next to each other and she started telling me all about her favorite thrift store that you have to take a bus and then walk about ten blocks to get to but it's always worth it. I told her I wanted to check it out. And I meant it.

"Okay people, chairs in a circle. Everybody now!" Mr. E. directed our lumpy blob of chairs into a tight perfect circle. Everyone pretty much sat next to their friends, which meant that I was in between Bean and Charlie.

"This is a concentration exercise. And it's one of my favorites. I think you'll quickly see why." As Mr. E. talked, he walked around the circle, pulling a guy out of one chair and making him swap places with a girl on the other side of the circle. He kept doing this until he had completely reorganized our careful seating. I looked around nervously.

"This exercise is designed to challenge your focus, so you'll really have to concentrate not to break character." He reached for my arm and directed me to switch seats with Svend, our one cool, totally pierced foreign exchange student, sitting between Cate Maduro and Clint Bedard. I didn't look at her, so I don't even know if she was still ignoring me. Clint smiled, raising his eyebrows and patting the seat next to him.

"If you maintain your concentration, each of you will get to be the Responder and then the Asker. If you break concentration at any point, you're out of the circle. Okay, here's how it works. The Asker says, 'Smile and tell me that you love me.' The Responder says, 'You know I love you, honey, but I just can't smile.'"

Some people groaned, but a lot of people just giggled nervously. Yes, I was one of the nervous gigglers.

"You must *commit* to the words. You get three chances to ask the other person to smile and three chances to respond—and *not* smile. You can use your body, within reason, whether you're the Asker or the Responder. You can touch the other person in a respectful PG-13 way, as long as it's in line with your objective. Any inappropriate touching"—he looked straight at Clint Bedard—"will get you a fast pass to the vice principal's office. Any questions?"

"Can I go to the nurse? I'm suddenly feeling ill," said Cate Maduro, all sweet and innocent.

More nervous laughter.

"No. Any other questions?"

You could feel the tension in the room expand as everyone realized who was sitting next to them.

"I want to see all of you committing to your objective. Choose a type of love—romantic, grandparent, best friend, teammate—and commit to it. I'll be paying close attention to everyone. And you *will* be graded." He paused. "One other thing. Your performance in this exercise will directly affect who I partner you with for your *Acting Out* scene study."

More groans.

"Okay." Mr. E. spun around the room with his arm pointing out at the circle. He landed on Mandy Mindel. "Mandy, show us how it's done."

Her eyes got really big behind her glasses. She took a deep breath, turned to Teddy Baedeker sitting next to her, and, like a nervous robot, said, "Smile and tell me that you love me."

Teddy Baedeker turned bright red and burst into hysterics.

"Ted, you're out!"

They both looked incredibly relieved.

I watched the tension move around the circle like slow, tortured knots of electric current. People tried different techniques—aloof, flirty, demanding, pleading, sweet, parental—with varying results and varying degrees of blushing, sweating, and uncontrollable nervous laughter. Most people stayed in their own safe physical space, and most people didn't stay in the circle.

And then Bean did something daring.

When it was her turn to be the Asker, she plopped right down in Svend's lap, casually crossed one long, lean leg over the other, and then threw her arms playfully around his neck like she was his girlfriend and did this all the time. "Smile and tell me that you love me," said Bean with total confidence. It worked. Svend was out like that. Then she scooted behind Charlie and started giving him a back rub. He responded and didn't smile. He didn't smile again. And then Bean started massaging up the back of his scalp in an innocent, hair-salon kind of way. His head sort of rolled back a little, his mouth fell open, and his eyes glazed over. When she asked for the third time, her mouth was just inches behind his left ear. He tried to answer, but nothing came out of his mouth.

"I'm out," he said in a high squeaky voice.

It got closer and closer to me. I had no idea what I was going to do except probably make a total fool of myself. Clint Bedard was about to say the love word to me. Guys like Clint Bedard do not say the love word to girls like me. They say the love word to bad girls, girls who smoke and drink, girls with tattoos, smokin' hot bodies, and no curfew.

Clint Bedard turned and faced me. Gulp. He sat back in his chair all relaxed and cocky, and flashed that naughty, flirty grin. "Smile. And tell me that you love me."

I was so nervous it was easy for me not to smile. "You know I love you, honey, but I just can't smile," I flatlined.

He leaned toward me and put on this sweet puppy-dog face, which was funny because he looked anything but sweet. He whimpered like a cute little puppy dog too. "Smile and tell me that you love me." He whimpered again.

I didn't feel at all sorry for him. But he almost got me. Almost. "You know I love you, honey," I said earnestly. "But I just can't smile." I shrugged, feeling this strange surge of energy.

He sat there for a second like he was stumped and then he scooted over. He was practically sitting in my chair. He slowly reached up toward my face. OMG! And stroked the side of my cheek. I felt the hairs on the back of my neck stand straight up. And I could feel myself turning bright red. A few people laughed and hooted. He reached up and ran his fingers down the side of my neck and down my necklace to my collarbone. More people hooted. My heart was racing—I could hear it pounding in my ears, but I didn't break concentration.

He looked me in the eyes. "Smile and . . . " He said it like he really, really wanted it. He gently tucked a few strands of my hair behind one ear and leaned into me. I was frozen. He smelled kind of sweaty but good sweaty, almost spicy. And then he whispered, "Tell me that you love me."

I got the chills from his breath in my ear. It shot down my spine and ended up melting in a warm pool somewhere below my belt. Whoa. I looked down at the floor, afraid to say a word. He touched my jaw, gently turning my face toward him so I had to look him straight in the eye. I must have had an out-of-body experience, because I don't even remember saying, "You know I love you, honey, but I just can't smile." All I know is that everyone was cheering and clapping and hooting.

Even Mr. E. was clapping. Clint was out. Wow. Maybe I *could* be good at this. I turned and faced Cate Maduro, actually glad to have anyone else to look at, even her. Concentrate. Concentrate. I pretended that she was my best friend and that my life depended on her smiling.

"Smile and tell me that you love me," I pleaded.

She didn't hesitate. "You know I love you, honey, but I just can't smile," she answered, ice cold.

She had her tough-as-nails thing turned up to full volume. So I figured the nicer I was, the more likely I would be to freak her out and break her. I turned my chair so it was facing hers and reached out for both of her hands and held them, really held them, imagining that I was her favorite grandma. I tried to make my eyes gentle and really loving. "Smile and tell me that you love me," I said.

She pulled away from me and shook her head. "You know I love you, honey, but I just can't smile."

I wasn't sure what to try next. But I was into this exercise and I was determined—determined to make her smile and determined to prove to these people that even a rah-rah like me deserves to be in Drama. Oh, what the hell. She doesn't like me anyway.

I reached out both of my hands and cupped her face like I could almost kiss her. Her skin felt really soft. People started hooting and whistling and making obnoxious catcalls. But I didn't budge. It just made me focus harder. I looked in her eyes, shifting from one to the other, searching for her deepest, darkest secret—that sweet, funny girl who had been so nice to me the other day. Then as plainly and as honestly as I could, I said, "Smile and tell me that you love me."

I saw this flash of fear or something crazy in her eyes. Then it was gone. She blinked a few times. She swallowed hard. Then in this small voice she said, "You know, you know I . . ." Then she pulled back and laughed like she was totally embarrassed. "Damn!"

"Cate, you're out!"

The room erupted with more cheers and claps and way more nervous laughter. Yes! I stood up and took a quick bow, then sat back in my chair feeling this giddy rush.

I was a drama queen rock star! I got her! I totally got her. I dared her to ever mess with me again. Or ignore me. Wow. Was I good at this? Maybe I was. Who knew I could concentrate like that? Who knew I could be weirder than the professional full-time weirdos? Ha! I smiled, thinking no one really knew me—not even me.

I looked around the circle, trying not to smile. And then I looked at Bean. We both cracked up. There were only seven of us left out of over thirty. Bean, five hard-core, weird-ass freaka-zoids, and me—Paisley Hanover, everyone's favorite rah-rah.

CHAPTER FIFTEEN

I was riding high until I realized it was morning break. No way was I going go buddy it up with Carreyn and Amy and Jen—assuming Jen even bothered to show.

So I decided to spend morning break in the library, coming off my Drama high—and staking out my locker. I'd figured last week's note was a fluke since I hadn't gotten another. But then right after Drama, I opened my locker and a *second note* was lying on my bio book. I grabbed it.

HOT 4 YOU!

Seriously, was this a joke?! And if it wasn't, then who? Who? WHO was hot 4 me?! Same handwriting. Same plain notebook paper. I looked around at the emptying hallway. Hmm. One thing was for sure—I wasn't telling Jen about this. No way was I telling her my secrets if she wasn't telling me any of hers. If she wasn't even *talking* to me.

When I got to the library, mostly I watched my locker from a seat by the window, but I also watched Clint Bedard, who was sitting at one of the computers. I know, Clint Bedard? In the *library?* He was slowly hunting and pecking. I wish I had the guts to go over there, sit on his lap, and whisper *Smile and tell me that you love me.* Suddenly he looked up, right at me.

"Red, you spying on me?"

I blushed big-time. Oh, perfect. No one had ever called me Red. I couldn't decide if I loved it or hated it. But my ears must have liked it. I could feel them burning. "No," I answered like it was the dumbest question in the world.

"Think you were." He grinned and raised his eyebrows.

"Think not." I turned away and looked out the window again, praying for my face to unblush immediately. Amy was sitting on our bench, watching Jen and Carreyn practice their cheerleading moves on the grass and looking extremely bored. Carreyn suddenly threw her arms out and popped some kid right in the chin. His smoothie went flying. Amy and Carreyn laughed hysterically while Jen went over and helped wipe down the kid. I smiled, feeling a little sad. That was the Jen I knew. I guess she was still in there somewhere.

"Hey Red? Check this out." Clint waved me over. "You're on YouTube."

I looked at him and rolled my eyes. "Okay."

"I'm serious. You've got your own music video." He smirked. I ignored him. "Says you're a fun of a kind girl, but I guess it's wrong."

"What?!" I ran over to the computer. "Show me!"

Clint hit the REPLAY button. I covered my mouth with my hands and almost had a heart attack. It was ME, well parts of me, doing a spastic jazz hands dance along with—and this was maybe the worst part—*me* doing this mortifyingly bad "Paisley Hanover: *Fun* of a Kind Girl" rap! I dropped into a chair, staring at the computer screen. Then I laid my head slowly on the table.

I knew who'd done it. Eric Sobel. It had to be. He was the only one who'd had a camera in Yearbook. Oh God. He must have videotaped me with his cell phone too. I started softly banging my head against the table. But why? WHY would he do this to me?

"Cool effects." Clint nodded. "The editing really pulls it together."

I lifted my head and glared at him.

"Wanna see it again?"

"No," I said coldly. Why had I wasted a single thought on Eric Sobel?

Of course I saw it again basically everywhere I went. Walking down the hall, Cate Maduro didn't waste a moment. "Hi, Paisley!" She jumped out and spastic jazzed me. "You crazy *fun* of a kind girl!" she said with a wink as she walked past.

Mr. Yamaguchi spastic jazzed our whole class when he announced a pop quiz in American History. Ugh. He was one of those teachers who tried so hard to be cool. I was embarrassed, but I was totally embarrassed for *him*.

At soccer practice, the whole defensive line spastic jazzed me when I was dribbling toward the goal. I ignored them, kept dribbling, and blasted the ball into the back of the net.

After practice, I ran a few extra laps. I didn't want to have to talk to Amy—about Jen or jazz hands or anything.

I was lost in my head space thinking about this stuff. Then I caught sight of Eric Sobel out of the corner of my eye. He ran halfway onto the girls' field, chasing a ball. When he saw me, he smiled and did his head-nod thing. Unbelievable. What a buttcap. I didn't smile back. I didn't wave. I didn't nod. I just kept running.

What did he expect?

CHAPTER SIXTEEN

When I walked past Jen the next day at morning break, she didn't say a word. She just stared at me as I walked by, then suddenly spastic jazzed me with this freaky-meanie smile, and then sunk into the splits. Jen was no Favorite Friend of mine either. But I wasn't going to let her know. So I served it right back to her.

"Hi, Jen!" I spastic jazzed her with a big, crap-eating smile. "You ready for cheerleading tryouts today?" I called cheerfully as I walked by. Carreyn and Amy were coming up from the other direction and— What?! I stopped dead, staring. "Oh my God, Carreyn! What happened?" I ran over to them.

The one—maybe the only—good thing about being in a fight with Jen was that I didn't have to deal with *cheerleading*. Jen and Carreyn were so caught up in their fantasy of impending fabulosity that it was dangerous to be anywhere near them— unless you liked getting backhanded in the face or your phone kicked out of your hand.

But this? I didn't even know what to say. The whole cheerleading thing had fried Carreyn's brain, and the evidence was right here. Carreyn looked—she looked . . . Well, she looked like a giant baked bean. What, had she slept all night in a tanning bed?

"She's been hiding in the bathroom all morning," said Amy. "Give her a break."

"What happened?" Jen asked, genuinely concerned. That was refreshing at least.

Turns out, Carreyn knew it was a stretch (ha-ha) for her to make cheerleader, even JV. So she came up with a secret weapon—body bronzing foam. The night before, she'd applied smooth, long strokes of foam all over her taut little bod, once, maybe twice, okay, three times—just to be sure. She was convinced that her body, bronzed to perfection, would make her stand out to the judges.

Cut to this morning: Surprise! Total disaster. She even pretended to be sick so she wouldn't have to come to school, but her mom forced her.

So now she was sort of standing behind Amy, with her permed hair brushed forward to cover her face. She was wearing a longsleeve turtleneck and jeans.

"Aren't you hot?" I asked, rubbing her back.

Carreyn just turned and glared at me, then looked around furtively. "I'm going back to the bathroom," she whispered, and took off through the crowd, head down.

Okay, so maybe that didn't help.

When the bell rang for lunch, Carreyn was still holed up in the handicapped stall, refusing to come out, much less try out. She texted Amy asking for a burrito, and then Amy texted me:

Crryn stl in toilet. Hlp! Pls?

I knocked on the bathroom door, and guess who opened it? Jen. I didn't want to be in the same room with her, much less in the same handicapped *bathroom*. But I wasn't some nasty sasshole, so I put my feelings temporarily on ice.

"But Carreyn, you've worked so hard. You have to," Amy was saying.

Silence.

I walked over. "You've learned all the moves," I tried, not knowing what else to say. "And . . . and you *rock!*" I looked from Amy to Jen, and shrugged. God, what was I supposed to say? Jen didn't have to stare at me like that.

"Carreyn, the Hornettes need you," said Jen. "They need your confidence and your school spirit, and your smile."

"Really?" Carreyn asked feebly.

"Really!" we answered. Jen looked at her watch. Tryouts started at 12:15.

"I still want to try out, I do. But I . . . I'm a little . . . I really need your support, you guys, okay?" she asked from inside the stall.

"Okay," we all said. Carreyn pushed open the stall door and stepped out like a proud Hornette, her frizzy, permed head held high.

"How do I look?" she asked, smiling uncertainly.

She looked like a giant baked bean covered in toothpaste and wearing a skimpy cheerleading outfit.

"Great!" I said. "You look great! How'd you do that?"

"You can hardly even tell," said Amy, who obviously hadn't been taking Drama.

"What *is* that?" Jen asked, touching Carreyn's skin.

"A little zinc oxide mixed with lotion. I had it in my purse."

"It works." Amy nodded. "It totally works."

"And your hair looks fab," said Jen.

Carreyn beamed.

Whew. Crisis averted. Right?

Wrong.

No one was allowed to watch the tryouts except for the judges and all the girls competing for a spot on the cheerleading squad. But Amy really wanted to see it for some bizzaro reason. I allowed myself to be dragged along—not out of camaraderie, I told myself, but out of morbid curiosity.

Amy and I pulled two empty garbage cans over behind the back of the small gym where the tryouts were happening and tipped them on their sides. We pushed the cans against the wall and climbed up. It smelled a little funky, but we had a perfect view through the open windows.

Carreyn did an awesome job. She kept her wrists straight and her shoulders down and she never stopped smiling. You could tell she believed in herself 115 percent. She didn't make it to the final round, but she sure stood out to the judges.

Jen stood out too. When she stepped into the middle of the gym with the other girls in her group, she was glowing with confidence. Really. Glowing. I rooted for her a little. I mean, what would you do? I didn't want her to *fail*. But oh yuck. Two of the cheerleading judges were her new best girls, BS1 and BS2. I watched distractedly as BS1 demonstrated the series of moves and then strung them together into a short routine.

BS2 punched a button on the sound system, stepped back, and yelled, "Ready? O-kay!" The music blared.

Jen's group started doing the routine, and Jen was doing all of these fabulous cheerleader moves with perfect form—except that they weren't the right ones. She bumped into a girl next to her, who bumped into the girl next to her. They both turned around and scowled at her.

BS2 turned off the music. "Okay. Okay! We'll show you again! *Watch* this time!"

BS1 demonstrated the routine again. "Kick left, step right, hips, punch it left, kick right, turn, low V, shake it, shimmy, turn, daggers, spastic jazz left, snap it, clean it up, spastic jazz right, snap it, clean it up, and splits!"

Wait. What?! Spastic jazz?!

Jen looked around, confused.

"Spastic jazz?!" I gasped out loud. "Oh my God! I can't believe . . . they *stole my move!*"

"I thought you hated that," said Amy.

"I did! I *do*. But still, they shouldn't steal my embarrassing move for their stupid cheerleading routine!"

The music blared again. Jen's group began the routine. At first she seemed to be okay. But then she started screwing up. And the more she screwed up, the worse it got, until you could tell she was totally freaked.

Amy and I looked at each other. What was up with Jen?

She was looking to the left and looking to the right, trying to get back in step: But I could see she was losing it. And then when I was finally like, Oh my God, I can't watch, Jen just stopped. She stood there, glaring at the judges' table. The music blared on around her. Her face was bright red. A couple girls bumped into her and shot her dirty looks. Finally, she took a few steps toward the judges' table and yelled something. She threw her hands down, then turned and ran out the back door of the gym.

Amy and I looked at each other, then ran around to the front of the gym to find her.

"Jen!" I yelled. She was running toward the playing fields. "Wait!"

She finally stopped and sat down in the middle of the field, her shoulders shaking. Amy and I caught up. And suddenly, I realized I didn't even know what to say to her. "Are you okay?" I asked lamely.

She glared at me. "No! God, I'm such an idiot!" She was crying, but she was more pissed than anything. "How could I have been so *stupid?*"

"What do you mean? I thought you looked really good," said Amy, trying to be positive.

Jen didn't even hear her. "They set me up. They *set me up!* Those skinny little brats taught me the wrong routine—on purpose!"

OMG. "But . . . That's so . . . Why would they do that?" I honestly didn't get why they would turn on her.

"What, are they jealous?" Amy asked.

"They're not jealous. They're *vicious*," Jen spat. "Candy's dying to get back together with Bodie. It's so obvious." She scrubbed the tears off her cheeks with the back of a hand. "She calls him and texts and hangs on him all the time when I'm not around and—and—and I'm gonna kill them. I'm gonna kill them!" Then she balled up her fists and sort of punched the ground, turning bright red again. It was scary.

Amy and I looked at each other.

Then suddenly Jen got all calm and Zen.

Carreyn ran up to us, panting. "What happened? What happened?!"

We all ignored her. "No." Jen exhaled slowly and softly. "Blowing roses. Blowing roses. That's exactly what they want. Bodie can't stand jealous girl drama." Jen smiled serenely. "Somehow, I've got to get *Bodie* to do it."

Jen had totally lost it. And I guess the expression on my face must have said as much. Because Jen looked at me and like, *exploded*.

"What? *What?!* God, you are so . . . " Jen scrambled to her feet. Her face was red and wet and all twisted up. "Just get away from me, Paisley! Go *away!* You're always telling me how I'm doing it wrong. You're always trying to make me feel like crap! I'm sick of it! I'm sick of you!" She looked from me to Amy to Carreyn, who were standing there totally stunned. And then she took off.

I was shocked. I felt this electric current like zap through me and make my head prickle. I looked at Amy and Carreyn. "Where did that come from?" I asked no one in particular.

"Where do you *think?*" Carreyn snapped.

I really didn't know. And frankly, I was starting not to care.

CHAPTER SEVENTEEN

There was a lot of avoiding going on that week. I was avoiding evil YouTuber Eric Sobel. Jen and Carreyn were avoiding me. Jen was also avoiding BS1 and BS2 and all of the other McNasty Poms. And, the big news—Bodie was avoiding Jen, and had been for a few days. Amy's cat sent me a text telling me all about it. Jen was totally freaking because she didn't know why. He said it was just because of the football game that night against our biggest rivals, the Cougars. But Jen wasn't so sure and she was getting all insecure and worried that Bodie was about to dump her.

Today was Friday and the first home football game and the first of the Pleasant Hill High insane pregame rallies, where the entire student body crammed into the gym and cheered like some crazy cult.

I spent lunch in the library, as I had for the last three days, trying not to get all pathetic about having to go to the rally by myself. Our rallies are not the kind of thing you want to endure alone.

I waited outside the gym for as long as possible, and even

thought about hiding behind the portable classrooms and not going at all. But I didn't want to get in trouble. I admit it. God, I hated being such a goody-goody.

Mr. Canfield, our vice principal, was closing the doors to the gym and pointed at me. "Hurry up, Paisley. You don't want to miss this."

Actually, I did.

Inside, the gym was a mob scene. The bleachers were packed with kids wearing black and yellow, and the band was already playing a sloppy version of "We Are the Champions." I looked around for someone I knew—anyone. Behind the band, a small group of anti-establishmentors were wearing Dumbe Blonde T-shirts. I so wished I had the guts to go sit with them and be a screaming, arts-loving activist. But so far, I'd only had guts enough to wear my Dumbe Blonde T-shirt to bed. How terribly lame.

The Dumbe Blondes were completely ignored by the popular kids in our class who were all huddled in one section of the bleachers, rocking together left and then right, in time—kind of—to the music. Jen, Amy, and Carreyn were right in the middle of them, which was kind of weird considering Jen's nightmarish cheerleading tryout. I looked around again. I had no idea where to go. I started to panic.

And then I saw Bean and Cate Maduro and some of the other kids from Drama sitting over to one side. Bean waved in my direction, so I headed toward them. All I knew was that I didn't want to be standing on the gym floor when the Ho'nettes paraded out. I was cutting across the gym floor when someone suddenly grabbed my hand.

"Come on, Red. We're gonna get trampled by cheerleaders!" Clint pulled me over to the bleachers and carved a path up to where Bean and Cate were sitting. "Little room, please!" He wedged in next to Cate, who sort of looked at me and nodded, and I squeezed in just as the action started.

"And now, give it up for Pleasant Hill High's award-winning Spirit Squad!" a voice boomed over the loud speakers.

"Do they give awards for drinking spirits now?" Cate asked, all doe-eyed and dopey. "Hurray?" I watched them all laugh.

The band started playing another off-tempo song and the baton twirlers high-kicked their way out into the middle of the floor wearing basically sequin-covered bathing suits. Everyone went wild, screaming and whistling.

"Nice butt-cheek action." Bean whistled like a guy. "Hello! Welcome to wedgies!" she shouted all counter-girl cheerful. We all laughed.

Clint flashed his bad-boy grin. "Can it ever be wrong to rock in a thong?" Then he yelled at the twirlers, "Be sure to butt-floss after every meal!"

"Ew!"

"Gross!"

"That's disgusting!"

We all cracked up.

The Spirit Squad did their routine with only two baton

drops, so they seemed pretty happy. I looked for Jen and Amy and Carreyn, but I couldn't see them from where I was sitting. I wondered if they even missed me, if they even noticed I wasn't sitting with them. And then I realized something. I didn't care. I was squished in between Clint Bedard and Cate Maduro, and I was fine. Actually, I was feeling even better than fine.

Then the Ho'nettes trotted out all bouncing with energy and holding their huge poofy pom-poms high. They stood in formation in the middle of the gym floor, dropped their heads, and froze. The whole gym fell silent. BS1 and BS2 were front and center. Then the band launched into a jazzy, semi-sultry tune, and one by one, the Hornettes came to life with electric smiles as if each of them had been poked by a cattle prod.

Everyone screamed. *Everyone*. It was insane. Cate Maduro did a fake school spirit shriek, pretending to be a lunatic like everyone else. She and Bean and LG Wong kept bursting into hysterics. Clint whistled, and it practically burst my eardrum. Then Bean tapped me on the shoulder and did this crazy teen girl scream and pretended to faint from excitement. I was laughing, this giddy, goofy feeling about to overwhelm me. But then I made myself stop because I didn't want to pee right there next to Clint Bedard.

We all started swaying to the right and swaying to the left with the music. Even though we were sort of making fun of the whole scene, we were having a great time. It had never occurred to me before that this was everyone's school, and everyone's band, and everyone's football team, and that the unpopular kids rooted for the same team as the popular kids, even if their school spirit was spiked with irony.

"Hey!" Bean smacked me in the shoulder. "That's *your* move. Cool!"

The Hornettes were doing spastic jazz hands as they kicked around in a circle and crumpled into a bud of butts. Everybody cheered.

I wanted to feel pissed, but I was kind of amazed. My weirdest, most embarrassing moment of high school life had been incorporated into Pleasant Hill High pop culture. I didn't know what to think of that.

The loudspeaker crackled and popped. "And now it's time to meet the men we're all cheering for, Pleasant Hill High's varsity squad!"

The bleachers erupted in cheers and screams and squeals as the guys ran out of the locker room wearing their jerseys and ran around the gym until they had circled the floor a few times. Most of the guys on the team seemed totally pumped, but Eric Sobel looked mortified to be out there. I almost felt bad for him. Almost.

When Coach Cave started introducing the first-string players by name, Clint leaned over and whispered, "Going to the game?"

His breath on my ear gave me that same strange tingly feeling up and down my spine. I pulled back, a little startled, and nodded.

He leaned in and whispered again, "Going to the dance?"

I pulled away again and looked at him. Was he *trying* to do this to me? Could he *tell* he was doing this to me? I nodded again. *Why* was he doing this to me?

Then he whispered, "Good. Dance with me." He flashed his flirty bad-boy grin.

Oh God. My face went red, and I quickly turned away, staring down at the far end of the gym. I don't know if his lip really touched my ear or if I just imagined it. But it sure seemed like it did. And if his lip really did touch my ear, did he do it on purpose or did it just happen because maybe the guy next to him leaned to the left and pushed him a little? I pretended to be extremely interested in the names of all our linebackers. Next time I looked over at Clint, he was gone, threading his way through the bleachers and out the door.

I turned back to watch the players, but I wasn't watching at all. I was thinking about Clint Bedard. Oh God, why was I thinking about Clint Bedard? He was a total flirt. He probably would've asked Mandy Mindel the same thing if she had been sitting next to him.

I tried to concentrate on Coach Cave's raspy voice. "Number thirty-seven, star wide receiver, Peter Hutchison!" Hutch ran into the middle of the circle, and everyone cheered. "Caught the game-winning catch last season. No pressure, Hutch!" People laughed and hooted. "Number twelve, All-Conference running back two years in a row, the one and only Bodie Jones!"

Bodie took a few steps out into the circle and smiled, a little shy, and then waved. The whole gym went nuts, cheering, and stomping, yelling, "Bodie! Bodie! Bodie!"

Some girl shrieked, "I love you, Bodie!" He got all embarrassed and went back to his spot in the circle. I wondered how Jen must feel sitting there knowing that she had to share him with the entire student body. Or maybe not, if he was still avoiding her.

The rally wrapped up with a "We've got spirit! Yes we do! We've got spirit! How 'bout you?!" cheering competition between the north and south sides of the gym. It was a tie because as Coach Cave said, "There are no losers at Pleasant Hill High!"

Ha. That was a good one.

Everyone cleared out of the bleachers and spilled into the courtyard next to the gym, mingling in their little groups. I wasn't sure where to go, so I stayed with Cate and Bean.

"That was scary," said Cate, holding her head. "I've got to get deprogrammed immediately before I do something insane like go to a football game."

"Hey Paisley, we're going thrifting this afternoon. Wanna come?" asked Bean.

"I can't. I've got soccer."

"Oh right, go team!" Cate made a fist and punched the air.

"Maybe next time," I said, and meant it.

"Right," said Cate, not sounding all that convinced, but looking like maybe she could be.

141

"Pains me! Show me some love!" Before I saw him coming, Hutch had picked me up off the ground and was spinning me around.

"Put me down! Put me down!"

"You're no fun," he said, setting me on the ground and pretending to mope.

I looked around for Cate and Bean, but they were already gone.

CHAPTER EIGHTEEN

By the time the game rolled around, Jen still wasn't talking to me, and every time I saw Carreyn, she would fling these weird verbal darts at me. Bizarre stuff like, "Betrayal is a cruel, cruel friend," as if she was quoting off the back of a trashy romance novel.

Amy kept her distance, but at least she was sill making goofy faces at me from afar.

The Dumbe Blondes were sitting together at one end of the bleachers cheering like maniacs and holding signs like GO TEEM GO! and HOMERUN! and GO FOR THE GOLE!

I sat with Bean and Charlie Dodd. It was a really close game—Bodie scored two touchdowns, Hutch caught a bunch of passes, and Eric Sobel kicked the winning field goal, which totally depressed me because now every girl in school would be crushing on him—as much as I hated to admit that I even cared.

After the game, tons of people were hanging out in front of the gym, waiting to get into the dance. I was standing there goofing with Bean and Charlie when Amy walked up, dragging Carreyn behind her.

"Hey," Amy said to Bean and Charlie, giving me a wacko smile.

"Hey," Bean said back. Carreyn looked totally uncomfortable, like there were at least a million other places she'd rather be.

And then Charlie said, "Hi, Carreyn. Are you going to the dance?"

"Maybe," she said, trying not to smile. Then she whipped her head around and squinted at me. "Paisley, why was *the bottle-rocket bomber* holding your hand at the rally?"

"Clint Bedard?" Charlie asked. "You were holding hands with Clint Bedard?"

I shrugged and smiled. "I wasn't holding hands with him exactly. He's just a guy I know from Drama class."

"He's kinda hot," Amy said.

"He is," said Bean.

"He is," I agreed.

Charlie rolled his eyes. Carreyn looked at us like we'd taken a big hit of helium and were speaking some strange foreign language.

Just then, Jen came running up. "Hey guys!" she said to Carreyn and Amy, giving Bean and Charlie a bizarre look. She grabbed my arm and pulled me away from the pack.

Oh, sure, Jen, just act like everything's fine, like you haven't been giving me the icy elbow all week.

"Look, I know this is going to sound weird," she said, "but just roll with me, okay?" So I did. I rolled my *eyes*. "Bodie and some friends are having a little pre-party before the dance out by the baseball field," she whispered. "I don't want to go alone."

No way. Was she serious? Was she asking *me*? She hadn't talked to me in like three days! And *this* was the first thing out of her mouth?! But all I said was, "Gosh, Jen, you don't have to go alone. Why don't you ask your best buds Carreyn and Amy?"

"You know." She hesitated. "The party's not for everyone. It's kind of *exclusive*."

"Oh, really? Well I'm kind of exclusive too. I don't hang out with people who treat me like crap." I stared at her, waiting. I was sick of being in this stupid fight, but I wasn't about to just totally cave.

She looked over at Carreyn and Amy, then back to me. "Sorry, Pais," she said, twisting her hands. For a second, I caught a glimpse of the real Jen. Or was it the *old* Jen? "Pleeease? I really want you to be there," she begged. "We haven't had any real qual time lately."

"Yeah, I wonder why." I shook my head.

Qual time? I started that one. I turned back to the group, still standing there awkwardly and looking everywhere but at each other. "Hey you guys, go ahead and go in. I'll catch up with you." They all looked so relieved. Carreyn and Amy went one way, Charlie and Bean went the other.

"Thanks, Pais. It'll be fun. Come on!"

Jen dragged me down a dark hallway behind the boys' locker

room and back around behind the pool, then out toward the trees near the baseball field. I could hear people talking and laughing, a few loud *Shhhhh*'s, someone reminding everyone to be quiet.

"Who's gonna be there?" I asked, totally unenthusiastically.

"Bodie's group. You know, guys from the team. I'll bet Eric Sobel will be there." She gave me an I-know-you-like-him smile.

Carreyn and Amy must have dished about my big "encounter" with Eric last week in Yearbook. But honestly? Whatever. I refused to crush on someone who'd uploaded that thing on YouTube, no matter how hard it was to *not* crush on him.

Jen stopped a little ways away from the group and pulled some lip gloss out of her purse. "Yeah. And a few junior and senior girls, some BPs, maybe even a few Poms. Here, try this color. It's yummy." She handed me the lip gloss.

Oh, now I got it. I was her backup in case any of the Varsity Poms got ugly with her again. And the worst thing was, I couldn't decide if I felt proud that she'd asked me or pissed, like I was only worth being a friend when she needed something from me. Actually, you know what? I *could* decide. I was pissed.

"Why do you even *want* to hang out with those nasty Poms after what they did to you?" I asked.

"I don't!" She sounded really frustrated. "Look, Paisley, you don't know *everything* about me anymore."

What did *that* mean?

"Sometimes you have to do things . . . " She sighed. "I *don't* like them, but they're Bodie's friends. So if I want to be with him, then I have to put up with them."

I had a bad feeling about this, but we were approaching the group. I couldn't just leave now. I'd look like a noob. Maybe it wouldn't be so bad, I tried to convince myself. Maybe I'd find the guts to confront Eric Sobel . . . or . . . or something.

There were about fifteen guys and girls standing in the shadow of the trees. It was too dark to see who all was there. But I saw a few guys wearing letterman jackets and two or three Ho'nettes, still in their foxy little uniforms. I could hear paper rustling, beer cans opening, guys talking in low voices, and lots of giggling.

"Hi, Jen." It was Bratty Sasshole #1 acting all fake friendly. She turned to me. "Well hello, Paisley Hanover. What a special treat. Hey, how's your brother?"

I was surprised that BS1 was talking to me. And that she even knew my name. "He's good." I sounded a little confused, like I wasn't sure I had a brother or didn't know what good actually meant.

"Your brother's such a cutie," said Bratty Sasshole #2. "I miss him *and* his fake ID. Be sure to tell him I say hi and buy. He'll know what that means." She laughed. I laughed too, even though I had no idea what she was talking about—and didn't want to.

"So," said BS1, sizing me up. "You're hanging with us now, huh?"

I looked at Jen. But I couldn't see her face in the shadows. Some girl handed her a bottle of what looked like peach schnapps. Jen took a sip.

"Tonight I am. I guess."

"By the way," BS1 said, half smiling, "I *loved* your YouTube video."

Was she serious?

"Big loved it," echoed BS2.

All the girls around me erupted in catty laughter. Of course she wasn't serious. What was I thinking?

"Dude! You're up again!" yelled Bodie, tossing a beer to Hutch.

He caught it with one hand, cracked it open, and chugged the whole thing. Then he let out this long disgusting burp. "Ahh. The sweet taste of victory!" The guys cheered and hooted. Then Hutch crushed the can in one hand and threw it out into the field. "Sobel, you're the man! You're the man! That kick was sick!" He picked Eric up in this big bear hug and lifted him off the ground.

"Okay," said Eric. "Thanks, man. Thanks. Enough." Hutch just laughed and dropped him to the ground.

Bodie kept tossing beers to everyone. "Gentlemen, down your beverages. Doors close at ten. And always remember, an empty beer can is an open container, but a crushed beer can is recycling." Everyone laughed.

Some BP girl passed the bottle of peach schnapps to BS1. She took a huge gulp, coughed a little, then passed the bottle to me.

"No thanks. I—" I hesitated for a second. "I'm so stuffed. I ate like two corn dogs at the game." OMG. What a dorkasaurus.

"Oh, you don't drink?" she cooed at me like I was a two-year-old. "That is *so* cute."

Jen looked alarmed. "Be cool," she hissed. "Anyone want a beer?" She walked away toward Bodie and the cooler.

Fortunately Candy Esposito came up to me right then. "Paisley, hey. How's Drama? I still feel really bad about that. I wish we both could've won."

"Drama's pretty fun. Not what I expected at all. How's Yearbook?"

"Kinda boring, actually. And a lot of work." She took a sip of her beer. "And Ms. Madrigal? She's evil. I was late to class a couple of times and she made me stand in a trash can like I was a piece of garbage. Can you believe that?"

"No way!" said BS2 with genuine horror.

"Way." Candy nodded grimly.

"Totally unacceptable," said BS1. "My parents would've so written a letter to get her fired."

"Done," said Candy smugly. "The letter part, at least."

So this is what the cool kids talked about on Friday night. Wow. I shoved both hands into my jeans so no one would be tempted to pass me a beer. Bodie had his arm around Jen and his hand in the back pocket of her tight jeans. I guess he wasn't avoiding her anymore—at least he wasn't avoiding her butt. So much for our qual time. I looked around for Eric Sobel. He had walked off to the side and was watching a couple of rowdy guys reenact the big plays of the game.

What the hell, I decided. I couldn't possibly embarrass myself any more than I already had this week. I took a deep breath and walked over.

"Hey," I said, trying not to squeak.

"Hey."

I waited a few seconds. "How's soccer?"

"Good." He nodded, looking a little uncomfortable. "How's the . . . the listening spot?"

I groaned and laughed, totally embarrassed. "I don't know where that came from. Too many head balls during practice."

He was laughing too, but in a nice sort of way.

"No. It was cool. It was . . . different." He laughed again.

"That's a generous way of describing it." We laughed a little more and then just stood there feeling weird. He took a sip of beer and stared at the ground.

You know, I wanted to ask, *why did you make that stupid video of me?* or maybe *Will you look for me at the dance?* But all I could squeak out was, "Well, great game tonight." Then I started to walk off.

"Hey," he said softly. I turned around.

He looked nervous, and awkwardly jammed his hands into his front pockets. "Look, um. Yours was better. In Yearbook. Your headline."

"What? Really?"

"Really."

"Wait, are you—? You're not just—" I stopped and pulled myself together. "Really?"

"Really." He nodded like he actually meant it. "Really."

"Thanks." I got all shy for a second. And then I got pissed. "Then why'd you post that completely humiliating video of me on YouTube?"

"I . . . I . . . Sorry. I didn't mean . . . It wasn't supposed to be humiliating. I didn't think people would—I didn't think—I didn't think anyone would even see it. It was supposed to be an homage."

A what? I had no idea what *homage* meant, but it sounded pretty good and kind of exotic and even a little bit sexy. So I played along. I'd look it up later. "An homage?"

"Yeah," he said, smiling kinda shy.

I smiled. God, I was such a goober. "Well, all right then. Apology accepted."

"Cool."

He took a few steps toward me, and my heart started to race. Where was this going? He looked down at his feet, then he tried to look into my eyes, but his bangs were in the way, so he flipped his hair and slowly, slowly leaned toward me, tilting his head just a bit. I couldn't move. Our lips were just inches away. OMG. Was this really happening? I closed my eyes and held my breath—

Actually no. It wasn't. It was just another flash fantasy. I admit it. But it was a really, really, really good one. Don't you think?

Okay, so here's what really happened. No, we didn't kiss or anything, but it was still our first beautiful moment together. And guess who ruined it? Candy Esposito. And to be fair, BS1 and BS2. They all came running over, yelling, "Eric! Eric! Can we get your autograph? We just love you! We love you!" They seemed more than a little buzzed.

Eric was so embarrassed, he didn't say a word. He just laughed nervously and took the black Sharpie that Candy was waving at him. Then all three girls lifted their tops enough so we could see their hard, flat, tan stomachs and screamed, "Sign me! Sign me!" What total McSleazy Skankmeisters. They kept giggling in a way that made me embarrassed to be a girl.

Eric took a few steps back, shaking his head.

"Dude, are you crazy?" Hutch pushed Eric back toward the girls. "There are perks that come with playing football, know what I'm saying? And these are three of 'em."

I turned and walked away. I couldn't watch Eric scribbling on their stomachs as they squealed with ecstasy. How could I compete with that? What was I *talking* about? I didn't *want* to compete with that. Fine. So, if that's what he was into, then whatever. No thanks. Even if he did like me—which of course he didn't.

But I couldn't help looking back over my shoulder.

Hutch was jumping up and down next to Candy Esposito holding his shirt up too, flashing his big hairy belly at Eric. "Sign me! Sign me!" he yelled. Eric seemed to have gotten over his discomfort. Now he was just signing away, one tan belly after another. And everyone but me was laughing.

CHAPTER NINETEEN

Our fun little pre-party wound down fast after that. Most people decided to head over to the dance. I could hear the muffled booming drums and shrill electric guitar in the distance. Jen was walking with Bodie a few feet ahead of me, so I had plenty of qual time to wonder what other ridiculous things she would do or say to keep Bodie happy.

I wanted to kick her in the butt as hard as I could. Lucky for her, Bodie's hand was still wedged in her back pocket. Now that he was back to acting like her butt barnacle, she was back to *ignoring* me! Why did I set myself up for this?

At least Candy Esposito was being nice, and I was trying to be nice to her even though she was all over Eric Sobel, telling funny stories and hanging on his arm. All I could do was stare at him—but not too obviously, I hoped—from a distance and pretend not to care. Twice he smiled back at me over her shoulder like the two of us were in on some Candy Esposito joke. Twice.

Bratty Sasshole #1 and Bratty Sasshole #2 were leading the charge down the hall when BS1 stopped suddenly and reached out both hands to slow the crowd. "Oh my God! Look!" she

blurted in a breathy whisper. She pointed ahead into the shadows. "Two NILs holding hands."

I peeked past BS1's head. There were Teddy Baedeker and
Mandy Mindel, sitting together on a bench.

Uh-oh.

"Ooooh," gushed BS2. "I just *love* NILs. They're *so* cute."

"*So* cute," echoed Jen, nodding like a brainless bobble-
head.

I looked at Jen like she was a total moron. She saw my face
and mouthed "What?" all annoyed, like I was the one who
had just said something cheerleader idiotic. I shook my head. I
wanted to get out of there.

Now Hutch pushed his way up to the front of the group.
"Special Ted! What up, dude?" Hutch was obviously drunk.
"Hey, is this your new babe?"

Teddy giggled nervously, wiping his palms on his pants. He
looked at Mandy, then back to Hutch. "I don't know."

"Wow, she's *pretty*," said some varsity jerk, stroking Mandy's
head like a dog. "Woof! Woof!" People laughed. I guess a lot of
people were drunk. Or just regular shidiots.

Mandy twisted away from his hand and stared straight at the
ground. "Just leave us alone," she whispered. Then she glanced
around for a few seconds with those sad, freaky-looking eyes.

"Hutch, let it go, man. Let's go," said Eric.

"Come on, we're just being friendly, dude."

"You think?" said Eric, sounding annoyed. He looked around
the group and I swear he was looking right at me when he said,

"Who wants to hit the dance?" He walked off down the hall. I started to follow, but Candy Esposito chased after him and grabbed his hand. I stopped. She was really starting to bring out the homicidal maniac in me.

Hutch yelled out, "Ted and I are buds! Right, bro?" He hung his arm around Teddy's shoulders and leaned into him. "Right, buddy?"

"Right." Teddy nodded.

Just like that, Hutch managed to get Teddy's wallet out of his back pocket. He waved it in the air above Teddy's head.

"Hutch, give it!" Teddy squealed.

"Dude, hope you're packing!" He flipped open the wallet and dug through it. "No way." He paused, looking Teddy in the eye. "Ted, man, you gotta be prepared for some action."

Mandy looked mortified.

"Hutch, come on," Teddy whined.

I couldn't believe this was happening. I was getting that sick, swishy feeling in my stomach. What were we all doing, just standing around watching like it was some kind of spectator sport?

"Hey!" I said to no one in particular. But it came out as a squeak. Jen turned and shot me a nasty glare.

One of the varsity jerks grabbed Mandy's purse and held it in the air. "They in your purse, bald eyes?" He tossed it to Bodie.

"Oh yeah. Bet she's holding! She's a smart girl." Bodie laughed and everyone laughed with him.

"No," cried Mandy. She looked around and caught my eye, then stared right at me.

"Hey! Come on, you guys!" I yelled. BS1 and BS2 turned around, cocked their heads, and stared at me like I was insane. I glared right back. I looked around for Eric Sobel, but didn't see him.

Hutch and all the other idiots started tossing Mandy's purse back and forth while Teddy jumped around between them, yelling, "Give it! Give it!"

Mandy stood there clenching her fists, tears streaming down her cheeks.

"Aw, Mandy, don't get all emo," Hutch taunted. "Your mascara will run. Oh wait! I forgot—you don't have eyelashes!"

Everyone, even Jen, howled at that one. It was disgusting. I started to back away from the group.

"Give it!" Teddy shrieked. "Give it back!"

"You scream like a little girl!" Hutch yelled.

"You're the girl, Hutch!" Teddy yelled back. "You're the one always looking at me in the locker room." He laughed feebly.

"What did you say, you sick freak?!" He took a swing at Teddy, totally missed, and almost fell over.

I kept backing away and backing away. And then I just turned around and took off. I wish I could say I was going to get help, but the truth is, I was just going. When I rounded the corner of the music building, I stopped. But I could hear it all through my breathing. The flap, flap, flap of Teddy's feet as he ran down the hall. Hutch chasing after him, yelling. The other varsity jerks cheering him on. And then an even bigger roar from the crowd as Hutch tackled Teddy, and Teddy squealing like a wounded animal, and the crowd just laughing and cheering.

"Hold his legs! Hold his legs!" some guy yelled. Then more scuffling and shouting. And then the thick heavy thud of Teddy falling hard against the cement.

I peeked around the corner. Teddy lay there in a crumpled pile, moaning while they pulled off his shoes and stripped off his pants.

"Nice skid marks, dude!"

More laughter.

"He shoots, he scores!" Hutch yelled as he did a hook shot and sent Teddy's balled-up pants flying up onto the roof of the covered hallway. I turned away and leaned against the lockers. A wave of nausea rolled over me. I put my hands on my knees. I could feel my pulse in my forehead. The hoots and laughter faded down the hallway. I stood there for a second, bent over, trying to think what to do, listening to Mandy quietly crying, and then I realized that it was Teddy.

So what did I do? I ran. I ran and ran and ran until I had to stop because I couldn't really see. I wiped my eyes and my nose with the back of my hands as I walked through the empty halls, trying to stay out of the light. I didn't even know exactly why I was crying. I ended up on the far side of the parking lot, nowhere near the gym, trying to fight back the urge to throw up.

I found a pole, a cold metal pole, to lean against and tried to look normal, like everything was just fine. But my head was swimming. From a safe distance, I watched people going into the gym in couples and small groups of look-alikes. What happened back there? I didn't want to think about it, but I couldn't stop. I kept replaying it over and over in my mind, trying to make sense of it, but there was no sense. What a bunch of shidiots. What a bunch of cruel morons. How could I have just stood there? How could I be so truly pathetic?

I pulled my cell phone out and called my mom. I was done.

"NQA Shuttle." I sighed. "I need a pickup. I'm at school."

My mom had no idea what I was talking about.

"Mom," I said, "it's me. N-Q-A, remember? The shuttle?"

Nothing.

I sighed, totally frustrated. "Mom, I need a ride home, no questions asked. Yes, right now."

I leaned there, waiting for my ride, absently watching the doors to the gym from across the parking lot. The music sounded pretty good. I so wished I hadn't gone with Jen to that stupid party. It was almost ten o'clock, and the doors were about to close. Just then, a motorcycle pulled up and screeched to stop. A guy and a girl hopped off, laughing as they took off their helmets.

My heart sank.

It was Clint Bedard and Cate Maduro. They danced like crazed teens for a few seconds next to his motor-

SIDEBRA

My parents have a lot of creative parenting ideas, like the Pick-Your-Own-Punishment Plan and the NQA Shuttle. You can call at any time of the day or night if you need a safe ride home for whatever reason. No Questions Asked. Period. Of course, I had never actually called for an NQA Shuttle pickup before. But still, you'd think my mom would have at least *remembered* what I was talking about.

cycle, then ran for the gym. I couldn't help smiling. Their idea of Friday night fun actually seemed fun. I so wished I was running into the dance with them.

Five minutes later, my mom pulled up. I could see Mrs. Merrill, Bean's mom, waving enthusiastically from the passenger seat. Great. Her window was rolled down and she shouted, "Paisley, you rock!" clenching her fist as much as anyone with long nails and a French manicure can. "I just want you to know how much I respect you and your good choices!" She was looking all gushy and weird.

"Thanks, Mrs. Merrill." What was she *talking* about? What good choices?

Before I could get into the car, Mom had jumped out and rushed around the back to hug me. She grabbed me by both shoulders. "Honey, are you all right? Are you hurt?"

"No. I'm fine."

"Have you been drinking?"

"What? No."

She leaned toward me, stared into my eyes, and whispered, "Are you on drugs?"

I rolled my eyes. "Mo-om. No! What happened to no questions asked?"

"Oh, honey. I'm so proud of you." She hugged me again. "And I'm so relieved. Would you mind driving home? I'd feel much better if you did. I really wasn't expecting to be the designated driver tonight."

"Vivienne? She doesn't even have her license."

"She has her permit. Right? You don't mind, Pais, do you, honey?"

Mind? Why would I possibly mind? I mean, why need your parent when you can *be* your parent. I got into the driver's seat and fastened my seat belt. "I thought tonight was book club night," I said, checking my rearview mirror twice, hands at ten and two.

"It is." Mom giggled.

"We're reading Hemingway," said Mrs. Merrill. "Love him. So spare, so masculine. But I always get a raging hangover when I read him." They both dissolved into giggles.

I hit the left turn signal, checked my mirrors again, and inched out into the lane of the parking lot. In case you're wondering, no, this wasn't the first time I'd had to drive, permit or no permit. What a perfect ending to a perfect night—driving my slightly buzzed mom and her friend home.

Mom reached over the backseat and stroked my hair in that the-wine-really-loves-me way. "Pais, what happened tonight?"

"Nothing."

"Nothing that you want to talk about or nothing that you don't want to talk about?"

I didn't answer.

"Did Jen go to the dance?"

I sighed. "N! Q! A!"

"Right, right. NQA, NQA. You let me know if you want to talk, okay?"

Mrs. Merrill wagged her head back and forth. "This is such a beautiful family moment."

Oh God. She looked like she was about to cry.

I turned up the radio. I just wanted to go home and go to sleep, for like the rest of my life.

CHAPTER TWENTY

I went straight to bed and curled up in a tight ball under my comforter. But I kept hearing Teddy's high-pitched shriek. And I couldn't get Mandy's eyes out of my head. She never said a word, but it was like she was asking me to do something. I tossed and turned and tossed and turned, feeling like scum. Like bottom-of-a-Dumpster scum.

I finally got up and flipped open my computer. I started typing. And no, it wasn't hate mail to Jen, for a change.

> Guess what, people? We do have losers at PH
> High. And most of them are wearing football
> jerseys and cheerleading uniforms. Why is it
> so cool to be cruel? Everyone down the social
> food chain gets eaten by the bigger fool and
> everyone else just watches and laughs. Why?
> Why?! WHY?!

I sat back in my chair, read it over, and then deleted it. My bedroom was dark except for the glow from the monitor.

What was I doing? I should just go to sleep. But my brain wouldn't shut off . . .

I got back in bed and opened up my notebook. I stared at the blank page, holding my pen. But I had no idea what to write.

Why *did* everyone try so hard to be popular? Why did we all compete in the brat-race? And why was it so cool to be cruel? Lately, I realized, I liked the *un*popular people at my school a lot more than the popular people. Most of the pops acted like nasty, brainless clones. At least the unpops had the guts to have their own style . . .

Oh, man.

That was it.

I sat up in bed and started scribbling frantically. I was totally on to something. I jumped out of bed and plopped down in front of my computer and started speed-typing. I typed and typed and edited and typed and edited and rewrote and rewrote and rewrote. This was a lot more fun than writing a vicious vent letter that I could never send. My whole body felt charged up. As I read what I had written one more time, I noticed the sky was getting light.

And then I was done.

Should I send it?

I went to the Pleasant Hill High homepage and linked to *The Fly* website. I found the submissions link, then cut and pasted my essay into the window. I sat back and thought for a minute. Then I clicked to the bottom of the page and deleted "Paisley

Hanover" and typed "Miss UnPleasant." I smiled. I hit SUBMIT.

I didn't think anyone would ever read it. And honestly? I didn't care. Just writing it made me feel like I had scored the game-winning goal.

And then I fell right to sleep.

If only I'd known.

CHAPTER TWENTY-ONE

On Monday morning, I was so dreading Drama class. I got there early and parked my butt on a windowsill at the far side of the room. I watched the door, but Teddy Baedeker never showed up. Mandy wandered in looking at the floor. She looked different somehow, smaller almost, like all of her pockets were filled with huge, heavy rocks.

I tried to imagine what it was like to be her, to be that shy, or anxious, or freaked out by life or whatever it was every single day. I mean, how did she even make it to school? And then I had this totally unexpected weird feeling. All at once, I suddenly admired her—Mandy Mindel had more guts than anyone in the whole school.

Bean loped over to me. "My mom won't shut up about you," she said. "It's so annoying. I'm afraid she's gonna make us go on a mother-daughter double date!"

I laughed. "That would be so hilarious. Oh my God, wouldn't it?"

"Really?"

"Sure, it'd be fun," I said.

"Okay, I'll tell her." She walked off and I was left with my dark thoughts.

I had to say something to Mandy. So when Mr. Eggertson said, "Partner up, people!" I ran straight for her. She just stood there, not saying a word. Unfortunately, it was a mirror exercise, so it was like looking at my shy, anxious, no-eyelash self.

We stood a couple feet apart, tracing each other's hand and leg movements. Her eyes looked puffy, like she'd been crying a lot. But the more I looked at her up close, the more I was starting to get used to the no-eyelashes part. It was just Mandy. That's who she was. That's how she looked. It was different, but it didn't seem all that weird anymore. I took a deep breath.

"Last Friday . . . " I whispered, and trailed off. She didn't say anything, but her eyes got really intense. "I—I'm so sorry about what happened, Mandy," I finally managed to get out. She focused in on me hard, the skin on her forehead pinching. But she didn't say anything. "And I'm so, so, *so* sorry I didn't do anything to stop it."

She froze. Her eyes started to water. "You should be so, so, *so* sorry," she said, gritting her teeth.

I was stunned.

And then she whispered, "Why?"

I got a big lump in my throat.

"And change partners!" Mr. Eggertson called out.

I don't even remember who my partners were during the next exercises. *Why. Why?* I don't know. Why does anyone do anything? Why does anyone do nothing? I don't know. I don't know!

I slumped down in my chair. Mr. E. was saying something about our big scene study coming up. I couldn't stop thinking about Mandy and Teddy, and how the biggest loser was probably me.

Me. Me. Me. Wait. What?

"Clint and Paisley," Mr. Eggertson said again.

Clint and Paisley. Clint and Paisley. OMG. WHAT?! Scene partners? Clint and *me?*

I tried my best to look cool and at the same time totally bored, like I couldn't care less, like I was even a little disappointed to get stuck with Clint Bedard as my *Acting Out* partner. But working together every day for two weeks? Blocking out an entire scene, staring purposefully into each other's eyes, speaking real words in complete sentences to each other? My heart was pounding in that way you read about in books but never seems to happen in real life. Why was I such an über goober?

I glanced at Bean sitting next to me. She reached up to push her long bangs out of her face and behind her hand shot me this you-are-*so*-totally-lucky look. I tried not to smile.

And then I didn't have to try, because my gaze shifted beyond Bean to Mandy Mindel. I'd totally forgotten about her. She was sitting across the room, rigid, her arms folded across her chest, staring down at her lap. It was like she wanted to squeeze herself into a little dot and disappear.

Mr. Eggertson handed me photocopied pages of the script for our scene. I pulled my eyes away from Mandy and—OMG. It was from *Taming of the Shrew*. Shakespeare. Yikes! I casually looked over at Clint. He was staring right at me with this odd expression on his face, like he was playing around with something sweet in his mouth. Oh God. I quickly looked down at my script.

Shakespeare? Why did Mr. E. have to give us *Shakespeare?*

I hadn't ever read *Taming of the Shrew*, so I had no idea what our scene was about. I speed-scanned it for clues. Okay, I play someone named Kate or Katherine. He plays Pinocchio? No wait, Petruchio and he's, he's . . . No. He's *wooing* me? To be his *wife?!* I suddenly felt a little warm inside.

Mr. E. continued going down the list of partners and passing out their assigned scenes. Some people groaned, some people laughed. I kept reading.

To tell you the truth, I couldn't understand everything, but it seemed pretty intriguing. Something about a wasp and a stinger and . . . a tongue! Whose tongue? Yikes—that's actually a line in the scene! I swallowed hard. The words were making less and less sense as I read. All I could get was I think he's a fool, but he says he's a gentleman, and I . . . I hit him? Then he's . . . Oh. Oh God. He's holding me—trying to *contain my rage*. And then I hit him *again*. I had to stop reading and look away because I was blushing big-time. I gazed out the window in a daze.

It was a lovers' quarrel. I had no idea that Shakespeare could be so exciting.

Thank you, God. Thank you, Mr. E. Thank you, Universe.

Thank you, William Shakespeare. Thank you, Candy Esposito, for getting the last spot in Yearbook.

I took a very slow, very deep breath. The leafy pattern in the tree outside magically morphed into a profile of Clint Bedard. I imagined the two of us onstage performing our scene, wearing fab Elizabethan costumes. Clint spouted something flirtatious and delicious and Shakespeare-ish that somehow I could understand. I smacked him, and he took me in his arms, then I smacked him again, and we kissed while I pretend-struggled to pull away.

"Hell-*ooh*." Bean tapped me on the thigh. "Hell-*ooh*? Earth to Paisley."

"Paisley. Paisley Hanover!"

What. What? Mr. Eggertson was waving a white slip of paper at me. "Your presence is requested in Mr. Canfield's office. Now."

"Ooooh!" The geek chorus hooted and jeered.

"Is somebody getting Canned?" Clint Bedard teased.

"You would know," I shot back all snarky as I calmly gathered up my stuff. "I'll tell Canfield you say hi." I waved to Bean and Cate and walked out the door, as if I got called to the vice principal's office all the time.

I never really got in trouble, so it didn't even occur to me that I could *be* in trouble. If I had stopped to think about it, though, I would have been worried. Way worried.

CHAPTER TWENTY-TWO

On the way to Canfield's office, it hit me. Mandy and Teddy. Ergh! How could I be so clueless? But what did Canfield want with *me*? My stomach fizzed nervously.

There's this line of yellow plastic chairs outside Mr. Canfield's office. I sat in the one closest to his door, which was closed. I could hear voices inside but I couldn't hear what they were saying. All I could think of was Mandy sitting in Drama like a clenched fist—and me so caught up in my own head space. I tried to distract myself by reading all of the stuff carved and scratched into the plastic.

I've got a detention headache
Bite me, fish lips
Squeal & Die!
Time to deface the music

And my personal favorite:
SUSPENSION IS FOR BRIDGES
I wrote that one in my notebook.

Of course, I would never deface school property, but who doesn't love a little public self-expression, especially in times of crisis?

After waiting a while longer, my belly went from fizz to gurgle. So I closed my eyes and said a little mantra in my head. *I didn't do anything. I am innocent. I didn't do anything. I am innocent. I didn't do anything.* But then it occurred to me—that was the whole problem. I didn't *do* anything. I didn't do anything wrong, but I didn't do anything right. I definitely didn't do anything to help Mandy and Teddy.

That's it. I was going to tell the truth. Did I really care if Hutch or Jen or any of the other pops or cheerleaders never spoke to me again? So what if Mandy Mindel became my best and only friend, and I ended up going to the prom with her and Teddy Baedeker because no one else would have anything to do with me?

Okay wait. Maybe I did I care. Let me think this through.

I mean, the damage was already done, right? I couldn't turn back time. I couldn't unhurt Mandy's feelings, I couldn't bring back Teddy's pants. If I ratted on Hutch and the other varsity jerks, then I'd just be causing more pain for a lot more people, including me. Right?

Ugh, what a pathetic, disgusting, lame rationalization. I was going to tell the truth. I *had* to tell the truth. Yes. I would definitely tell the truth.

I dropped my head between my knees to stretch out my lower back and get some blood flowing to my brain. That's when I noticed a bright clean copy of *The Fly* under my chair. OMG. It must have just come out! I wonder if they printed my . . . No. That was crazy. I reached for it. But they might have. They could have. What if they . . . No, of course not.

I stared at it for a second. Then I grabbed it and frantically started flipping the pages.

Just then, Mr. Canfield's office door swung open. I popped up out of my seat and dropped *The Fly* on my chair. I brushed invisible fuzz off the front of my jeans.

"Yes sir, I understand," some guy was saying to Canfield. I leaned over a few inches, just far enough to see into his office. OMG. Eric Sobel was standing just inside the door. He pushed his bangs out of his eyes and clenched his jaw muscle a few times. Oh, he's even cuter when he's in trouble. Ugh, I'm so gross.

"You know where honesty comes from, Eric?" asked Mr. Canfield. "Honor. And you've got it. But get it right next time. I don't want to see you in here again."

"Thank you. I will," he answered, throwing his backpack over one shoulder. I leaned against the wall next to the door and held my breath.

Eric stepped through the door, saw me, and paused for a split second. As he passed by, inches from my face, he stared me straight in the eyes and lifted his index finger to his lips. Then he walked out the door.

Wait! What did that mean? Don't say anything? Don't tell the truth? If I did say something, *whisper?* How could he do

172

this to me? I watched him walk away. And no, he didn't look back. Was he really telling me to stay quiet? That had to be it. I couldn't believe it . . . Could Eric Sobel really sink this low?

"Well, well, well, Paisley Hanover," said Mr. Canfield, zapping me back to reality. He welcomed me into his office with a big fish-lipped smile. "I never thought I'd have to call you in for something like this."

I'd never been in Mr. Canfield's office, but I had heard plenty of stories. Over in the corner was the old glass phone booth, affectionately known as the Fink Tank, where he made students who wouldn't cough up a confession sit for hours and "wait for a call from your conscience."

"Sit down and make yourself comfortable." He sat on the front of his desk and leaned back, crossing his arms so his biceps would look as big as possible. Gross. "We might be here for a while," he said.

"Do I need a lawyer?" I chuckled nervously, only half kidding.

"No, Paisley. Just the courage to tell the truth."

"Okay." I smiled, sinking into a chair that was about three inches lower than normal—on purpose, I'm sure. "No problem," I said, crossing my arms over my gurgling belly. I leaned back and jerked suddenly as the chair wobbled. Canfield had probably sawed off half an inch from one of the back legs to keep the presumed guilty off balance, so they'd fink faster.

"Good. Guess who I got a call from this morning."

I don't know. Your conscience? I didn't say it. I should have.

"Mandy Mindel's parents, on speaker phone. And they were not happy," he said.

He waited. I waited. Was I supposed to say something? "Well, it's so hard to be happy these days. I mean, the world is in such a distressed state," I offered.

"Don't get smart with me, young lady. I know you were there Friday night."

I put on my trying-to-remember face while I quickly ran through my options. Lie. Say nothing. Say, "I don't recall," which always seemed to work on Court TV or for people testifying to Congress. Or tell the truth and be iced out for the rest of my life by my so-called friends and the most popular people in school. Miss UnPleasant wouldn't care, but I still did. Much as I hated to admit it.

"Friday night?" I asked vaguely.

"Don't even bother. I've seen every evasion in the book." He pointed his finger in my face. "I know what happened Friday night. I know *everything* that happens on this campus." He leaned into my face, flaring his hairy nostrils.

And then something weird happened. I looked at Canfield's smug, bullying face, and any desire I had to tell the truth went, like, *poof!* I wasn't going to give him the satisfaction.

"Really?" I asked, all pleasant. "Well, then why are you asking me, Mr. Canfield?"

He cocked an eyebrow at me. After a short pause, he said, "You know where honesty comes from, Paisley?"

Jeez! What was that? Page thirty-two from the lame vice principal's handbook? I thought for a second, then looked at him sincerely. "Honor?" I asked.

He looked surprised for a second. Then he walked around his desk, dropped into his chair, and leaned back. The springs squeaked and pinged under his weight. "That's right," he said. "Honor. And if you have any, Paisley, you'll tell me exactly what happened to Mandy Mindel after the football game on Friday night."

"After the game . . . ?" I felt a fizzy wad of nausea rise, remembering Teddy lying there. I willed it down.

"Yes," Canfield said slowly. "After . . . the . . . game." He leaned across his desk, looking at me like I was some kind of mutant life form.

I didn't know what to do, or who to do it for. I only knew I wasn't doing anything for Canfield.

"I don't know what happened to Mandy," I said, looking him in the eye. Even as I said it, I wanted to grab the words out of the air and shove them back in my mouth. But I didn't. "After the game, I started feeling really gross. I think it was the corn dogs. So I called my mom, and she came and picked me up. We drove home and I puked a few times and then I went to bed. I didn't even go to the dance. You can call her if you want." I reached into my bag and offered him my cell phone.

He smacked his big fish lips together and stared hard at me. "So you don't know Mandy Mindel?"

"Sure, I know her from Drama." I calmly uncrossed one leg and crossed the other. The non-breathable vinyl seat cushion was making my butt sweat. "But I didn't see anything. Maybe she's mistaking me for someone else." Sorry Mandy. "She wears glasses, doesn't she?"

"And you don't know anything about an angry mob?

I sat up straight. "An angry mob? At school? What happened?"

Wow. I think I missed my calling as a bad kid. I was really good at this.

Canfield told me that Mandy Mindel's parents had reported the whole ugly incident. But Mandy could only identify two people in the angry mob by name—her secret crush, Eric Sobel, and her new friend from Drama, me. Mandy wasn't wearing her glasses Friday night and apparently, without her glasses, all nasty popular girls and big jocky idiots look pretty much the same. Glasses or no glasses, I tended to agree with her. But Mandy couldn't ID anyone, and Teddy Baedeker wasn't talking. Clearly, he wanted to live.

I sat there, trying to think things through. So Mandy only named Eric and me. Eric had left before things got really nasty. But maybe someone told him what went down? If Eric knew and didn't tell Canfield what really happened, and I did, then Eric would totally know it was me who narced, and he'd probably never talk to me again.

Wait. Did I even *care* if he ever talked to me again? Ugh. *What did Eric say to Canfield?!*

I just shook my head. "The cruelty among teenagers today is shocking." I sighed. At least that part was true.

"You got that right. It spreads like a disease. Makes me want to crush those little maggots with my bare hands." Canfield had this crazy look on his face. "Now even good kids like Eric Sobel are getting sucked into this crap."

Eric Sobel? But he wasn't even *there* when it got ugly. He left. What was going on?

Canfield mashed his fish lips together. "Well, Paisley, I know you've got a lot of friends, so if you hear anything about this incident, anything at all, please let me know."

I nodded, wondering, *did* I have any real friends?

I left Canfield's office with a sour stomach and an aching brain. As I walked down the hall, my crazy vigilante courage wore off. I'd had my chance to stand up for Mandy and Teddy. And I hadn't—again. And why? Because . . . because I couldn't stand Mr. Canfield? Because I had a crush on some shidiot guy? How horribly, hideously lame.

I wandered into the main quad in a daze. It was still third period. No one was there. It was empty and safe. I sat down on the low brick wall around the bronze hornet and dropped my head into my hands. It felt painfully heavy. The sun beat down on me.

Then my phone rang. Unknown caller. I answered it anyway.

"Hello?"

"Hi, this is your conscience calling." It was Eric Sobel. I suddenly felt exhausted.

"I'm not sure I have a conscience anymore."

"What'd you say?"

"I'm not sure I have a conscience anymore."

"No. What'd you say to Canfield?"

"Nothing. I didn't tell him anything."

There was a long silence.

"You sure?"

"Yes, I'm sure."

"Cool. Thanks."

Another silence.

"So." I hesitated. "So what do we do now?"

"Nothing. Don't say anything else. No matter what, okay?"

"Okay. But what did you—"

"Sorry, I gotta go." And he hung up.

I shook my head. I couldn't believe I'd gotten sucked into this. Now I was just as guilty as the rest of them.

CHAPTER TWENTY-THREE

The bell rang for morning break and snapped me back to reality. There was no way I wanted to be in the quad when the jocks and pops flooded in. Unfortunately, there was no escaping them, as I was about to find out.

I speed-walked back to sophomore hall. Amy was already parked on our bench, sipping her breakfast—a delicious, nutritious Diet Coke. I waved to her and quickly opened my locker.

I was shoving my books inside just as Carreyn rushed over like last week's stream of verbal darts had never happened. She almost dropped a huge Cindy-Kutcher-boob-sized sticky bun, she was so excited. "Did you hear about Eric Sobel? Suspended for a week!"

A tightly folded note fell to the ground in front of me. Uh-oh. I stepped on it before anyone could see. Wait. What did Carreyn just say? Did I hear that right?

"No way!" Amy exclaimed.

"Way." Carreyn nodded ominously.

I turned around. "Why? For what?" I asked, feeling the blood drain from my face.

"I dunno—yet. It's all very hush-hush. But something definitely went down Friday night after the game. And Eric Sobel got busted."

I dropped a pen on purpose so I could bend down to pick up the pen *and* my latest locker stalker note, which I casually slipped into the pocket of my hoodie sweatshirt.

It took a second for this Eric news to sink in. Then—oh no. Oh crap! He must think I squealed! I wasn't sure how I was supposed to feel about Eric Sobel anymore, but . . . but I knew I didn't want him to think I'd narced on him to Canfield. I pulled out my phone.

we nd 2 tlk

I hit SEND, and then I had another horrifying realization. Did this mean I would be suspended too?! I was telling myself to stay calm, when I looked up and saw Jen and Bodie walking up to our bench like they wandered into sophomore hall together every day. Ergh!

"Hi guys," said Jen all chipper. Amy and Carreyn were ogling Bodie like he was some kind of rock star. I so wasn't buying it anymore.

"Hey, Paisley." Bodie nodded, working his smile magic. "How you doing?"

"Hey, Bodie," I said with a chill. Frankly, I wasn't at all sure how I was doing, but Bodie wasn't going to charm me with that smile.

"Hey, can we steal Paisley from you?" Bodie asked Amy and Carreyn.

"We need some personal qual time," Jen added.

Carreyn and Amy both looked at me a little weird, then nodded. "Sure, yeah," Amy said.

"Come on, Pais." Jen grabbed my hand.

I shook it free. "You know, no thanks, Jen. The last time I fell
for that? Not so fun."

"Pais, this is different." She looked at me really seriously.
"We just need to ask you something. Two minutes. I promise."

It had better be some sort of apology—maybe for getting
me dragged into Canfield's office? Had she heard about that? I
nodded reluctantly. "Okay. Two minutes. That's it."

As we walked off, I turned back to Amy and Carreyn and
mouthed "Qual time," rolling my eyes.

We headed away from sophomore hall and toward freshman
hall. And guess where we ended up? On the exact same bench
where Mandy Mindel and Teddy Baedeker had been holding
hands. Jen and I sat down while Bodie leaned against the lockers
across the hall, watching us.

Jen turned to me and got all serious. "You know you can't say
anything to Canfield or anyone, right? Promise me you won't."

"I *didn't* say anything."

"And you won't, right?"

I looked at Bodie. "Why?"

"No reason. I just need to know you won't," she said.

"Someone already did," I pointed out. "I mean, Eric got suspended."

There was a pause. Then Jen and Bodie looked at me like I
was some clueless noob and laughed.

"No one narced," Jen finally said.

I must have looked as confused as I felt.

"Eric took the fall. He told Canfield *he* threw Special Ted's pants on the roof, and he wouldn't name anyone else. I thought you knew. God, I love that guy. He's a total stud hero."

Wait. What? "Eric Sobel took the fall? *Eric?* He wasn't even there. He left!"

"I know. Isn't that cool? When he gets back from suspension, I'm going to give him a big kiss."

"Better not, Sweetland." Bodie grabbed her around the waist, and they both laughed. Ha ha ha.

I sat there not even believing this. Why?! Why would he take the blame for those guys? Oh . . . At least that explained the whole finger-to-the-lips thing. Ergh! He was such a moron.

"And you guys think this is okay?"

"What?" Jen asked, pulling away from Bodie. "Yeah, it's better than okay."

"No. No, it's not. It's totally shady."

Jen looked a little concerned. I glanced at Bodie, who had suddenly taken an intense interest in his shoes. I couldn't believe these two.

Jen grabbed my arm. "Paisley, you can't say *anything*. You promised."

"I didn't promise."

"Hey, Red." I looked up. Clint Bedard was striding toward us. "What're you doing out here in Siberia? Missed you at the dance," he said suggestively.

"Hey, Clint." I smiled, pretending everything was fine. He missed me at the dance? "Just having a little private *qual time* with my best girl." I patted Jen on the leg.

Jen gave him a half wave, then shot me a why-are-you-talking-to-*him*? look.

Clint noticed Bodie and stopped. "Hey, Bodie Jones, some game. Two grind-up-the-middle, humiliate-the-defense TDs. Right on." Clint nodded at him.

"Thanks, man," Bodie said, looking surprised. "Didn't realize you were into football."

Jen and I sat there, speechless. People don't normally just walk up to Bodie and start chatting. I loved it.

"You serious, dude? Yeah. It's the last form of sanctioned tribal warfare."

Bodie laughed. "Yeah, I guess."

"See you, partner." Clint pointed at me and walked off down the hall.

My phone buzzed.

listnin spot 6:30 wear ur cleats

Normally this would have made me melt. But now? Argh! I flipped my phone shut.

"Red? Partner?" Jen wrinkled her nose. "Why is the bottle-rocket bomber even talking to you?"

I stood up. I was so ready to get out of there. "We're doing a scene together in Drama, that's why. Is that okay with you?"

"Oh," she said, making this pukey face.

I rolled my eyes. How old was she, like five? Cate Maduro

was right. Popularity *is* poison. It was turning Jen into a mean Bratty Sasshole. "Wait," I said, imitating her brattitude. "Why am I even talking *you*?" God, I should have just told Canfield everything in the first place, hairy nostrils or not.

"Wait." Jen grabbed my arm. "Where are you going?"

"Canfield's office."

"Paisley, hey! I admit it was really bad judgment. But don't make it worse. I'd appreciate it," Bodie said. He did not look happy.

Jen grabbed my arm again. "Paisley, come on! Show some school spirit. We can't lose Hutch and Bodie and the other guys for the next game."

"School *spirit*?" I pulled away, looking from Jen to Bodie and back to Jen. "Are you Pleasant Hill *high*?"

I turned and walked off down the hall, shaking my head. That was it. I was done with her. I was done with all of them. I was going back to Canfield's office. And I was going to tell the truth.

CHAPTER TWENTY-FOUR

I burst into Canfield's office without even knocking.

"Good to see you again, Paisley," Mr. Canfield said, hardly looking surprised. "Please, have a seat."

I dropped down into the wobbly Fink Fast chair. Canfield raised his eyebrows, waiting.

I tried to seem composed. "Look, it wasn't Eric Sobel," I blurted. So much for composed. "He wasn't even there Friday night. I mean, he was there but he left. It was Peter Hutchison and some of the other varsity football players."

"Really?" Mr. Canfield leaned back in his chair with a big fish-lipped grin on his face. "I thought you weren't there. Didn't you tell me you and your corn dogs went home early?"

Oh, crap. "Well, I . . . I did. Yes. But that was before I knew Eric Sobel would get suspended for what Hutch did."

Canfield laughed like a barking seal.

"What? I'm serious," I said.

He sat up in his chair and played with a pen, tapping it on the padded corner of the desk blotter. "You'd better be serious— you're making some very serious accusations, Paisley Hanover."

"I realize that. I wouldn't say it if it weren't true."

He leaned back in his chair and put his arm behind his head like he was watching a football game on TV. "Now, if you'd said it was Clint Bedard or rather someone with a history of pants-snatching and other delinquency, no problem. But I have a *very* hard time believing that Peter Hutchison, a fine student, a star player, and a team leader, would be involved in this."

"I *saw* him." I sat up as tall as I could in the Fink Fast chair. "I *saw* Hutch strip off Teddy's pants and throw them onto the roof like he was shooting a basketball."

"Really?" Canfield looked like he was fighting back a smile, then pinched his nose and sniffled. "I'm also having a very hard time believing *you.*"

What? It had never occurred to me that Canfield wouldn't believe me. I mean, I always tell the truth! Except sometimes when I don't, which is very, very rare and only for extremely good reasons.

"Well, you either lied to me before or you're lying to me now." He smiled. "So either way, you're really not a credible witness, now, are you, Paisley?"

"I am! I am. I'm telling the truth now. I . . . I didn't before because—look, Eric Sobel is totally innocent! I'm just trying to make things right."

Canfield folded his arms and swiveled back and forth in his chair. "Do you have any evidence? Cell phone photo? Video clip? Will anyone corroborate your story?"

I sighed. "No, no, no, and probably not."

"That's what I thought." He stood up and leaned over his desk. "Next time you try to malign another student's reputation, young lady, I suggest you consider how it will reflect on *your* reputation."

"Mr. Canfield, I am *not* my reputation," I said as politely as possible. "And I'm pretty sure you can't *malign* someone if you're telling the truth about them."

He *laughed* at me. Can you believe it? Canfield was such a condescending pig. And obviously not particularly bright. There was no way I was going to let him shut me down.

"Maybe we should look it up," I said, smiling.

He leaned into my face, hairy nostrils flaring. "Don't you dare mouth off to me unless you want to get suspended too."

Okay, so maybe there was one way to shut me down. Still, I had an idea.

I got out of there as fast as I could. Fine student? Star player? Team leader? Hutch was a jerk, plain and simple. Obviously, Canfield wouldn't have asked for evidence if I had named someone who wasn't a star football player, someone like Clint Bedard. God, even the faculty at this school were desperate for the popular kids' approval. Pathetic.

But I wasn't done. No way. In fact, I was just getting started. I marched out of Canfield's office and straight into the quad. It was almost the end of morning break now, and the quad looked a lot different than it had a half hour ago. It was packed with pops. I stopped after a few steps as a wave of adrenaline surged through me.

There they were—Jen and Bodie, the varsity jerks, Candy Esposito, BS1 and BS2, and Hutch, laughing and smiling and talking. Good thing Hutch looked in high spirits, because I was about to bring him down.

CHAPTER TWENTY-FIVE

I stood motionless in one corner of the quad, psyching myself up. Where was the soundtrack in my head when I needed it? I concentrated hard, summoning some personal power music. Yeah, there it was. My brain-speakers cranked. I started across the quad doing my baddest power strut.

"Hey! Nice hip action, Hanover!" someone yelled.

Everyone in the entire quad stopped talking and turned to stare at me. Well, not really. But it felt that way. Jen looked terrified. Bodie frowned. Candy looked like she was trying not to explode with laughter.

I kept walking.

"Peter Hutchison?" I yelled, just a few feet away.

He turned around, looking startled. "Jesus Christ! You sound like my mother."

"Eric Sobel got suspended!" I totally got in his face, only, because he's so tall, it was more like in his chest. "He got suspended for the disgusting crap *you* pulled on Friday night!"

Everyone in the group took a step back like they were afraid my rage would splatter on them. Then someone started giggling.

"Oooh, watch out, Hutch!"

Hutch laughed it off. "Yeah, it sucks about Sobel." He fake sighed, shaking his head.

I was horrified. "Is that the best you can do?"

"Oh, wait. You *are* my mother."

Bodie and a few other varsity jerks laughed.

"What is so funny?" I asked, looking around.

"Paisley, please," said Jen. "You're embarrassing yourself."

"*I'm* embarrassing myself? What, like you did when your super cool shidiot friends tortured those kids, and you and everybody just stood around laughing because you're all too cool to care?"

Silence.

BS1 cocked her hip. "Whatever. It was kinda funny."

"You know, *you* were there too, Paisley," said Candy Esposito, pointing her manicured finger at me.

"Yeah, but I was *not* laughing." Okay, I know. I didn't do anything to stop it either. I know that! But I wasn't . . . I wasn't *like* these people. I turned to glare at BS1. "And FYI—it was *not* funny."

Hutch stepped between us. "Paisley, is it that time of the month for you? Because if it is, I can understand why you're so irritable. But I'm pretty sure there's a pill for that now."

"Why don't you grow a pair, Hutch! Go tell Canfield what really happened!"

"Ooooh!"

"Eric Sobel shouldn't have to take the fall for you," I said.

"He didn't *have* to, Pains Me, he *wanted* to. It was his idea." Hutch shrugged, shaking his head. "Whatever. He's fine. No school, watching soccer all day. Sobel's lovin' it."

It hadn't occurred to me that Eric might have volunteered for this. I stood there, all of a sudden unsure. Should I defend my point? Or just run for the middle of the quad like a naked girl wearing a tuba? If Eric volunteered, did I even have a point to defend? Oh, he was such an idiot!

"Why don't you go find some other stupid cause to fight for, Hanover?" Hutch walked off laughing. Jen was staring at me like I had absolutely zero comprehension of reality. Bodie and Candy were trying not to laugh. Too hard.

"Fine, maybe I will!" I called lamely.

"This is hilarious. Have you guys seen this?" BS2 had her nose buried in *The Fly*.

Oh, God. *The Fly!*

She held up the page. "'How to Be UnPopular'? Yeah right," she snickered. "Like anyone would *want* to know how."

Suddenly, it was like listening through the wrong end of a telescope—everyone sounded tiny and far away . . . In my wildest weirdest flash fantasies, I honestly never thought my essay would be printed in the school paper. I thought maybe Miriam Goldfarb and Logan Adler would get a good laugh, but . . .

BS1 leaned in and glanced at the headline, then snorted. "Who cares?" She pushed the newspaper down. "Wanna split a burrito?"

I casually strolled off the quad, and then broke into a full-out sprint as soon as I was in the main hall. I found a stack of newspapers outside the main office, grabbed one, and slipped out the doors to the front lawn. But I didn't get the chance to read the Miss UnPleasant essay because I kept hearing bursts of laughter and snippets of conversations—

"UnPop Culture?"

"Love it!"

"Kiss anyone who's different!"

"Hilarious."

OMG. OMG! OMG!!! Uns were reading Miss Unpleasant's essay!

I walked casually out onto the grass and roamed aimlessly through the various pods of unpops, trying to overhear what people were saying.

"Big kiss, class dismissed!"

"That's perfect!"

"It's about time."

"Adopt-a-Pop! It even rhymes!"

"Who do you think she is?"

"Cate Maduro?"

"But what the hell is a *sidebra*? You think this Miss UnPleasant chick has three boobs or something?"

What? *Three boobs?* I skimmed Miss UnPleasant's column. Whoops. Typo! I meant side*bar*. But I immediately liked sidebra much better. It has a sassy swing to it.

Whoa. *Tons* of Uns were reading Miss UnPleasant's essay— and laughing and talking and quoting it and . . .

This was amazing.

This was so freakin' *cool*.

This was riding the fast train to fabulosity.

HOW TO BE *UN*POPULAR

Okay, people—listen up! Let's all move our chairs into a circle. Welcome to the first day of UnPop Culture, Pleasant Hill High's sick new social studies class. Please note: This class will be graded on a slippery slope, just like life.

Okay, who wants to share first?

Me! Me! Me! (Surprise! I'm the teacher *and* a student!)

Can I just say, I absolutely *love* Pleasant Hill High more than life itself, but I feel so, so, *so* sorry for the Pops at PH. The Jocks, the Poms, the BPs—all these poor rah-rahs are living a too-cruel-for-school nightmare.

Why? Because they're trapped in a no-fun house of mirrors where all they can see is their own reflection. Poor, poor Pops. How boring it must be! No variety pack and no imagination. All those shiny, happy, zit-free freaks talk alike, walk alike, dress alike, think alike— oh wait, you're not allowed to think when you're popular. Silly me.

Tragically, the Pops don't get to explore the free world or enjoy the fun fringe benefits of being an outsider. They don't get to frolic in the freedom that comes with being ignored and invisible. They don't get to know anyone with strange ideas, strange clothes, or strange secret obsessions.

Instead, the big boys brag by stripping the pants off the helpless—then pitching those pants onto the school roof. So brave, so strong! And the mean girls set up their sweet "friend" for a cheerleading choke by teaching her the wrong routine. So cool, so classy!

Worst of all, when you're a Pop, there's no place to go but down. Uh-oh. Do I hear the

SIDEBRA

Gosh, It's *Really* Hard Being Popular!

Don't think the Populars need your help? Read on, people!
It's painful being popular.
Things You Get to Do When You're . . .

POPULAR	UNPOPULAR
Pretend to be invincible	Pretend to be invisible
Get a fake ID	Get a real identity
Act like everyone else	Act out!
Dis anyone who's different	Kiss anyone who's different
Hide your real feelings every day	Hide your real feelings every day
Stress! Everyone's watching you— even though they aren't	Relax! *No one's* watching you— even though they are

sound of a cracking mirrored floor? Oh well, never mind. Have to go to Pep Squad practice!

It breaks my heart (really!) when I see the Pops gossiping in the halls or puking up lunch in the girls' bathroom or spitting on nerds outside a school dance. Poor little Pops. They don't stand a chance in the real world. They have no real skills and (whoops!) they peaked way too early.

But I'm determined to change all that! I believe that everyone at PH deserves the chance to be UnPopular—even the meanest, shallowest, cutest, best-dressed, and most entitled. Yes, I'm here to help.

Every underprivileged Pop can learn how to be UnPopular in just four easy steps:

1. Own a brain and know how to use it.
2. Have the guts to stand up for yourself and what you believe in, especially when everyone else is acting like a total moron.
3. Be weird—make weird friends, do weird things, wear weird things, say weird things, date weird things.
4. Be yourself. (OMG! Is that allowed? What will everyone think?!)

Okay, people! Here's your homework assignment:

If you're one of the fortu-

194

nate UnPops at Pleasant Hill High, please reach out to one of the needy students and adopt a Pop. Be sure to keep a picture of your adopted Pop in your locker or on your phone to remind you of their pathetic rah-rah daily existence. By sharing your mental wealth with a Pop, someone less fortu-

nate than you will have at least three well-balanced thoughts a day. Hooray!

And maybe, if we're lucky, one day Pleasant Hill won't feel like Pleasant Hell.

Big kiss, class dismissed!
Miss UnPleasant

CHAPTER TWENTY-SIX

At practice, I was brutal. Slide tackling everyone. Winning every loose ball, elbowing, bumping, grunting. I was so pumped after seeing my words in print *and* seeing all the UnPops so into it, I even scored three goals in our scrimmage—without Jen. Coach Sykes loved me.

We did our moronic Lady Hornets cheer, and then everyone else trotted off toward the girls' locker room. I headed over to my sweatshirt on the side of the field.

"So who do you think wrote it?" Amy asked me, wiping the sweat off her forehead with her sleeve.

"I have no clue." I shrugged. "Someone very angry and deeply tortured."

"Well, that could be anyone at this school." Amy smiled.

"It was probably some Pop trying to be deep. Maybe the Bratty Sassholes put their airheads together." We howled at that one.

Amy kicked a ball toward the locker room and chased after it. "Pais, you coming?"

"Gonna run a few laps. Go ahead."

"You're crazy, but okay. See you later."

I waved and pulled on my sweatshirt. The fields were clearing out, but I didn't see Eric Sobel anywhere, so I started jogging. I only ran one lap and then I walked over to one of the goals and waited there for a while, doing stretches against the goalpost. He probably wasn't coming. I wandered toward the middle of the field and my best guess for the listening spot and flopped down on the grass.

I always see faces in the clouds. Always. No matter how I'm feeling, I can find a cloud face that mirrors mine. There it was. I growled up at a fierce face in the sky. "Errrghh."

This whole Miss UnPleasant thing was, like, wow. I had never imagined that anyone would even *read* what I wrote, much less care enough to quote Miss UnPleasant. The UnPops seemed to love her. The Pops were . . . well, they were the Pops.

I slid my hands into my pockets and felt the locker stalker note. I'd forgotten all about it. A thrill went through me as I carefully unfolded it like I was unwrapping a precious gift.

WANT TO KISS YOU ALL OVER

I kind of gasped. Really. OMG. OMG! I felt tingly. This was getting serious—and we hadn't even gone on a single date yet!

"Hey!" Eric Sobel jogged up, wearing a backpack.

"Hey." I quickly folded up the note and stashed it in my pocket.

"Sorry. Running five miles from my house takes longer than I thought." He was dripping with sweat. I hoped he wouldn't take his shirt off. I didn't think I could handle it. He unzipped his backpack and dropped a soccer ball on the ground. "Come on."

We dribbled and passed the ball up and down the field a few times, not saying anything. Then when I was getting near the penalty box, he yelled, "Shoot! Shoot!"

I touched the ball one more time and kicked it as hard as I could, keeping my head down and my body over the ball.

"Goooooooooal!" he yelled, running into the back of the net to get the ball.

What a goober, what a totally adorable goober. Stop it!

"Nice shot! Upper left corner. Perfect placement," he said.

I laughed. "Thanks. I was aiming for upper right."

"Yeah, I bet." He juggled the ball with his feet as we walked toward the middle of the field, keeping it alive for about thirty kicks. Finally, he caught the ball in his hands. "Last one to the listening spot is a—"

"Double-wide buttcap!" I yelled.

He laughed and took off running.

"Hey!" I sprinted after him.

He slid to a stop. "I win!"

"Wrong spot!" I ran past him and slid down at a different spot. "I win!"

"Really?" He put his ear to the ground and listened. "Nothing. Well, I guess you would know because the earth is *your* friend."

I laughed like a total dork.

He log rolled over to me and stopped a few feet away. We both just lay there looking up at the sky.

"Dragon!" I pointed up at a cloud.

"Yeah." He rolled over on his elbows. "I heard you gave Hutch the smack-down today. He texted me."

I cringed.

"I see why you did it. I mean, I get it. But . . . yeah, it's kind of . . . embarrassing."

I looked at him. I knew what he meant. But it wasn't really about him, I realized.

"I don't need you to stick up for me, okay?" he said.

"Okay. Sorry. I was . . ." I turned back to the sky. "I wasn't really sticking up for you. It was more like I was trying to take Hutch down. Even though he basically laughed at me."

There was an awkward pause. "So, um . . ." Eric finally said. "You wanted to talk?"

Oh God. I suddenly realized—when I sent him that text, I thought that *he* thought that *I* had squealed on him. But now . . . what *did* we need to talk about? I sighed and rubbed my forehead.

"What?"

"Nothing. I just . . . Well, why *did* you tell Canfield that you did it?"

"Oh man." He rolled onto his back.

"Really. I don't get it. Why?"

He didn't say anything.

I rolled onto one elbow. "Why would you cover for them?" He plucked a piece of grass and bit the soft white end. "It's like you think it's okay, what they did. Or that you're trying to protect them." He closed his eyes and chewed on the grass. We lay there in silence for what seemed like minutes. I sighed. No response. Okay, I was starting to get pissed. I sat up. "Hell-*ooh?* Eric?"

"What do you want me to say?" He sat up too. "I was busted! And no one else was, except for you. I don't know—it seemed like the right thing to do."

"I was there! If you had seen what really happened that night, you would *not* have taken credit for it. It was ugly. Hutch is such an unbelievable jerk."

"He's not a jerk. Well, yeah, he is a jerk sometimes, but he can't help it. He doesn't mean to be."

"Why are you even friends with those morons?"

"Who am I supposed to be friends with? The debate team?" he snapped.

I didn't say anything. Maybe Eric Sobel was more like me than I'd realized.

He lay back down. "And I *don't* think it's okay. But getting half the first-string suspended for the next game wouldn't fix the problem."

I sat there hugging my knees.

"Giant rat eating a cat." He pointed up at the clouds.

"Where?" I lay back onto the grass.

"Two o'clock."

"Looks like the social food chain at our school."

He laughed. "Yeah."

The colors in the sky were beginning to change from blue to pinks and violets as the fading sun hit the edges of the clouds.

I studied Eric's profile, watching his jaw muscle clench and unclench. He has cute little ears with attached lobes. I couldn't hear anything but my heart pounding and Eric calmly breathing. Why do I always say the wrong thing? I closed my eyes, wishing again that I could just melt into the center of the earth.

"Did you read *The Fly* today?" he asked. I tried not to squirm. "I read it online. There was this column, 'How to Be UnPopular.'"

"Really?" I lay there waiting to be slammed. I didn't care about the other Pops, but I wasn't so sure I wanted to hear Eric Sobel rip me to bits.

"It was pretty cool. You should check it out."

What?!

He rolled onto his elbow, facing me. His other hand was on the grass, about half an inch away from mine. "Do you ever wish you were unpopular? So you could fly under the radar and just do your own thing and not have everyone watching everything you do all the time—or have to sign anyone's stomach?"

OMG. I love this guy. "Yeah, sometimes." I rolled onto my back. Staring into his intense green eyes was freaking me out. "I hate it when people ask me to sign their stomachs."

He laughed and flicked my arm. "You know what I mean." Even though it seemed highly unlikely, I was getting the feeling that Eric maybe liked me—*liked me* liked me. But I couldn't be sure because he never did anything or said anything. Shy guys . . . ugh!

We were quiet for a long time. But I think the earth was giving me special powers, because I suddenly felt fearless.

"So, are you and Candy Esposito like a thing now?"

"What? No way. She doesn't like me. She just hangs on me to make Bodie jealous."

I popped back up on my elbow. "Really?"

"Oh yeah. She's dying to get back together with him. Don't tell Jen. Candy's not my type anyway."

"I thought she was everybody's type." I brushed the grass in front of me with the palm of my hand, trying to decide if I should ask what I really wanted to know. Would it make me seem totally desperate? Or maybe I'd seem refreshingly direct and confident? Or maybe I'd seem refreshingly desperate. Oh, what the hell. "So, who is your type?"

He looked at me. "I dunno." Then he closed his eyes and smiled like he was embarrassed or thinking of some inside joke. "Someone cool, someone doing her own thing, someone bad-ass like that Miss UnPleasant chick."

"What?"

What?! OMG. That's *me*—or at least a part of me. He likes part of me?! He thinks I'm bad-ass? He thinks I'm cool? I had to try very hard to be cool at that moment.

"Wait, the snarky girl who wrote that UnPopular thing?"

"Yeah, she just seems . . . funny and smart and . . . " He scratched his eyebrow, thinking. "She calls people on the BS that everyone else at this school ignores," he said, turning to look at me.

I smiled. "Some geeky guy in computer lab probably wrote it." I poked him in the arm.

"Nah. It's got a lot of chick energy. She's probably some edgy indie babe who just moved here, *or* some geeky computer guy with a lot of chick energy." We both laughed. "But I'm gonna figure it out."

"Figure what out?"

"Who wrote it, who she really is."

Oh, wait. Of course. He doesn't *like me* like me. He likes my made-up character! "How are you gonna do that?"

"Access *The Fly's* web log somehow and track the IP address of the computer she used to send the column. Shouldn't be too hard."

Holy crap! "They can do that?"

He nodded. "Hey, are you going to the carnival thing next weekend?" he asked.

"The Walnut Festival?"

He nodded again.

"Yeah, I was planning to go. Wouldn't want to miss the festival of nuts."

"Cool. Maybe I'll see you there?"

And he didn't say that like a statement. *Maybe I'll see you there.* It was a question. *Maybe I'll see you there?* You know, like an invitation.

"Sure." I smiled.

OMG. Could Eric Sobel be my locker stalker?

CHAPTER TWENTY-SEVEN

On the way to school the next day, I was busy doo-dling a very detailed rendering of the Fink Fast chair in my notebook when Charlie Dodd turned to me with this really serious look on his face. "Can I talk to you about something?"

He looked like he was in pain. "What? Are you okay? Do you have cancer? Genital herpes?" We had just learned all about STDs in Health.

"No! I just have a question." The sleeping-braces-kid next to him slowly fell over onto Charlie's shoulder. Charlie pushed him back toward the window. "I'm giving you permission to be hon-est, brutally honest." He looked at me with this tortured expres-sion and then finally whispered, "Am I popular or unpopular?"

I couldn't help laughing.

"What? What's so funny? I'm serious!"

"Nothing. Sorry. I just wasn't expecting that." I tried not to laugh.

"It's not funny! I really need to know because some people think I'm popular, you know like super-geeks and Library Girls, but other people would most likely call me unpopular. So?"

He paused, looking like his whole life depended on my answer. "Which am I?"

He just told me to be brutally honest but still, I didn't want to insult him.

"You are . . . You're . . ." What was the right nice-person answer? I didn't know.

"Just be honest. *Please?*"

"Charlie, you're like in your own category. It's not popular or unpopular, it's . . . it's like *neo*-popular. You can exist in both worlds happily and thrive."

"No! I don't want to be popular. I don't want to be popular of any kind. I can't peak too early. I'll never get into Princeton if I am perceived as peaking too early!"

Sleeping-braces-kid woke up and looked around the minivan. "What? What?"

"Go back to sleep," said Charlie. "This is all just a minivan nightmare."

Charlie kept talking and I pretended to listen while I doodled, but I was really thinking. It was so weird. After the Miss UnPleasant column, two people in the last twenty-four hours had told me they would rather be unpopular than popular. Their reasons were totally different, but still. Maybe there was something to this whole UnPop Culture thing.

"Hey, are you gonna run for class office?" Charlie asked.

"What? Why?"

"The sign-up sheets are up in the main hall. You should definitely run for something. Admissions directors really look at your accomplishments sophomore year. I'm running for class secretary. I wanted to run for treasurer but LG Wong already signed up and everyone knows she's a math freak—I heard she dreams in numbers. Is that possible? Anyway, I really need to win. So this year it's secretary. Next year I'll run for treasurer."

"Well, I'd been thinking about maybe running for class vice president. Does that sound insane?" I hoped not. It was a building block for my seven-point plan.

"Not at all. I'll be your campaign manager if you want."

"But won't you be kinda busy running for secretary?"

"Yeah, but it'll look good on my college apps."

So before class, I walked over to the sign-up sheet. I wasn't signing up yet or anything. I just wanted to check out my competition. Charlie had signed up for secretary, and LG Wong was the only name under treasurer. There was also only one person signed up for sophomore class president—but you'll never guess who.

Peter Hutchison!

I wanted to scream. So I did—fortunately, at the exact same moment that the warning bell rang for homeroom. So no one was tempted to call 911.

Maybe I should run for class president instead of vice president . . . Hmm . . . It seemed like the perfect way to kick Hutch's butt. *And* it would look good on my college applications. I could beat Hutch, couldn't I?

Couldn't I?

CHAPTER TWENTY-EIGHT

Drama that day was intense—for a few reasons. First, when I walked into class, Cate Maduro practically ran over to me.

"Smile, Paisley! Say Brie cheese!" She snapped my picture, even though I was looking like a total goober trying to figure out why she would want a picture of me. "I'm adopting you for the Adopt-a-Pop program."

What?!

"No!" yelled Bean, stepping in front of Cate. "She's *my* Adopt-a-Pop. I knew her first. Paisley, look at me. Okay, now look really sad." Bean took my picture too. This was weirdly amazing.

"What are you guys doing?"

"We're reaching out to help a less-fortunate popular student," said Cate.

"And sharing our mental wealth," Bean added, trying not to laugh.

I could tell they were joking. At least I *thought* they were joking.

"Don't be afraid. We just want to help you," said Cate really sweetly.

"I'm *not* one of those popular people!" I snapped, playing

my part. Although I kind of was, but, honestly, I didn't think I needed anyone's help.

"Maybe we can share her," Cate said to Bean, looking hopeful.

"Yes, let's share her." Bean smiled, throwing her arm around Cate's shoulder. "Two unpopular brains are definitely better than one."

"You guys! I am not some freaky rah-rah! Really!"

Cate and Bean looked at each other, shaking their heads.

"Paisley, it's okay." Cate touched me gently on the arm.

"Acceptance is the key to inner peace," Bean said, smiling kindly.

"I'd better not see any of those pictures online—or anywhere else, especially on YouTube." I was kind of pissed, but I was also secretly flattered. I couldn't believe that anyone would actually take Miss UnPleasant's homework assignment seriously. How cool was that?

Teddy Baedeker was finally back in school, looking basically the same. I debated whether or not to say anything to him about last Friday night. I kind of wanted to, but then it might really embarrass him if he knew that I saw him in his underwear, crying. Besides, my apology to Mandy Mindel hadn't gone very well. Teddy seemed okay, so I sent him a brain-wave apology and hoped he would get it.

"Okay, people!" Mr. E. announced. "Let's pull our chairs into a circle—wait, where have I heard that before?" he asked, all dramatic with a British accent.

My butt clenched. Uh-oh.

"I'm hearing a lot about this 'How to Be UnPopular' column," Mr. E. said, holding up a copy of *The Fly*. "Let's talk about it."

What? We all looked around at each other, but nobody said a word. Mandy was looking at the floor. Teddy chewed nervously on his lower lip.

"Okay, so is Miss UnPleasant serious or kidding or maybe both?"

A Library Girl raised her hand.

"Louise?"

"I think she's serious and I think she's . . . mean."

Mean?! A rolling wave of snickers and laughs.

"Mean?!" Cate asked, all perturbed. "Everything she wrote was dead on."

"Yes!" yelled Bean and a few of the AV Guys. A few others mumbled agreement.

"It's divisive," said Charlie Dodd. "It calls attention to the problem but it also contributes to the problem."

"How so?" asked Mr. E.

"Well, making it unequivocally clear that there are two groups at this school—the Pops and the UnPops."

"Yeah dude, because there are," said Clint, shaking his head.

Mandy Mindel raised her hand uncertainly.

Mr. E. pointed at her. "Mandy?"

"I like her. I . . . I like the way she uses irony to make a point." Mandy talked at the floor with her hands folded neatly in her lap. "There's a huge divide between the popular students at this school and everyone else," she said, glancing up for a second and catching my eye. "And some of them are vicious. They treat us . . . They act like we're only here for their amusement." She mushed her nose around with the back of her index finger.

"What I can't figure out," Cate said, "is who *thinks* like an UnPop but *acts* like a Pop."

I gulped, glancing around the circle, waiting to see who would speak next.

"Paisley, what do you think?" asked Mr. E.

Oh crap. "Well . . . I'm pretty sure I know the real identity of Miss UnPleasant." I had my serious face on, waiting until everyone in the room was looking at me. "It's Mr. Canfield."

Everyone burst into hysterics, even Mr. E.

"All right. That's enough for now," Mr. E. said. "But this is interesting stuff, and worth thinking about. Personally, I hope we'll see more from Miss UnPleasant."

OMG. Mr. Eggertson was a fan!

The rest of class, we were working with our scene partners shooting lines. So I got to sit facing Clint Bedard, which wasn't such a bad way to spend time. But it was a little hard to concentrate—Clint was wearing some girl's lip gloss again.

SIDEBRA

Shooting lines is not as violent as it sounds. It's basically just you and your scene partner saying your lines back and forth quickly without trying to do any acting. It really helps you memorize your lines and get a sense of the flow of the scene before you start thinking about blocking.

BTW—*blocking* is what you call figuring out where you move and what you do in a scene. It's sort of like choreography for actors. None of the movement in a scene happens by accident—at least it's not supposed to. (More on that later!)

"So, I'm handsome and dashing and delightful, and you are . . . kind of a total b—"

"Babe?" I cocked my head, smiling.

Clint laughed. "Yeah, that too." He leaned in. Our knees almost touched. "Otherwise I wouldn't put up with that nasty-ass sharp tongue of yours."

"A sharp tongue comes from a sharp mind." I smiled smugly.

"Excellent. You're already in character. I guess I'll start then."

Clint slowly read from his script. It sounded like he was reading a foreign language.

> CLINT AS PETRUCHIO:
>
> Good Morrow, Kate—for that's your name, I hear.
>
> ME AS KATHERINE:
>
> Well have you heard, but something hard of hearing.
>
> They call me Katherine that do talk of me.
>
> CLINT AS PETRUCHIO:
>
> You lie, in faith, for you are called plain Kate,
>
> And bonny Kate, and sometime Kate the curst . . .

"No way I can memorize this." Clint slapped his script on his knee. "I don't even know what I'm saying."

"Just try. We'll figure it out."

He shook his head but kept reading.

> And bonny Kate, and sometimes Kate the curst,
>
> But Kate, the prettiest Kate in Christendom,
>
> Kate of Kate Hall, my super-dainty Kate—

"Great. At least I know what super means. Who knew *super* was such a Shakespearean classic?"

"Keep going," I said. "You're doing great." Clint sighed. I was feeling a little frustrated too—I just wanted to run my hands through that hair. Oh, maybe I'd get to do that in our scene! That could count as blocking, right?

> For dainties are all Kates—and therefore, Kate,
>
> Take this of me, Kate of my consolation:

I watched him read, wondering what his bedroom looked like. I hoped we could rehearse at his house sometime—not in his bedroom, of course. I just wanted to see where he lived and see his stuff and what he had on his walls . . .

> Hearing thy mildness praised in every town,
>
> Thy virtues spoke of, and thy beauty sounded—

"I have *no* idea what I just said." He shook his head.

Frankly, neither did I, but I folded my arms and stared at him until he continued.

> Yet not so deeply as to thee belongs—
>
> Myself am moved to woo thee for my wife.

"What?! No way I'm marrying *you*. You're a total . . . *shrew!*"

"Well, yeah, that's kinda the point. Have you even read this scene yet? You have to win me over. You have to *persuade* me to like you."

He sighed.

"You know, if you're not even gonna try, then forget it."

"Wow. You really *are* in character. How could I not want to win you over?" he said, batting his eyelashes.

I sighed and looked away. Bean and Cate were working on a scene from *The Odd Couple*. Clint was hot, but suddenly it seemed like a lot more fun to be working with a girlfriend on a comedy. Why did we get stuck with Shakespeare?

The bell rang and everyone scrambled for their stuff.

I was headed out the door when Clint started walking with me and threw his arm around my shoulders.

"Hey Red, wanna do something next Saturday night?"

Whoa. I stopped. "What?" *What?!* "Um, you mean like a date?"

He pulled me along and we kept walking up the main hall together, his arm still around me. "Yeah, but kinda home-work too. Don't you think our scene will be a lot better if we actually get to *know* each other?" He gave me that smirky flirty grin.

"I guess." OMG. Clint Bedard just asked me out—on a date! I was giddy and giggling on the inside but extremely cool on the outside. Then suddenly, I started to sweat. Could I handle being alone with Clint Bedard? My head might explode—or worse. "Um . . . Hey, the Walnut Festival carnival thing is happening that weekend . . . "

"Well, yeah. We could stop by," he said, smiling.

I was excited but completely unprepared. Never—even in my dreamiest, most delusional flash fantasies—had this crossed my mind. Suddenly this romantic soundtrack soared through my brain-speakers. This feeling melted from my brain—down, down, down.

And then Jen, Candy Esposito, and Bodie stepped into the main hall from the quad, just as we were walking by.

I remember it as this beautiful slow-motion moment. Jen did

a full-on double take, her mouth fell open, and a wad of pink gum flew out. Candy froze, looking sick like she had accidentally taken a huge gulp of Coke instead of Diet Coke. Bodie just stared at me looking totally confused—or was it amused? Whatever.

Clint and I passed by them without breaking our stride. And it felt . . . *good*.

"So, what do you say?" Clint asked.

"Yeah. Okay, sure," I said with a big grin.

"Cool. I'll pick you up on my bike around seven thirty. You're not afraid of motorcycles, are you?"

"Course not." I shrugged. That might have been a lie. "This is me." I peeled off to the right toward my locker and waved like a dorkasaurus. He winked at me and kept walking.

Holy shiitake mushrooms! I had never been on a motorcycle before. But more to the point—I had never been on a real date before. You know, where the guy actually comes to your house and picks you up?

Wait. Wait! WAIT!!!

Didn't I kind of sort of tell Eric Sobel that I would meet *him* at the Nut Festival?

Oh crap.

SIDEBRA

Guys who wink fall into two categories.
1) The skanky, trying-too-hard category, when . . .
- they don't have a clue what to do next after they say something stupid.
- they actually think a wink will persuade you to do something you don't want to do.
2) The effortlessly cool category, when . . .
- they know exactly what they're doing and how charming they really are.
- they don't care about trying to persuade you because they love the thrill of the flirt—which makes them, of course, totally irresistible.

CHAPTER TWENTY-NINE

YOU'RE SO CUTE WHEN YOU'RE MAD

Ugh! I slammed my locker shut. Normally, I would be happy to get a locker stalker note. But not today. For starters, no one wants to be told they're cute when they're mad. Really. What an insult. And secondly, *everyone* has seen me mad lately—Jen, Bodie, Eric, Hutch, Mr. Canfield, Cate, Bean. So it could be *anyone* writing these notes—except for Canfield. I hoped. Ew.

I slipped the locker stalker note into my notebook and slammed it shut.

Jen was back to serving me up a double ice-berger with cheese, which was fine. I didn't have anything to say to her anyway. Amy and Carreyn were terminally inconsistent, one day choosing sides, the next, trying to build a bridge of peace by running messages back and forth between us.

"No! Tell her again I don't have her green sweater at my house." I was seriously annoyed. "I've looked. I never even borrowed it!"

"Okay, okay." Amy backed up. "Jeez, don't shoot spit on the messenger."

"Sorry." I wiped my mouth with my sleeve.

"Why are you wearing that old ratty shirt?" Carreyn asked me.

I was wearing the cowgirl-cool shirt that Bean had given me. "It's not ratty, it's vintage—and it's *paisley*." I spastic jazzed her. "Get it?"

"Um, not really. It looks like it smells."

I decided right then to go with Bean the next time she invited me thrifting.

Amy flipped open a copy of *The Fly*. "Any new ideas on who wrote this 'How to Be UnPopular' thing? I'm searching for clues."

"Oh my gag, I read it again last night in the tub before I loofahed," Carreyn answered. "It's sooo sad. Whoever this Miss UnPleasant is, she's obviously filled with self-hatred because she's not popular."

My mouth fell open. But I quickly covered with a very convincing yawn.

"I don't know," said Amy, looking back at *The Fly*. "She makes some pretty good points."

"I'm so sure. Like what?" Carreyn snapped.

"Like how all the Pops walk alike, talk alike, and dress alike. Like how the UnPops have more freedom . . . to be weird or unweird or whatever."

"Well, I don't want to be weird," said Carreyn, so missing the point.

"I do." They both looked at me. "I *do!* Don't you?" I asked Amy.

"I *am* weird. You have no idea how exhausting it is to appear this normal all the time."

I laughed. "This is you trying to be normal?" I made the uh-oh face and we all fell off the bench giggling.

Bean and Cate were weaving their way through the crowd in sophomore hall, taping flyers to the wall and handing them out. Oh man, did they stand out. Bean was wearing her vintage power polka-dot suit with white, shiny, wet-look go-go boots. Cate was in her usual retro drag. I think it was more forties that day, a pencil skirt and tight little shawl-collar blouse on top with these open-toe platform sling-backs.

"Hey, Drama Mamas!" I called.

Carreyn wrinkled her nose, giving them the up-down.

"Hey Paisley." Bean handed me a flyer. "Join the revolution!"

"Doubt you know her," Cate said, looking from me to Amy to Carreyn. "But if you do, *please* beg her to write again."

MISS UNPLEASANT—WRITE ON!

We desperately need your insightful,
snarky commentary.
If you want it, you've got an ongoing column on
UnPop Culture at Pleasant Hill High.
Contact me, please!

Miriam Goldfarb, editor
The Fly

OMG. Was this for real?!

"You have *got* to be kidding." Carreyn was reading over my shoulder. "Miss UnPleasant is a crazy you-know-what."

"You say crazy you-know-what." Bean did this hip-hop girl, finger-wagging head wave, pointing right at Carreyn. "I say crazy what-you-know."

Everyone laughed, except for Carreyn, who didn't know what to do. She just gave Bean the stink-eye.

"So, girls." Cate fingered her tight pearl choker and looked from Amy to Carreyn. "Has anyone adopted you yet for the Adopt-a-Pop program?"

Amy and Carreyn shook their heads. I think they were a little afraid of her.

"Oh, I'm sorry. That's too bad." Cate tried to look sorry for them. "We'll put the word out to all our unpopular friends."

"We've adopted Paisley," said Bean, hanging her arm over Cate's shoulder. They both smiled at me like goobery proud parents. "With the proper mentoring, we believe there's hope for her." I smiled back like any hopeful UnPop protégée would.

"Hey!" Bean yelled suddenly, pointing down the hall. "Peter! What are you doing?!" Hutch was ripping down all the flyers that Bean and Cate had just taped up. What a brainless buttcap!

"Just cleaning up some trash in the halls," he answered innocently, walking over to us.

Carreyn laughed like that was the funniest thing she'd ever heard.

Cate leveled her eyes at Hutch and draped her hands on her hips. "Miss UnPleasant is not trash, Peter. She's a valuable hidden resource at this school. We've got to find her."

"Her BS is boring. I don't want to read any more of that

crap in *The Fly*." Hutch tossed a big wad of crumpled flyers at a garbage can like he was shooting a free throw. It hit the back rim and bounced over onto the ground.

"More arc," said Amy.

Hutch just laughed. "Hey girls, I'm running for class president. Will you vote for me?"

What nerve! And he didn't even pick up his trash.

Bean cocked her hip out and put her hand to her mouth, pretending to contemplate his question. "Hm . . . Nope. Definitely not." She smiled.

"I will," Carreyn chirped. "Absolutely!"

"I'd rather go on a roller-skating date with the entire JV football team," said Cate matter-of-factly.

Amy gave her a funny look.

"Oooh, that sounds hot. Need a chaperon?" Hutch chuckled like the creep he knew he was.

Carreyn giggled. The rest of us did not.

Cate smiled warmly. "Gosh Peter, that was so thoughtful and clever. Maybe I *will* vote for you. Oh wait. You're a misogynistic philistine. Never mind."

"Yeah, I'm sure it's mutual." Hutch turned to Amy and me. "What about you guys? Gonna vote for me?"

"Maybe," answered Amy.

"I'm not sure yet. Who's running against you?"

"No one. Guess they're all afraid of me." He shrugged and walked off down the hall.

Bean stared after him. "Someone better run against that

cretin." She turned back to me and did the prom queen wave. Elbow, wrist. Elbow, wrist. "See you later, Pais."

"Cute shirt, Paisley." Cate winked at me as she turned to go.

"Oh my gag. Did you see that?" Carreyn whispered. "That lesbianic chick winked at you."

"She's just trying to freak you out."

"It's working," Amy and Carreyn said at the exact same time.

"You guys!"

"Excuse me, but why were they even talking to us?" Carreyn asked. "I do *not* want to be seen with girls like that."

"Like what?"

"You know. Like weird and loserish and . . . gangly."

"Carreyn, you're such a snob."

"Thank you."

I let that one go. I had bigger things to think about—like my new campaign for sophomore class president.

That's right.

Game on!

CHAPTER THIRTY

I couldn't wait to start brainstorming my campaign strategy, but first, this flyer. An ongoing column on UnPop Culture?! I read and reread the flyer as I walked to the library. Wow. Maybe this could replace Yearbook and be the new seventh point on my seven-point plan? *This is Paisley Hanover, UnPop Culture columnist, reporting live from the gym.* Oh wait. It's by Miss UnPleasant. Not me. And did I even know anything *about* UnPop Culture?

Bean ran up next to me, still clutching her stack of flyers, and fell into step. "Really. Come on. Who do you think it is?"

"Really? I think Miss UnPleasant sounds a lot like Cate Maduro," I said.

Bean's eyes got all big. "I *know.* I thought that too. But don't tell her I said that. Gotta go," she said, waving her flyers and hurrying off in the other direction.

And if I *did* write more Miss UnPleasant columns, how would I keep people from finding out it was me—and then *hating* me? If tracking an IP address is as easy as Eric Sobel made it sound, then I couldn't send anything from my laptop. If people found out, I'd have to change schools or . . .

I had a traumatic flash fantasy of being chased down the hall by an angry, screaming mob of Pops lead by Candy Esposito, Bodie, and Jen. They cornered me in the quad near the base of the bronze hornet, shouting ugly accusations as they pelted me with chicken nuggets. Carreyn was especially vicious. She dipped her nuggets in honey barbecue sauce and *then* fired them at me.

Oh God, if people found out, I was going straight to Pleasant Hell.

I looked up just then and saw Eric Sobel walking out of the library. Perfect! I had an idea.

"Hey, Eric," I said, running to catch up. "Have you seen this?" I waved the Miss UnPleasant flyer in his direction.

"Hey." He grabbed the flyer and read it. "Wow."

"Yeah, wow. How's your plan to expose her coming along?"

"Um . . . slowly." He sighed. "*The Fly*'s weblog is password protected. I'm still working on it. Know any good hackers?"

I laughed. "Nope. Sorry." Like I would say anything if I did. I shrugged and waved. "But I'll keep thinking."

I went into the library and casually leaned against the windowsill, keeping an eye on my locker. At the same time, I scribbled in my notebook, making a list of pros and cons for doing the ongoing column.

Charlie Dodd was speed-typing at one of the library computers nearby. Come to think of it, Charlie was kind of a computer brainiac. I'd have to keep that to myself. I looked around. These computers were a good twenty-five feet from the magazine lounge. Two of the five computers were basically concealed behind the end of a reference shelf. Hmm. I could hide in plain sight. If I typed my columns at home and transferred them to a jump drive, then I could quickly submit them to *The Fly* website from one of the library computers. I checked around for security cameras . . .

No! This was crazy. It would be too much work on top of homework and soccer and Drama and running for class office. But it sure would be fun to keep empowering the UnPops and see what Miss UnPleasant could inspire them to do next week. Hmm . . .

"Hey, Paisley," said Charlie, waving the "Miss UnPleasant— Write On!" flyer. "Have you seen this?" He shook his head. "Gold. Pure college-admissions gold."

"What do you mean?"

"Shhhhh! Library voices, please," said Ms. Whitaker softly, waving at us. I waved back.

"Are you kidding?" asked Charlie, trying to whisper. "I'd kill to be Miss UnPleasant. To have a platform to write satirical social commentary about high school while you're *in* high school—and do it anonymously? Gold. I've been trying to write a 'How to Be UnPopular' column. It sucks. I thought maybe I could ghost it for her, but her voice is snarky, and snark is not my forte. Whoever she is, if she accepts this offer, I bet she can write her own ticket to any college in the country."

"You think?"

"With the grades and the test scores? Definitely. Assuming

that she lives through it and doesn't get stripped and duct-taped to the bronze hornet by a mob of angry Pops."

"Yeah . . . " I nodded slowly, picturing that exciting possibility.

"Have you signed up for vice president yet? Three people are already on the list."

"Actually, I've decided to run for president instead."

"Really?" He sounded shocked. "You really think you can beat Hutch?"

"Yes, I do—and I look forward to it." I left Charlie sitting there speechless, looking quite envious of my newfound confidence.

When I got down to the main hall, I scoped out the sign-up sheets. Good thing I changed my mind. Now there were *four* people signed up to run for vice president of the sophomore class. And it was only the second day of sign-ups. LG Wong was still the only name under treasurer. Some C-list girl had signed up under Charlie for secretary. I scanned over to the list for president—and stopped dead.

There was a new name on the sign-up list for sophomore class officers.

OMG.

Miss UnPleasant was running for president.

CHAPTER THIRTY-ONE

It took all my self-control not to mention anything to Cate and Bean when I went thrifting with them that weekend. It was just too surreal to think about me running against . . . well, my pen name.

Cate and Bean were calling this our first Adopt-a-Pop field trip and I played along mainly because I needed to find something to wear for my *Taming of the Shrew* scene. And Bean said she wanted to take me to her favorite second-hand clothing store. So we hopped a bus and entertained ourselves playing the "where are they going?" game. Every time a new passenger got on the bus, we made up stories about them. It basically went like this.

A young man wearing a baggy suit got on carrying a small bouquet of flowers.

"He's going to visit his girlfriend in the hospital," Bean whispered. "Her appendix almost ruptured, but she's gonna be fine. And then in three weeks, he's gonna dump her."

Cate leaned in toward us. "He's going to the cemetery to put flowers on his father's grave." Her eyes got all big. "He goes every Saturday afternoon and he always wears his father's suit—

because he murdered him and has to pretend to be grieving to keep the cops off his trail."

"You guys are dark," I said. "I hope he's just going to Nordstrom to buy a suit that fits."

Finally we got off the bus and started walking through this semi-sketchy neighborhood. We passed an old bowling alley that was boarded up and a self-storage place where a few people with shopping carts were organizing their stuff.

"So, how's it going with Clint Bedard?" Cate said his name like it was a dirty word—the good kind of dirty.

"Fine." I tried not to blush, but I couldn't help it.

"Pais, what?" asked Bean, smiling. "Come on, dish."

For some reason I felt safe talking to them. "It's kinda crazy," I said, laughing, a little embarrassed. "Promise you won't say anything to anyone?" I pressed the crosswalk button.

"Promise!"

"I have a major below-the-belt crush on him. I can barely concentrate when we're practicing our blocking and he's whipping me around in his arms." I sighed, blowing out a mouthful of air. "I don't get it."

We ran across the street.

"What's not to get?" Cate asked. "He's sexy."

I nodded. "He's definitely different from other guys at our school, you know?"

"That's because he's confident," said Bean. "And he doesn't care what anybody thinks. And he's tall."

I nodded. "But it's more than confident. It's like he's . . ." I struggled to find the right word. "It's like he's *man*fident. He just *knows* what to do with a girl."

"Ooooh," said Cate provocatively. She and I laughed. Bean just looked at me.

"But Clint and I don't have anything in common, other than our scene."

"Are you sure?" Bean asked coldly. Cate raised an eyebrow.

"Are you saying I'm manfident?" I smacked Bean on the arm. "Thanks!"

"I'm not saying anything." Bean shrugged.

"*I'm* saying you should spend some time with him and *find* something in common." Cate winked.

"There it is!" Bean shouted. "The Second Coming thrift store. Prepare for miracles, girls!"

Cate and I followed Bean inside. It was kind of dark and smelled like my Grambo's glove drawer.

Cate immediately took charge. "Okay, so I'm seeing you in something long, of course, maybe with an empire waist, with either poofy sleeves or sexy little straps."

"Or something with a tight little lace-up bodice," Bean suggested.

"Sexy? I can't be sexy."

"Everyone can be sexy. It's all up here." Cate tapped the side of her head. "Okay, fan out and start flipping hangers."

We found six long dresses that might work, but one didn't pass the stink test. Then we holed up in a dressing room. Cate sorted the possibilities while I got undressed.

"You guys, I signed up to run for class president." I looked at Cate and then Bean. "What do you think?"

"Yes!" Bean cheered. "You've got to beat that pompous sexist buttcap."

"That's so weird!" Cate practically jumped. "Yesterday at lunch, I signed up Miss UnPleasant for class president!"

"That was you?"

Cate nodded, raising an eyebrow.

"Isn't that the best idea?" Bean asked. "Miss UnPleasant infiltrates the establishment and brings it down!" Bean and Cate burst into hysterics.

"I'll be managing her write-in campaign for class president." Cate added.

I stepped into the first dress, feeling a little freaked. Did they know? Were they making fun of me? Was this a trap? Wait, how *could* they know? "Genius." I nodded. "Pure genius. Of course, she doesn't stand a chance against *me*." I smiled, but I meant it. Miss UnPleasant wasn't real. No one would actually vote for her. "Hey, can you zip this?"

Bean zipped up the back of a purple velvety dress. I looked at my reflection in the full-length mirror and cringed. "It's huge. I look like Barney."

Bean unzipped it, nodding, and handed me the next dress.

"Canfield immediately crossed Miss UnPleasant's name off the list. But I'll just sign her up again and again and again."

This was fascinating. I mean, why would anyone want to act

like Miss UnPleasant really existed. "Why? Just to bug Canfield?" I asked.

Bean giggled. "Cate's in love."

"It's true. Miss UnP is a goddess. I worship her."

OMG! Miss UnPleasant has a better social life than I do! "Cate, what if she's butt-ugly?"

"It doesn't matter," Cate mooned. "I love her for her mind, her wit, her deep social insights."

I burst out laughing. This whole thing was just too bizarre. "You are way weirder than I thought!"

"Love is the flower you've got to let grow," Cate responded wistfully.

"That's beautiful." I rolled my eyes. "I never realized you were such a romantic. So, you think I should run?"

"You should definitely run," Bean urged. "It'll be fun to run against you. And Peter Hutchison is scum of the universe. Miss UnP will kick his butt! Or, you know, you will." She smiled.

Cate stood in front of me, lacing up the black bodice part of the next dress. "Take a big breath and exhale." She pulled really hard on it and tied it in a bow.

"I can't breathe," I gasped, taking a quick breath. Stitches popped. Oops. "Well I hate to burst your bubble, girls, but *Miss UnP* can't run for class president. She isn't real."

Cate cocked her head and looked me in the eye. "She may not be real to you. But she's very real to me."

"Me too." Bean studied the dress I was wearing. "That's the one!" she squealed. "Turn around. I love it! Don't even try the others."

"What do you think, Cate?"

She nodded slowly. "Elizabethan hottie. Clint's gonna like you in this."

I looked in the mirror. Bean was slouched against the wall behind me while Cate tried to hold my hair up. That bodice was holding most things in and pushing a couple of things out, making it appear like I actually had some shape. Wow. I didn't look like me at all. I hardly recognized myself.

On the walk back to the bus stop, I casually mentioned that Clint Bedard had asked me to go to out with him next Saturday night.

Bean stopped suddenly. "Like . . . like on a date?"

"Yeah, kinda. But also like homework for our scene. I think we're going to the Walnut Festival."

"Clint is going to the *Walnut Festival*?" Cate asked, grinning.

Bean shushed her. "What did you say to him?"

"I said yes."

"Oh my God!" Bean walked around in a circle, huffing.

"What?" I asked. "You said he was hot."

"He is, and *tall*! It's one thing to be crushing on him from a distance, and another to start dating him!" She glared at me and marched off down the sidewalk.

I turned to Cate. "What? I don't get it."

Cate and I stopped, watching Bean stalk off to the bus stop at the end of the block. Cate turned to me and sighed. "If girls like you start dating guys like Clint Bedard, then who will girls like us have to date?"

What? I blinked a few times trying to do the math in my head, but I was totally confused. "Wait, I thought you liked *girls*?" I asked.

"That's not the point!" She shook her head, then looked me hard in the eyes. "Why do you care anyway?"

"Because we're friends."

"Since when? Seventh grade? Or last week?"

I looked at her, trying to understand what she was saying. And then it hit me. Oh my God. She was hurt—of course, she'd never admit it. Did I ice her out after seventh-grade Spanish? Did I ice her out just like Jen was icing me out? God, what a buttcap. "Cate, I'm sorry. I—I just hope we're friends now— friends enough that we can be honest."

She looked away, slowly shaking her head. "You want me to be honest? Okay. Guys don't like me. I don't know why. Whatever." She shrugged. "So this one girl kissed me, and it was pretty damn fun, and then I told everyone I was a lesbian—basically to freak out my parents. But they were *soo* accepting, *soo* supportive, *soo* there for me." She threw up her hands. "And I was *soo* annoyed. You have no idea." She sighed. "I don't know what I am. I guess . . . I guess I'm still undecided."

For the first time since seventh-grade Spanish, I felt like the real Cate Maduro was actually talking to me. I gave her a big hug.

She looked at me kind of awkwardly. "Thanks. FYI, I'm pretty sure Bean has a major below-the-belt crush on Clint Bedard too."

I looked at her to see if she was kidding. She wasn't. "Oh no. I had no idea. I thought . . . I just—"

"There's the bus. Come on!" Cate pulled me up the sidewalk and we ran a half block to the bus stop.

The three of us climbed on the bus and worked our way to the back row.

"Bean, hey, I didn't know you were into Clint, like for real. I wouldn't have—"

"Whatever." She rolled her eyes at me. "Girls like you never know."

Girls like me? God, who does she think I am? I looked at Cate hoping that she would say something to back me up. But she looked away and then pulled out her phone and started reading her text messages.

The three of us rode back on the bus in silence. I stared out the window replaying over and over what Cate had said. *If girls like you start dating guys like Clint Bedard, then who will girls like us have to date?* Sure, there were never enough popular guys to go around, I knew that. But it never occurred to me that there weren't enough *unpopular* guys to go around either, or that there was some sort of unspoken boundary. If I went on a date with Clint, would I be just another piggy insensitive Pop? *Am* I even popular anymore? Do I want to be? I couldn't figure out anything or anyone anymore, especially myself.

CHAPTER THIRTY-TWO

I pushed all of that out of my mind. I had work to do. Because that night, I decided to take my first stab at answering Miriam Goldfarb's rally cry. Better me than Charlie Dodd, I figured—though I *did* admire his crafty thinking.

I sat in bed with Dyson on my lap and brainstormed into my notebook. I wanted to write something even better than before—something that made people really think. But it wasn't coming together. At all. I just wasn't sure what I was trying to *say*. I put on my Dumbe Blonde T-shirt for inspiration. I didn't have the guts to wear it to school yet. But I always had the best bizarro dreams when I wore it as a sleep shirt.

What *is* UnPop Culture anyway? I guess I knew, but I didn't *really* know. And so far, I'd scratched out everything I'd written. It all sounded stupid or forced or whatever. So I got out of bed and I went online to Wikipedia, typed in "Pop Culture," and read the definition. Basically, it means everything that's popular right now. So that would make UnPop Culture everything that *wasn't* popular right now? Oh, crap.

I started a new text file and typed, "Miss UnPleasant's Ongoing Column," except that I'm not the best typist and so I actually typed, "Miss UnPleasant's Ungoing Column." I was about to fix it, but then I stopped. Wait a second. Maybe UnPop Culture isn't just about *being* unpopular or *feeling* unpopular . . . Maybe it's about being *un*-everything—unpredictable, unapologetic, unperfect, unappreciated, undiscovered, undecided.

A flood of excitement rushed through me. OMG—that's it!

I started speed-typing. Miss UnPleasant's second column— "Un Is More Fun!"—practically flew out of me. I submitted it to *The Fly*'s website and was in bed by midnight.

I was lying there, petting Dyson, listening to his power-purr and trying to fall asleep. But I couldn't shake this thing about Bean. I buried my nose in Dyson's black fur. I loved the way he smelled, sweet and dusty.

So Bean was crushing on Clint. How much did that suck? I mean, no—not that she was crushing on him, but that I felt like I had to *do* something about it now. Because Bean was, like, my friend. Oh, that was weird. Three weeks ago, just the idea of being friends with Bean—the idea of Bean *wanting* to be friends with *me*—would have been totally crazy. And now the crazy thing was that it wasn't crazy at all.

I didn't blame her for being surprised and mad. There aren't a lot of hot desirable UnPop guys—especially guys as tall as her. And she couldn't exactly go out with some rah-rah guy or some jock. She'd lose all credibility.

But truthfully? It kind of bugged me that she was crushing on Clint. There, I said it. I'm an awful person. Still, I had to call it off. I *had* to. Even if I did have a major below-the-belt crush

and desperately wanted to know him better. I would do something nice for my friend. Besides, lots of guys are taller than I
am. And there was Eric Sobel, who was more and more a real
person and not just a lickable torso in one of my flash fantasies.
And hey, there was always my locker stalker, right?

I started to drift off. And then I remembered what Cate had
said as we were walking to the bus stop. Did guys really not like
her? She was so pretty and confident and clever. Or was that
just her way of explaining things to me—and maybe explaining
things to herself?

CHAPTER THIRTY-THREE

Charlie Dodd was my official campaign manager, but Amy and Carreyn were helping out too. I guess Carreyn had decided that I wasn't so bad after all, or more likely, that helping me run for president might somehow help her. So on Sunday, they all came over to my house to brainstorm. The night before, Carreyn had dyed her hair red in a show of solidarity with me. I screamed when I opened the front door.

"Okay, for starters, we need posters, locker stuffers, and a really memorable slogan," I said, sitting down at the kitchen table.

"I have a few ideas." Charlie pulled out a yellow legal pad and showed us his list. Charlie's great, but his slogans were not.

Paisley for President!

Pais for Pres!

Hand the reins to Hanover!

Good Ideas—Great Leadership!

"Leadership, scholarship . . . " He tapped his pen on his yellow legal pad.

"Chip and Dip?" I laughed. Charlie snorted and Amy nearly spit up her Diet Coke. Carreyn glanced at Charlie and giggled.

"I was thinking of something a little more offbeat. Maybe a play on words?" I pulled my notebook out of my bag and flipped to the last scribbled pages and read from a list of possible slogans.

Building Sophomore Bridges

Connect the Dorks

Redhead & Shoulders Above the Rest!

Go Red to Get Ahead!

Paisley Hanover—Not Just Tho—

I stopped. I was suddenly having a painful flashback of my Yearbook headline disaster.

"A Pattern of Success!" my mom yelled from the other room.

I groaned as loudly as possible. "How about 'Cool, Calm, and Connected'?" I tossed out.

"That's pretty good," said Amy. Carreyn nodded in agreement.

"I know!" Charlie blurted. "'*Fun* of a Kind Girl!'" They all fell out of their chairs at that one.

I rolled my eyes. Hilarious.

"Or maybe I should go with 'Spastic Jazz Hands Working for You!'" I spastic jazzed them.

Charlie pulled back and tilted his head like a dog trying to understand. "I kinda like that."

"It was a joke."

"Wait, what's this?" Amy grabbed my notebook.

Oh God, please don't let it be another doodle of Eric Sobel kicking a heart-shaped soccer ball.

"'Spastic Jazzed for the Job!'" she read from my list. "It's perfect!" She set my notebook on the table and drew an arrow and smiley face pointing right at "Spastic Jazzed."

"I like that one too," Charlie said, sounding surprised. "Yeah, I think that works! It shows that you can laugh at yourself. Plus, it's memorable and it's *ownable*. Hutch can't use a tagline like that. And no one's gonna confuse that slogan with Hutch's slogan, you know?"

"What's his slogan anyway? Do we know?" I asked.

"Yeah." Charlie flipped through his yellow legal pad. "Go with a Proven Winner. Go with Hutch—I'm Open!"

I read it a couple of times. My shoulders fell. "Damn. That's good."

"Yeah." He nodded. "It's pretty perfect for a star wide receiver running for president." I nodded. He was right.

We were all silent for a second.

"Paisley—Power to the People!" Mom shouted again.

"Thanks, Mom!" I crossed my eyes and everyone laughed.

"I think that's sweet." Carreyn shrugged.

"No."

"Speaking of sweet. Did you guys see the necklace that Bodie gave Jen?" Amy asked.

"And when exactly would I have seen that?" I asked sarcastically.

"Oh, right." Amy shrugged. "Sorry."

"It looks *really* spendy." Carreyn nodded with obvious envy.

"Guys like Bodie shouldn't get to have money too," said Charlie. "It's just not fair to the rest of us."

"Jen's *so* lucky." Carreyn sighed.

"Whatever." I flipped the pages of my notebook, looking for other slogan ideas.

"Hey, how's your website coming?" Charlie asked me. "Mine's in beta, we're going live on Monday."

"My website? What website?"

"Paisley, come on. You've gotta have a website these days. Voters expect it. And college admissions officers love it. Total competitive advantage." Amy and Carreyn were looking at Charlie like he was an alien life form. "A personal website is like a college app on steroids. You gotta do it."

I nodded, trying to process what he was saying without laughing. Was he serious? Did I really need my own website? Was PaisleyHanover.com even available? With my luck, some web geek in Scotland had already bought the domain name. "Okay, good suggestion. I'm on it as soon as we nail my fabulous, memorable slogan." I so didn't have time to worry about it right now.

Amy jumped out of her seat. "Spastic Jazzed for the Job! Spastic Jazzed for the Job!"

"Spastic Jazzed for the Job," I repeated. "Paisley Hanover— Spastic Jazzed for the Job! What do you guys think?"

"Let's do it," said Charlie. Carryen nodded.

"Yay!" Amy ran a victory lap around the table, giving me a low five as she rounded my side. I tried to imagine that my official campaign slogan was "Spastic Jazzed for the Job!!!"

Oh man. It was crazy enough that it might work. Or maybe I was just crazy.

UN IS MORE FUN!

Okay, people—let's all move our brains into a circle for a lively class discussion! Today's topic:

What is UnPop Culture?

Who wants to share first?

Me! Me! Me!

Yes. That's correct. UnPop Culture is all about *you*!

It's about listening to the *Un*Usual all-in-your-head voice and grooving to the *Un*Predictable tunes of your own personal soundtrack. It's about throwing a big bash every day for what makes you *Un*Normal and letting your freak flag fly! It's the art of being *Un*Popular, *Un*Perfect, *Un*Forgettable, *Un*-Decided, *Un*Sane, *Un*Cool, *Un*Discovered, *Un*Apologetic.

Sound familiar? That's right. It's UnEquivocally YOU.

Aren't you sick of scrambling up the Pleasant Hill Higherarchy? I know I am. Come on, people! Let's quit this Brat Race, because I've got the inside dish—there *is* no finish line!

Come on, people!

Just say "No!" to that popularity poison pill.

Just say "Whoa!" to that too-cruel-for-school brattitude.

Just say "I don't think so" to those perfectly plasticky popular clones and hunky homogenerous varsity jerks.

SIDEBRA

*Un*Pleasant Questions to Ponder for Future Class Discussions:

1. Ever wonder why the Pretty-in-Pop girls act like we're just extras in their *fabulous* lives?
2. Ever wonder why some Pop bullies are too cruel for school, as if we're just here for their vicious amusement?
3. Ever wonder how some Pop varsity jerks get away with murder, and never even mess up their hair?

I have. It's called *Preferential Treatment* by the oh-so-Pleasant Hill administration. Yep. Hate to pee in your bubble bath, kiddos, but our star athletes get all the perks, and they make this a Pleasant Hell for the rest of us.

240

Take a hall pass on the in crowd and join the *Un* crowd instead. Everyone's welcome and everyone's got the power—it's called UNdividuality. What a concept.

Okay, people, listen up! Your homework assignment this week is multiple-choice:

1. Tap into your UnPop Power—wear your *Un*-side out.
2. Be yourself—Be Un of a Kind and be proud!
3. Take back the quad—it's not just for Pops!
4. Take back Pleasant Hill—it's your school too.

Big kiss, class dismissed!
Miss UnPleasant

LETTERS TO THE EDITOR

Dear Flies,

Miss UnPleasant needs to get on meds and get a life. What a miserable beyatch. And if she really feels so strongly, than [sic] why is she hiding behind some stupid fake name?

Keep up the bad work, Flies—

A Varsity Hornette, Junior

Dear Editor:

I was extremely disappointed to read the column by Miss Un-Pleasant in the last edition of *The Fly*. Do we really need this kind of negativity in our school newspaper? I don't think so. I consider myself popular and all of my friends are popular too,

and we are NOT trapped. The next time that you are tempted to run a piece like this, you should remember that popularity is <u>earned</u> by people who have style and confidence and social skills and athletic ability. Too bad the bitter, untalented, unpopular students at this school don't get this.

Signed,
Anonymouse [sic]

PS: Popular students have feelings too.

Dear Madame Editor,

When I read "How to Be UnPopular" by Miss UnPleasant, I laughed out loud. Finally someone is calling these snotty bullies and brats on their entitled behavior. I hope she will write another column, because this school needs to hear from someone who has the guts to point out what makes Pleasant Hill feel like Pleasant Hell.

Sincerely,

Cate Maduro, Sophomore

Dear Fly Paper Editor:

"How to Be UnPopular"—what a provocative op-ed piece! When I consider the true identity of its author, Miss UnPleasant, I am reminded of the Jackson 5 hit "One Bad Apple."

After my first reading of "How to Be UnPopular," I was quite certain that this anonymous author was a disgruntled, unpopular loner, the type of person who lurks in the shadows of PH and does nothing more than take up space on our crowded bleachers. Upon further readings and reflection, however, I now suspect that the real Miss UnPleasant is actually a disgruntled, *popular* loner. While that may sound like an absurd oxymoron, I assure you that it is not. In fact, I myself am a popular loner.

Having said that, I too prefer to remain anonymous.

The primary support for my thesis is reflected in Miss UnPleasant's keen knowledge of certain events, events that only an in-the-know Pop could possibly be aware of and, therefore, reference.

I would caution Miss UnP not to dismiss the merits of all popular students simply because of the unsavory and selfish behavior of a few, which I admit can be quite odious. In conclusion, let me refer your readers, including Miss UnP, to an excerpt from the deliciously addictive chorus of "One Bad Apple":

One bad apple don't spoil the whole bunch, girl.
Ooh. I don't care what they say.
I don't care what you heard now.
Ooooooh! Ooooooh!

Yours truly,

Sir Pleasantly Laughs-a-Lot

CHAPTER THIRTY-FOUR

After the second Miss UnPleasant column ran in *The Fly*, things got crazy. That day at lunch, I was in the main hall hanging one of my campaign posters when I noticed Candy Esposito and a bunch of other Pops marching into Canfield's office, looking outraged. I don't know what they said, but I'm pretty sure they weren't nominating Miss UnPleasant for homecoming queen.

When they all marched out, I overheard Hutch asking Bodie, "And what the hell does she mean by *homogenerous*?"

"Dude, what do you think?"

They were heading toward me, so I quickly turned to face the wall, adding another piece of tape to my poster.

"I'm gonna crush her!" Hutch sounded really mad. "I'm gonna out her and I'm gonna bring her down."

Yikes.

Homogenerous? I pulled my copy of *The Fly* out of my bag and skimmed my Miss UnPleasant column. Whoops. Typo! I'd been going for homogeneous. Different thing *entirely*.

The next morning at carpool, some dweeby freshman climbed

into the minivan wearing what looked like his dad's undershirt over his clothes—except it had "UNDISCOVERED" written across the back with black electrical tape.

In Drama, three Library Girls showed up wearing matching cute baby-doll tees, "UNIMPRESSED" written across the front in black felt pen. Cate Maduro swished her hips around, pointing out the slab of duct tape stuck to her butt. "UNDECIDED" it said. Bean Merrill was wearing a cowgirl-cool belt with a big "UN" buckle made of aluminum foil.

And at morning break, I kept passing people in the halls— kids I didn't know and, frankly, had never even noticed before— with "Un" signs safety-pinned to their backpacks.

UnNormal

UnDetected

UnApologetic

UnSane

It was everywhere. It was endemic. It was historic. It was *unbelievable.*

It had to be a really, really long flash fantasy.

But no. LG Wong had brought a bunch of stick-on name tags and was handing them out to people. Throughout the day, I kept seeing *Hello, my name is . . .*

UnPerfect

UnEven

UnAppreciated

UnForgettable

I didn't know what to think, and I sure wasn't going to say anything. I just watched in amazement. And then I remembered—that day at the first *Fly* meeting? Ms. Whit was so totally right. Writing is *power*.

The next day was even better. Because the next day was Backlash Day. A bunch of Pops showed up at school sporting signs and name tags and T-shirts that said things like:

UnTouchable

UnDisturbed

UnDaunted

UnTarded

UnFazed

UnAffected

UnShakable

The fact that even the Pops couldn't ignore it? That they had to get in on it in order to defend themselves against it? It was like a small, seriously viral miracle.

And then came the day when the Uns took back the quad.

I was sitting in the main hall at lunch, trying to get caught up on my American History homework, when there was this crazy roar. I stood up and looked out over the quad. The Pops were swatting and screaming like they were being attacked by a swarm of bees. A corner of the quad—the sunny corner, the corner nearest to senior hall—was totally and completely overrun by a flash mob of colorful, weird Uns in all shapes and sizes, laughing and talking. Hey, there was Mime Guy juggling with Teddy Baedeker! Someone must have sent out a text message

---

that spread like bad news and got the UnPops to the quad en masse the second the lunch bell rang. In a few minutes they'd all be lining up for the conga.

Yep, the conga. See, all week, Cate and Bean had been rolling out Miss UnPleasant's write-in campaign for sophomore class president. Canfield kept crossing Miss UnPleasant off the sign-up list, but that didn't slow down Cate and Bean—they signed her up fourteen different times. And every day at lunch, there was a Miss UnPleasant conga line. They marched and danced from one end of sophomore hall to the other and back again, waving signs, cheering, and chanting that day's UnSlogan. And every day, the parade got bigger and bigger and bigger. Even Uns from other grades joined in.

If I had spent all summer coming up with a master plan to promote UnPop Culture and the whole Un thing, I doubt I could have come up with something that would have worked nearly this well.

But I was starting to worry that maybe it was working *too* well. With a growing following of Library Girls, Mathletes, AV Guys, and weird-ass freakazoids, Miss UnPleasant's message was attracting

SIDEBRA

UnSlogans!
Monday: "Vote for Miss UnP to Support Diversity!"
Tuesday: "Join the Un Crowd!"
Wednesday: "UnNormal and Proud!"
Thursday: "The Power of Un Is Way More Fun!" *

* On Thursday, the Miss UnPleasant parade/conga line danced all the way down to the main quad and halfway through it before the Pops attacked them with water balloons and everyone screamed and scattered, laughing all the way back to sophomore hall. Which only proved their point—the power of Un *is* way more fun.

a lot of people no candidate had even noticed before, much less tried to reach.

I did my best to act really annoyed by the whole thing. I mean, I kind of had to or I'd blow my cover. But secretly, I was all butterflies and rainbows inside. I was even a little jealous—Cate and Bean and the whole Miss UnPleasant crew were having so much fun! A lot more fun than us boring candidates, all taking ourselves so seriously. As I passed out my paisley-patterned playing cards stamped with "Paisley 4 Pres!" that my mom had found online, I had to wonder if my pen name was jeopardizing my own candidacy. But no one would really vote for her, would they?

Then Cate and Bean started a membership drive. If you signed up to join the UnCrowd, this *un*official club they were starting, you got to choose three Un stickers that they'd had printed up. By Wednesday, people had started wearing them on T-shirts and slapping them on binders and lockers just because they were funny, even if they had no intention of voting for Miss UnPleasant—even if they weren't in our class.

Hutch was pissed. But his dad is in like marketing or promotions or something, so he had a few hundred little yellow plastic footballs printed with HUTCH FOR PRESIDENT. When Hutch passed them out at lunch one day, it was like the most brilliant idea. I was totally annoyed. But then Hutch's little balls turned into a big, chaotic game of Tweak the Freak, and one of the Trost twins got smashed in the head and needed stitches.

Canfield confiscated all of the footballs and threw them away in two giant trash cans. Oh, poor Hutch. Guess he'll just have to go buy more balls.

On Thursday, we heard about the campus-wide assembly to discuss the whole Miss UnPleasant thing. Apparently the principal had received a number of complaints from outraged Pop parents and students who were demanding that Miss UnPleasant be silenced and whoever was responsible be punished. They were even calling for the resignation of the *The Fly's* editor and faculty advisor.

The forum would take place in the quad during third and fourth periods on Friday—which meant no Drama. Secretly, I was relieved. Over the last week, every day in Drama with Clint had been excruciating. Our big *Acting Out* performance was coming up on Monday night, and our scene together was getting better. At least now we both sounded vaguely Shakespeare-ish, even if Clint still didn't seem to know what he was saying half the time. But even with our amateurish fumbling, there was something . . . *yikes* about the whole thing. Every time Clint grabbed me and pulled me up against his chest and whispered, "Nay hear you, Kate: in sooth you scape not so," I totally dissolved. Which, of course, made it hard to be like, "Um, yeah, so the Walnut Festival on Saturday? Sorry. Can't make it after all. Bean loves you."

Off topic, off topic. So anyway, the forum. It was going to take place in the quad on Friday before lunch, and there would be equal time for people speaking for and against Miss UnPleasant. Whoever wanted time at the mic just had to sign up in advance either Pro Miss UnPleasant or Anti Miss UnPleasant.

And then I had this brilliant idea.

The best way to hide from any suspecting minds was in plain sight, right?

So I signed up to speak.

CHAPTER THIRTY-FIVE

Friday morning, things were insane. Almost all of the PH student body had squished into the quad, probably for the first time ever. Most people were just milling around waiting to watch the action. But some people were holding signs. "Miss UnPleasant for President!" "Shun the Uns!" From where I stood up near the podium with all the other speakers, I could see that there was even a local news team doing a live report from our parking lot.

Ms. Whit was in a very animated discussion with a few of the faculty members. Canfield was standing with his arms crossed, talking to our principal. They both looked stressed and annoyed, like they'd much rather be off at McDonald's chowing down on Egg McMuffins.

The Dumbe Blondes had taken over the circle around the base of the big bronze hornet. The bongo guy was drumming and they were all softly singing, "Kumbaya, Miss UnP, kumbaya. Kumbaya, Miss UnP, kumbaya."

Ms. Whit stepped up to the podium and quieted everyone down. The Dumbe Blondes would not be silenced, but they did bring their Kumbaya down to a haunting whisper. Then Ms.

Whit thanked everyone for attending and introduced Miriam Goldfarb, editor extraordinaire of *The Fly*.

"Hello, peoples!" Miriam announced in her nasally voice. "Is this great or what?! When was the last time anyone got pissed enough to gather in the quad and duke it out? Right on, peoples!"

Peoples from both camps cheered because, hey, she was right.

"I am here speaking today because I am the"—pause—"editor of *The Fly* and thus, the decider. Yes, I approved Miss UnPleasant's columns."

A wave of boos and cheers filled the quad.

"Okay, all right, pipe down, peoples. Obviously, you don't *all* agree with Miss UnPleasant's point of view. And that's cool. She doesn't"—pause—"agree with all of you either. But can't we agree today that anyone should have the right to express his or her views—as long as they are nonviolent? I mean, hey, this is a democracy! This is the United Screwed-Up States of America, and every voice counts! I say give Miss UnPleasant's piece a chance! Thank you."

Miriam bowed a few times and then stepped to the side. In the meantime, a yelling war had broken out between the Pops, who were booing, and the UnPops, who were screaming and cheering. It was hilarious, and incredible. I couldn't believe I had started this. I couldn't believe we were all here because of something I had *written*.

The first to speak out against Miss UnPleasant was the tag

team of BS1 and BS2, wearing their cheerleading uniforms. Of course.

"Hello, fellow Hornets," said BS1.

A lot of people clapped and yelled "Hello!" back.

"Thank you for your support. We are here to say that we have been deeply wounded by Miss UnPleasant's hurtful words. As you know, we are Varsity Hornettes, so we know what it's really like to be popular. And I just have to say that we are not trapped, we are not bullies, we are not brats. We are happy, nice people—and we *do* have power at this school. We have power because we have *earned* it!"

The Pops cheered and whistled.

"Obviously," BS1 continued, "this Miss UnPleasant person is clueless. We don't think that someone who has no idea what they're talking about—and obviously *no* school spirit—should be allowed to write mean lies, and hurt so many good, beautiful people. Thank you."

The Pop crowd cheered like maniacs.

When they finally quieted down, BS2 leaned into the mic. "Ditto," she said with a smirk, igniting another insane explosion of cheering and stomping.

Then Cate Maduro stepped up. She was wearing a T-shirt that said "UnEven and Proud."

"I don't agree," she said, leveling her gaze at the crowd. "Yes, I realize it's *shocking* that someone like me doesn't agree with two *Hor*-nettes. I think Miss UnPleasant has a ton of school spirit— but she's disappointed and she's pissed off! She cares enough to write that Pleasant Hill *does* feel like Pleasant Hell. And for those of you wondering, no, I didn't write those columns—but I sure wish I had. Miss UnPleasant has shined her high beams on the bad behavior of the Pops at this school and the bad-ass behavior of the UnPops. She has empowered the UnPops by encouraging them to let their freak flags fly. I say, Miss UnPleasant's got the power!" Cate raised her hand in a fist and saluted the crowd. "Power to the UnPops! Power to the UnPops! Power to the UnPops!"

The UnPops went crazy, picking up the chant and screaming and stomping and waving signs, holding their clenched fists high in a show of UnPop solidarity.

Cate had a huge smile on her face as she passed the mic to Bentley Jones.

"Good morning! I'm Bentley Jones. Sophomore. I'm here to show my support for Miss UnPleasant."

"Boo!" someone shouted.

"This debate is not about whether or not you agree with Miss UnPleasant's opinions. I certainly don't agree with everything she's written. This is about freedom of speech, which is one of our inalienable rights as freshmen, as sophomores, as juniors, as seniors, as people of this world. Without freedom of speech, we cannot have an open dialogue. And an open dialogue is vital for a healthy society."

The Dumbe Blondes cheered and raised their signs high.

"PH may be a small society, but it *is* a society nonetheless. It's important for us to hear diverse voices that raise our awareness of social issues and raise our consciousness. I applaud Miss UnPleasant. Yes, she has criticized us, but I ask you, if we can't handle criticism from an *insider*, then how can we possibly handle criticism when we're out in the real world?"

A bunch of people cheered at that. Not the Pops, though.

"Let us look at her criticism as an opportunity to improve ourselves. I ask you to focus not on where Miss UnPleasant is wrong, but rather on where she is right. Thank you for being here and for having a voice in freedom."

I really liked that Bentley Jones. I realized I had to spend more time with her, even if she *was* the next generation of Yearbook Royalty.

Then suddenly it was my turn to speak. OMG. I'd gotten so caught up in everyone else's speeches that for a second a blanked on whose side I was on. Cate nudged me toward the podium. I pulled myself together and stepped up.

"Hi, I'm Paisley Hanover," I said, smiling out at the crowd. "I'm speaking today because I think Miss UnPleasant is a *coward!*"

The Pops cheered.

"And I'm not just saying that because I *am* a Pop. Or at least, I'm close to being one," I said, catching Candy Esposito's eye and winking.

"Sure, Miss UnPleasant raises some good points about our school, but I think the way she's doing it is pathetic. She's hiding behind the safety of anonymity. She's hiding behind this bogus Miss UnPleasant name! If she has something to say to us, then I invite her to step forward—right here, right now—and identify herself. I'll be happy to give up my time and pass her the mic." I squinted at the crowd. People started looking around suspiciously.

Ooh, this was fun. Then I had an even better idea. "Given her obviously twisted brain and tweaked sense of humor," I said, "she's probably even one of the speakers today. She's probably standing up here right now." I cocked an eyebrow and turned to Miriam and Bentley and Cate and Ms. Whit, who were all looking nervously at each other.

"Come on, Miss UnPleasant! Come clean! Who are you?"

I waited. I was really into it.

"Take responsibility for your words!"

A few voices from the crowd joined in.

"Yeah!"

"Right on!"

"Step up, coward!"

A few more clumps of people cheered and yelled.

I waited a little longer, feeling giddy with podium power. And then I kind of went off the deep end.

"That's what I thought. Miss UnPleasant, you're a gutless, two-faced coward! Whoever you are, don't mess with Pleasant Hill's best!" I paused for dramatic effect, slowly raising *two* clenched fists. "*More* power to the Pops! *More* power to the Pops! *More* power to the Pops!"

I smiled in triumph as the crowd went crazy, cheering and clapping and whistling. It was like a wall of sound being pushed on top of me. I looked out and saw Bean and Charlie, and over there, Amy. And suddenly my smile felt stamped on my face. They all looked just . . . stunned. My eyes swept over the quad. I caught sight of Jen and Bodie, laughing and clapping, and Hutch whooping. My stomach swished dangerously. Uh-oh. I hadn't thought this through very well. I took a step back from the podium—I spotted Eric Sobel taking pictures. Then he lowered his camera, and my eyes locked with his. But I couldn't read his expression. What *was* that? I took another step back and bumped into someone. I turned to apologize, and there was Cate, glaring at me.

When I first came up with this idea, I thought I was pretty darn clever. And that line about Miss UnP being one of the speakers? Genius, right? No one in a million years would think she was me. But now this gross feeling was creeping up my arms and legs and making my scalp prickle. My stomach twisted as I realized, finally.

That look on Eric's face? It was disappointment.

He may not have known that I was Miss UnPleasant. But I knew.

I was the gutless, two-faced coward.

CHAPTER THIRTY-SIX

I couldn't face anyone at lunch. I mean, really. What had I been thinking? So instead I started walking down to the deserted end of sophomore hall where I almost never go—and nearly tripped over Clint Bedard. He was stretched out on the grass reading.

He covered his eyes from the sun and squinted up at me, smiling. "Hey, Red."

How could it be that I'd literally trip over the first and last person I wanted to see right now? That warm feeling was spreading again somewhere below my belt and—God, who was controlling the heat settings in my body? I just stood there for a second, trying to figure out what to do. I knew what I *had* to do. Finally, I dropped down onto the grass next to him.

He kept squinting at me. "What's up?"

"You weren't at the assembly?" I asked, pulling out a blade of grass.

He flashed me that what-do-you-think? look. But all he said was, "I've been reading."

Well, that was a relief at least. He hadn't seen me cluelessly toss aside my morals—and my friendships. "Is it good?" I asked, gesturing at the book.

"It's okay," he said, flipping it over and resting it on his chest. "What's up?" he asked again.

Well, no time like the present, I guess. I took a deep breath. "Um, I know I said yes last week, but . . . but I don't think I can . . . go out with you."

"What?" He laughed, and then looked over at me a little confused. "Wait, this weekend or ever?" he asked, sitting up.

Oh, this sucked. I didn't want to lie to him, but I couldn't really explain the real reason. And the truth was, I *did* want to go out with him. I *so* wanted to go out with him. If only he *knew* how much I wanted to go out with him. But at the same time, it kind of scared me. I mean he kind of scared me. Well, not him really, it was more me around him that scared me.

"This weekend . . . " I said, trailing off. Coward.

"Really?" he asked. He could tell I was totally hedging. He scratched his beautiful thick head of hair. "Why not?"

Oh man. I should have planned this better. "Well, I just . . . I don't know. I just don't think it would be a good idea."

"What, did you run it by your popular posse, and they didn't sign your permission slip?"

"No! No, it's not like that at all. It's just that . . ." I scrambled for something to say.

"Yeah, okay." He shook his head. "I know how it works." He snapped his book shut and stood up. I looked down at the grass, waiting for an onslaught of angry words. But they didn't come. When I looked up again, Clint was already halfway across the lawn, headed for the lockers.

I'd done this thing for my friend, right? I'd done this for Bean. I should feel good about it, right? So why did I feel so much worse?

CHAPTER THIRTY-SEVEN

I just sat there, out in the boonies of sophomore hall, slumped over with my chin in my hands. No matter what I said, it always seemed like the wrong thing. The wind was starting to kick up now, blowing the grass around me in twisting waves. I looked up just as the sun disappeared behind a big dark cloud. Then it started to sprinkle. Perfect.

I leaned back and closed my eyes. The light rain felt cool on my face, and I didn't care if I got a little wet. I *wanted* to get wet. I wanted to wash this feeling away, this feeling of dumbness and dread. I felt like I had really blown something that could have been—I don't know. Like different and real and special.

I thought about my Drama scene with Clint. Could I fix this? Probably not. Clint and I were supposed to perform on Monday night. Ugh! Now with him feeling completely disgusted with me, thinking I'm some ridiculous rah-rah clone who can't think for herself . . . Who would want to woo that?

It started raining harder, so I got up and ran for the covered hallway. It was bad enough to *feel* like a rat. I didn't want to *look* like a wet rat too.

I wandered down the hall toward the crowded section and my locker, so in a depressed daze that I almost bumped right into Jen.

"Pais, hi." She touched my arm. "God, I've been looking all over for you." Jen was trying to smile, but I could tell she was upset. "Your speech was really great. You put the screws to that Miss UnPleasant. You're so right. She is a gutless coward."

I tried to smile back. I knew she was trying to be nice, but her compliment just made me feel worse. Was that even possible? Yes.

And then I noticed her necklace. It was a small but chunky silver *j*—with a sapphire or something as the dot—hanging from a short silver chain. Wow. Bodie's got money *and* style.

It was almost the end of lunch, and the halls were getting really crowded because of the rain. I watched Jen's face brighten.

"Hey, Hutch," she said all perky. Ugh. I didn't turn around.

Jen grabbed my arm and led me away from the crowd back toward the sophomore boonies. When we were a safe distance away, she burst into tears.

"What?" I stopped. "What is it?"

She shook her head, trying to cover her face with one hand, pulling me along past the few loners and dweebs and outsiders who stared at us as we walked by. When we got to the end of the hall where it was deserted, she rounded the corner and collapsed against the wall, sobbing.

"Jen, what happened?"

She shook her head. "It's bad, Pais, really bad."

I tried to imagine what could be so bad. Not so bad that she would cry but that she would come to me after everything that had happened. And to tell you the truth, I wasn't completely sure I trusted her. Was this just another setup?

"Why are you telling me?" I asked.

"You're the only one I trust. You're the only person I *can* talk to."

I eyed her. That was a switch.

"I did something . . ." She let out this big sigh. "I did something really . . ."

I waited for her to finish, but she started crying again, so I put my hand on her shoulder. I didn't know what to say. I still wanted to be mad at her, but Jen hardly ever lets her guard down. I was starting to worry. "You did something . . . bad?" I asked, trying to get her talking again.

"No!" She wiped her nose. "I mean, yeah, I did something stupid, but that's not the bad part."

The rain was coming down hard by then, hitting the roof like dancing pebbles. "What's the bad part?"

She gritted her teeth and sort of growled. These weren't sad tears. She was crying because she was angry, frustrated.

"Jen, what? What? Tell me."

"Oh, that stupid, stupid party. I hate those people! If only I hadn't gone. I so wish I had never gone."

"What party? Hutch's party?"

She nodded, dropping her head into one hand.

Okay, wait. That really confused me. I thought she *loved* those people. I thought that party was where she bonded with her new best girls and hooked up with Bodie.

"God, I'm such an idiot, I'm such a fool." She wiped under her eyes, careful not to smear her mascara. "There was this bathroom in the pool house." She shook her head. "Before the party, some sick creep—"

The warning bell for sixth period rang. Crap!

She wiped the tears from her face and tried to sniffle herself together. "Damn! I've got a test in sixth. I have to go."

We ran back toward our lockers, weaving our way through the crowded hallway.

"Want to talk tonight?" I asked, spinning the combination lock on my locker.

"Yeah. Can I come over?"

"Sure." She hadn't come over since before Labor Day weekend. I gave her a big hug. "Yeah, that'd be great." I wondered for the thousandth time what happened at that party. Whatever it was, it couldn't have been good.

I opened my locker—and another folded note fell out. I looked at it there on the ground. Jen looked at it too. Then she looked at me, puzzled.

Finally, I picked it up.

RIGHT ON, BABY.
MORE POWER TO THE POPS!

"I have a secret admirer." I shrugged, feeling more embarrassed than proud. "I've been getting anonymous notes in my locker since the first day of school."

"You're kidding." She tilted her head, thinking. "That's weird. I've been getting anonymous notes in my locker too."

"You have?" Damn. Suddenly I didn't feel so special.

"Yeah. But they're definitely *not* from a secret admirer."

CHAPTER THIRTY-EIGHT

I slammed my locker closed and took off for Biology. On the way, I passed a scraggly group of UnPops. OMG! They flipped me off! Whoa. And then all of them flashed the UnPop Power fist. I almost ran right into a pole.

I ran all the way to class and dropped into my seat, panting, just as the final bell rang. I was so distracted by what Jen had told me that I forgot to turn off my phone. About ten minutes into sixth period, it buzzed in my pocket.

I discreetly slipped it out and flipped it open. It was a text. From Charlie Dodd? That was weird.

Hutch bought his speech online!

No way! Was that true? I texted back under my desk.

Hw do u kno?

He told me.

Disgusting. What a lazy, pathetic cheater. I had to think about this. No way was I letting him get away with that on top of everything else. But what could I do? It's not like I could just run through the halls screaming, "Hutch bought his speech online!" Like anyone would even care. No. I had to be able to prove it.

· I stared at the whiteboard, not thinking at all about how cells multiply.

And then it hit me. Maybe I *wouldn't* have to prove it. Maybe all I had to do was get people wondering . . .

Suddenly, I knew what to do. And I knew I had to write it that day if it was going to make it into the next edition of *The Fly*, which would be coming out right before the election.

And honestly, I was so charged up I couldn't wait. Besides, my weekend nights were becoming weirdly UnSocial with all the time I'd been spending writing "How to Be UnPopular" columns. So in Biology, I got to work. I pretended to be attentive, taking detailed class notes, but really I was scribbling a bunch of UnPleasant ideas in my notebook. By the end of class, I knew I had a killer secret weapon.

I waited until the end of the day. Then about halfway through final period, I stuffed my notebook into the back of my jeans and pulled my top over it. I asked to use the hall pass to go to the bathroom. But this was no bathroom break.

I speed-walked down the hall and ducked into the library. It was pretty dead in there. But I couldn't risk Ms. Whit seeing me. I quickly ducked behind the magazine rack and hauled booty for the reference shelves. Then I opened my notebook.

When the coast was clear, I crept out from behind a book-shelf. I checked over one shoulder and then the other. Then I slid into the chair in front of the computer closest to the book shelves—the one with the most protective cover. I knew I had to move fast. I went to *The Fly* website, clicked on SUBMISSIONS, and started speed-typing right into the submissions window. I finished in less than two minutes, and leaned back to double-check my bad typing. I made a few corrections and hit the SUBMIT button.

I stood up, feeling pretty darn pleased. Maybe everything would work out okay after all. I turned to leave, but then stopped. I had this weird feeling. I looked around and didn't see anyone. I turned the other way—and there was Ms. Whit, staring at me from across the room with her arms folded over her chest. I'd already used my Get Out of Jail Free card on the first day of school. What could I do? I smiled, shrugged, and bolted.

As I rounded the corner into the hall, I ran smack into Charlie Dodd.

He seemed surprised for a second, or maybe just preoccupied. But he wouldn't look me in the eye. Then he shook his head. "Nice one, Paisley."

I didn't know if he was talking about my disastrous speech at assembly this morning or me running into him just now. "Uh, sorry," I said lamely. "Hey, thanks for the tip about Hutch."

"Yeah, no worries." He looked at his feet, tugging nervously on the bottom of his black XXL polo shirt like he was trying to decide what to say. And for Charlie, that was bizarre. When he finally looked at me, he had this weird expression on his face. But all he said was, "Good to know the real you, Paisley." Then he turned and walked into the library.

Talk about mixed signals. What was up with Charlie Dodd?

And then I had this horrible sinking feeling. I remembered Charlie's stunned expression at the assembly . . . and I groaned. Oh no. Thanks to my brilliant More-Power-to-the-Pops speech, had I just lost my campaign manager too? Or was it more than that?

CHAPTER THIRTY-NINE

It poured rain all weekend—there were flood warnings and everything. I sat on the couch eating like a whole bag of Pirate's Booty, watching bad reality TV, while I worked on my campaign speech for president.

I felt totally crappy.

I'd managed to alienate practically all of my friends and romantic possibilities in a single day. Was that like some kind of world record?

And Jen never showed up Friday night. She ignored my texts and my calls. God, I was such a sucker. And by Saturday afternoon, it was clear the Walnut Festival wasn't happening. The TV news said it was being postponed till next Saturday.

It's not like I was going anyway. Who would I go with? Not Cate, not Bean, not Carreyn, not Amy, not Jen, not even Charlie Dodd. Eric thought I was a shallow idiot after hearing my totally UnInspired anti–Miss UnPleasant speech. God, the look on his face when he lowered his camera . . . I'd never forget it.

And what *about* Eric? I still liked him. Was that so bad? Was it bad to like two guys at once? It's not like I could just switch my feelings on and off like a floor lamp. And Clint—Clint thought

I was a total Pop snob. Ugh, I couldn't even begin to imagine what our *Acting Out* performance would be like on Monday. Total disaster.

I must have fallen asleep on the couch. I don't know. I just remember being startled when my dad came bounding down the stairs in his running gear, including his dorky neon yellow vest over a rain jacket. I sat up, my heart pounding.

"Hey Pais, come on! Let's go for a run."

"Dad," I grumbled. "It's *pouring* out there."

"I know! It's gonna be great!" He started doing his quad stretches. "Nothing better than a run in the rain to clear your head. It's a meditative outdoor shower. It's an endorphin-powered brain rinse. Come on!"

I just looked at him. "No thanks." I sighed. I was so inside my own head space that if I cleared it, I wasn't sure I'd even exist anymore.

"We could talk while we run?" he suggested.

"Yeah, but I really have to work on my speech," I said. "Thanks anyway." I waved and fell back onto the couch, closing my eyes.

"Can't wait to hear it!" He ran out the back door and into the pouring rain.

By Saturday night, I was stuffing handfuls of Pirate's Booty into my mouth. Just stuffing and stuffing, I was so mad. I couldn't believe the mess I'd gotten myself into. I really wished that Mom wasn't off at a Yogilates retreat. I actually *wanted* to talk to her for a change.

Then I stopped. I was having this horrible, dawning realization as I listened to the rain coming down.

OMG, I didn't even *have* to cancel with Clint. I didn't even *have* to make it into this whole big thing. The rain would have taken care of it for me. Oh God, this was the worst. I wish I hadn't even thought of it. I dug back into the bag of Pirate's Booty.

Wait.

No.

Of *course* I had to say something to him on Friday. I mean, I wasn't just calling off our date. I was calling off *Clint*. And I was doing it for Bean. It wouldn't have been fair otherwise . . . I mean, that's why I'd done it, right? For Bean? Or was I just telling myself that? I mean, I knew I was sort of afraid, you know, of the way Clint made me *feel*. But if I was going to be totally straight with myself, I guess I was also sort of afraid of . . . of what some people might think.

Suddenly my bones felt like lead. Oh God, I really was the worst of the gutless cowards. What was I going to do?

CHAPTER FORTY

On Monday morning, I was still feeling so crappy that I didn't even want to go to school. It was only *Acting Out* and my curiosity about Miss UnPleasant's latest column that got me out of bed.

Carpool was painful. No one would sit next to me. Two Library Girls scowled at me over their shoulders, whispering back and forth. Sleeping-braces-kid flashed the UnPop Power fist with a nasty grin, then closed his eyes and went back to sleep. The dweeby UnDiscovered freshman turned to me. "*More power?*" He shook his head sadly. "Really? I thought you were one of the *nice* ones."

Ouch. That one really hurt.

Charlie Dodd wasn't in carpool. Charlie Dodd was *always* in carpool. I guess he didn't want to get stuck ignoring obnoxious, podium-power me all the way to school. I couldn't really blame him.

I stared out the window, trying to focus on my day. *The Fly* probably wouldn't be out until just before lunch, so I should spend all morning campaigning wherever I could—especially in the outer limits of sophomore hall. The election was only a day away, and I had a lot of damage-control to do. I really needed to score big with the fringe factor if I was going to crush Hutch. And after my crazy speech in the quad . . . Oh God. Would we find out the fate of Miss UnPleasant today, I wondered, or would the administration wait to read her next snarky column and then decide? I shook my head. Ugh, I didn't want to think about it.

Fortunately my shipment of PAISLEY POWER temporary tattoos had arrived on Saturday along with my bags of custom-ized pink and green M&M'S. Half of them said *Paisley 4 Pres!* The other half said *Spastic Jazzed!*

Yes, it's true. Hutch had inspired me—I refused to let him be the only one with shameless self-promotional treats and toys.

Before homeroom, I set out for the far end of sophomore hall. As I was handing stuff out, I got some major UnPop brattitude from a bunch of girls. They actually flung my M&M'S back at me. Then a few AV Guys flashed the UnPop Power fist—one of them even turned his clenched fist around like he was threatening to hit me. OMG. Creepy. But most people were like, "Thanks, cool, whatever," just happy to be getting candy for free.

Not LG Wong. She was standing with a clump of dog-eared Library Girls. She took one look at the temporary tattoo I gave her and laughed in my face. "*Paisley Power?* How perfect," she said all snarky. "*More* power to you, Paisley."

The Library Girls all snickered.

I got out of there fast—and ran into Bean and Cate near the far end of the hall. The air between my teeth hissed as I sucked in a breath. Uh-oh. This might hurt.

They were rehearsing their scene. I watched them for a few seconds until Cate noticed me and stopped. I stood there awkwardly. She put her hand on her hip and raised her chin. "Miss UnPleasant is *not* a coward," she said, zapping me with her crazy laser-beam blue eyes.

I glanced at Bean and then back at Cate. Then I heaved this huge, heavy sigh. "I know. I know," I finally said. "I got a little carried away up there. I'm really sorry. Believe me."

"Why did you even say that?" Bean asked, looking at me in total disbelief.

I couldn't tell them the truth. I so wanted to, I realized. But I couldn't. So I stood there, not knowing what to say. They looked at me. I looked at them. And then I just blurted, "It was for my campaign. You know, for visibility. I—I didn't mean all that stuff. I just wanted to . . . to stand out and be . . . um, controversial."

Cate gave me this long yeah-right look.

"Hey, here's a peace offering." I handed each of them a few temporary tattoos and a bag of Spastic Jazzed M&M'S. "Don't hate me, okay?" I asked, looking from one of them to the other.

"Don't worry," said Cate. "I don't care enough about you to hate you."

Um, did that mean she was still mad at me?

"Yum, chocolate! Thanks, Pais." Bean ripped open her bag of candy and dumped half of it into her mouth. "I don't agree with *all* your campaign tactics," she said around a mouthful of

M&M'S, "but I do agree with some. You need any help passing stuff out?"

"Actually, yeah. That'd be great," I said, thinking of the UnPops who'd flung my M&M'S back at me. "Thanks. Come by my locker at lunch, okay? See you guys in Drama." I waved, heading back down the hall toward Popularity Place.

Lunch. OMG. I'd almost forgotten. *The Fly* would be out. I was dying to read my little UnPop Quiz and see how people reacted—nothing like juicy gossip to get tongues wagging. By the end of lunch, practically everyone in our class would know that Hutch didn't write his own campaign speech. What a skeezy creep cheater. And who would vote for him then?

CHAPTER FORTY-ONE

Clint wasn't at school. Or maybe he just cut Drama because he was too disgusted to look at me. I wondered if he was even going to show up for *Acting Out* that night.

I sat on a windowsill doodling in my notebook, watching the others rehearse their scenes for the last time. Charlie Dodd and Teddy Baedeker were still using their scripts a little. Bean and Cate were having a hard time rehearsing because they kept cracking each other up. Svend, the cool foreign exchange student, was rehearsing with Mandy Mindel. She actually looked like she was having fun for a change. I smiled.

Mandy saw me and gave me a shy smile. I waved back, surprised. I was even more surprised when they got to the end of their scene and she walked over to me. "Hi," she said, twisting her hands in front of her. "Um . . . did Miss UnPleasant ever . . . ever um, say anything to you?" she asked, looking up at me for a second. "I mean, after the assembly?"

"Nope. Not yet," I said, shaking my head. "I was kinda harsh, though. I'm not sure she'd *want* to talk to me." I laughed like, *Oh, silly me and my crazy podium-power.*

"Well, if you um, if you figure out who it is, will you . . . will you tell me?" she asked. "I really want to talk to her."

I nodded, wondering what Mandy wanted to say to Miss UnPleasant.

"Okay, um, thanks." She gave me this little wave down by her hip, and then walked back to Svend.

At the end of class, I found Bean and Cate. "Hey, you guys feeling ready for tonight?"

"Yeah, ready to burst into hysterics!" Bean said giddily. "What about you?"

"I don't know. I don't know where Clint is. I hope he shows tonight."

"I'll call him," said Cate. "He'll show." She looked at me but didn't smile.

Was she still mad? I couldn't tell. Then I remembered something, and my heart started beating fast.

"Oh, hey Bean," I said, feeling awkward all of a sudden. "Um, Clint and I decided to bag our date on Saturday. It seemed kind of stupid. I mean, other than *Taming of the Shrew*, we don't really have much in common. And after tonight, you know, that'll be over, so . . ."

"Really?" She looked super happy. "It seemed stupid?"

The damage was already done with Clint, I'd decided. I might as well share the good part and make Bean happy. "Well, I mean, we're so . . . different. What would we even talk about?" I said. "Just thought you'd want to know."

Cate shot me a knowing glance and then smiled. "Maybe there's still hope for you."

I smiled back.

At lunch, I made a beeline for *The Fly* stack in the main hall, trying not to walk too fast.

When I saw the headline, I caught my breath. "Miss UnPleasant Writes On!" Yes! I didn't bother reading the article and skipped straight to my column.

MISS UnPLEASANT'S UnPOP QUIZ

Okay, people. Heads up—pencils down! It's time for your first UnPop Quiz.

1. Which incredibly popular hottie has a secret crush on sweet, adorable me?
2. Which candidate for sophomore class president bought his speech online?
3. Which BP flirts shamelessly with one hot guy just to make another—the one she *really* likes—jealous?
4. Which Varsity Pom stole her mom's credit card to get a nose job?
5. Which sophomore rah-rah is getting love notes in her locker?
6. Which brainy babe ignored an invite to speak at the assembly because she has way more power if she stays UnNonymous?

Pop goes the weasel!

Big kiss, class dismissed!
Miss UnPleasant

After about five minutes, it was clear that my Miss UnPleasant plan had worked—only, maybe a little *too* well. I ran back to my locker to meet Bean and pass out more Paisley promo paraphernalia. But all during lunch, I couldn't help listening in on people's conversations everywhere we went.

"Number three," said Carreyn, sitting with Amy on our bench reading *The Fly*. "'Which BP flirts shamelessly with one hot guy just to make another—the one she *really* likes—jealous?'"

"That would be *all* of them," said Amy matter-of-factly.

I saw Charlie run up to Hutch at his locker and show him *The Fly*. Hutch said an unpleasant expletive very loudly and slammed his locker. I suppressed an evil chuckle.

Then Eric walked up to Hutch and Charlie. I couldn't hear them, but it looked like they were talking about something serious. Eric turned and stared at me. He looked, I don't know, worried or something. He didn't smile or wave. Then he looked back to Hutch. Weird.

But I didn't think much of it. I was too distracted. The UnPop Quiz had caused this delicious cacophony of speculation and accusations. It started slowly, like popcorn popping, and then got faster and louder and crazier. I couldn't help but smile.

"How could any popular hottie have a crush on *her*?"

"Hutch."

"Of course it's Hutch. He's the only guy running for president."

"Are you getting love letters in your locker?"

"No. Are you?"

"Hey, I'm not a rah-rah!"

When Bean and I turned the corner, BS2 and BS1 were heading toward us on their way back to junior hall. And they were really going at it.

"I didn't tell *anyone* you stole her card. Not a single person!" cried BS2.

"You liar!" BS1 snarled. "You're the only one who knew!"

OMG. That one I just made up!

"It's true! She *does* have more power if she stays anonymous."

"A lot more power."

"Yeah, but if anyone finds out who she is, she's totally dead."

And my smile totally faded.

CHAPTER FORTY-TWO

Acting Out started at 7:00. It was 6:50, and there was still no sign of Clint.

I peeked out through the side of the curtain. The audience was really filling up. People were chattering away. Logan Adler and a bunch of Dumbe Blondes had gathered in the back, holding up signs in a silent protest. "THE ARTS ROOL!" "DRAMA QUEENS GIVE ME THE CLAP!" "I SUPPORT PERFORMANCE ANGZIETY!" "HOMERUN!"

Grambo and my parents were in the third row, sitting next to Mr. and Mrs. Merrill, studying the program, probably reading my mini bio over and over. OMG! A few rows back on the other side, I spotted Jen and Amy and Carreyn—and *Eric Sobel!* What was he doing here?! Oh right, probably just taking photos for Yearbook.

Even so, I got a jolt of chills and pulled back from the curtain. Now I was sort of relieved that Clint hadn't shown up. I wasn't sure I wanted Eric to see me wrestling around in Clint Bedard's arms. I wasn't sure *I* wanted to be wrestling around in Clint Bedard's arms. Okay, who was I kidding? I wanted to. I so wanted to. But it totally freaked me out at the same time.

I wouldn't have to worry about it if Clint didn't show up, though.

I found Cate and Bean backstage doing relaxation exercises in front of the girls' dressing area. I almost squealed, they looked so great. They were both dressed like old men with funny hats and neckties and plaid pants. They were even wearing men's dress shoes! I love those guys.

"Break a leg!" I said to them.

"You too," said Bean.

Cate shook out her arms. "I am so damn nervous!"

"Don't worry. Your scene is hilarious. Everyone's gonna love it."

"Have you seen Clint yet?" Bean asked.

"Nope." I sighed. "I'm pretty sure he's not coming."

"No, I mean, he's here. He's right behind you."

Was she kidding?

I turned around. Clint was standing right there, holding a garment bag over one shoulder.

"Hey!" I broke out into a huge goobery grin, but I couldn't help it. I was so happy to see him. "You're here?!"

"Yeah, I'm here. You think I'd blow this off just 'cause you blew me off?"

Cate and Bean looked at each other, then at me. "Clint, I'm sorry I—"

"Save it. Whatever." He walked away to the guys' dressing area and went inside.

Cate and Bean looked at each other again.

"Holy molé," said Cate. "You blew him off? I thought you said you both decided it was stupid to go out."

"Well . . . "

"Pais, he likes you," Bean whispered, sounding like she had just solved a big mystery.

"No, he doesn't. Not anymore, if he ever did. Trust me."

"No, I think he does." Cate nodded. "I've never seen him like that. Oh, I can't wait to watch you two go at it in your scene!"

Bean didn't seem all that disappointed, actually. I guess maybe it had never occurred to her that guys like Clint Bedard could ever like girls like me. Frankly, it had never occurred to me before either.

"Well, I guess I should come clean," Bean said, blushing. "I feel kinda bad now, after what you did, Pais . . . But you know Svend, the exchange student? He just asked me out today at lunch. Can you believe it? Apparently tall gangly blondes remind him of home. And Svend told me he's *very* homesick."

What?! OMG. Well, that explained it. I couldn't believe that I'd killed my date with Clint! *Aaaaaaah!* I could have screamed. Instead, I gave her a big hug.

Mr. Eggertson gathered us all together and delivered a quick pep talk. Then he went onstage to introduce *Acting Out*. And then the curtain went up.

Charlie Dodd and Teddy Baedeker opened the show with their "Who's On First?" scene. Teddy was playing this dopey ding-a-ling who couldn't get anything straight, and Charlie was playing this over-thinking, frustrated control freak. And I have to say they were both *really* good. Even though they screwed up some lines, they really got the crowd laughing.

Then a few other groups did their scenes—some were pretty good and a few were pretty awful. Then Cate and Bean did their *Odd Couple* scene. I watched from the wings, so I couldn't see the audience but I could sure hear them, and they were laughing like crazy. I could hear my mom, and I just knew she and Mrs. Merrill were crying with laughter.

I looked across the stage. Clint was standing in the wings in the shadows on the far side. A huge tidal wave of nervousness smacked into me. We were next! *Aaaaaaah!*

Cate and Bean's scene ended, and the audience went nuts, clapping and cheering. I was so nervous. I already had swamp pits. Cate and Bean took a quick bow. Then the lights went down. As Bean moved offstage and I moved on to my position, Bean whispered, "Go Pais!"

I took my place, waiting for the lights to come up. And when they did . . . OMG! Holy molé was right! I blinked a few times. The audience hooted and whistled. Clint was standing across from me looking like some sexy, bad-ass swashbuckler. He was wearing these tight black pants tucked into knee-high black boots. And his off-white shirt was loose and billowy and—I swear to God—open practically to his belly button. Talk about an Elizabethan hottie! I started to pant with fear. At least I think it was fear.

"Good morrow, Kate," said Clint in his stage voice. "For that's your name, I hear."

"Well have you heard, but something hard of hearing." I walked around him in a half circle, and then cocked my head, full of attitude. "They call me Katherine that do talk of me."

He laughed in his mocking yet flirtatious way. "You lie, in faith, for you are called plain Kate, and bonny Kate and . . . "

Thank God, the minute I started speaking my lines, my fear transformed into energy. I was totally in it. And Clint was right there with me. He became Petruchio like I had never seen in our rehearsals. He was dashing, charming, flirtatious, confident, and really Shakespeare-ish.

We didn't just deliver our lines. We moved around the stage like we were sparring and dancing and flirting all at the same time. It was intense. I couldn't tell if I was just one hundred percent in character or if he was really making me *feel*. And then we got to the really, really intense part of the scene.

Of course, we were speaking Shakespeare. But Clint was basically saying, "I really dig you. You're hot, and I want to marry you." And I was all, "No way! You're not good enough for me—even though I'm way hot for you. But I'd never admit it in a million years." And it was full of all this sexual innuendo and plays on words like tail and stinger and tongue. Oh boy, that William Shakespeare!

Then Clint grabbed me and pulled me up against his chest and whispered in my ear, "Nay hear you, Kate: in sooth you 'scape not so." He had tiny beads of sweat on his forehead. I wanted to reach up and wipe them off, but I had to stay in character.

"I chafe you, if I tarry," I replied, struggling a little to get away—but not too hard since, let's face it, both Katherine and I kind of melted whenever he whispered in our ear.

Clint spun me around and held me in his arms while I struggled to break free. His chest felt warm against my back, and I could feel him breathing hard. I kept struggling to get out of his grip. And then? I heard my dress rip.

Uh-oh.

I looked down as the front of my dress pulled away from the poofy shoulder part. Good thing I was wearing a really cute bra! A few people in the audience laughed. I heard a camera speed-clicking. But I didn't break. I just clutched the front of my dress, holding it up, and looked at Clint like I was furious.

"No, not a whit," he said. "I find you passing gentle." I struggled again and spun around, but he grabbed both of my wrists and stared into my eyes, holding me close. "'Twas told me you were rough and coy and sullen, and now I find report a very liar. For thou are pleasant, gamesome, passing courteous, but slow in speech, yet sweet as springtime flowers . . ."

I was so caught up in the words, and the emotion *behind* the words, that I began to lean toward him. God, I wanted to kiss him. And I almost did. But then at the last possible second I remembered that we were up onstage in front of my parents, my grandmother, and about a hundred other people, including Eric Sobel. I suddenly pulled back, turning my head to the side. Wow. That was close.

It went along like that for a few more steamy minutes. I struggled—holding my dress together—pretending not to like him, trying to push him away, while Clint tried to wear me down with his honesty and his charm and his open shirt. And boy, was it working. Whoops! Did I say Clint? I meant Petruchio.

And then before I knew it, our scene came to an end. Clint held me in his arms, leaning over me like he was about to kiss me. My head was dropped back, but still our mouths were just a few inches apart. He was panting. I was panting. I looked into his eyes and they were hungry. And for a second I thought he really was going to kiss me. And honestly? I hoped he would. I really didn't care who was watching anymore.

But then the audience began to clap and scream and cheer. Someone whistled like a teenaged boy. I'm pretty sure it was my Grambo, because she does that kind of thing. Then Clint drew me up so I was standing, and he let me go. I almost fell over. I was so . . . so . . . I don't know what. But then he grabbed my hand and pulled me back next to him, and we did our little bow. When we straightened up, he turned and hugged me, lifting me up so that my toes came just off the floor.

I could barely breathe. I was having a major below-the-belt meltdown.

Then the lights went down. And I'm sure this time—his lips brushed my cheek.

CHAPTER FORTY-THREE

Backstage, Clint and I didn't talk. I hung out with the girls and he went over to the guys. I had a lot to think about, and maybe he did too. I don't know.

After the show, Amy came up to me and gave me this big hug. "Pais, that was amazing! You're a really good weird-ass drama freakazoid!"

"Thanks," I said, laughing. Maybe I was.

Carreyn came over and gave me a quick hug. "Wow. That was *hot!* I've got to read more Shakespeare. Okay, well, any Shakespeare." She laughed.

My parents and Grambo came up and did the whole proud parent and grandparent thing. It was a little embarrassing, especially when Grambo high-fived me. But fortunately Bean's and Cate's and everyone else's parents were doing the same proud parent thing. I looked over at Clint, but I didn't see anyone who looked like his family. And then, thank God, the parents retreated to a safe distance where they could swap embarrassing parenting stories or whatever it is they do.

I was sort of hoping that Eric and Jen would come over and

say something to me, but they didn't. I watched them walk out the door toward the parking lot. Oh well.

Then Clint grabbed me from behind. I could smell it was him. Mmmm. I closed my eyes and melted back into his arms. "That was fun," he said, lifting me up and spinning me around. "Maybe even more fun than a regular date."

I didn't say anything for a second. I just inhaled and smiled like a goober and nodded. I was a little afraid of what might come out of my mouth. But at the same time, I was like really feeling the emotion behind the words. And you know what? That was it. I decided I was going to say it. So what if I sounded like an idiot? At least I'd sound like a fearless idiot.

I turned to face Clint. "Hey, um . . . I know I called off our date. You know, the date that the rain probably would have called off anyway and I, um . . . I'd kinda like to propose a rain date. You know, I mean . . . if you're up for it."

I looked at him hopefully, waiting for some response. But he just stared at me, eyes squinted.

And then he finally said, "Red, you are *trouble*." He picked me up and swung me around again. We both laughed. I felt like I was going to melt and slip right through his arms.

I had a hard time sleeping that night. I lay in bed with Dyson, mainlining my customized "Paisley 4 Pres!" M&M'S while so many thoughts and questions swirled through my head. Mostly I was wondering why Jen had reached out to me like that, then never showed up at my house and now wasn't talking to me again.

I traced a pink M&M in my notebook and then wrote "Why" in it. And what happened in that bathroom at that stupid party? I was almost tempted just to ask Hutch. He must know *something*. It happened at his house.

I traced another one and wrote "What happened?" and chased it with an arrow, then scribbled "Flush Hutch!"

And then I kept rehearsing my speech in my head, especially the big audience laughs. I knew it was going to be a tight race and I didn't want to be insanely nervous. Hutch probably never got nervous. At least he never seemed nervous. Ugh. I hated Hutch.

And what about Eric? Eric. Eric. Eric. I so blew it with him when I made that drunk-with-podium-power anti–Miss UnPleasant speech. God, what could he think of me after that steamy scene with Clint? If he even thinks of me at all.

But what was really keeping me awake was Clint. I couldn't stop playing the mental movie of our scene over and over and over again trying to relive the experience—and I mean the *whole* experience.

I'm pretty sure when I *did* fall asleep, it was with a smile on my face.

CHAPTER FORTY-FOUR

Something felt weird the day of the speeches. For starters, Hutch was being really nice to me. At morning break he came up to our bench, acting all friendly.

"Hey, Team Paisley!" he said, interrupting my speech—I'd been practicing all morning. "Brought you guys a good-luck sticky bun." Carreyn's eyes lit up, but Amy and I were instantly suspicious.

"Is it poisoned?" Amy asked, poking it with her finger.

"Are you hoping I'll choke on it and not be able to give my speech?"

"Choke? No way. The speeches are gonna be fun today. I know yours is gonna be crazy good."

"Thanks," I said uncertainly. "You too."

I saw Eric Sobel in the hall at lunch while I was passing out our *I'd Vote for Paisley* buttons.

"Hey," I mouthed to him across the crowded hallway.

He didn't say anything. He just stared at me, like maybe he recognized me but wasn't quite sure. I guess he was still annoyed at me for bashing his imaginary girlfriend Miss UnPleasant at the assembly last week. Either that or . . . or he felt weird about me after watching my steaming hot scene with Clint. Ergh.

After lunch, everyone in our class started gathering outside the gym for the speeches assembly sixth period. It was a warm sunny day, so everyone waited until the last minute to go inside. Carreyn and Amy were both doing their best to pump me up.

"You're gonna do great!" Amy cheered. "Just be the Fun of a Kind Girl we all know you are!"

I laughed nervously. "I'll try," I said.

Carreyn nodded and gave me a little pat on the back. "Don't get all freaky nervo. Your speech is awesome. Really. I know because I've heard it like ten times. High five!"

As we goofily high-fived, I caught sight of Hutch and Charlie Dodd talking. "Since when did those two become friends?" I asked.

Amy and Carreyn turned to look. "That's beaucoup bizarro," said Carreyn. "I thought Hutch hated Charlie."

"And in reverse," added Amy.

"Yeah," I agreed, watching Hutch and Charlie get into it. "Weird."

"Hey, Pais, good luck!" Bean chirped as she and Cate walked by on their way into the gym. "I'll be vibing you positive energy." She wiggled her fingers at me.

I just laughed. What a goof.

Cate stopped and gave me a quick hug. "You know I love Miss UnPleasant, but I still like you as a friend. Kick Hutch's butt for us, okay?"

"Looking forward to it," I said, smiling.

Mr. Eggertson and a few other teachers were trying to herd all of us into the gym. He smiled at me and tapped his chest three times. That was Drama class code for "feel the emotion behind the words."

I tapped three times back.

I kind of hoped I'd see Jen walking in, but it didn't happen.

"Come on people, take your seats," Mr. Canfield barked into the microphone. "We've got a lot of speeches to get through."

All of the candidates running for sophomore class office were seated in a row of chairs in front of the bleachers. I was between LG Wong and Hutch. Ugh. The gym was buzzing. It was so noisy, I couldn't think—which was probably a good thing because thinking made me more nervous, and more nervous made me have to pee.

I turned around and waved at Amy and Carreyn sitting in the front row of the bleachers, then scanned the crowd for Jen. I finally spotted her a few rows up, but she was all caught up in a conversation with Eric Sobel. Fortunately, Bean was sending me more positive vibes with her wiggling fingers.

Clint Bedard was practically the last person into the gym. He probably got busted trying to skip the assembly. I watched him climb up the side of the bleachers and squeeze in next to Cate. He caught my eye and gave me a clipped military salute. Whoa. Certain parts of my body did the wave. God, how does he do that to me?

I had practiced my speech so many times that I basically had it memorized, but I still wanted to be able to look at it just in case I had a total brain freeze. Even though I felt solid about my message and my jokes, I still had butterflies in my butt. And my sweaty palms kept rolling my speech up into a little paper baton.

I leaned down the row of jumpy, twitching candidates and mouthed "Good luck!" to Charlie Dodd. He looked particularly uncomfortable and winced more than nodded in my direction. Why did he have a laptop on his knees? Oh, I hoped he wasn't going to do some obnoxious flow-chart presentation with his speech.

I snuck a peek at LG Wong's notes on her lap. They looked like some math equation. She probably *does* dream in numbers. Then she turned to me. "Don't you just love the democratic process? I think I'm gonna puke."

"Me too," I said with a nervous giggle. That was funny. Was LG Wong funny? I couldn't figure out why *she* was nervous about her speech. No one was even running against her. She could stand up there and do an interpretive dance of the Pythagorean Theorem and win.

Just then, Mr. Canfield stepped back up to the podium and explained how it all would work. The candidates for secretary would go first, then the treasurers, then the VPs, and then the presidents. Great. I had plenty of time to make myself queasy.

Kirby Scarborough went first. I really tried to listen, but she lost me when she started connecting her childhood butterfly collection to her being a social butterfly now, and somehow that made her the most qualified to be secretary.

Charlie went next, but he left the laptop on his chair. Was he going to be the AV guy for Hutch's speech? That was weird. Why would he do that?

But Charlie was great. His entire speech, he acted like he was running for secretary of state instead of secretary of the sophomore class. He talked about his plan to negotiate a peace alliance between the sophomore and junior classes and his desire to spend as much time in face-to-face talks with Poms and BPs as possible because popularity was definitely a foreign policy to him. And his big idea was to impose economic sanctions on the freshmen by forcing them to pay a toll every time they walked through sophomore hall. It was good. Everyone laughed. I was definitely voting for him.

Keep it funny. Keep it funny. Keep it funny. I exhaled deep breaths, trying to pay attention to the other candidates' speeches. But I couldn't stop rehearsing mine over and over. I was stuck in my head—and there was no indie-groovy soundtrack playing this time. It was more like fingernails on a chalkboard.

Finally—thank God—it was time for the presidential candidates. I snapped to and sat up straight in my chair.

"The first of our two candidates for sophomore class president hardly needs an introduction." Mr. Canfield chuckled, smacking his fish lips together. "I'm sure you all know Peter Hutchison! Come on up, Hutch!"

The audience clapped and whistled and cheered. Canfield clapped like a total suck-up.

Hutch bounded up the stairs, pretending to trip at the top step, which got everyone laughing. Crap. Physical comedy. Everyone loves physical comedy. He stepped behind the podium and launched into his speech, raising both arms.

"Friends, Hornets, countrymen, lend me your ears!" He looked down at his notes. "Whoa! Wrong speech. I bought that one online last week but it seemed a little too old-school."

People laughed. Not me.

"Seriously, I'm running for president for three simple reasons—all things I truly believe in and genuinely value. Leadership, scholarship, and chip and dip!"

More laughing.

Hey! I shot Charlie an evil look. That was *my* line! He didn't look at me. What was going on?

"Okay, I guess that's four reasons, but you get the idea." Hutch chuckled.

"I'm a leader on and off the field, I'm a serious student—even though I don't always act like it outside of class, *and* I throw killer parties!" People laughed again. "So if I am elected class president, each and every one of you will be invited to my next party!"

Everyone went nuts at that one, whistling and whooping. Except for me.

"Because bringing people together is one of my favorite extracurricular activities. Know what I'm saying?" He nodded with sort of a creepy grin.

More laughing and whistling.

"Okay, okay, but I'm not up here because of me—I'm up here because of *you*. I want to work for you! I love this school and I want to make this class the best sophomore class in history! And I can do it. I'm a guy with connections and I can get things done. Trust me with the awesome responsibility of being your class president, and I promise you, I will not drop the ball." He laughed at his own bad joke. "I'll totally be open to your ideas, your suggestions, and your propositions—especially if you're a really hot babe."

Laughs, then a few of boos, and then more freakin' laughs!

"Go with a proven winner, go with Hutch—I'm open!" He faked catching a football and doing a touchdown spike on the stage. "Thank you! Thank you!"

The audience clapped and cheered.

What an idiot. What a cocky jerk. I had this thing in the bag.

Hutch was beaming as he hopped down the steps. He gave a few people in the front row of the bleachers knuckle knocks and then strutted back over to his seat and plopped down next to me, flashing a big ol' winner's smile. Then he laughed, like he was in on some private joke.

"And now our second and final candidate for sophomore class president, Paisley Hanover!" Mr. Canfield clapped politely.

I confidently climbed the steps to the stage while the audience clapped and cheered. Of course, my friends were hooting and whistling and screaming like rowdy lunatics. I had a hard time un-smiling as I flattened out my speech on the podium.

I was just about to begin when Hutch hopped back up onstage and grabbed the mic off the stand in front of me. "Before you get started, Paisley, a few of us varsity jerks have a special treat for you."

He turned to the audience. "I think you're all *really* gonna like this."

CHAPTER FORTY-FIVE

The audience was suddenly going nuts. People were talking, then booing at Hutch and yelling.

"Sit down!"

"You had your turn!"

"Come on, man! Give her the mic!"

What was going *on?* I turned to Canfield and spread my hands, like *do something!* He stood up but looked as surprised as I was.

"Hutch, sit down!" Canfield yelled over the crowd. "You gave your speech! We're on a schedule here. This is Paisley's time."

I tried to grab the mic back, but Hutch held it up over his head. So then I tried to be cool, acting like maybe I had a clue what was going on.

The audience started stomping and chanting. *"Paisley! Paisley! Paisley!"* The gym filled with this deafening, chaotic roar. It was pretty cool, but I was so pissed at Hutch, it was hard to enjoy the moment.

Hutch seemed to be pleading his case to Canfield, but I couldn't hear a thing he was saying. Canfield just kept shaking his head.

Then Hutch turned away from Canfield. "Charlie, roll video!" he yelled into the mic, pointing at Charlie Dodd. "Roll it! Now!" Charlie looked completely terrified.

The audience was still chanting and stomping. *"Paisley! Paisley! Paisley!"*

And then everyone went totally silent. Hutch and Canfield turned to look up at the screen behind me.

Okay, seriously. What. Was. Going. On?!! I traced the cord from the projector to . . . Charlie Dodd's laptop?!

No. No. This couldn't be happening. Charlie Dodd?!! What—? Unless . . . Were they showing that stupid Spastic Jazz Hands video on YouTube? Oh, please. That was so old. Get over it, people. I looked at Eric Sobel, frowning. He saw me and quickly looked away.

I refused to turn around. It was so stupid. I couldn't believe that Hutch could get away with this, or that Charlie was in on it. Fine. I'd just stand there until it was over and then calmly start my fabulous speech.

I watched the audience. Everyone was looking at the screen behind me. It was actually kind of cool. In their faces, I saw confusion, fascination, boredom, curiosity. Some people were shaking their heads.

Wait. Why wasn't I hearing the humiliating, ridiculous rap that went with the video?

This tangy, sour, metallic taste started bubbling up from my stomach. But the voice in my head kept me focused. *I will not turn around, I will not turn around, I will not turn around—*

I couldn't help turning just a little, just enough to see Hutch looking up at the screen. He was sporting a big ol' smile.

I will not turn around, I will not turn around, I will not let Hutch screw with my confidence! I turned back to face the audience.

Cate and Bean and Clint were all staring up at the screen with confused, curious expressions. Amy and Carreyn were leaning forward, their mouths hanging open. Jen held her hand up to her mouth, watching in total fascination. Eric Sobel looked like he was in physical pain.

Don't look. Don't turn around. Just keep breathing. Just keep breathing. Don't look. Don't turn around. Just keep breathing. Just keep breathing. Whatever it is, it'll all be over soon.

Suddenly, the audience erupted. "No way!" someone shouted. People were gasping and pointing at the screen, yells, boos, hisses, laughter. "Oh my *God!*" Carreyn screamed. Everyone in the gym, even the teachers watching from the side, started talking all at once.

"What?!"

"No!"

"Oooooh!"

"Rewind!"

I couldn't stand it anymore. I turned and faced the screen.

It was . . . It was hard to be sure what it was at first. It looked like the back of my head and part of one shoulder. And there was a little red flashing graphics arrow, pointing at a few barely legible words on the computer monitor in front of me.

I tilted my head to read them.

Big kiss, class dismissed!

Miss UnPleasant

Oh, God. No.

The audience was going crazy, hissing and booing and screaming.

I watched the image of myself peek over one shoulder, looking utterly guilty, and type a little more. Then I stood up from the computer, looking quite pleased with myself, and stuffed my notebook into the back of my jeans. I turned to leave. But then I tensed—you could see me do it. I looked around furtively, like a criminal. And I froze. You could see my eyes looking off beyond the camera. My face slowly got really huge as the camera zoomed in, giving everyone a nice view up one nostril. It stayed like that for a second before suddenly pulling back to show me all bug-eyed. Then I smiled this weird smile, shrugged once, and ran off. The screen went dark.

There was some laughter, some shouts, more chatter, more confusion.

"Fellow classmates!" Hutch boomed into the mic. "I give you . . . Miss *UnPleasant!*" He gestured grandly toward me, then slipped the mic back on the stand. He clapped, nodding at me with a huge crap-eating grin on his face, and hopped off the stage.

My heart pounded and my ears got all hot. I felt my nose break out in a cold sweat. And I swear, it felt like my stomach had shot out my butt. The audience kept blasting me with a strange mix of nasty sounds—mostly boos and angry hoots and heckles, some stomping and laughter and yelling, and a few lonely cheers and claps. It even smelled really nasty. Maybe it was just my BO, but the whole place suddenly reeked of teen revenge.

Mr. Canfield glared at me. I think his head was actually vibrating.

Everyone was talking and shouting and making these weird, angry faces. My ears rang. I breathed fast and hard. And even though everyone seemed to be saying something, the only words I could hear crashing around the gym were:

"Paisley Hanover! Miss UnPleasant?"

"Paisley Hanover? Miss UnPleasant?!"

"Paisley Hanover! Miss UnPleasant!!!"

It was like being trapped in the spin cycle of some nightmarish washing machine. I wanted to run off the stage and out the door and never come back *ever*. But I couldn't move. I started feeling dizzy. Soon I was praying that I'd just pass out or die. Then this would end and I could be carried off to the nurse's office on a stretcher.

Mr. Canfield had stepped up to the microphone. He was trying to quiet everyone down. "People, that's enough! That's enough! Okay, okay, okay! Let's give Paisley a chance to speak." The room got quiet. The only sound left in the whole gym was this gigantic, excruciating silence.

Canfield turned to me. "Paisley? Do you have something you'd like to say to us?"

Um. I stood there blinking at the audience. My head

really hurt. Then I finally realized that the only way to end my pain was to start my speech. So I gripped both sides of the podium and looked back out at the crowd, searching for a friendly face. Some were mocking me, but most looked like they couldn't wait to kill me with their bare hands. The look on Jen's face actually made me want to kill *myself* with my bare hands.

But then I saw Bean beaming at me with a big, proud, goobery grin. And I remembered the advice my dad had given me at the breakfast table: "Even if you make a mistake or forget to say something, no one will notice but you—so just keep on going with a smile on your face."

So I smiled. But my mouth was so dry that my upper lip stuck to my front teeth. I casually tried to un-stick my lip while smoothing my speech out on the podium.

"Hi," I squeaked into the microphone. Whoa. I cleared my throat. "Hi! I'm Paisley Hanover and I'm running for class president."

Silence.

"Good thing I have a big mouth, because I have some really big ideas for you."

More silence.

"Doesn't a hula hoop–athon fund raiser for homecoming sound like fun?"

Nothing.

"Or how about a sophomore hall clean-up-party-slash-scavenger-hunt?"

Silence.

Oh crap.

"I'll bet you're gonna love this idea"—I really tried to sell it—"Smoothie Tuesdays!"

A few snickers followed by another long silence.

Help. Help! HELP! I'm dying up here.

I looked down at my speech, trying to flatten the curled edges, and skipped ahead to the next paragraph. "Have you ever wondered if your biggest embarrassment could turn into your biggest break? I sure have." I jumped out from behind the podium and spastic jazzed the crowd.

The audience groaned and hissed.

OMG. OMG. OMG. OMG! I'm screwed. I'm so totally screwed.

Some guy yelled, "You got a new biggest embarrassment, Hanover!"

Sure, *everyone* laughed at that. Ha ha ha.

I looked down at my typed speech. "Um . . . Have you ever felt frustrated because you couldn't find Pirate's Booty or . . . or other tasty snacks in the . . . "

I took a deep breath and crumpled my speech into a tight sweaty wad. For a while, I just stood there, feeling everyone's eyes on me. Waiting. Waiting. And then . . .

And then I kind of lost it.

"Surprise!" I spastic jazzed the crowd. "Yep. Yep." I nodded, taking it all in. "I am Miss UnPleasant."

A few people whistled and yelled not-so-nice things.

"Yes, me. I am scary, bad-ass Miss UnPleasant . . . *Boo!*" I shouted. "Big kiss! Class dismissed!"

I started to giggle. All of a sudden, this felt like the most hilarious, absurd moment of my life.

"I didn't plan this. I mean, who could plan this? No one!" I grabbed the mic off the stand and walked around the stage like Oprah, only I was giggling way more. I jumped out at the audience again. "*Boo!*" Then I went into absolute hysterics, laughing so hard I could barely get the words out. "No one could. No one would! I was just . . . crazy one night. *Crazy pissed off!*" I let my smile fade. "It just happened . . . one Friday night . . . It happened by accident." I stared out at the crowd. A lot of people were looking really sorry for me. But I didn't care.

I realized then that I was holding a microphone, on a stage in front of almost four hundred students—and I could say *anything*.

"Okay, people—listen up!" I snapped my fingers. "Let's all move our brains into a circle!" I walked to the front of the stage. "Have you ever seen something go down at this school, something *really* ugly, and you wanted to do something to stop it, but you didn't? And you know you only wimped out because you didn't want to be the quote-unquote *uncool one* or break some unspoken social rule?"

Nobody said a word. I sat down on the front edge of the stage and looked right at Hutch. He didn't flinch.

"I have," I said. "And I felt like total crap. And I . . . I just couldn't shake it. I was pissed! So I started typing. And I typed and typed and typed all night. I know, I know, you're thinking, big deal, Paisley, so you're bitter and you couldn't sleep. You should've taken an Ambien or one of your mom's Valium, but don't trash our beloved school!" I thought about it for a few seconds. "Yeah, I dunno. I was surprised too. But I didn't want to sleep—I wanted to *wake up!*

"Because what is up with all these *stupid* rules?! I am *so* sick of them! I am *so* sick of who's in and who's out, who it's okay to talk to and what it's okay to wear, who you can date and who you can't date, who gets to sit where at lunch and what classes make you cool and what classes make you a geek or a freak or a loser." I took a breath. "God, aren't *any* of you sick of this crap too?"

Some scattered claps and cheers.

"Who even makes these rules up anyway—and why do we *all* follow them?"

More solitary claps and cheers from various pockets of the crowd. Oh, thank God—Eric Sobel was clapping. Amy and Bean both screamed, "Yeah!" And LG Wong let rip a series of loud whistles. I liked that girl more and more.

I looked down at my hands while the smattering of clapping faded. Wow. I've got to stop biting my cuticles.

"So, why am up here?" I stared at the row of candidates sitting in the front, each looking at me completely baffled and/or disturbed. Even Hutch. "Oh, right. Yeah. Would I make a good class president? I dunno. I really don't." I shrugged. "All I know is that I care about this school and I think about this stuff. And I think about everyone, really—not just the popular people, or the unpopular people."

If this had been my Academy Awards acceptance speech, the music would have started right about now. But it wasn't, and it didn't. So I stood up and kept talking.

"Popular. What does that even mean? All I know is that I don't want it. I don't *want* to be more popular. I just want to be more *me*. I'm a *closet weirdo!*" I shouted.

A lot of people laughed.

"Sure, I can pass for normal, but why should I want to? Why should I *have* to? What is normal, anyway?" I looked out at the crowd. "Does anybody out there hear what I'm saying? Is *anyone* getting this?"

A small burst of hoots and applause.

"I don't just want to go to school every day. I want to go to my *life*. And if that makes me *unnn* . . . cool or *unnn* . . . popular, well then, good! Because some days I feel really *unnn* . . . *every-thing*. I mean, I can't be the only one, can I?" I scanned the entire audience. Uh-oh. Maybe I can be. I hadn't thought of that.

"Come on, people! I've *seen* you over the last couple weeks! I *know*. If you've ever felt a little *un*normal or *un*sane or *un*discovered or *un*cool, *un*perfect, *un*apologetic, *un*decided, *un*fashionable, *un*forgettable, *un*predictable, *un*usual, *un*whatever, then maybe you can relate to why I wrote that stuff! Maybe you can even relate to *me*. Un *is* way more fun!"

The gym was totally silent again.

Crap. I seemed to be going backward.

I stood there in the middle of the stage and looked down at my feet. Oh well. I tried. I should just end it. "Okay, well, that's all I have to say." I started to put the mic back into the slot on the stand, when I realized something and grabbed it back. "But whether I'm Miss UnPleasant or Paisley Hanover, I'd vote for Paisley. And I hope you will too."

The crowd started to grumble and rumble and gurgle and churn. A few people started clapping. A few more started standing up. Then Bean and Clint and Amy and a bunch of Library Girls and AV Guys started yelling, *"Paisley! Paisley! Paisley!"* And— OMG, I couldn't believe this! More and more people stood up, and then this whole chunk of the audience was clapping and cheering, and chanting. I couldn't even understand what they were saying at first. Then it came clear, and I smiled the hugest, most goobery smile I've ever smiled in my life.

"Un! Un! Un! Un! Un! Un! Un!"

Even some of the teachers joined in. What *was* this? Like some crazy teen movie?! I just stood there looking out at the crowd, completely amazed.

Before I could think what to do next, Canfield grabbed the microphone from me and said something about how everyone should be sure to vote tomorrow and get hustling to seventh period so classes could start on time. And then the assembly was over.

I went straight for Charlie Dodd. He looked like he was going to crap in his pants.

"Et tu, Charlé?" I asked coldly. He tried to laugh, but he

couldn't even convince himself it was funny. "You suck." I turned and walked back to my chair to get my stuff.

A lot of people came rushing up to me, mostly people I had never really talked to before. And they said all these things to me all at once. But the one comment I'll never forget was Mandy Mindel saying "Thank you." That's all she said, then ducked out of the crowd and out the door.

Bean gave me a great big hunched-over hug. "I knew you were a closet weirdo! I knew that's why I liked you!" she squealed. "I'm a closet weirdo too!"

"No. You're just a weirdo!" And we both laughed.

Amy stood a few feet away, watching some Uns swarm around me. When things calmed down, she finally came over. "I can't believe it was you all along. It seems so obvious now. Who else could have known all those things?"

I didn't know what to say to her.

"I'm really mad at you," she said.

"Sorry."

"No, I'm mad because you never *talked* to me about this stuff before! I can totally relate."

"You can?"

"You have no idea. And you're a hella good liar. That's kinda scary, actually."

But a lot of people kept their distance. Carreyn and Jen stood back with their arms crossed, watching Amy and me, and obviously dishing. Eric Sobel was getting into it with Hutch, who looked like he was trying to explain himself. And Cate hadn't moved from her spot on the bleachers. She was the only person still sitting there. Clint was long gone. I waved to her. But she didn't wave back. She just stared at me, upset or mad or disappointed. I couldn't tell.

I walked over to Eric and Hutch. "Hey Eric, what did you think?" I asked, buzzing with adrenaline.

Eric turned from me to Hutch and back to me. He seemed embarrassed. "Not really sure what I think yet . . . But the speech was pretty cool. Nice save."

"Thanks." I slid my gaze over to Hutch. "Thanks again for the sticky bun, Hutch," I gushed. "It was *crazy* good just like you said." I smiled and turned to go. "And great speech!" I called over my shoulder.

I was headed for the gym doors—and that's when Canfield tapped me on the shoulder.

"Meet me in my office, Paisley. Now."

CHAPTER FORTY-SIX

On the way to Canfield's office, people were looking at me really weird. Some kids smiled and stared, like we were in on some geeky secret. A few flashed me the UnPop Power fists with big grins. But others acted like I'd just turned them in for cheating on their American Lit test. It was a rush having this UNderground connection with so many people I really didn't know. But I also felt exposed. Okay, totally naked— like not-even-wearing-a-tuba naked.

When I got to Canfield's office, he was talking on the phone. He waved me in, so I sat down in the low, wobbly Fink Fast chair and waited for my butt to start sweating, wondering what brilliant clichés were going to come out of his fish lips this time. Finally he hung up.

He looked at me, shaking his head. "That was quite a show, Paisley."

I smiled. Was he serious?

"Very *un*pleasant to watch."

Duh. Of course not.

"I called you in here to let you know we'll be reprinting the ballot for sophomore class elections—and your name won't be on it."

What?! I was shocked. "Why not?"

"Frankly, you amaze me. How anyone could write such ugly, mean-spirited words about our exemplary school and student body and then expect to represent this school and its students is beyond me." He was cold. "You have really disappointed me, Paisley. And you've disrespected this school and your classmates. I'm sorry. But you are clearly *not* leadership material. I'm terminating your candidacy as of right now."

My mouth fell open. "You can't do that! I have all the signatures required to run." I felt my nose break into a sweat.

"Oh yes, I can. The administration has the right to deny any student running for class office at Pleasant Hill High. Check the school bylaws."

"But I *am* leadership material! Didn't the audience at speeches prove that? I mean, don't you think it takes a real leader to challenge things, and . . . and inspire people, and point out what's wrong with something and try to make it right?"

He gave me his big fish-lipped smile. "I didn't read a lot of hope in your Miss UnPleasant negative propaganda."

I wasn't exactly sure what propaganda meant, but I sure wasn't going to let him know. I'd look it up later. "It's not propaganda. I think it's called satire, Mr. Canfield. You know, using irony and sarcasm to make a point?"

"You can call it whatever you want, but you're off the ballot. And another thing." He pointed at me, hairy nostrils flaring. "You won't be writing anything ever again by Miss UnPleasant. Got it?" He waved me out of his office. "Ba-bye."

I stormed down the hall. What a pig. Just because he couldn't stand being criticized, he was going to shut *me* down? I didn't think so. Check the school bylaws? Yeah, I thought I would.

I marched straight to the library and up to the front desk.

"Ms. Whit, can you help me find a copy of the Pleasant Hill High bylaws? I need to see them right now." I pounded on the countertop. My heart was thumping hard and fast in my chest, and I could feel the sweat on my nose cooling in the air-conditioned library air.

"Paisley, what's wrong. Are you okay?" Ms. Whit asked, looking alarmed.

"No! I'm not okay! Mr. Canfield just told me I that can't run for class president because I'm not leadership material! He's reprinting the ballot—and my name won't be on it!"

"All right, all right, calm down."

"And that means Hutch will automatically win even though he's a bully and a liar and a cheat! Is that what Canfield considers leadership material?" I was nearly panting, I was so mad.

"Paisley," Ms. Whit whispered. "Library voice please. Let's go into my office."

She closed her door. "Why would Mr. Canfield not let you run for class office?"

"Because I'm Miss UnPleasant."

"What?" She suddenly looked very excited. "*You* are Miss UnPleasant?"

I nodded.

She covered her mouth, then laughed, and I mean laughed hard. "Right on, sister! You're a little radical trapped in the body of a popular girl. Cool. Good for you for stirring the pot. Good for you for making people think."

"Really? Thanks. I guess. People are really pissed, though. Not just Canfield." Then I told her everything Canfield had said to me.

Ms. Whit stood up. "Wait right here."

I had never thought of myself as a radical before. But Miss UnPleasant is definitely a radical, and she came out of my brain, right? So part of me must be a radical. Why are there so many parts of me? It's so confusing. There's the popular me, the unpopular me, the rah-rah, the closet weirdo, the radical, the girl who just wants to be liked, the girl who likes Clint, the girl who likes Eric. Who was the real me anyway?

Ms. Whit came back in carrying a thick binder and started flipping through it. "Okay, here it is. Class elections."

I sat up eagerly watching her read. She shook her head slowly. "Hmm. He's right. Damn! Oops." She looked up at me. "Sorry. The bylaws state that the administration has the right to terminate the candidacy of any student deemed to be an inappropriate student leader. Inappropriate is defined as unlawful, negligent, below a C minus average, or inclined to influence other students in a negative manner."

Ergh! I clenched my fists super tight. I was so angry, and—and I hated that Canfield was doing this to me! I hated feeling helpless. Then I burst into tears—not because I was sad but because I was furious, and indignant, and, well, PMS-ing a little. It's true.

"I'm so sorry, Paisley."

"It's not fair! I've worked hard for this and now . . . " I blubbered a little more. "I can't believe Hutch is going to win all because of Miss UnPleasant! He's such a jerk. He's the whole reason I wrote the column in the first place. And talk about unbelievable? Miss UnPleasant has a thriving write-in campaign for president— which is completely ridiculous! And now *I* can't even run!"

Ms. Whit looked up from the binder, like she had just thought of something really interesting. She quickly scanned the bylaws again. "That's it!"

"What's it?" I whined.

She jumped up out of her chair. "Paisley, you have to launch your own write-in campaign. The bylaws don't say a word about write-in candidates and who may or may not be eligible."

"Really?" I blew my nose. "Really?!" I started to feel a lot better. "But the election's tomorrow!"

"You'd better get going. You've got a lot to do!"

"Yeah, I do!" I was feeling pumped up again.

Ms. Whit left me in her office so I could pull myself together and formulate a plan. What was I going to do? And who could I get to help me? And more importantly, would anyone even vote for me now that they knew the real me?

I texted my mom. I had to get out of there and away from school, fast.

NQA shtl pls!

She called me right back. Mom's not the best texter.

"Horrible," I said into the phone. "Yes, please! Right now. I'll be by the vending machines. Thanks, Mom."

I ran to my locker to grab my stuff. It was almost the end of seventh period, and I really didn't want to be caught in the halls when the bell rang. I opened my locker, grabbed my bag, and shoved in a few books—not that I'd have any time for homework tonight. And that's when I saw it.

Another locker stalker note.

I looked around, really fast, checking both ways down the hall. Then I opened it quickly.

I'D VOTE 4 ANYONE BUT YOU.
YOU'RE UNDERLIEVABLE.

CHAPTER FORTY-SEVEN

What?! OMG. My locker stalker had turned on me! And he was obviously a sophomore. *And* he must have just stuffed this in here!

I looked into all the classroom windows across the lawn to see if anyone was spying on me, but I didn't see anything suspicious. The bell was going to ring any minute. So I just stuffed the note in my pocket, slammed my locker shut, and took off jogging down the hall with my bag bouncing awkwardly against my hip.

On my way down the main hall to the vending machines, you'll never guess who I ran into coming out of Canfield's office.

Peter Hutchison.

He had this big dumb-ass grin on his face. Canfield must have just told him that my name was not going to be on the ballot.

"Hey Paisley, I heard you're history."

I stopped. "Oh yeah? I'm a lot of things, Hutch—but I am *not* history."

"Come on, Pais, don't be mad. Look, I'm ... I'm sorry. Really. I didn't know *this* would happen. Come on, peace!" He threw open his arms, like he wanted to hug me. "Share the sugar."

I snorted out my mouth like a horse. "What?! Yeah right. Like that's ever gonna happen."

"Don't be mad. Come on. Don't be mad 'cause I'm gonna win. I can't help it, dude. It's genetic."

I just laughed at him. He was such a clueless social loser that I almost felt sorry for him. But no. I was too pissed. "*Dude*, I'm not mad—I'm motivated. So watch out."

I left him standing there trying to figure out what I meant.

I guess he couldn't think of anything smart to say because he yelled after me, "Are you just PMS-ing again?"

I sat on a wall at the front of the school waiting for my mom, scribbling in my notebook.

I am not history.
I am *not* history!
I am NOT history!
I am not a loser.
I am not giving up.
I am not going away.

And I felt really good, like superhero good, so I kept scribbling in this frustrated manic rant that Miss UnPleasant would have been proud to call her own.

I am not who I was last year.
I am not who I was last <u>week</u>.
I am not a rah-rah.
I am not my reputation.
I am not who the vice principal thinks I am.
I am not perfect.
I am not <u>trying</u> to be perfect.
I am not afraid to say no.
I am <u>not</u> just PMS-ing.
I am not kidding.
I am not falling for that.
I am me! (If only I knew who that really was!)

On the way home, I started telling Mom about my disastrous speech and everything else that had happened, but I didn't get very far. Mom totally freaked.

"*You're* Miss UnPleasant? No." She practically stopped the car. "No!"

I nodded at her, like *Yes I am! I just said so!*

"*You* wrote those biting, sarcastic, popularity-bashing columns?"

"Mo-om, whatever, yeah! I just said that!"

"Paisley Hanover." She sounded seriously stern, like I was in big trouble. But then she started to giggle and she kept giggling like she was about to lose it." This is going to be a little embarrassing for me."

"Embarrassing for *you*? Mom, this isn't about *you*! And by the way, I'm proud I wrote those columns. Miss UnPleasant is way cooler than I'll ever be."

"Oh honey, no! I'm proud you wrote them too. Really, I'm impressed—surprised, but impressed. It's just that . . ." She started to laugh again. "It's just that I've said some rather pointed things to a few parents about Miss UnPleasant and her obviously rotten parents."

"What?! You've been talking about her? I mean me?" I started laughing a little too. It all seemed so surreal. "Saying like what?"

"Like . . ." She turned to me, making one of her funny whoops-I-really-blew-it faces. "I said she's clearly an intelligent but extremely angry girl who needs therapy immediately."

My mouth dropped open. "Mo-om! That's so harsh."

"I didn't know it was *you*." She shrugged. She looked at me all sweet and loving. "Honey, *do* you need therapy? If you do, it's perfectly okay. You know how I feel about therapy. It's always better to ask for help than to suffer in sil—"

"Mo-om, no!" I rolled my eyes. But then I thought about it for a second and got very serious. "Well, after today, maybe I do need therapy—I need *speech* therapy!"

We both howled at that stinker. Mom loves bad puns almost as much as I do.

"What did your friends think when they found out?"

"Well . . . I don't know really. Bean thought it was cool, and

Amy, but everyone else . . . not so cool. No one wants to talk to me. I guess I'm officially unpopular with almost all my friends."

"Oh honey, I'm sorry. But you can't always be who your friends want you to be." She squeezed my leg.

We drove on in silence for a while and I thought about what Mom had just said. It finally hit me. As much as I wanted everyone to like me, I realized that everyone wasn't going to like the *real* me. I loved my friends and I needed my friends, but I was never going to be just who they wanted me to be. And that was okay. I mean, no one was who they seemed to be on the surface. Nobody was the person they wore to school every day.

I looked down at my notebook in my lap and put a big bold X through the E. That was the moment my notebook became my *not book*. Totally *not* what it seemed—just like me.

I opened it to the page of my "I am not" rants, adding:

I am not just who my friends want me to be.

"So, Mom? Did you ever think you'd have an unpopular little radical trapped in the body of a popular girl?"

She laughed. I love it when I can make Mom laugh.

"Actually, yes, even if you do scare some people. But Pais, look on the bright side. You know what? Our gossip street-value just went way, way up. We are gossip rich!" she screamed, honking the horn like we had just won the lottery. I slid down in my seat, trying to hide. My mom can be so over-the-top weird sometimes.

When we got home, I went straight to up my room, closed the door, and turned on some music. Part of me wanted to curl up with Dyson and listen to music till I fell asleep. It had been an off-the-chart, Stressy-Bessy day. I was fried, but I knew I needed a plan. I needed a strategy. I needed to make a lot of noise in a short period of time and I had no idea how. So I sat down at my computer and started typing ideas, anything that came to mind.

But suddenly, it's like my phone wouldn't stop buzzing.

Amy texted.

Whr ru?

I didn't reply.

Eric texted.

Listnin spt 6:30? Nd 2 tlk

I didn't reply—but I wanted to.

Jen texted.

Cnt bleev u did dis 2 me! hu RU Nyway?

Wow. I thought I was dreaming when I got that one. And no, I didn't reply. It made me feel so sad. I was starting to wonder if Jen and I would ever be real friends again. But I couldn't think about it right now.

I started typing a bunch of ideas:

Locker stuffers telling people to write me in.

New signs?

Name tag stickers?

Something to make a lot of noise?

I dug through the drawers of my desk and night table, looking for anything that might help. Safety pins, binder clips, paper clips, nail polish, a mini harmonica. What could I use to reach four hundred people that I already had at my disposal? I found a plastic whistle. That could help. No. I grabbed the wad of sticky notes. These could work.

I knew I definitely needed a good locker stuffer. So I started thinking. What do I say? What do I say?! WHAT DO I SAY?! Just keep it simple, just keep it clear, and don't sound like a bitter loser. I started typing.

VOTE PAISLEY HANOVER!

I'm off the ballot but I'm not out of the race—
I'm still spastic jazzed for the job!

Please WRITE IN Paisley Hanover
for sophomore class president.

I hit SAVE and transferred the file to my jump drive.

Dyson had hopped up onto my lap, and I was curling my fingers under his neck, getting his power-purr going. And then I felt his name tag. I pulled it up and looked at it. Hmm . . . I could make a bunch of these tonight at Pet Stuff.

Then I speed-texted a message:

Realy nd yr hlp W campain!
Sofmr hall @ 9:00 2nite. Pls?

I sent it to Bean, Cate, Amy, Carreyn, Eric, and Clint. It

would be interesting to see who, if anyone, showed up. Really interesting.

Mom and Dad were way into the idea of my write-in campaign.

"Glen Canfield is a boob." Dad looked up from the mail he was opening. "He always has been. I know, I went to high school with him."

"Glen? Gross." It creeped me out to think that Mr. Canfield was a real person with a first name.

I explained my plan to them and asked if they would drive me around, then over to school to stuff lockers. Dad couldn't wait. He changed his clothes and came downstairs wearing jeans and a black turtleneck. He pulled a black knit cap down really low and slipped on sunglasses.

"Dad, what are you doing?"

"I'm driving the getaway car, right?"

"You are so embarrassing. I'm driving with Mom."

"Oh no, no. I'm staying home. Someone has to be here when you call from the police station."

"Come on, Viv. We're not doing anything illegal, just making a little adventure out of it."

She shook her head. "No thanks. You kids have fun!"

Dad drove me to Kinkos and I had them print out five hundred flyers on bright pink paper. Then we drove straight to Pet Stuff, where I made twelve round, pink dog tags. The machine engraved this in each tag:

I'D VOTE
FOR
PAISLEY

Wow. They looked pretty cool. These were for my core supporters—whoever agreed to pass out flyers at school tomorrow.
But first, we had to get through tonight.

CHAPTER FORTY-EIGHT

When Dad and I got to school, it was quiet and dark. We parked at the far edge of the parking lot, then made our way up to sophomore hall. Amy and Bean and Eric were already there, standing in the shadows talking. I could have screamed, I was so happy to see them.

"Hey you guys!" I gave each of them a hug. "Thanks for showing up!" OMG! Did I just hug Eric Sobel?! I did!

My dad whispered, "Shhhhhhh. This is a commando mission." My dad could be such a goober.

I gathered everyone into a little pod. "I need your help," I whispered. "I've been canned. Canfield took my name off the ballot for class president because of Miss UnPleasant."

"No way!" said Amy and Bean.

"Way." I handed each of them a stack of pink flyers, and they started reading. "I have a ton of these. So we need to get a flyer into every sophomore locker."

"Cool." Eric nodded.

Amy joined in, "Write on, Miss UnPaisley!"

Bean gave me another hug. "Yes! Power to the UnPops! We're bringing Peter Hutchison down!"

But just as we were about to spread out and start stuffing lockers, there was this loud noise. It came screaming up the hall. So much for our commando mission.

Clint Bedard on his motorcycle. He screeched to a stop. We all stood there a little shocked as he got off his bike and pulled off his helmet.

"Hey, sorry I'm late." He smiled at me, then noticed Eric Sobel. He ran one hand through his hair, looking a little perturbed.

I was speechless to see him there at all.

Fortunately, Dad jumped in. "No problem. We're glad you made it." He patted Clint on the back. What? No! "Right on! Power to the UnPops," Dad cheered the group. OMG. I couldn't wait until I got my license.

Clint read the flyer, digging it. "I love an anti-authority chick. Yeah. Let's make this happen."

Eric Sobel gave Clint a cold, scrutinizing stare, like he was eyeing his competition. But he didn't say a word.

We spread out, going up and down sophomore hall, stuffing every locker with my pink flyers. Little conversations kept suddenly igniting and ending.

"Can I talk to you?" Eric asked me after a little while. "Look. Sorry about the video. Sorry about what happened at the assembly."

"You were involved in that?"

"I was before I knew it was you. And then when I found out, I was a little freaked. But the whole thing snowballed out of control. I didn't want it to go down like that, really. But Hutch is a stubborn bastard. So, you know, I just wanted to say sorry."

Wow. "Thanks." I'd have to process all this later. There was way too much to do right now. But I smiled at Eric Sobel like a total goober.

Amy came up to me. "Oh my God," she whispered. "Jen's mortified and beyond mad. She said you really embarrassed her and trashed her in front of all her Pop friends. I don't agree, but she thinks you wrote those columns just to hurt her."

"That's ridiculous!"

"I know. But everything that happens to anyone these days is all about Jen. Don't tell her I said that, okay?"

"Don't worry. We never even talk anymore." I couldn't see Amy's eyes. It was too dark. But I was pretty sure she understood why.

I walked over to the box of flyers, shaking my head. It sounded like Jen was lost in space. Or more like lost in her own head space.

Bean reached in for another bunch of flyers. "Hey Bean, have you talked to Cate?" I asked, using my library voice. "Is she mad? She looked mad after my speech."

"Well, not mad really, I don't think." Bean twirled a piece of hair over and around her index finger. "It seems more complicated than that. You should talk to her about it. I know she wants to talk to you. I just think she's still trying to figure it all out for herself."

We went back to stuffing lockers. Every time I stuffed a flyer into a locker, I thought about my locker stalker. I guess he didn't like the Miss UnPleasant side of me. That had to mean he was a Pop. Hmm . . .

When we were finally finished, Dad took us all to Millie's for a late-night breakfast. He was even cool enough to sit at the counter and pretend not to know us. Thank God.

We were all sitting in one of those big round booths, scribbling "WRITE IN PAISLEY" on bright-colored sticky notes as quickly as possible. Then I talked strategy while everyone chowed down.

"Okay, tomorrow morning, I need boots on the ground early, passing out more flyers, slapping sticky notes on lockers and poles, making noise, making sure everyone knows to write me in, and showing support." I reached into my Pet Stuff bag. "I got these for you guys." I passed out the pink dog tags. "Chokers for the girls and, I don't know, belt loop thingies for the guys?"

"Yay! I love jewelry," Bean squealed.

"Dog tags? Nice." Amy nodded. "Very Un . . . Expected."

"No way," Clint said adamantly, putting up his hands. "I'm not wearing this on my belt loop." Then he flashed that smile. "I'm wearing mine as a choker too. Chokers are sexy." He raised his eyebrows seductively.

We all laughed, except for Eric, who was staring at Clint. "Oh yeah? Dude, you think you're so bad-ass. Well, I'm wearing mine as an *earring*." He held it up to one ear, smiling like a goof, the same goof I had seen doing that crazy dance on the soccer field.

Everyone screamed at that one. I laughed so hard I thought I was going to pee. But then I reminded myself that I was sitting at a table with Eric Sobel *and* Clint Bedard—plus Amy, an old friend, and Bean, a new friend. Wow. I watched them all talking and laughing and eating while I was secretly having a warm and fuzzy, people-are-beautiful moment.

So much had already happened this year. I looked at Clint and then Eric, then back to Clint, realizing that a whole lot more was *still* going to happen this year—I just didn't know what. But I did know that whatever happened with the election tomorrow, I *was* living the best year of my life.

CHAPTER FORTY-NINE

The day of the elections was a crazy Hornets' nest of activity. Posters were up on every wall in all the halls, and everyone—especially me!—was excited, buzzing around and passing out buttons and flyers and stickers.

The ballots wouldn't officially open until the beginning of lunch. But that didn't stop us all from campaigning like overcaffeinated overachievers. Amy and Bean were great, shamelessly getting the word out about my new write-in status. Eric and Clint were much more on the down low, but still slapping sticky notes on people, working opposite ends of our class's social food chain.

I guess Eric chickened out on his earring idea, which was kind of a relief. I didn't want him to feel too weird supporting me. I just appreciated his help. I mean, he could have just hung with Hutch like all of the other Pops in our class.

But Clint was wearing his pink choker with pride. And he was right—he did look sexy.

Hutch and a bunch of his varsity jerk and Pop buddies had taken over the lawn in sophomore hall, tossing around a new load of soft and squishy, hospital-safe mini yellow footballs, all printed with "Vote Hutch—I'm open!" Jen and Carreyn were helping to pass them out and—oh my gag!—wearing tight little baby-doll T-shirts that said "I'm a Hutch's Honey" across the front. That explains why Carreyn didn't show up last night—not that I really expected her to. By the looks of it, she was probably in the bathroom all night anyway—poor Carreyn was sporting tragic Easter-egg pink hair. I guess her home-salon effort to remove her red-hair-show-of-solidarity hadn't quite worked out.

And wow. I didn't know why Jen was so mad at me for trashing her reputation. She seemed to be doing a pretty good job of trashing it herself.

Amy walked up to them and casually patted Jen on the back. OMG. She put a WRITE IN PAISLEY sticky note on her back! I love Amy.

Charlie Dodd ran up and down our hall, frantically passing out pens that said *Vote Charlie Dood for secretary!* Bean showed me hers. Perfect. That one was going to stick. He tried to hand me a pen. I ignored him.

The voting stations for all four classes had been set up in the quad, each at a table in a different corner. It was pretty much the only day of the year when it was safe for any student at our school to cross into to the sacred ground of the quad.

At morning break, I ran straight out there to check out the action. The bronze hornet was covered in signs for various candidates from all classes. It was a tradition. But still, the pink paper plate that I had tied around the hornet's neck like a choker definitely stood out. "I'D VOTE FOR PAISLEY!"

Yes! Even the Pleasant Hill Hornet was behind me.

I ran back up to sophomore hall. We were already out of flyers and sticky notes, but I still wanted to be there, urging people to write me in. I spotted Amy sitting on the grass sharing a sticky bun with Bean and Clint. Aw, that's so cute.

I was going over to join them, but then I saw Cate and a bunch of Uns marching down the hall in a sloppy but enthusiastic clump, blowing on party noisemakers and chanting "Join the Un Party!" "A vote for *Un* is a vote for Fun!" "Write-on, Miss UnP! Write-in Miss UnP!"

Oh man, this had to stop. I raced over to Cate, waved her down, and pulled her out onto the edge of the lawn where we wouldn't get bonked by a yellow football.

"Cate, come on, why are you *still* doing this? I really appreciated it before, when it was all just a joke but now—"

"It's never been just a joke," she snapped. The Un Party moved on without her, chanting and weaving down the hall.

"But now you're just hurting my chances of beating Hutch. Come on—*no one's* actually gonna vote for Miss UnPleasant!"

She looked me in the eye. "I'm not doing this for you, Paisley. I'm doing this for me."

"What do you mean?"

She squinted and frowned and finally shrugged. "I don't know what I mean."

There was so much chaos going on around us, it actually

seemed like the perfect place to be having a personal conversation. "Cate, Miss UnPleasant isn't real. *I'm* real."

She blinked her eyes a few times and looked away. Oh no. Oh God. I hoped she wasn't going to cry. "Yeah but who *are* you? I'm still trying to figure that out."

"Well, that makes two of us." I kinda half laughed. "But don't be mad at me, please. Help me out here."

"I'm not mad at you, I'm just . . . I'm just . . . " She looked away, then finally turned to me. "I'm just kinda heartbroken, I guess." She wiped underneath each eye and exhaled hard, trying to pull it together. "That freaked me out yesterday."

I was surprised. "Why? I thought you'd like me *more.*"

"I do." She tucked a piece of dark hair behind her ear, looking really sad. "But I sort of had this fantasy that Miss UnPleasant was a lot like me, and that we'd become best friends, and that I wouldn't feel so lonely in this Pleasant Hell." She wiped her nose and looked away. "And that maybe, maybe she even liked girls." Oh wow. I hadn't thought of that. Cate twirled her party noisemaker around in her hand, then pretended to smoke it like a cigarette. "But now . . . I don't know. That fantasy is over, up in smoke," she said, fake exhaling.

I felt like I had somehow let her down. "Sorry if I disappointed you."

She shook her head. "That's okay. It's not your fault. It's me. I get disappointed all the time."

I gave her a hug. "Me too." Over her shoulder, I could see Jen acting like a brainless bimbo. "Cate, I need your help. I really

336

don't want to lose this election. Is there any way you could get the Uns to endorse me and start chanting about writing in *my* name for president? Otherwise, Hutch is gonna win this and then we'll both be disappointed."

Cate looked a little better. Then she laughed. "Okay, but only if you give me one of those foxy pink chokers."

"Deal!"

At the beginning of lunch, Team Paisley sprinted down to the quad and staked out a choice yelling spot right next to the sophomore voting station. We stood on the bench, chanting, "Write in Pais-ley! Write in Pais-ley! Write in Pais-ley!"

Our group got bigger and louder and way more diverse as Miss UnPleasant's supporters gradually joined in. I was smiling and waving to Hutch, who had gathered with his Pop posse near the hornet. They were all staring at us like we were freaks, especially Jen and pink-haired Carreyn. Poor Carreyn.

As Hutch walked up to the voting station, he scratched his eyebrow, giving us the finger. What a classy guy, what an exemplary leader.

Our chant got even louder. *"Write in Pais-ley! Write in Pais-ley! Write in Pais-ley!"* He swirled his finger in circles a few inches from his ear, and mouthed "Crazy!" I just laughed, watching him grab a ballot from the stack and lean over to vote.

He looked up suddenly with this crap-eating grin on his face. "Hey Paisley, have you seen the ballot yet?" He waved it at me. No, actually, I hadn't. So I snatched it out of his hand.

I gasped—yes, I really gasped. Holy shiitake mushrooms! Oh

crap. Oh no! Canfield was more of a pig than I ever imagined. He was a rabid revengeful fetal pig! Amy and Bean and Cate were all trying to read over my shoulder. Eric and Clint grabbed their own copies of the ballot.

I felt the bottom fall out of my world and sank down onto the bench. Under *Class President,* there was a box to vote for Peter Hutchison. Under that it read: *Any write-in votes for Paisley Hanover will not be counted and will automatically disqualify your entire ballot. None of your votes will count.*

Everyone slowly stopped chanting my name, trying figure out what was going on.

The Pops all started chattering and laughing. Yup, Jen and Carreyn were front and center. Jen was all leaning into Bodie in the submissive-needy-girlfriend pose.

Hutch stood there laughing at me.

Some girl yelled, "Hutch, you suck!" OMG. It was Mandy Mindel.

"This is no election," Bean said to him. "It's *Preferential Treatment* by Pleasant Hill." She bounced her hand under her blond hair with this dopey vacant smile.

"Whatever, Beano."

Clint stepped into Hutch's face. "Dude, be a man. I'm pretty sure this isn't how a democracy works."

"Oh, thanks for the tip, dude."

"You play filthy dirty, you scum sucker," Cate said coldly.

Hutch didn't say anything. He just tried to laugh it off.

Then Eric stepped up and calmly asked, "Hutch, do you

really want to win like this? I mean, seriously, I've always thought of you as a winner. This isn't how a winner plays the game."

Yells of support popped around the crowd that had gathered.

Hutch looked a little confused, like he was actually thinking about what Eric had said. "Yeah, dude. This blows. I want to win, but not like this."

I wanted to pound on him so bad, and I would have if he hadn't weighed like twice as much as me. "Oh really? Then why'd you set me up like that at the speeches?"

"I thought it'd be funny! That's all. And yeah, I was sick of all your Miss UnPleasant crap."

"You know what? That's really hilarious. Miss UnPleasant never would've existed if it hadn't been for you and your shidiot behavior."

He looked at me puzzled.

"What you did to Mandy and Teddy that night after the game."

Hutch's face showed a flash of recognition, then he looked away, scratching the side of his nose with his knuckle. The crowd around us was silent, waiting for him to say something. But I knew he wouldn't.

"Hutch, why don't you do the *right* thing for a change?" I called.

He turned and stared at me like he was thinking hard, trying to figure out what to do. And then I realized something. Hutch had no idea what was the right thing to do—and he probably never did. For a second I almost felt sorry for him. Almost.

"So . . . um. Well, what do you want me to do?" he said, suddenly frustrated. "I can't change the ballot!" Hutch looked at all of us and then at his Pop buddies, who had gathered around.

"I have an idea," said Eric. "You write in Paisley Hanover. And you get everyone else to do it too." A bunch of us cheered at that. OMG! He's gorgelicious *and* a genius! "We'll force the administration to do the election over again."

He looked at Eric and sighed. "Dude, I *don't* want to win like this. I don't." He turned back to me. "So if I do that, what do I get from you, Paisley?" he asked in his trying-to-be seductive, creepy way.

"Nothing," I snapped.

Bean and Cate clapped politely. Then Amy joined in.

"Dude, listen. This way, you get the chance to, like, win for real," said Eric.

Hutch shook his head. "Crap." He leaned over and started writing on his ballot. Then he held it up and showed his vote to everyone, starting with the Pops. "Everyone write in Paisley Hanover!" he yelled. "We're throwing the election!"

A wave of reactions followed—from angry shouts of "Dude, no!" to cheers of support for Hutch from our side.

Eric smiled at me. And yes, I was smiling at him too.

Hutch slowly turned around until I could see his ballot.

I craned my neck. I squinted.

Under Class President, Hutch had written

PAISLEY HANOVER

What? WHAT?! I could feel my eyes bulging.

He dropped his ballot into the box and walked off.

No! NO!! *Aaaaaaaah!* The soundtrack to the shower scene from *Psycho* blared from my brain-speakers in these sharp pulsing shrieks. No. No! NO! I felt this creeped-out icky feeling, thinking of all the times Hutch had teased me or grabbed me and tried to hug me. Gross! Yuck. Hutch was my locker stalker? Hutch?! No. I wanted to puke in a purse! No!!!!!!!!!

I stumbled away from the bench, grabbing my head. I felt completely disoriented. Clint caught me as I was about to tumble to the ground. Then Clint and Amy and Bean and Cate were talking to me in slow-mo-underwater-speak that made no sense. What? What were they trying to say? I didn't even care. I just wanted to get out of there. I took a few steps back from the group and then I ran from the quad as fast as I could.

CHAPTER FIFTY

Eric eventually found me at the listening spot, stretched out on the grass with my ear to the ground.

"Hey," he said. "You okay?"

I opened my eyes. He was panting like he'd just finished a run. I closed my eyes again. "I dunno."

I had been lying there for a good half hour or so, trying my best to have an out-of-body experience.

Eric stretched out on the grass next to me. Neither of us said anything for a long time. I liked that about him. We both just lay there looking up at the clouds. The warning bell rang for sixth period, but I didn't budge and he didn't either. And then the starting bell for sixth rang.

I closed my eyes again. But I kept seeing Hutch's all-caps handwriting. Uck! So I opened them again.

Why do I always want to know everything and have everything all figured out? Lying there, I realized that sometimes it's much better not to know.

I didn't care about the election anymore. I didn't care if I won or lost or got any votes at all. I didn't want to be like Charlie "Dood," so obsessed with planning my future that I couldn't enjoy what was happening right now. A lot of great things were happening *right now* and I hadn't planned any of them!

Eric pointed up at the clouds. "Dumb varsity jock chasing a cool indie chick."

I laughed.

"UnSane redhead chasing her tail. Two o'clock."

We both laughed.

"It was pretty crazy in the quad after you left."

I didn't want to think about it anymore.

"Jen voted for you."

I looked at him. "You're kidding."

"She showed me her ballot before she stuffed it in the box."

Wow. That was a shocker. Maybe she did still like me a little—or maybe she just wrote in my name because Hutch did and she was a "Hutch's Honey." I'd never know. All I knew was that if we somehow got to be friends again, it would never be the same as it had been before school started. But I guess that was okay. Neither were we.

"Hey." Eric rolled over on his stomach. "Wanna go to the dance Friday after the game?"

OMG. Was he serious? I turned to look at him. He seemed serious. But he did have that crush on his idea of cool, edgy Miss UnPleasant. "Are you asking me or asking Miss UnPleasant?"

He smiled. "I'm asking you."

I smiled too. But on the inside, I felt like a screaming, wind-blown, frizzy nerve. I'd been riding this crazy emotional roller coaster for so long without a safety bar, holding on for dear life. I turned to him. "Don't be too nice to me, okay? I might burst into tears."

Eric didn't say anything. Finally, he reached over and grabbed my hand and just held it. "That'd be okay," he said at the clouds.

Wow. This guy could melt my heart. I remembered the first time I really liked him, when I saw him almost cry after getting the MVP award at the soccer championships. For a change, I didn't want to melt into the earth and hide from embarrassment. I kind of wanted to melt into him. OMG. Did I just say that?! Yes! I totally did!

You're probably wondering if this was all just another flash fantasy—I know I was for a second. But it wasn't. It was real. I was going out on a date with Eric Sobel on Friday night. And I was spastic jazzed for it! And then I suddenly remembered something else. I had a Nut Festival rain date with Clint Bedard on *Saturday* night!

I had a date with my above-the-belt crush *and* my below-the-belt crush all in the same weekend? OMG! How was I going to manage that?

In the movie version of my life, this is where the camera pulls up and away to a high crane shot (or a helicopter shot, pending budget) and the soundtrack swells, but it's not just in my head for a change—it's in digital surround-sound. And you can see two small people lying in the middle of a big green soccer field smiling and holding hands.

And then my voice-over would say something smart and kind of deep like, *Have you ever had the feeling that you were destined for greatness? And that the whole reason you're even on the planet is to do something unique and totally amazing? Not that you would ever admit that to anybody. Whoops!*

The UnEnd

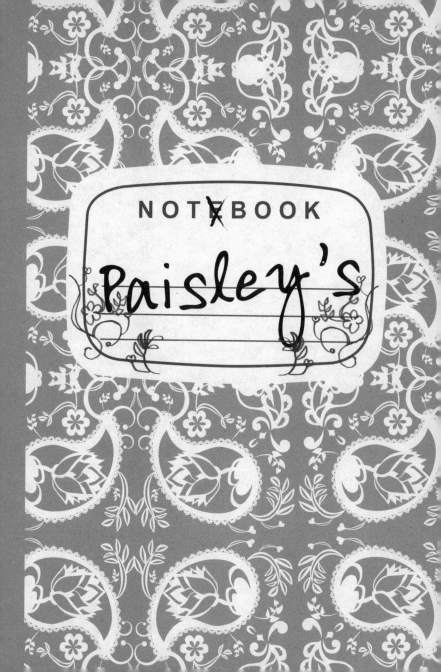

Paisley's NOTEBOOK

NO PEEKING!!!!

Paisley Hanover—
Something clever
Something clever
Something <u>cleverer</u>
Anything!
Welcome to Never Clever Land
Clever is Crazy Being Polite
Paisley Hanover—Crazy in Polite Ways
Ugh.
Brainy Babe
Quirky Turkey
Strange but True
Hope on a Rope
Dork on a Fork
Fun for All, All for Fun!
A Punny, Funny Friend
Funny Weird
Funny Ha Ha
Funny Weird <u>and</u> Funny Ha Ha
More Laughs than a . . .
More Fun than a Barrel of
Sophomores
Sophomore of the Good Stuff
Sophomore of a Good Thing
Paisley—Not Just Those
    Sperm-Shaped Thingies
Focused on Fun
Focused, Fun, Fabulous!
Little Miss Funshine
Freckles and Funshine
Freckles are Fun
One of a Kind
Fun of a Kind
Fun of a Kind Girl
Fun for Your Life

Tickled Think
The Sizzle <u>and</u> the Steak
Functional <u>and</u> Fashionable
Smart, Stylish, and . . .
    totally stupid!
Shigoogley!
<u>What</u>?
Irony. Irony. Try irony.
Paisley Hanover—
    I Should Have Overslept!
That's good. That's kind of funny.
No, not so funny.
Paisley Hanover—Write On!
Will Write for Clothes
I'm Dying Here!
Not as Popular as Candy
Will Write for Candy
I'd Vote for Candy

Sidebra

When I bought this at the beginning of school, it was a totally normal notebook. Now it's my NOTbook and totally un-normal like me. But I won't tell you why. You'll have to read it to figure that out. I will tell you it's kind of my journal, my sketchbook, and my scrapbook all in one doodle-icious mess. It's filled with secrets, notes, confessions, daydreams, and a lot of things I probably never should have said. Basically, it's a peephole into my life and my slightly tortured brain. I'll bet you can relate.

Write on,

Paisley Hanover

REASONS MY LIFE IS OVER TODAY:

• Made a TOTAL fool of myself trying to get into Yearbook class.

• Got stuck in Drama with the socially disabled and hair-impaired! (my so-called best friend!)

• Jen basically dumped me.

Why? WHY?! What did I do?

(((The CRAZY·OMETER)))

TODAY I FEEL . . .

"A Little Un-Sane"

"A Little Manic"

"Totally Bonkers"

"Totally Paranoid"

"Totally Sane"

A sign of brilliance and creativity.

But, hey! I'm getting a lot done.

I MUST STILL BE ASLEEP,

But looking FAB quivering in my new suede boots.

SOLUTION: More chocolate and shopping.

I AM NOT A RAH-RAH. I AM NOT MY GPA. I AM NOT SURE.

THINGS I WISH I'D SAID:

"Hey, no worries.
I'll just take Drama."

THINGS I WISH I'D NEVER SAID:

"Paisley Hanover—FUN of a kind girl!"
(Punctuated by me doing spastic jazz hands.)

Don't ask.

I AM NOT JUST PMS-ING. I AM NOT MY REPUTATION.

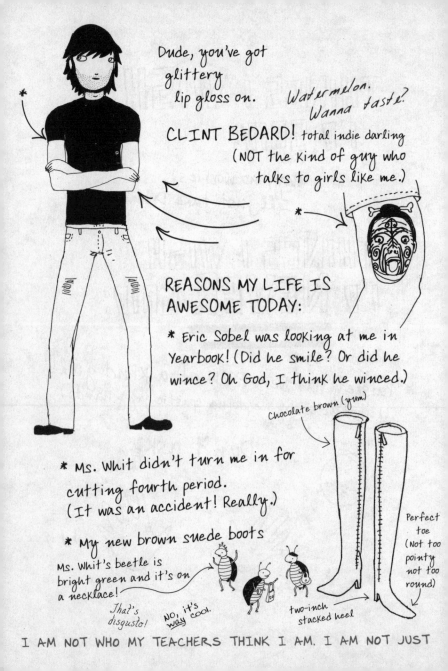

Dude, you've got glittery lip gloss on.

Watermelon. Wanna taste?

CLINT BEDARD! total indie darling (NOT the kind of guy who talks to girls like me.)

REASONS MY LIFE IS AWESOME TODAY:

* Eric Sobel was looking at me in Yearbook! (Did he smile? Or did he wince? Oh God, I think he winced.)

Chocolate brown (yum)

* Ms. Whit didn't turn me in for cutting fourth period. (It was an accident! Really.)

* My new brown suede boots

Ms. Whit's beetle is bright green and it's on a necklace!

That's disgusto!

NO, it's way cool.

Perfect toe (Not too pointy not too round)

two-inch stacked heel

I AM NOT WHO MY TEACHERS THINK I AM. I AM NOT JUST

Secret crushes:
ERIC SOBEL
Not-so-secret crushes:
ERIC SOBEL

He never speaks!
He can't help it. He's SHY.
Like THAT's ever going
to happen, Pais!

*Eric Sobel! SO pop,
sweet, adorable, shy, sexy.
(NOT the kind of guy who talks
to girls like me—for so many
different reasons.)*

WEIRD PLAY
(My vocab prep for SATs)

WEIRD OF THE DAY:
in·sa·tia·ble [in-sey-shuh-buhl]
  -adjective
not satiable; incapable of being
 satisfied or appeased:
She has an insatiable hunger for
~~sticky buns, gossip,~~ shoes.

SOMEBODY'S GIRLFRIEND. I AM NOT JUST SOMEBODY'S EX.

PEOPLE WHO SECRETLY WANT TO **KISS**/KILL ME:

Eric Sobel?

Clint Bedard?

My new secret admirer?
(Affectionately known as my _locker_ _stalker_)

PEOPLE WHO SECRETLY WANT TO KISS/**KILL** ME:

Ms. Madrigal!

Candy Esposito!

Whoever pinched my butt during the
so-called TRUST exercise in Drama.

BM?

CB?

CM?

Ugh!

I AM NOT MY HAIR. (THANK GOD!!!) I AM NOT A WIMP. I AM NOT A

POP QUIZ!

1) Who's been getting notes in her locker from a secret admirer?

2) Who thinks she's going to become "mucho popularo" by trying out for cheerleading?

3) Who did fifteen perfect pull-ups with his shirt off while I watched his gorgeous shrink-wrapped torso and totally forgot to breathe?

FRECKLES ARE SEXY

Who wrote that?!
(must figure out who makes E's like backwards 3's!)

PICKLES ARE SEXY

That's disgusto

3) Eric Sobel (Yum!)

Answers: 1) Me! 2) Jen (my soon-to-be-ex best friend!)

LOSER. I AM NOT GOING TO BE QUIET. I AM NOT GOING TO HIDE.

UNPOP QUIZ!

1) Who basically asked me to kiss him on the first day of Drama?

2) Who got dropped on her butt by a bunch of geeks, losers, and Library Girls? OUCH!
Bummer
Sorry Pais!

3) Who said, "I don't hate you, Paisley, you're just _so_ Pleasant Hill?"

NOTE INTERCEPTED IN CLASS
Found this under my chair in Drama. Real subtle.

PH is not only so PH, she can't even act. How did this no-talent rah-rah get into our class?

I heard she got bounced from Yearbook because she dances like a total freak.

What? That makes NO sense.

Answers: 1) Clint Bedard (He's like some delinquent.) 2) Me!
3) Cate Maduro (Duh. Obviously she hates me. See above. But why?)

The bottle-rocket bomber? No way!

I AM NOT WHAT ANYONE SAYS ABOUT ME BEHIND MY BACK.

THIS FLYER CHANGED MY LIFE.
(It's a long story.)

Hey,
I thought **I** changed your
life! It was
my idea to go the Fly
meeting.
-Bean

THE FLY IS OPEN!
for business this year

Despite senseless draconian budget cuts,
The Fly is still in business.
Come to a lunch meeting to learn how you
can join our new all-volunteer staff
and discover the many joys of journalism—
long hours, no pay, great parties.
We need writers, editors, field reporters, columnists,
photographers & coffee sherpas.
No experience or scruples required.

"Zipper or button?"
Thanks, Charlie! Duh.

Come on, *peoples!* Step up!

WHERE: Room 107
WHEN: Friday @ noon

You can KILL the budget
but you CAN'T silence the pen . . .
or the computer . . .
or the website . . . or whatever.

Or the Kumbaya singers.

OR the bongo players!

I AM NOT PERFECT. I AM NOT TRYING TO BE PERFECT.

AM I CRAZY??

or did Cindy Kutcher get a boob job over the summer?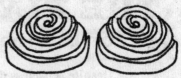

Gotta get the scoop.

They were a b-day present from her parents!

Disgusto!!

WAYS MY MOM IS

CRAZY:

Fake tap-dances when she's happy or nervous.*

Always tries to hug and kiss me.

Obsessed with Yogilates.
(What is that anyway?!)

***OMG**. Maybe that's where spastic jazz hands came from! It's GENETIC!

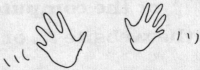

I AM NOT GOING AWAY. I AM NOT WHAT SOME GUY WANTS ME TO

RUMORS I
HEARD/ IGNORED/ STARTED:

Ms. Whitaker, our new librarian,
is a radical socialist. (Heard it.)

Not true. She's actually
a radical socialite.

Foxy Señor Abbott is married to
a Bolivian heiress. (Started it.)

I got kicked out of Yearbook class because I
dance like a freak. What?! (Tried to ignore it.)

*Well Pais,
you kind of do!*

INCREDIBLY BORING
Personal **REFLECTIONS:**

I KNOW SOMETHING HAPPENED TO JEN AT HUTCH'S
POOL PARTY. BUT WHAT I DON'T KNOW IS WHY SHE HASN'T
TOLD ME ABOUT IT. SHE USED TO TELL ME <u>EVERYTHING</u>.

BE (OR DO). I AM NOT WHAT SOME GIRL WANTS ME TO BE (OR DO).

I AM NOT FALLING FOR THAT. I AM NOT FALLING FOR HIM. (AM I?)

IDEAS FOR HOW TO BE
MORE POPULAR?

Get super cute
new boyfriend (jock? BP?).

Buy more clothes.

Bigger boobs? ←

Like THAT's ever going to happen!!

If it does, call me! —Clint

Happened! Total humiliation. → Get on YouTube.

Start catchphrase or trend.

Me too!! ox Cate

Start a club.

Lose 10 pounds.

Brilliant idea... Popular but D.E.A.D!

Lose 100 pounds.

Be mean to everyone below me
on the social food chain. —

Candy

Candy Esposito
So pop.
So perfect.
<u>SO</u> ruining my life!

I AM NOT WHO I WAS LAST YEAR. I AM NOT WHO I WAS LAST <u>WEEK</u>.

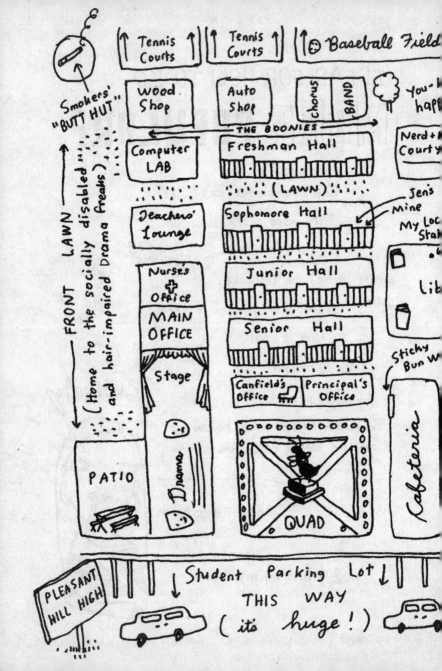

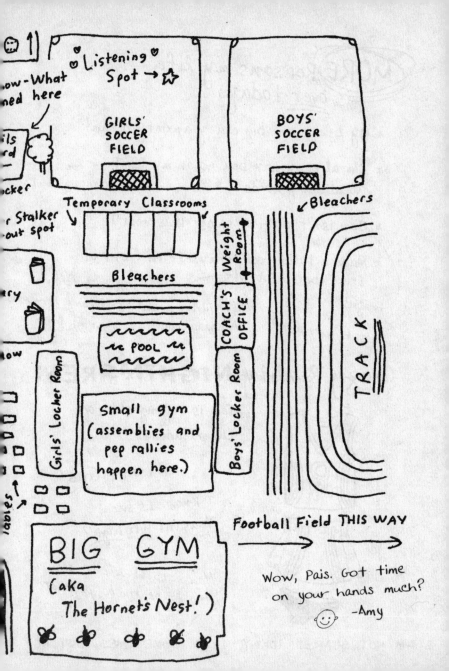

ow–What
ned here

ils
rd

cker

r Stalker
out spot

ry

ow

♡ Listening ♡
Spot → ☆

GIRLS'
SOCCER
FIELD

BOYS'
SOCCER
FIELD

Temporary Classrooms

← Bleachers

Weight Room

Bleachers

COACH'S OFFICE

POOL

Small gym
(assemblies and
pep rallies
happen here.)

Boys' Locker Room

Girls' Locker Room

TRACK

BIG GYM

(aka
The Hornet's Nest!)

Football Field THIS WAY
→   →

Wow, Pais. Got time
on your hands much?
–Amy

(MORE) Reasons my life is over today:

* My life is one big crazy anxiety dream!

* I'm already way behind on my PSAT vocabulary words.   Look up repugnant.

* Jen isn't playing soccer this year!!

* Made a total fool of myself in front of Eric Sobel! AGAIN! ←

So tragic! She's one of our best forwards!

Silent library scream Aaaaaaaaaaah!

Already told you. Offensive. Repulsive. Disgusting. Duh! —Charlie

Crazy Reality **NIGHTMARES:**

Jen is trying out for cheerleading!

Oh my Gag!

I know. Is she Pleasant Hill <u>high</u>?

You guys!!! We're all going to be mucho popularo!

I AM NOT SCARED. (OKAY, I AM SOMETIMES, BUT NOT

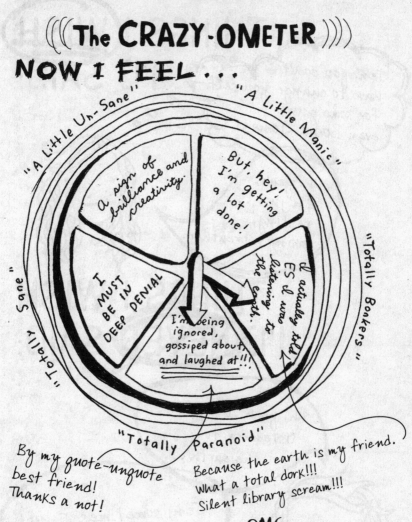

THAT SCARED.) I AM NOT APOLOGIZING FOR WHAT I WANT.

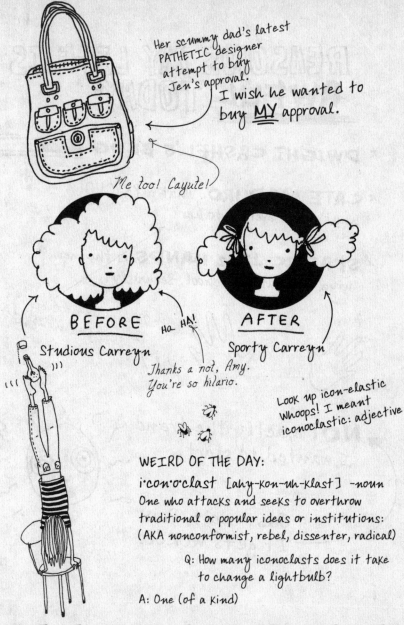

Her scummy dad's latest PATHETIC designer attempt to buy Jen's approval.

I wish he wanted to buy **MY** approval.

Me too! Cayute!

BEFORE

AFTER

Studious Carreyn

Sporty Carreyn

Ha HA!

Thanks a not, Amy. You're so hilario.

Look up icon-elastic WHOOPS! I meant iconoclastic: adjective

WEIRD OF THE DAY:
i·con·o·clast [ahy-kon-uh-klast] -noun
One who attacks and seeks to overthrow traditional or popular ideas or institutions: (AKA nonconformist, rebel, dissenter, radical)

Q: How many iconoclasts does it take to change a lightbulb?

A: One (of a kind)

I AM NOT JUST A GIRL. I AM NOT MY BRA SIZE. I AM NOT A SNITCH.

REASONS MY LIFE IS ~~AWFUL~~ TODAY:

* **DWIGHT CASHEL'S BLOG**

* **CATE MADURO.** What a PSYCHO! What did I ever do to her?

* **SPASTIC JAZZ HANDS** is the new "hiya" wave at my school. Seriously.

Think about it. Tu hablas denial?

NOT exactly the trend I wanted to start.

Just wait, Pais. It gets WORSE.

some sort of clerical error, Ms. Madrigal announced. OMG! That never even occurred to me.
Highly suspicious, I thought immediately. But no one else
seemed the least bit suspicious. Were I a betting man,
which I am not, I would wager that Ms. Madrigal, our
beloved yet masochistic yearbook advisor, had planned
the whole thing—the mix-up and the headline slam-off. I
suspect that after a long, hot summer, she had developed
quite a hunger for student suffering, craving the acrid
smell of our mental anguish much like a vampire craves
pulsing, warm blood and will do anything to get it. (Please
note: my brother was in Yearbook for three years. I've
heard all about Ms. Madrigal's devious ways.)

SPUNKY?!
What an insult!

Despite my suspicions, I thoroughly enjoyed watching
that spunky Paisley Hanover sweating it out, pitted
against the lovely, gifted, caramel-coated Candy Esposito.
(Who says that God doesn't give with both hands?) The
headline slam was quite a revelation as fine sport and
entertainment. (I am going to suggest that we do it as an
icebreaker at the next Scrabble party.) It was reminiscent
of the gladiators of ancient Rome. Only these gladiators
were thrown to the literary lions armed with no weapons
save their wit—and they were super cute.

What a total dork!

I love Scrabble.
Who wrote that?

they?

After a three-minute brainstorming period, during which
poor Paisley looked like a frightened, disoriented beagle
caught in the headlights of an 18-wheeler, and Candy
looked...well, you all know how Candy looks, Paisley
bravely went first. Her headline, Fun of a Kind Girl, wasn't
bad. But she had some sort of spasm or petit mal seizure
as she announced her headline to the class and kept
flapping her hands around uncontrollably. It was weird.
Of course, Candy won the last spot in Yearbook with her
outstanding headline, "Sweet, Nutty, Mouth-Watering
Candy." I voted for her. Twice.

BEAGLE?!!!
Okay, okay,
I'll take
spunky.

Uptight & annoying—yes!
Squeaky clean....not so much!

THINGS I WISH I'D SAID:

"Teddy! Howdy partner!"

 "Gosh, thanks, Cate. You're just . . . so _Unpleasant._"

THINGS I WISH I'D NEVER SAID:

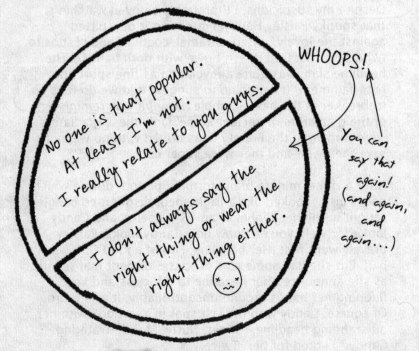

No one is that popular.
At least I'm not.
I really relate to you guys.

I don't always say the right thing or wear the right thing either.

WHOOPS!

You can say that again! (and again, and again...)

I AM NOT WHO MY PARENTS WANT ME TO BE SO THEY CAN BRAG TO

KILLER QUOTES FROM THE GEEK CHORUS:

(Bean Merrill, Charlie Dodd, Cate Maduro, LG Wong (and her LG posse))

"So, Paisley, what's it like being one of the chosen people at PH?" —LG Wong

"Leave her alone." —Bean

"Does it hurt your head being so popular? Does the pressure just make you want to kill yourself?" —Cate

"She's not that popular." —Charlie

And I thought the POPS were the only McNasties at my school.

Tu hablas denial?

Who keeps writing this?!!

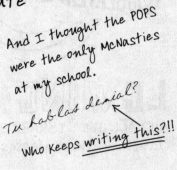

ALL THEIR FRIENDS. I'M NOT EATING THAT! I AM NOT KIDDING.

PEOPLE WHO SECRETLY WANT TO (KISS) KILL ME:

NOBODY

PEOPLE WHO SECRETLY WANT TO KISS / (KILL) ME:

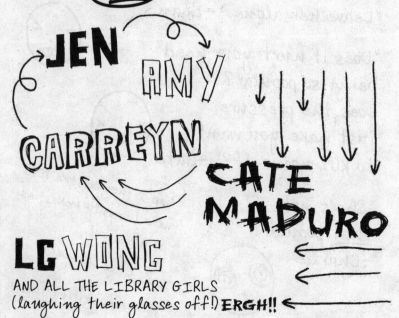

JEN
AMY
CARREYN
CATE
MADURO
LG WONG
AND ALL THE LIBRARY GIRLS
(laughing their glasses off!) ERGH!!

I AM NOT WHAT I WEAR. I AM NOT A TEASE. I AM NOT DESPERATE.

THE FLY

HORNETS STING COUGARS

Wow. This looks just like The Fly! You're good, Pals.

I'm going to Princeton. Don't burst my bubble!

Freshman Charlie Dodd marches to his own beat at the car wash fundraiser for new band uniforms

Sophomore standout Bodie Jones catches air before dunking the ball at the buzzer for the varsity victory over Cougars hoopster rivals.

PLEASANT HILL PROFILE:

What a PERV!

Football Coach Dave Cave builds summer personal training business and muscles for moms at Bigwood Athletic Club.

I think he's kinda toxy.

CAN'T WE ALL JUST NOT GET ALONG? By Miriam Goldfarb pg 10-11

oh my gag!

NOTES FROM THE FLY LUNCH MEETING:

1. The Fly is no longer an accredited class. It's a <u>club</u>!

   — Pun intended!

2. The Fly has sick parties.

3. Miriam Goldfarb is a weirdo. (But a cool, independent weirdo. Hmmm...)

4. OMG! The budget for Drama was almost cut too?!

   Thank God that didn't happen!

   I know!

Look up jingle-ism
Whoops. I meant jingoism! noun

It's kind of like fanatical (football) patriotism. (I looked it up.) ox Bean

♡ They're a couple!

How do you know?

Read his blog. It's hilarious!

Black and yellow just like our school colors! Very clever.

FYI: You don't need blond hair to be a Dumbe Blonde. You just have to be an authority-questioning, arts-loving activist.

PS FYI: Dumbe is misspelled on purpose. You know, it's like satire?

I don't get it.

but I just laughed at her, staring her down through her thick eyeball-distorting glasses. And then she said in her adorable, nasal voice, "Logan, you imbecile, you need three (pause) credible sources, and (longer pause) Wikipedia is not one of them." We debated that point for a good hour while we made punctuation mosaics out of macaroni. That night, I lay in my narrow, swayback upper bunk tossing and turning and tossing and turning but I couldn't get her adorably nasal voice out of my head. And suddenly, I knew it was looooove. That was a fact. But there was no fact-checker on the planet who could prove it.

Aw!

Check out Carreyn's new tote bag!

OMG! How bizarre... It's just like Jen's.

Yeah!!! It's made of <u>imitation</u> leather.

POP QUIZ!

1) Who's turning into a freaky-meanie cheerleading zombie?

2) Who's turning into the freaky-meanie cheerleading zombie's clone?

3) Which popular sophomore found another note from her locker stalker?

HOT 4 YOU!

It's Teddy Baedeker!

That's disgusto!

Who? Who?! WHO?!
E? CB? CM? CD?
Must set up a stakeout and spy on my locker

Answers: 1) Jen (duh!) 2) Carreyn (Double duh!) 3) Me! (Yay! Someone really likes me!)

I AM NOT AFRAID TO TRY. I AM NOT AFRAID TO FAIL.

UNPOP QUIZ!

1) Who's jealous of Clint Bedard?

2) Who can juggle like a total pro?

3) Who thinks that Paisley Hanover is
   A-list popular? (Hilarious!)

Answers: 1) Charlie Dodd (But he totally denies it.) 2) Teddy Baedeker
(Wonder what other things about him would surprise me?) 3) LG Wong

Oh gosh, maybe I _am_ A-list popular!
Wow! Wouldn't that be super-duper?
Let me think...Hmmm...I have lots
of really cute clothes, a really big
mouth, and super small boobs,
and...Oh, never mind.
Definitely <u>not</u> A-list popular!

PAISLEY'S PERSONAL POP QUIZ:
(I told you you'd be tested later.)

I am named after ...

a) my grandmother who loves to sew ← Sew what?!
b) those sperm-shaped thingies
c) my older brother, Gingham — Ew. Gross!
d) Paisley, Scotland

He's very comfortable
with himself, but kind
of plain and often
"checked-out"! (Ha ha!)

Great city, but
named after those
sperm-shaped thingies!

REASONS MY LIFE IS AWESOME TODAY:

NONE. ZERO. ZIP.

THINGS I WISH I'D SAID:

(Still too stunned and sad to think of anything smart...or clever...or funny...)

I kind of want to puke, but every time I try, I keep seeing my own reflection!

THINGS I WISH I'D NEVER SAID:

Let's have a powwow pig-out party.

Static clingy.

I'm not sure I really trust Bodie. I know he's supposed to be a great guy and all. But what if he's just using Jen?

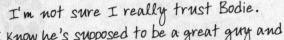

I AM NOT MY BAD HAIRCUT. I AM NOT MY BAD HAIR DAY. I AM

(((the CRAZY-OMETER)))

"A Little Un-Sane" "A Little Manic"

A sign of brilliance and creativity.

But, hey! I'm getting a lot done!

Solution: GET ALL NEW FRIENDS!!!

"Totally Bonkers"

I must be having an out-of-body an experience.

"Totally Sane"

Why wouldn't, I.e., somebody who considers.

"Totally Paranoid"

POWERFUL PERSONAL DISCOVERIES:

Never leave the house without...
shoes and a cell phone!

No one is always who they seem to be!!!

OUCH!

NOT MY AVATAR. (BUMMER! SHE'S SUPER HOT AND SUPER BAD!)

CRAZY ANXIETY DREAM:

Crying... Crying... Crying... Crying

→ Puddles of Tears

My quote-unquote friends will cry oceans of tears at my funeral, then fall into deep depressions and go on to live very long, unfulfilling, loveless lives because they can never escape the memory of how unbelievably nasty they were to me.

And it was all PREMEDITATED!

Am I CRAZY?

Or was Cate Maduro actually nice to me? I think she's kind of cool.

Uh, yeah! What did you think?

And modest!

And shy!

Don't forget clever!

And HOT.

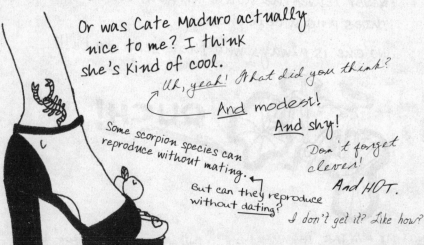

Some scorpion species can reproduce without mating.

But can they reproduce without dating?

I don't get it? Like how?

COOL (ANCIENT) MOVIES TO RENT:

Heathers

Say Anything

The Breakfast Club

Dazed and Confused

Ferris Bueller's Day Off

Fame

Dirty Dancing

10 Things I Hate About You

(OMG! It's based on <u>Taming of the Shrew</u>.)

UNPOP QUIZ!

Who doesn't?!

Um, like Jen, Carreyn, BSI, BS2, Bodie, Hutch, Candy Esposito...

1) Who thinks that popularity is poison?

2) Who has the best goody-goody schoolgirl act of anyone?

3) Who performs road-kill surgery like a cool, calm pro?

My sweet, snuggly, crazy Kitty Dyson. (Yes, he was named after that vacuum cleaner. I know, I know. It's a long story...)

ACTUALLY, NO.

This is how I feel. Yikes! Crap.

OMG

OMG

OMG

OMG

PUKE in a purse!!!

Dyson sent my angry vent letter!

Answers: 1) Cate Maduro 2) LG Wong (Wonder what she's really like outside of school?) 3) Cate Maduro

REASONS MY LIFE IS OVER TODAY:

→ old

* My friends aren't talking to me!

There. I added "old." — What am I? Your sidekick?!

My OLD friends aren't talking to me.

REASONS MY LIFE IS AWESOME TODAY:

OLD

* My friends aren't talking to me!

* Bean! (She gave me this cowgirl cool
vintage paisley shirt. How sweet!)

Thanks Bean. I love it!
You're a great sidekick.

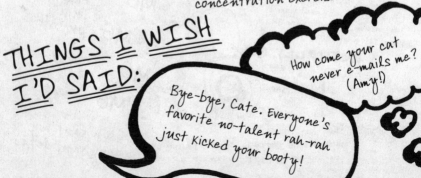

* Drama class!
(CB said the love word to
me, and I said it back!

OMG! No way!

WAY! But it was only during a
concentration exercise in Drama.

THINGS I WISH I'D SAID:

How come your cat
never e-mails me?
(Amy!)

Bye-bye, Cate. Everyone's
favorite no-talent rah-rah
just kicked your booty!

POWERFUL PERSONAL DISCOVERIES:

I am a drama queen
ROCK STAR!

* Eric Sobel is so vicious.
No, he's beyond vicious—he's EVIL!

(Nerds in love)

SECURE CRUSHES: ♡ ♡

Teddy Baedeker on Mandy Mindel (?)

OMG NIhs! Love them.
They're cuter
than Muppets.

Oh my gag! Disgusto.

*Excuse me, but nerds
need love too.*

I AM NOT HOW MY BUTT LOOKS IN THESE JEANS. I AM NOT GOING THERE.

PEOPLE WHO SECRETLY WANT TO ~~KISS~~/KILL ME:

GLINT BEDARD?

→ (Is that even possible?)

Don't take this the wrong way but...NO.

Thanks a not!

I so hope you're kidding.
He's disgusto.

MY LOCKER STALKER?

↖ Your *what*?!

PEOPLE WHO SECRETLY WANT TO KISS/~~KILL~~ ME:

↑

Duh!

Um, Pais. I don't think it's a secret.

JEN

CATE MADURO

Carreyn

???

· · ·

?

Incredibly Boring Personal Reflections:
LAST NIGHT...I HAD A DREAM
(YES. *THAT* KIND OF DREAM!)
ABOUT: CB!!
(OMG. WHERE DID THAT EVEN COME FROM?!)

I AM NOT CRYING. I AM NOT TOO SENSITIVE. I AM NOT

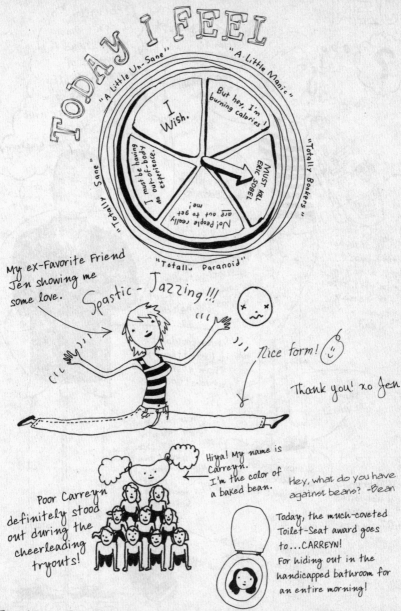

TALKING TO YOU <u>OR</u> YOUR CAT. I AM NOT JUST A TYPO.

ZZZ CRAZY ANXIETY DREAMS:

Sorry, Pais.
That wasn't
a dream.

Okay, so I'm standing up in front of the class doing this totally embarrassing spastic jazz hands dance and singing this utterly humiliating beat-box-like rap song that makes me sound like a total idiot and I'm in a video on YouTube!!! Aaaaaaaaaaaaaaaah!

Rock on, Red!
And that editing
was mad. ← Don't you mean bad?

No, little dude,
it was mad.

CRAZY REALITIES:

I swear to God, Jen totally lost it
and ACTUALLY said this to me.

"Just get away from me, Paisley! Go <u>away!</u>
You're always telling me how I'm doing it wrong.
You're always trying to make me feel like crap!
I'm sick of it! I'm sick of you!"
What is up with her? Whatever. I am SO over her.

I really like your friends.

Me too!

I AM NOT MY YEARBOOK PHOTO. I AM NOT BETTER THAN

zzz

AM I CRAZY

Or did the Hornettes steal my spastic jazz move for their cheerleading routine?!

You are crazy AND the Hornettes stole your spastic jazz move for their cheerleading routine.

Hey, I thought you weren't talking to me?!

I'm not. I'm writing.

RUMORS I HEARD/ IGNORED/ STARTED:

- I'm secretly dating the bottle-rocket bomber. Me! Paisley Hanover!! (HEARD IT.)
- Cate Maduro goes to a therapist to be deprogrammed after every pep rally. (STARTED IT.)
- Candy Esposito is way into Eric Sobel. (IGNORED IT.)

Who even cares?!

ANYONE ELSE. I AM NOT WORSE THAN ANYONE ELSE.

POP QUIZ!

1) Who claimed she wanted "qual time" with me but really just wanted backup? Ergh!!

2) Who was hanging all over ES all night?

3) Who scored the game-winning field goal and uses words like "homage"?

Answers: 1) Jen (I'm never falling for that one again!) 2) Candy Esposito (Ew! Hate her! She gets everything I want! Whoops. Did I just write that? I did.) 3) Eric Sobel.

WEIRD OF THE DAY:

hom·age [hom-ij or om-ij] –noun

A tribute or formal public acknowldgment

of reverence or respect: ←

His totally humiliating video paid homage

to her totally humiliating moment in

Yearbook.

Not homage like the ho'nettes. It's a soft "h" or silent "h," like ohmage. Like OMG.

Wait a minute. Reverence? Respect? Was he kidding?

Like OMG! When did YOU turn into such a total nerdathon?

INCREDIBLY BORING PERSONAL REFLECTIONS:

ERGH! I SO CAN'T FIGURE OUT ERIC SOBEL. I DON'T WANT TO LIKE HIM—BUT I DO. BUT SO DOES EVERY OTHER GIRL AT THIS SCHOOL. AND I SO HATE BEING ONE OF THE CROWD. HATE IT! I AM NOT GOING TO LIKE HIM. IT'S DONE. IT'S DECIDED. BUT WAIT, WHAT IF HE LIKES ME? NO, THAT'S TOTALLY RIDICULOUS. BUT...WHAT IF HE DOES?

I AM NOT ON A BUDGET. (WHOOPS. NEVER MIND.) I AM NOT

UnPOP QUIZ!

1) Who held up hilarious misspelled signs at the football game?

2) Who will burn to a crisp in the popular wing of hell with all the other cute, well-dressed wimps for what she didn't do after the football game?

3) Who danced in the parking lot like goofy crazed teenagers?

Answers: 1) The Dumbe Blondes (Love those guys!) 2) Me (Hate myself! And Hutch!!) 3) Clint Bedard and Cate Maduro (I so wish I had been with them Friday night.)

FAKING IT. I AM NOT SIGNED UP FOR THIS CLASS. (NOT AGAIN!)

I CAN'T SLEEP!

(WHY? I'M SOOOOOOOOOOOOOO TIRED.)

Why? Why? Why? Why? Why? Why? **WHY?**
Why did that happen? Why didn't anyone do
anything? Why didn't _I_ do anything? I'm such
a wimp-out loser. What am I afraid of? What
are we ~~ALL~~ so afraid of? The popular people? The
MORE popular people? That's insane!!! That's
sad. They're sad. I'm sad.

<u>Sad</u> + Mad = **BAD**

Varsity Jocks. Varsity jokes. **VARSITY JERKS!**

Boozers vs. Losers

Uncool but Uncruel

Popular. Popular. Popular! Popular?

If you write it enough times,
it doesn't look like the same word
or even mean anything!

Gotta be popular! More. More! **MORE!**

Poor. Bore. **SNORE**. Got to be more Popular.

Why does **EVERYONE** try so hard to POPULAR?

POOPULAR is more like it.

I AM NOT UNPOPULAR. I AM NOT POPULAR. I AM NOT

Popular = mean, cruel, cloney, phony

FUN Popular = different,
cool, weird,
unweird

Do I even WANT to be popular?

Does anyone really?

WHY? WHY? WHY?!

Why try so hard to be popular
when I can be...

UNPOPULAR

Hmmmmmm...

PLAYING THAT GAME. I AM NOT ASLEEP. I AM NOT A SHEEP.

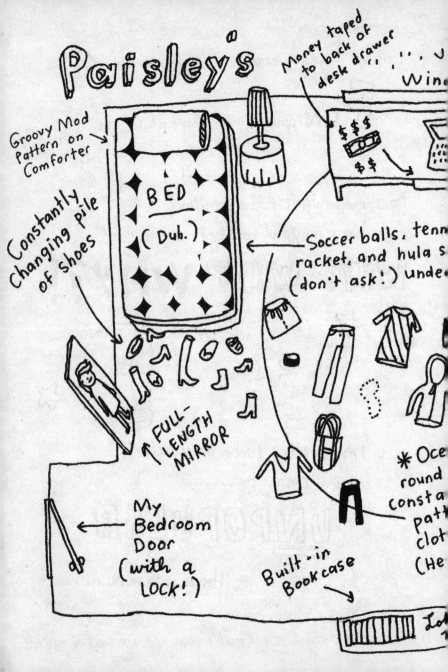

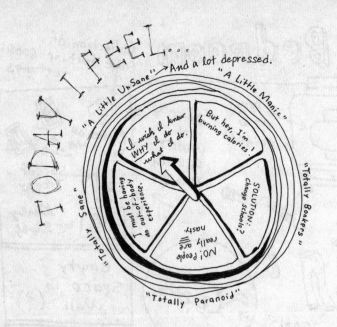

TODAY I FEEL...

And a lot depressed.

"A Little UnSane"   "A Little Manic"

"Totally Sane"   "Totally Bonkers"

"Totally Paranoid"

I wish I knew WHY I do what I do.

But hey, I'm burning calories.

SOLUTION: change schools?

No! people really are nasty.

I must be having an out-of-body experience.

REASONS TO HATE MYSELF/ MY LIFE/ MY SCHOOL TODAY:

* That look on Mandy Mindel's face when I apologized.
* The fact that Teddy Baedeker didn't even come to school.
* The way I feel right now.

I AM NOT THE STUFF IN MY PURSE. I AM NOT PUKE IN A PURSE.

Dear Mom and Dad,
Today I learned a lot at school...

1) Eric Sobel is possibly more of
   a creep than I ever imagined.
   Unbelievable!

2) Mr. Canfield (our lame, ridiculous
   vice principal) has this self-contained
   torture chamber in his office.
   I call it the Fink Fast chair.
   (Get it?)

That's pretty funny, Red.
I always just called
that chair "friend."

Seat covered in sticky, non-breathable
vinyl to make your butt sweat.
(It's probably a fire hazard!)

Oh the stories I
could tell...
I should write
a memoir!

This leg
is shorter

One back leg is a
little shorter
to keep you—the
presumed-guilty—
off balance.

Lower than most chairs
to keep you feeling small!

And now I call
the Fink Fast chair
"friend" too.

3) I think I missed my calling as a bad kid.
   I'm a really good liar!

REASONS TO LOVE MYSELF / MY LIFE / MY SCHOOL TODAY:

Don't forget STICKY BUNS!

* At least I apologized. Well, I tried.

* Drama! & Mr. E. & William Shakespeare & Clint Bedard! OMG!!!

  You are so friggin' lucky!

* Thank you, Candy Esposito, for getting the last spot in Yearbook!

  I hate you! (In that I-love-you-and-wanna-be-you kind of way!) ox Bean

Wait. I thought you hated her?

Does anyone really need a reason to love? —Cate

She's such a weird you know what!

Smart punster troublemakers!

You say weird you-know-what, I say weird what-you-know! (Picture my finger wagging in your face, girlie.)

SUSPENSION IS FOR BRIDGES.

Write on!

I AM NOT A FAD. I AM NOT A PHASE. I AM NOT A MISTAKE.

AM I CRAZY

OR

IS ES REALLY THE GOOD GUY HERE?

CRAZY REALITIES:

Oh here it is. I found it!

• Jen has totally lost it. <u>School spirit?!</u> She's confusing school spirit with the truth. Is she Pleasant Hill <u>high</u>?

• Canfield didn't believe me—even when I finally told the TRUTH. That's no surprise. He's Pleasant Hill low!

• Canfield is as desperate to be liked by the Pops as everyone else!

I AM NOT DOING <u>THAT</u>. I AM NOT JUST WHO MY FRIENDS WANT ME TO BE.

POWERFUL PERSONAL DISCOVERIES:

* If you lie once, it's really hard to get someone to believe you next time.

THINGS I **WISH** I'D SAID:

> Mr. Canfield, may I suggest that you purchase a nose-hair trimmer? It's very hard to show you the respect you deserve with those little gorillas crawling out of your nostrils.

THINGS I WISH I'D **NEVER** SAID:

I am such a lame-ass loser wimp.

But wow—I'm a really good liar.

I don't know what happened to Mandy.

An angry mob? At school? What happened?

Maybe we should look it up.

HEllA good liar, as we'll all later discover!

And I was right! I looked it up.

I AM NOT MY TATTOO. I AM NOT MY TEMPORARY TATTOO.

ma·lign [muh-lahyn] -verb
to speak evil, harmful untruths
about someone; slander, defame:
There are many people in line to malign
PETER HUTCHISON.

I thought it was underlined untruths?

There is no one in line to   Oh right. Whoops!
malign Bentley Jones.

She's awesome.

Awesome?
She's PERFECT.

Charlie!
I know you wrote
that! ——→ I know. I hate her.

PEOPLE WHO SECRETLY
WANT TO KISS/(KILL) ME:

HUTCH

I AM NOT THE SONGS ON MY IPOD. I AM NOT A CLONE.

PEOPLE I SECRETLY WANT TO KISS/~~KILL~~:

HUTCH   MR. CANFIELD

JEN

BODIE   ALL THE POPS

PEOPLE I SECRETLY WANT TO ~~KISS~~/KILL:

→ MISS UNPLEASANT

ALL THE UNPOPS

MY CAT DYSON

Me too!
Me three!
She's baaad.

You are so weird!

What?! He's really handsome.

Disgusto!

what the hell is a SIDEBRA?

Sidebra?

HOW TO BE UnPOPULAR

Okay, people—listen up! Let's all move our chairs into a circle. Welcome to the first day of UnPop Culture, Pleasant Hill High's sick new social studies class. Please note: This class will be graded on a slippery slope,

zit-free freaks talk alike, walk alike, dress alike, think alike— oh wait, you're not allowed to think when you're popular. Silly me.

Tragically, the Pops don't get to explore the free world ~~on~~ the fun fringe benefits

Okay, people! Here's your homework assignment:

If you're one of the fortunate UnPops at Pleasant Hill High, please reach out to one of the needy students and adopt a Pop. Be sure to keep a picture of your adopted Pop in your locker or on your phone to remind you of their pathetic rah-rah daily existence. By

People actually did this!!

sharing your mental wealth with a Pop, someone less fortunate than you will have at least three well-balanced thoughts a day. Hooray! *Wow! That Miss UnPleasant sure is clever*

And maybe, if we're lucky, one day Pleasant Hill won't feel like Pleasant Hell.

Big kiss, class dismissed!
Miss UnPleasant

These must be the ideas that pop into your head at 4:00 AM.

I AM NOT MY PHONE. I AM NOT GOING TO DIE WITHOUT MY PHONE.

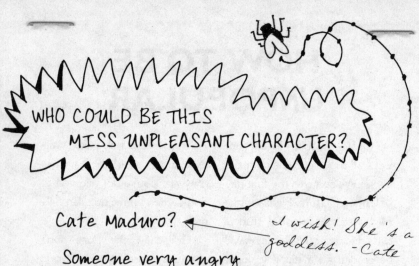

WHO COULD BE THIS MISS UNPLEASANT CHARACTER?

Cate Maduro?

I wish! She's a goddess. -Cate

Someone very angry and deeply tortured.

Like I said, that could be anyone at this school!

Ms. Whit?

Who?

LOCKER STALKER

WANT TO KISS YOU ALL OVER.

Is that from your cat? Can I get his number?

Ha Ha!

Double disgusto!

I AM NOT LOST IN MY OWN HEAD SPACE. I AM NOT A BUTTCAP.

I'M SO CONFUSED...

NO! NO! NO! NO!

That Miss UnPleasant is such a cool bad-ass—or some geeky guy in the computer lab!

YES! YES! YES!

SECRET CRUSHES:

Eric Sobel on Miss UnPleasant

OMG! Candy Esposito still has it for Bodie! (I wonder if Jen knows?)

She does. DON'T bring it up. She's feeling insecure enough already. Seriously. —Amy

* Amy on Dyson

Me on ES (It's back!) (Could ES be my LS?)

*PS: It's no crush. It's true love.

I AM NOT A BENCHWARMER. I AM NOT ABOUT TO GIVE UP.

WEIRD OF THE DAY:

ne·o·pop·u·lar [pop-yuh-ler] -adjective
new and different type of popular characterized
by individuality rather than commonality:
If everyone in school would just be themselves,
then we'd all feel neopopular.

Just made that one up in carpool!

But I kind of think it works.

It definitely works.

Can I use that on my
college apps? -Charlie

Ditto

Double ditto

Paisley, you're sooo deep.

Double ditto!

OMG! People are really doing
Miss UnPleasant's homework
assignment!

ADOPT-A-POP

Cate and Bean
adopted me!

PEOPLE THINK MISS UNPLEASANT IS... SERIOUS

MEAN

DEAD-ON

DIVISIVE ← Hmmm...

A POP WHO THINKS
LIKE AN UNPOP

OMG. He's wearing
some girl's
lip gloss again!

What can I say?
Chicks dig me.

POWERFUL PERSONAL DISCOVERIES:

I LOVE Shakespeare,
especially when I'm staring at CB.

See?

SILENT LIBRARY SCREAM!!!!!!
How did he get my notebook?!

I AM NOT PROCRASTINATING. (WELL, MAYBE JUST A LITTLE.)

INCREDIBLY BORING PERSONAL
REFLECTIONS: OMG! OMG! OMG! OMG!
OMG! OMG! OMG! OMG! CLINT BEDARD
ASKED ME (ME!) ON A DATE! MY HEAD IS
ABOUT TO EXPLODE. OF COURSE I SAID YES.

Red, relax. It's just homework for our scene.

EXTREMELY <u>NOT</u> SILENT LIBRARY SCREAM!!!!!

*I let him borrow the mirror
in my compact. Sorry. -Cate*

MUST
BE
MORE
CAREFUL

MUST BE MORE
CAREFUL WHERE
I LEAVE THIS
NOTEBOOK!

Yep. I found another one.

YOU'RE SO CUTE WHEN YOU'RE MAD.

I HATE MY LOCKER STALKER. HE'S GETTING OBNOXIOUS.

Bean handed me one of these today. I couldn't believe it! They were everywhere...

MISS UNPLEASANT— WRITE ON!

We desperately need your insightful, snarky commentary.
If you want it, you've got an ongoing column on UnPop Culture at Pleasant Hill High.
Contact me, please!

PROS
COULD REPLACE YEARBOOK
ON MY SEVEN-POINT PLAN
EMPOWER AND
INSPIRE THE UNPOPS
MAKE CHARLIE DODD
INSANELY JEALOUS

Miriam Goldfarb, editor
The Fly

CONS
A LOT OF WORK
DO I KNOW ANYTHING ABOUT UNPOP CULTURE?
DEATH BY CHICKEN NUGGETS IF FOUND OUT

I just might love Miriam Goldfarb. **HOW COOL IS SHE?**
Hutch **HATES** Miss UnPleasant.
Makes me **LOVE** her even MORE!
Hutch is running for class president?!
Makes me **HATE** him even **MORE** . . .
and inspires me to...   puke in a purse? ☺
Cate called Hutch a misogynistic philistine.
Makes me **LOVE** her even more! But wait. What is a
misogynistic philistine? Gotta look that up.
AND MOTIVATES ME! I'M RUNNING FOR PRESIDENT TOO!

Basically, it's a woman-
hating idiot. - Cate
PS: Love you too!

RUMORS I HEARD/ IGNORED/ STARTED:

* Miss UnPleasant is full of BS. (Heard it.)
* Miss UnPleasant is really Cate Maduro (Started it.)
* Miss UnPleasant will be pelted to death by an angry,
  screaming mob of Pops hurling chicken nuggets and
  then go straight to Pleasant Hell. (Started it in my
  own head and then tried to ignore it but couldn't.)

OMG! You'll never guess
who's running for sophomore
class president:
  Peter Hutchison
  Me
And...Miss UnPleasant!!!
Hilarious.

OMG. Cate
signed her up!

She couldn't help it.
She's in love.

It's true. She's a goddess.

I AM NOT <u>SO</u> BACK-IN-THE-DAY. I AM NOT MY FRENCH HORN.

WEIRD OF THE DAY:

man·fi·dent [man-fi-duhnt] -adjective
Bold, sexy, and self-confident, especially
when it comes to knowing how to treat a woman:

He whipped me around in his arms like a manfident
rogue until I felt weak in the knees and
delicately collapsed against his chest that
rose and fell with his every hot breath.

Sigh...I better sit down. Oh wait.
I am sitting down. -Bean

Hmm...Let me think. Do I want to look like
an Elizabethan hottie onstage with CB or
do I want to look like Barney?

X

Purple and velvety
and HORRIBLE.

Elizabethan hottie dress.
(Even I looked
almost sexy in it.)

I AM NOT DISGUSTO. I AM NOT JEALOUS. I AM NOT THE ENEMY.

THINGS I **WISH** I'D SAID:

Hey Cate, wanna eat lunch with me?
(Like three years ago in seventh grade!)

THINGS I WISH I'D **NEVER** SAID:

Hey you guys,
guess who asked me out?
Clint!

Dear Mom and Dad, **NOT**
Today I learned a ~~lot~~ at school...

1) Cate is actually <u>undecided</u>.

2) Bean has a major below-the-belt crush
on CB too.

3) "If girls like you (me) start dating guys
like Clint Bedard, then who will girls like
us (Cate and Bean) have to date?"

*Why would anyone want to date
guys like Clint Bedard?*

Wow. Never thought about it
that way before.

Because he's HOT!   Me neither!

Like a pile of steaming dog crap.

*Girls, please—there's enough of me
to go around.*

OMG! I hate him!
What a snoop.

I AM NOT YOUR COMPETITION. I AM NOT GROUNDED! (PLEASE?).

Different by design

Break out of the mold. Break your own mold.

Break out and break free! ← ——— Brilliant! Sounds like an ad for zit medicine.

Color outside the lines. Live outside the box.

Don't repeat...something. Don't compete...something again.

Don't be a sheep. Don't be asleep. Don't...ERGH!

Okay. Think like a Dumb Blonde.

How to be...

What am I trying to say?????

Be YOU-nique!

That's kind of funny.
No, not so funny.

www.PaisleyHanover.com
?????

Dare to be different. Dare to scare. Dare to shave your hair. Oh crap.

UnPop Culture??????? What is that anyway?

IT'S OFFICIAL!

I AM RUNNING FOR CLASS PRESIDENT!

I need a GREAT slogan. And locker stuffers and posters and...and I don't have much time!

Building Sophomore Bridges

Connecting the Dots

Connect the Dorks

Head and shoulders above Hutch

Redhead & Shoulders Above the Rest!

Go Red to Get Ahead!

Paisley Hanover—Not Just Those sperm-shaped thingies!

Spastic Jazz Hands Working For You!

Spastic Jazzed for the Job! ←

Spastic Jazzed to crush Hutch!

Don't you need at least a little CLASS for that job? (Arg! Arg!)

carreyn's hair is so moody!

OMG! Carreyn dyed her hair RED!

Carreyn Hates Me Hair

Carreyn Likes Me again Hair

No it's NO!!

Un IS MORE FUN!

Take a hall pass on the in crowd and join the *Un* crowd instead. Everyone's welcome and everyone's got the power—it's called UNdividuality. What a concept.

Okay, people, listen up! Your homework assignment this week is multiple choice:

1. Tap into your UnPop Power—wear your *Un*-side out. ← *They actually did this!*
2. Be yourself—Be Un of a Kind and be proud!
3. Take back the quad—it's not just for Pops! *AND this!*
4. Take back Pleasant Hill—it's your school too.

LETTERS TO THE EDITOR

and we are NOT trapped. The next time that you are tempted to run a piece like this, you should remember that popularity is <u>earned</u> by people who have style and confidence and social skills and athletic ability. Too bad the bitter, untalented, unpopular students at this school don't get this.

Hi! I'm Mickey Mouse's invisible shy cousin!

Signed,
Anonymouse [sic]

bullies and brats on their entitled behavior. I hope she will write another column, because this school needs to hear from someone who has the guts to point out what makes Pleasant Hill feel like Pleasant Hell.

Sincerely,
Cate Maduro, Sophomore

Good thing they have social skills!

Love her!

One bad apple don't spoil the whole bunch, girl.

Ooh. I don't care what they say.

I don't care what you heard now.

Ooooooh! Ooooooh!

Yours truly,
Sir Pleasantly Laughs-a-Lot

Love HIM! (whoever he is...)

OMG! OMG! OMG! OMG!
THINGS ARE CRAZY! MISS UNP HAS STARTED AN UNOFFICIAL REVOLUTION! UNS ARE EVERYWHERE! (WAIT. IS THIS JUST A REALLY LONG FLASH FANTASY?)

NO ONE SUSPECTS IT'S ME! AT LEAST I DON'T THINK.

Life is happening SO fast,

I barely have time to write anything!

Backlash day was amazing!

UnTouchable
UnDisturbed
UnDaunted
UnTarded
UnPhased
UnAffected
UnShakable ← Yeah, right!

HELLO
my name is
UNFORGETTABLE

MISS UNPLEASANT'S CAMPAIGN IS A LOT MORE FUN THAN MINE.

UNSLOGANS!

Monday: "Vote for Miss UnP to Support Diversity!"

Tuesday: "Join the Un Crowd!"

Wednesday: "UnNormal and Proud!"

Thursday: "The Power of Un is Way More Fun!"

HELLO my name is
UnPerfect

HELLO my name is
UnEven

HELLO my name is
UnAppreciated

I just signed up to speak out against Miss UnPleasant at the school forum. (Am I a genius or what?!)

I'd say you're an OR WHAT!

Um... Yeah! What's up with you?!

Most definitely. Actually, calling you an OR WHAT is very kind.

I AM NOT EASY. I AM NOT EASILY DEFINED. I AM NOT MY SHOE SIZE.

PEOPLE I WANT TO KILL:
BS1 & BS2
JEN & BODIE
HUTCH
MYSELF! (What was I thinking?!!)

PEOPLE I WANT TO KISS:
MIRIAM GOLDFARB
BENTLEY JONES (Love her!)
THE DUMBE BLONDES, ESPECIALLY BONGO GUY
CATE MADURO

~~AM~~ I CRAZY...

Or did Jen just say that I'm the only one she
can trust and really talk to?
I must be crazy.

NICE NECKLACE! ⟶

What in the hell happened at that party?!
I'm going to explode if I don't figure it out !!!!!!!!

I AM NOT MY SHOES. (BTW, MY SHOES ARE SUPER CUTE!)

YES. I GOT ANOTHER ONE...

RIGHT ON, BABY.
MORE POWER TO THE POPS!

Now I know my LS has to be a Pop—or maybe just
a moron. Probably both.

But the really weird thing? Jen's been getting
notes in her locker too.   ???

But NOT from an admirer. Hmmm...

I'm sitting in biology trying
to pay attention. **SNORE!** A text from CD?
That's kind of weird. (He better not be my locker stalker!)

OMG! Hutch is such a skeazer, lame-ass,
slime-bag, scum-of-the-universe CHEATER!

I am not just going to sit here and take this.

I HATE HUTCH!!!!

Guest columnist?

How to be UnEthical   How to be UnFair

How to be UnBelievably Lazy
by Peter Hutchison

MISS UNPLEASANT'S CRYSTAL BALL?
MISS UNPLEASANT'S VOODOO DOLL?
MISS UNPLEASANT'S AGONY QUIZ?

I AM NOT MY FAT POCKETS. I AM NOT WHAT I ATE TODAY.

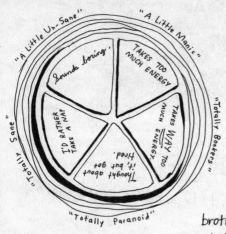

"A Little Un-Sane"   "A Little Manic"

Sounds boring   TAKES TOO MUCH ENERGY

"Totally Sane"   I'D RATHER TAKE A NAP   TAKES WAY TOO MUCH ENERGY   "Totally Bonkers"

Thought about it, but got Tired.

"Totally Paranoid"

TODAY I FEEL...
TOO DEPRESSED TO FEEL ANYTHING.

It's raining. I have NO friends, at least no friends that I like or like me. I have NO boyfriend. I have NO dates. My mother doesn't love me anymore—she only loves Yogilates. My brother never returns my calls. My dad just went running in the pouring rain. I'm depressed. Totally depressed. I should be working on my speech but I can't concentrate—and I can't stop stuffing my face with Pirate's Booty! If I eat any more I will turn into one big giant Pirate's Booty. What is that anyway? "Pirate's Booty." A pirate's butt? I don't know—but it doesn't sound pretty. If I ever have any good ideas for my speech, they'll go right here:

I AM NOT THE POSITION I PLAY. I AM NOT KEEPING SCORE.

I WONDER IF

Miss UnPleasant will get the boot
or get to write again?

Ooh, wondering that really made me tired. I
have to put my head down. The mail just arrived.
Should I get up?

No. It'll take too much energy.

The doorbell just rang.

OH CRAP...

OMG! Guess what just arrived?! My shipment
of temporary tattoos and Paisley for Pres,
Spastic Jazzed M&M's. Yes. Chocolate! Wahooo!!!

My shameless self-promotion.

How cool is that? ⟶
Thanks for the inspiration, Hutch!

Carpool was painful this morning.
But not half as painful as
being pelted by M&M's.
Those Library Girls have   OUCH!
surprisingly strong
arms. Must be from
lugging all those
books around.

OUCH!

OUCH!

I AM NOT MY BAD MOOD. I AM NOT WEARING THAT.

THINGS I WISH I'D NEVER SAID:

More power to the Pops! More power to the Pops!

I don't think I can go out with you.

Podium power is a gateway drug.

MISS UnPLEASANT'S UnPOP QUIZ

Okay, people. Heads up—pencils down! It's time for your first UnPop Quiz.

1. Which incredibly popular hottie has a secret crush on sweet, adorable me?
2. Which candidate for sophomore class president bought his speech online?
3. Which BP flirts shamelessly with one hot guy just to make another—the one she *really* likes—jealous?
4. Which Varsity Pom stole her mom's credit card to get a nose job?
5. Which sophomore rah-rah is getting love notes in her locker?
6. Which brainy babe ignored an invite to speak at the assembly because she has way more power if she stays UnNonymous?

Pop goes the weasel!

Big kiss, class dismissed!
Miss UnPleasant

IT WORKED! (ALMOST TOO WELL.) EVERYONE WAS GOSSIPING LIKE CRAZY!

Clint's not in Drama. Everyone's rehearsing but me.

This is what I would look like in my Taming of the Shrew Elizabethan hottie dress if I get to wear it onstage which I probably won't because I'm an idiot and insulted my scene partner, and now he's not talking to me or even coming to Drama class and he probably won't show up tonight for Acting Out!

He showed up. Oh my God...

Oh my God is right!

He more than showed up! He showed his whole chest! *Girls, girls, girls, get a grip!*

WHY?

WHAT HAPPENED?

Will I ever find out what happened at that stupid party?! It's killing me!!! (And maybe killing my friendship with Jen.)

→→ FLUSH HUTCH! ←←

It's speeches day. I have butterflies in my butt. Something feels weird...

OMG OMG OMG
OMG OMG OMG OMG OMG O
OMG OMG OMG OMG OMG
OMG OMG OMG OMG OMG
OMG OMG OMG OMG O
OMG OMG OMG OMG
OMG OMG OMG OMG OMG O
OMG OMG OMG OMG OMG
OMG OMG OMG OMG OMG
OMG OMG OMG OMG

I'D VOTE 4 ANYONE BUT YOU.
YOU'RE UNBELIEVABLE.

Everyone hates me!
Even my locker stalker has turned on me.
!!!!!
Is that "OH MY GOD" or "OH MY GAG"?

I am not history.

I am _not_ history!

I am NOT history!

I am not a loser.

I am not giving up.

I am not going away.

I am not who I was last year.

I am not who I was last _week._ — Good. Who were you last week anyway?

I am not a rah-rah. ←

I am not my reputation.

I am not who the vice principal thinks I am. — Excuse me! What's wrong with that?

I am not perfect. ←

I am not _trying_ to be perfect. — Thank God. That would be boring!

I am not afraid to say no.

I am _not_ just PMS-ing.

I am not kidding.

I am not falling for that. — Are you sure?

I am me!

(If only I knew who that really was?!)

I am not just who my friends want me to be.

— But are you falling for him?

They're pink. →

I'D VOTE FOR PAISLEY

FOXY!

I love jewelry!

For my core supporters. Love those guys! ♡

(You never know ♡ ♡ who's really there for you until you need them!)

♥ ♥ ♡ ♥

I AM NOT MY MOST EMBARRASSING MOMENT. I AM NOT

GUESS WHAT?
I <u>AM</u> LIVING THE
BEST YEAR OF MY LIFE.

Every year is the best year
of your life! ox Bean

You're so deep. I know.

The day of class elections
WAS **INSANE**!

And that was before
I found out about...

POOR CARREYN. ANOTHER
HOME DYE-JOB DISASTER.

No, not Carreyn's pink hair

Something much MUCH

WORSE!

Puke.

SOPHOMORE
CLASS PRESIDENT

( ) Peter Hutchison

✓ PAISLEY HANOVER

OMG
HOLY SHIITAKE
MUSHROOMS!

THAT'S DEFINITELY "OH MY GAG!"

MY MOTHER'S DO-OVER. I AM NOT A DISAPPOINTMENT.

I AM NOT ALONE. I AM NOT HISTORY. I AM NOT FINISHED.

Big thanks to many—the legendary, loving, and lovable Charlotte Sheedy; her ace assistants, Meredith Kaffel and Hilary Costa; my trusted and beloved readers: Angela Drury, Wendy Merrill, Sasha Cagen, Julie Mason, and Lisa Webster; my inside high-school spy Michael McAlister; my unofficial but not unappreciated editor Andy Garrison; my friends and family who propped me up and/or ignored my absence while writing this book; the incredibly enthusiastic, talented, and patient team at Dial Books (AKA Team Paisley): Lauri Hornik, Regina Castillo, Lily Malcom, and design-goddess Jasmin Rubero; and the amazing illustrator Alli Arnold who created the visuals for Paisley's world.

Special thanks to everyone who has ever lived through high school, especially the Pops and UnPops who lived through it with me. You are all an inspiration!

My biggest thanks goes to my editor Jessica Garrison, who transformed my dirt clod into a sparkling gem. Without her vision, tenacity, support, smarts, to-do lists, friendship, and undying positive energy, Paisley Hanover would not exist. Thank God we found each other! OMG. Did I just say that? I totally did.